HORSES
ON
THE STORM

WILLIAM ALTIMARI

IMPERIUM BOOKS

"Horses On The Storm," by William Altimari. ISBN 9780972872652 (Softcover); 9780972872645 (Hardcover).

Published 2012 by Imperium Books. ©2012, William Altimari. All rights reserved. No part of this publication may be reproduced, stored in a retrieval system, or transmitted in any form or by any means, electronic, mechanical, recording or otherwise, without the prior written permission of William Altimari.

Manufactured in the United States of America

FOR MY BARBARIAN QUEEN
WHO CHANGED MY LIFE

AND FOR

CAROL BROCK—
SPECIAL FRIEND, WISE MENTOR,
HORSEWOMAN EXTRAORDINARY

ACKNOWLEDGEMENT

I thank my niece Veronica Altimari for employing her editorial skills in the preparation of the manuscript.

**MALO TE SAPIENS HOSTIS METUAT
QUAM STULTI CIVES LAUDENT**

**CHOOSE THAT A WISE ENEMY
FEARS YOU
RATHER THAN THAT FOOLISH COMPATRIOTS
PRAISE.**

FABIUS MAXIMUS CUNCTATOR

1

THEY DO NOT FEAR THE WHEEL OF FORTUNE.

CICERO

Judaea?

The tribune's gaze raced down the letter, and then he lowered the sheet and stared off into the falling snow.

Judaea — searing wasteland crawling with scorpions and vipers and half-mad prophets. Ulpius Crus brushed the snowflakes off his head and pulled up the hood of his red cloak. He felt as anxious as he had last year when he had galloped across a German battlefield, even though he was now walking down the Via Praetoria. The icy air sliced his nose and throat. Yet the spring storm's assault he ignored as a trivial pain.

All around him, the five thousand men of the Twenty-fifth Legion carried on as if the snow did not exist. The horses, too, many of them Sequani mounts, were impervious to the Gallic blast. A spontaneous snowball fight had erupted among a few younger soldiers at the edge of one of the barracks blocks. A stray missile sailed by the ear of a passing cavalryman. His steed reared and a barrage of curses pelted the snowballers. Yet a centurion nearby waved off the angry horseman. The centurion's smile showed that he was recalling his own carefree youth, before he had been battered into calluses by the toughest job on earth.

Crus relished the snow. Odd for a man whose ancestors hailed from Neapolis, where palm trees grew. Yet it soothed him like a mandrake elixir. The purity of the white and the hush of its muffling blanket — a sacred mantle in a world scarred by the profane.

He stopped in the road that bisected the fort and absorbed it all in one great vision. He wanted to freeze the legion in his mind precisely at this moment, for he feared that Fortuna had decreed he would never see it this way again.

He strode back up the Via Praetoria. Two men in this fort he trusted more than any others in the world. To one of them he knew he now had to go for guidance.

Guards at the door of the Principia acknowledged their tribune as he passed and went inside. The flagstones of the open-air forehall were still crunchy with snow as he crossed to the rooms beyond. Three Sequani elders were coming out of the Legate's office. They greeted the tribune and went on their way.

"Sit down," the commander said when he looked into his tribune's eyes.

Is it that obvious? Crus pushed a wicker chair closer to the warmth of one of the glowing braziers.

"Give me a moment," Marcus Aemilius Sabinus said and made some notations on a document.

The war with the Suebi had aged the handsome Legate, but in an attractive way. Seasoning more than aging, like a marble bust with a hint of darkening or a bronze graced with the trace of patina.

"What's the matter?" Sabinus asked, pushing aside the papers.

Crus stood and pulled off his cloak and handed Sabinus the letter.

Crus sat back down and watched him read it with that deceptively casual focus the commander brought to everything.

"This is deep," Sabinus said as he read.

"Yes."

"Why didn't the senator write to me first?"

"I don't know, commander."

"We should know soon enough. He's probably been held up by the storm."

Crus leaned forward and rested his forearms across his knees. "I need your advice, commander."

"It's a daunting task. Do you want to go?"

"No, I want to stay here and learn more from you."

"Well, I don't know how valuable that is," he said with a smile.

"You're ten years older than I and a thousand years wiser." Crus smiled back. "And you know I'm no flatterer."

"I suspect there's more to it than that."

Crus could feel Sabinus's gaze piercing his mind like a blade.

"Yes. These men. When I first arrived, they looked at me as if I were a skinny wastrel—which I was. Now they honor me. I try not to get soggy about it, but it means a great deal."

"You distinguished yourself in battle. They don't expect you to be a soldier—they know you're not. But they expect you to act like a soldier, because they know you can. And you have."

Crus stared down at his hands. "I don't want to leave them."

"You must eventually."

"I know, but not now."

"Then don't."

"But how can I turn down a commission like this and retain my honor?"

Sabinus eased back and placed his fingertips on the edge of his desk. "An interesting dilemma."

Crus shook his head hopelessly and stared off at nothing.

"If you took it, how would you go about it?"

"That's another question entirely." He hated the exasperation he could hear in his own voice. "I don't even speak the language out there."

"You speak Greek. That would be enough. At least for a while."

"Are you encouraging me to go?" he asked in surprise.

"I'm encouraging you to serve Rome—and yourself."

"Could I return to the Twenty-fifth?"

"Certainly."

The wind moaned as Crus gazed at the waves of heat rising from the iron brazier. "I've never been east of Brundisium. I don't even know anyone who has."

"Of course you do."

Crus looked back at his commander.

"Rufio," Sabinus said.

"I didn't know that."

"He served several years in one of the Syrian legions. Though I don't know if he's ever been to Judaea."

Sabinus called to one of the guards to bring some heated wine.

"But what does it matter?" Crus asked. "You'd never let him go."

"I might. Temporarily."

Crus was stunned. "Why?"

"For you. As a friend. And for Rome."

"I owe you so much, Marcus."

"Give thanks to the gods who favor you, not to me."

"But would he go?"

"Difficult to say. An enigma, that man. And I'd certainly never order it."

"That baffling man has done so much for me. I'd have no idea how to ask another favor of him."

"Do it the Roman way. Lay it out, put the question, accept the result."

"How do you always make everything sound so simple?"

"I'm a simple man."

"Oh, yes. Simple as a sorcerer."

2

GRAVE MATTERS ARE NEVER MANAGED BY FORCE OR HOPE BUT BY WISE COUNSEL.

ROMAN SAYING

Though the storm had intensified, Crus mounted his horse and rode through the heavy snow near the eastern edge of the fort. Even the flakes clogging the air could not dull the smell of bread coming from the outdoor ovens by the turf rampart wall. He inhaled the aroma, the soothing flavor of home and hearth.

"Tribune!" a soldier shouted.

Crus looked to his left. One of the bakers, his brown cloak covered with snow, smiled and tossed him a hot round loaf. It almost burned his fingers, but cooled quickly in the air.

"Thank you, soldier. The civic crown for you!"

Crus heard the soldier laughing as he rode out of the fort.

He passed through the gate over the pair of ditches that surrounded the fort like the arms of Mars. Yet there could be no enemies in this soundless world. There seemed to be no one else on earth.

He made for the woods in the distance and was quickly surrounded by the great frosty pines. Soon he had come to the edge of the lake near the Sequani village. With the loaf of bread still under his left arm, he dismounted and spread his cloak beneath him and sat under the trees near the bank.

The gray horizon appeared to end at the far edge of the lake. Heavy flakes fell with eerie silence and disappeared like melting honey on the surface of the water. Crus was certain that the absolute purity of this scene could have made even a cynic shed a tear.

Motion at the edge of his vision distracted him. A rabbit was digging through the snow for some surviving scrap of green. Crus broke off a piece of the crusty bread and tossed it to him. He scurried toward Crus and snatched it and began devouring, always keeping a big eye on the tribune. Apparently even rabbits respected their superiors. When he finished, he scooted forward about half the remaining distance from the man. Crus smiled as the rabbit gazed at him with the surety of a Sequani maiden behind lowering lashes. He had obviously worked the hearts of gruff old soldiers before. Crus tossed him another piece, but the little fur ball was only partly done when crunching hoofbeats startled him. He hurried off with his prize.

Crus stood up. A cloaked Roman came toward him on a black Numidian stallion.

"Still riding that little African stud?" Crus asked.

The creases in the man's cheeks deepened in a smile. "Best horse in the legion."

"I've heard the Arab's horse is even finer."

"Not true," he answered as he dismounted.

"Rufio," Crus said simply and reached out.

They gripped each other's right forearms.

"Thank you for meeting me," Crus said.

"A word from you is an order."

"It wasn't an order. A request."

"You're my superior."

"Oh, yes," Crus laughed. "As if I ever could be."

"You're a tribune"—he made a mock bow—"and I a lowly centurion."

"Lowly centurion? That's a self-contradiction. The centurions are the spine of Rome."

"Never say that in the Senate."

"The Senate be damned. Sit with me."

Though Romans considered trousers distastefully effeminate, suited only for eunuchs in eastern harems, most soldiers in these northern fastnesses had long since smothered their pride. Beneath their short tunics they sometimes wore bracae, snug Celtic pants of wool or leather that went halfway down their shins.

But not so with Quintus Flavius Rufio. Crus noticed his legs were bare as the centurion spread his red cloak beneath him and pushed his sword out of the way and sat down. Only his cloak and bright blue tunic shielded him from the harshness of a Gallic winter. No feminine pants for him. And yet he wore a Sequani woman's bronze torque on his left wrist. As always, Sabinus had been right. An enigma.

"I wanted to meet you here because this isn't a legionary matter. It's personal. Between men."

"I can think of warmer places to meet."

"As if the cold could ever bother you."

Rufio pushed back the hood of his cloak. "What is it?"

"Is it true that silver hair of yours came from the cares of war?"

"I tell people that to see if they're silly enough to believe it," he said with smile. "My father had hair like this by the time he was thirty."

"But he was a great soldier, too, wasn't he?"

"Greater than I. Stop dallying and tell me what you need."

Crus turned and stared out across the lake. "An uncle of mine is a senator. He's also a longtime friend of Agrippa. The old soldier told my uncle that the Nabataeans are causing trouble at Judaea's southern gate. Bandits and raids. Herod is feeling shaky so—."

"Herod is always feeling shaky."

Crus looked at him in surprise. "How do you know that?"

"Go on."

"Herod wants to smash the Nabataeans. Augustus won't have any of this. He doesn't want that kind of upheaval out there. So he told his right hand man to get a rope around Herod. But the king wasn't pleased with being choked, even by an old friend like Agrippa. He asked Agrippa to have the Romans build and garrison a fort at the edge of the Judaean desert. That would keep the Nabataeans away from him. They'd never challenge Romans."

"True."

"My uncle got me the commission from Agrippa. To construct the fort. Good for my career, he says. Sabinus has approved, too."

"Take it. You're young and vigorous. A desert adventure while still in your twenties. Never say no to life. More important, never say no to Rome."

"But to build a fort in that desolation? I have no talent for that."

"Some people think you'll find the talent. Within yourself."

"Do you?"

"I wouldn't encourage you otherwise."

Crus sighed and picked up the loaf of bread from the snow. He broke off a piece and handed it to Rufio. It was a shocking act of deference to a social inferior that he would never have dared before others.

"Centurion, I didn't ask you here for advice. . . ."

Rufio set down the bread and gazed into the tribune's eyes. His stare made Crus uneasy.

"You want me to go with you," Rufio said.

"Yes."

"I plan to finish my career in Gaul—not among a pack of squabbling Judaeans."

"It would only be temporary."

"Life is temporary."

The finality in Rufio's voice closed the topic like a bronze door.

"Very well," Crus said with a nod. "Thank you for listening."

They sat together in silence.

"This is the spot where I spared Demetrius," Rufio said.

"Is it? Seems like a hundred years ago. Whatever became of him?"

"He tutors my nephew in Rome."

"Ah, Rome," Crus said with the wistfulness of a dying man. "I want to tell you a story. I might not get another chance. Back in Rome, there's a woman I love named Lucia. I think she loved me since we were ten. I have no idea why. Others far handsomer and nobler than I have fawned on her. She spurns them. When I left for Gaul, her eyes told me she'd wait for me. Yet I'd made no commitment. I was certain a better man would take her. I knew her love for me had its roots in ignorance—."

"Yet she knew you since you were ten."

"Yes. Then after the war with the Suebi, I went back. Remember last fall when I was gone for a few months?"

"Were you? I didn't notice."

"Nice to be missed," he said, giving Rufio a sour look. "Lucia said I'd changed. I assumed she meant for the worse, because of the horrors I'd seen, but that wasn't it. She said I was gentler, more reserved. More confident and more forgiving. She told me those were the qualities she'd always seen but which I'd scorned within myself. Do you understand what I mean?"

"Yes."

"It took that terrible battle along the Rhenus to wipe out the pompous fool who'd left Rome. And to teach me to see the value of the love of this adorable woman. To show me how important it is to cherish her."

"I've seen things in war that could curdle a Spartan's stomach. And acts so tender they'd put a lump in the throat of Mars."

"No one who has never seen battle can have any idea," Crus said.

"War is a strange furnace. It can melt and destroy or temper and ennoble. Everything depends on the raw material that gets thrust into the forge."

"I know that now. But no forge is that powerful. That magical. If I've changed, it's also because I've been touched by others."

"Don't be absurd. We have no such power."

"You have power far greater." Crus rose and mounted his horse. "Live and be well, my friend. And good fortune."

He tapped his heels against his horse and rode away through the forest.

Out of the woods he went and up a low rise. Below him sprawled the magnificent turf and timber fort of the Twenty-fifth Legion. The heavy snow softened the edges, but beneath it lurked the iron will of Rome. Not simply buildings did he see, nor only the ten cohorts of men toiling in a strange land and sworn to the cause of Caesar. Here was the furnace of his great testing, the forge that had purified his soul.

No lover ever left his beloved with the heartache he felt now.

3

EVERY LOVER IS A SOLDIER.

OVID

"I love afternoon love," Flavia managed to say, breathless as a runner who had just raced to the top of the Palatinum.

Rufio leaned down and kissed her damp forehead. The flush across her breasts had begun to fade, but she still cast the heat of a young woman in the full glory of her passion.

"Where did you learn to love like that?" She curled a leg around him and pulled up the soft Egyptian blanket.

"There was this dark Spanish temptress. . ."

She pressed her lips quickly to his. "That's enough," she said with the half-girlish smile that was hers alone.

Rufio luxuriated in the eyes of the forest spirit who had conquered more of him than had all the barbarian armies of Gaul. He thanked Victoria and unconsciously thumbed the image of his patron incised in the cornelian of his signet ring.

"Do you know you have an eye smile?" Flavia asked.

"What's that?"

"Sometimes your expression is completely blank except for your eyes—they have the most amazing smile."

He laughed. "It's funny that no one has ever told me that."

"Everyone probably thinks you already know."

"Well, I never did until now."

"You look into me so deeply," Flavia said. "What are you seeking?"

"The reason for you."

"It's the will of your goddess."

"I honor her."

"When you look into me with love, I often think I see some sadness, too. Why?"

"You deserve the robes of a princess, not the old cloak of a soldier."

She murmured and rested her head in the hollow of his shoulder. "I want only my centurion. So don't say that again. I command it."

"And who would dare disobey Flavia?" he said with a gentle laugh.

She placed a hand over his left breast. "Something else troubles you today, I think. Share it with me. My heart beats with yours."

"A man has an enormous task to perform, but he's young. Downy as a hatchling. He goes to an older man. Wiser in the agonies of the world. He asks his help. A very great favor."

Flavia pushed herself up and swept the long black hair away from her face. "You say yes because your honor demands it."

"It's a faraway place with many dangers."

She smiled a smile that could have melted granite. "Then your Sequani protectress has to accompany you. To see that you return safely to your haven in the forests of Gaul."

Overwhelmed, Rufio crushed his lips to hers and squeezed her so tightly he felt as if every pore of her body were joined to his.

"I'll never let you be apart from me," he whispered.

"Our spirits are fused." She pressed her face into his neck. "Forever."

He smiled and pushed her back and touched his lips to each of her dark eyebrows.

"What is this faraway land?"

"A cauldron called Judaea. I'll tell you about it later. I have to return to the fort now. But first I have something to give you."

As Rufio rose and dressed, Flavia got out of bed and stood naked by the hot brazier near the window. Rufio could hear her sigh as she watched the snow falling in the central garden around which the house had been built.

He gazed at her from behind. Her black hair hung halfway down her back and contrasted stunningly with her pink skin. A bronze torque encircled her right biceps. Her body seemed as soft as doeskin, and yet she was muscled like a huntress. The sweep of her back and the contour of her hips and bottom could have been born only in the mind of divinity.

"This is such a lovely villa," she said, still looking onto the snowy scene. "These rugs and hangings remind me of your rooms at the fort. Who is your friend?"

"A cotton merchant from Alexandria. He built this house here on the edge of the settlement to be close to his customers. But it's far enough out to be peaceful and to give his horses space to run."

She turned toward him. "We should have a place like this, my love. A home where we can be together away from the fort. A place to share each other." She smiled. "Where we can hear birds sing far from the noise of marching men. And where my mare can graze outside my window."

"Here is your gift." He handed her a small bronze key.

"But where is the strongbox that goes with it?" she said and tapped him playfully on the end of his nose.

"You're in it."

Her smile vanished and her lips parted slightly. "This house?"

"We need heavy walls to contain your wails of passion."

She simply stared at him.

"My friend retired to his estate in Italy. I gave him more than he asked before he changed his mind. But that smile in your eyes is worth a dozen slabs of gold."

She yelped in pleasure and bounded toward him and wrapped him in her arms. She pulled him toward the bed and pushed him back and leaped on top of him.

"You rogue—you set me on fire! Get this tunic off and burn once more in the arms of your protectress!"

4

LET HIM WHO DID THE FAVOR BE SILENT. LET HIM WHO ACCEPTED IT SPEAK.

SENECA

Rufio stepped into the crowded changing room of the bathhouse just as Arrianus's fist crashed into the face of another soldier. The man collapsed like a sack of wheat. On the way down, he banged his head against the edge of a bench, scattering coins and dice across the mosaic floor.

"Centurion!" a soldier yelled in warning, but it was too late.

Rufio looped his towel around Arrianus's neck and jerked him back. He twisted brutally and wrenched Arrianus sideways and sent him tumbling to the hard tiles.

The other soldiers retreated to the edges of the room.

Rufio dropped to one knee beside the fallen man. Conscious but dazed, the soldier gaped at him like a child struggling to pull himself out of a bad dream.

"Relax," Rufio said soothingly. He eased the man's head back against the wall. Above him in a niche, a statue of Fortuna gazed down with that inscrutable expression that so maddened all those who sought her favor.

"He was cheating me," Arrianus shouted from across the room, but Rufio ignored him.

"Rest a bit," the centurion said. "Then have one of your friends take you back to your barracks."

"Thank you," he managed to croak.

"He was palming coins," Arrianus said and hurried over to Rufio to plead his case.

A backhand from the centurion rocked his head rearward, but he managed to stay on his feet.

"You embarrass my century with this kind of nonsense?" Rufio said.

Arrianus was as feisty as a ferret, and, like most short men, prone to see enemies and plots coiling behind every sidelong glance.

"Is this true?" Rufio asked the other soldier.

"Yes," he said, unable to lie before that searching gaze.

"Why?"

"I got drunk in the settlement and was robbed. I have no more money until the next stipendium."

"All right. Talk with your signifer. If he's as good a man as mine is, he'll advance you something until then. Were you winning tonight?"

"Yes, centurion."

"Count up your honest winnings and give back one coin in twenty to Arrianus. That's your fine for palming."

"Yes, centurion."

Rufio turned toward Arrianus. His upper lip had already swollen to the size of a plum.

"My office, fifteen minutes."

Rufio settled back in the comfortable wicker chair behind his desk and took the cup of Setian wine from his slave. Rufio was wearing the off-white tunic he favored in the evening after the pleasures of the bath.

"Thank you, Neko."

The Egyptian lowered his head in acknowledgement.

"You decorated my house as beautifully as you did my quarters here," Rufio said, gesturing at the rugs and hangings and bronze oil lamps that Neko had arranged as deftly as an artist.

"I want to make all your rooms cozy ones. Warm refuges from the fierce cares of war."

"You're indispensable to me," Rufio said and sipped his wine.

"A master should never say that to a slave." He smiled. "But then, you are not just any master."

"How could I be when I have a servant who tells me that his people had created a great civilization when Romans were still living in huts?"

"I don't believe I've ever said such a thing."

"You say it with your eyes every day." Rufio smiled at him over his cup.

Neko lowered his head an inch in acquiescence.

"We're going to return to the desert, my friend."

"Indeed? Egypt?"

"Judaea."

"Ah, the Jews. A strange people."

"None stranger. Ready for a journey?"

"I have but one role, to be within call of you."

Rufio's eyes smiled. "Go to bed now."

"I sleep when you sleep. And you are awake late tonight."

"I have much thinking to do. Go to your room. I'll call if I need you."

After Neko had left, Rufio turned his chair around toward the corner behind his desk where the bust of Julius Caesar presided from a plinth draped with purple cloth. Neko had arranged an ornate triple lamp stand in such a way that the three flames illumined the great Roman's face with an eerie, otherworldly light. It was the perfect vision for silent contemplation.

Rufio did not turn around when he heard Arrianus enter the office.

"You made a fool of yourself and your century over a dice game," he said without looking at him. "Suppose you'd broken his jaw. Or blinded him. Over a handful of coins? Or to puff up your shrunken manhood? You broke discipline. Until you regain it, you're not entitled to share a barracks with these men. For the next three nights you'll pitch your tent in the snow outside the fort. And no wheat or fruit or meat. You'll live on barley." Rufio turned and drilled him with his eyes. "Understood?"

"Yes, centurion."

"Is that enough time to find some discipline?"

"I'm not sure, centurion. Three nights I could do standing on my head."

"Good—I'm pleased my soldiers are so tough. I'll give you three more to get you back on your feet. Six nights under leather. Barley and water. Dismissed."

Arrianus left without another word, and Rufio turned to his contemplation of Caesar.

Yet it was not to be, at least not yet. The last man he expected to see at this time of night strode into his office.

"Commander," Rufio said and stood up.

Sabinus peeled off his red cloak and looked casual as a bathhouse lounger in his off-white tunic with no sash of rank. He waved Rufio back down and pulled a chair before the desk.

"I enjoy spending time in your quarters more than in those of any other soldier in the fort." He gazed at Caesar brought to life by the flickering yellow light. "I wish I were old enough to have known him."

"My father did."

"I didn't know that."

"He served in the Tenth."

"Did he tell you many stories?"

"Oh, yes. And if I'm in need of guidance, I come here to try to draw something of Caesar's spirit. His wisdom. And when I'm in Rome and feeling restless, I go down to the Forum at night. I stand in front of his temple before the altar built outside. On the spot where they cremated him. And there I feel peace."

Sabinus smiled.

"And how ironic that is," Rufio went on. "Peace was the one thing his enemies would never allow him. When those butchers cut him down, they had no idea they were performing an act of mercy."

"Now he belongs to the annals of Rome."

"Here," Rufio said quietly, "in the dark of the night, he belongs only to me."

Sabinus nodded his understanding. "Now how about some of that excellent wine you have stashed away?"

"Forgive me, commander. Neko!"

But the Egyptian was already on his way in with a pitcher and a plate of fruits and cheeses.

"Let's get more comfortable," Rufio said, and he led Sabinus into his small dining room.

Neko had lit the lamps and gotten the big iron brazier going.

"Your choice." Rufio pointed to chairs and couches.

"It's been a long day," Sabinus answered and stretched out on one of the three couches arranged around a low central oak table.

Neko came up to the open fourth side of the table and set out the food and drink and then stood in the background.

"Not many of my centurions have couches for dining."

"I think more clearly when my body is at ease."

"Do you think even when you're eating?"

"I think even when I'm sleeping."

Sabinus looked around at the Oriental rugs and the lush wall hangings. "I like that one." He pointed behind Rufio.

A golden leopard against a deep green forest struck a startling note in a room dominated by the dark reds of the rugs.

"My favorite. I bought it from a Persian trader in Antioch. No one weaves like the Persians."

"Why do you refuse to return to the East?"

"Ah," Rufio said and took sip of wine. "You've been speaking with Crus."

"Yes, but he doesn't know I'm here."

"I've had enough sand between my teeth to last me the rest of my life."

"What else?"

"Nothing else. I'm happy here."

"I see." Sabinus reached for a wedge of cheese. "Well, I'm happy to have you here, but why not do a favor for a deserving young man?"

"A favor?" he said with a laugh. "It's not like buying him a cup of beer in the settlement. Have you ever been to a desert?"

"No."

"I thought not."

"He'll be lost out there without someone like you. You know that."

"Yes, he will."

Sabinus searched Rufio's eyes. "I don't believe I've misjudged you. You're not that cold."

Rufio remained silent.

"Would you do it as a favor for me?"

"Yes," Rufio said calmly as he scooped an olive from the bowl. "As a favor for you and for Crus and for Rome."

Sabinus stared at him warily, looking for a leg snare. "It's that easy for you to change your mind?"

"Nothing is that easy. You must do a favor for me. I don't want to go alone."

"Flavia," Sabinus said, smiling. "All right. I'll break the rules for you. But I cannot allow all your officers to take their women as well."

"That's not the reason"—Rufio smiled—"not the only reason anyway. The horse and the bow are the weapons of the East. I might need Flavia to teach those skills to others. Horses I can do, at least to some extent, but the bow is Flavia's weapon. She's the finest archer I've seen outside of Africa."

"Very well."

"Something else. I want my cohort, too."

"Now I see! You laid the trap before I walked in the door."

"I'm just a simple soldier."

"How can I send your cohort? It's become one of the finest in the legion. I need them. And a vexillation of that size is unreasonable. You know we're undermanned."

Rufio split the olive with his teeth and popped out the stone and set it on the table. Then he chewed the fruit and washed it down with wine.

"No answer?" Sabinus asked.

"Certainly there's an answer," Rufio said with the hint of a taunt. "Order me to go. Against my will."

"You know I never would," Sabinus said in exasperation. "It was a twisted fortune that brought you here to me."

"Why not do a favor for a deserving older man?"

5

SO GREAT IS THE STRENGTH OF HONESTY THAT WE SHOULD ESTEEM IT EVEN IN OUR FOES.

CICERO

Sharp sun glancing off the snow felt like the edge of a blade of grass being drawn across the eyeballs. The soldiers squinted at the glare as they labored through their afternoon weapons drill. They were armored with helmets and mail but wore no cloaks, despite the chill.

Rufio observed from a distance as Valerius, his optio, goaded them through their exertions. Though only in his twenties, Valerius was as relentless as a centurion in his pursuit of perfection.

"Arrianus looks like a tortoise today," Rufio said as he came up behind Valerius.

"Very sluggish. It's difficult to get any sleep when you spend all night shivering."

"How many more nights for him?"

"Two."

Rufio folded his arms and watched his men assault the training stakes. "Draw their records. I want to know how many have served in hot climates."

"Are we leaving?"

"For about six months. After this weather breaks. Eager for a frolic in the desert?"

Valerius smiled. "I've heard that the women along the Nile have a technique of squeezing with their—."

"No, not Egypt. Judaea—land of burnt offerings and bad food."

"Isn't Herod on the throne there?" he asked in surprise. Why would—?"

"My thoughts, too. Is Metellus still enraptured by that Sequani woman?"

"Oh, yes—Calpurnia. And her little girl worships him."

"I cannot imagine what it's like to be worshipped by a child."

"Neither could he until it happened."

"Authorize him three days' leave."

Rufio bent down and scooped up some melting snow. He pressed it into a ball as hard as alabaster and drilled it into the spot behind Arrianus's right knee. His leg crumpled like a dead leaf.

"Wake up, soldier!"

Arrianus stopped himself before he had spun completely around, and then he thrust back at the oak stake with renewed fury.

"I'm having supper tonight with Sabinus and Crus and the noble senator Bulla. I won't see you at dusk when you take an extra blanket and a bowl of stewed venison to our wayward gambler camped in the snow."

Valerius smiled.

Rufio gazed at the clearing sky and inhaled the crisp air. "The longest snowfall always seems too brief. And yet nothing is more pleasant than the first scent of spring." He shook his head to himself. "Men are such strange creatures."

He turned away and headed back to the barracks.

Paki was curled up on his desk but stood up as soon as she heard him come in. Already purring, she stretched her back legs out languidly behind her and then walked to the edge with her tail high in the air.

Rufio extended a hand and she rubbed her face hard against his fingers. He leaned down and let her lick his nose vigorously several times.

"Tribune Crus was here to see you," Neko said as he glided in from one of the other rooms. "He seemed happy and bewildered—if one can be both at the same time."

Rufio removed his dagger belt and hung it over a chair. "I'll see him later. Now I need a nap."

Ah, Flavia, were the words written all over Neko's face, though he uttered not a sound.

Rufio gave him a mock-angry glare and then went off to the blessed peace of his bed.

Darkness had already fallen by the time Rufio made his way to the Praetorium. Without a cloak and wearing his usual bright blue tunic, well wrinkled from the day's toil, he did not appear to be the guest of a distinguished senator. He carried several papyrus sheets with him.

"I'm sorry, commander," he said as he entered Sabinus's dining room. He set the papers onto the table.

"I understand," Sabinus said. "Neko told us you would be late. Please greet—."

"Are we low on your list of priorities, soldier?" The chubby senator lay on the dining couch and reached for a sweet cake. "Supper is finished."

"I just left the hospital, senator. One of my men ate in the wrong popina in the settlement. He's been returning his meal to me for the last hour." Rufio pointed to the bottom edge of his tunic. "Would the senator like to examine this stain more closely?"

"Centurion Rufio is very solicitous of his men," Crus said quickly from his couch at the opposite side of the table.

"Centurion, meet Senator Vibius Spurius Bulla," Sabinus said, but the senator ignored the introduction and reached for his wine.

"Please join us, Rufio," Crus said and gestured beside him.

Rufio settled onto a couch covered with wine-colored drapery. He noticed Sabinus shoot him a look that told him to use restraint.

Rufio's eyes smiled back, but Sabinus was clearly not reassured. Rufio's tongue was like an unbroken horse. One was never quite sure where it might go.

A half-dozen Sequani servants flitted about, and Rufio asked one for some spiced wine.

"My nephew tells me you'll accompany him to Judaea."

About fifty-five, the senator had indulged himself far too long. The fat in his florid face squeezed his eyes into a pair of puffy slits that he seemed to struggle to keep open.

"I told him I'd consider it," Rufio said with perhaps a hint of tact. "There are many details that need discussing."

"Proceed," Bulla said.

"We're not in the senate now," Rufio said. "A place where they shave the truth like a carpenter with a plane."

Bulla's rheumy eyes narrowed even further. "What are you implying?"

"Nothing. I'm stating outright that you dishonor your nephew by lying to him. And I'll have nothing to do with this venture until I'm given the truth."

Out of the corner of an eye, Rufio saw Sabinus wriggle like a hatchling that had just tumbled out of its nest onto a pile of thorns.

A servant presented Rufio with his cup of wine and hurried away.

Bulla's thick lips threatened to twist into a sneer, but he seemed to be fighting it.

Rufio set down his cup. "It's well known that Agrippa visited Herod last year. They're friends, and like any wise man Augustus likes to use friends as emissaries. Not to mention his top soldier. But Agrippa never came away from that scorpion's nest with a request from Herod for Roman troops. Herod would never ask that."

"Why not?" Sabinus said.

"Because the old fox knows that if Roman soldiers march in, they might not march out. Ask us to come? Never. We'll see Minerva shit pearls before we'll see that day."

Polluted by the lies and pomposity of the senate, Bulla was clearly unaccustomed to knife-edge talk.

"Uncle?" Crus asked.

"Evidently our centurion here pretends to have a greater knowledge about these matters than the senators in Rome."

"I pretend nothing," Rufio said, cool as marble.

"Then where do you get this profound insight?" Bulla asked.

"I've met Herod. When I was with the Sixth Legion in Syria, he paid an official visit. He came with some of his wives and his bodyguards and his sycophants. A whole baggage train of leeches. He reviewed one of the cohorts and selected ten soldiers for the honor of hunting lions with him. I was one of them." Rufio sipped his wine and stared calmly back at Bulla. "Have you ever hunted lions with Herod, senator?"

The silence of the tomb shrouded the room and seemed to last a week.

"Uncle," Crus said at last in a conciliatory tone, "tell us everything we need to know and we'll go to Judaea and build a fort for Caesar."

Surprisingly, Bulla seemed relieved the artifice was over. "Augustus has always liked Herod, even though Herod sided with Antonius years ago. But these days he's disgusted with the Idumaean. When he isn't threatening to crush the Nabataeans, he's running around looking under every bed for conspirators, even among his own family...."

"Is he justified in that?" Crus asked.

"Probably. His sons are a nest of vipers. In the past when he's felt threatened, he's killed members of his family as casually as if they were rats in the gutter. He even executed his beautiful wife Mariamme.

According to Agrippa, he regretted that and has never recovered from it. Some say he still calls out for her in despair in the middle of the night...."

"Are any of the sons conspiring against him now?" Crus asked.

"I don't know, but if he suspects them, their time is short. The Judaeans, you know, don't eat pork, and Augustus once remarked that it was safer being Herod's pig than Herod's son."

"And Augustus wants a Roman presence there to put a bridle on all this?" Rufio asked.

"Yes. To calm these dynastic squabbles and to stop the Nabataean bandits from embarrassing Herod at his southern gate."

"But it goes beyond that, does it not?" Rufio said.

For the first time, the senator smiled at the centurion. "I see you do know the East. The Parthians are out there, like wolves beyond the door. Instability in Judaea is raw meat to them."

"I don't understand," Crus said. "Why don't we just smash the Parthians?"

Rufio smiled but remained silent.

"Because, tribune, it's not so simple," Bulla said. "Crassus tried and he and his men were slaughtered. His head was presented to the Parthian king. Caesar planned a campaign to settle accounts, but he was killed three days before he was to take the field. Antonius tried, too, and his army was shattered. The remnants crawled back."

"I see," Crus said quietly.

"Tribune," Rufio said, "Parthia is the greatest empire in the world—not including Rome. And their troops are the greatest defensive warriors that exist. Because they're mostly cavalry, they can stay out of reach of infantry and just wear them down to nothing. Offensively, they're less formidable. But that's true of most cavalry armies, although not all."

"I understand," Crus said.

"The Judaeans are always fighting among themselves," Rufio said. "That makes them easier prey. During the last upheaval, about twenty-five years ago, the Parthian horse archers swarmed into Judaea and sacked Jerusalem. They cut off the ears of the High Priest, among other entertainments."

"Precisely," Bulla said. "Augustus wants no repeat of that. We need stability at our eastern door. Herod is the key. Many of his own people hate him, but at least he can control them. Augustus respects that. You almost have to be a magician to control ten Judaeans, let alone a whole country of them."

"What exactly does Agrippa want?" Crus asked.

"A small fort. Just enough for a cohort. A Roman presence there to deter the Nabataeans and to send a message to the Parthians."

Rufio nodded. "That's what I assumed. But you have to understand, senator, that if the Parthians choose to ignore the message, we're doomed out there. We'll all be killed or enslaved."

"You don't believe we can deter them?" Bulla asked.

"Simply by our presence, no matter how small that is? The Parthians are proud and brave. Collapsing before a bluff—I wouldn't bet Judaea on that."

"I won't ask these men to commit suicide, senator," Crus said.

"Nor would I," Bulla answered.

"If it's just a small Parthian action," Rufio said, "a probe to test the rank waters of Judaea . . . well, who knows? But a major horse army? Then we're finished. We won't come back."

"Are you saying you fear them?" Bulla asked in surprise.

"Senator, only fools don't fear them. And all the fools are dead."

Silence followed for several minutes.

"Who'll garrison the fort?" Sabinus finally asked.

"Mostly Herod's own troops. But it'll be a Roman-built fort with Roman officers there for a while. That should be enough of a statement."

"Who pays?" Rufio asked.

"Herod."

"Well, that should endear us to him," Rufio said. "What about the labor?"

Bulla hesitated. "I don't know. I hadn't thought about it."

"This isn't like building a thatched hut," Rufio said. "This is a complex undertaking. Unless someone detaches some cohorts from one of the Syrian legions—and they're not the best soldiers in the Roman army—we'll need to hire hundreds of skilled Judaeans to do the job."

"Is that possible?" Crus asked.

"Anything is possible," Rufio said. "But that doesn't mean it's simple." He slid his cup out of the way and picked up the papers he had brought. "When I was with the Second Legion in Spain, we had to build a fort from the ground up. I kept notes." He looked down at one of the sheets. "The fort was about twenty hectares. About the same as this one. It took almost three thousand men a little over a hundred days. We usually worked between eight and nine hours a day. We lived under leather for quite a while."

"I had no idea of the size of this task," Bulla said in the first respectful tone he had used all evening.

"I've done a few calculations." Rufio flipped to another sheet. "To house a cohort we'll need a fort of at least two hectares. That would include all the buildings necessary for it to function as an independent unit. If we're generous to ourselves and allow four months of construction time, we'll need between four and five hundred men working eight to nine hour days, six days a week. And, in fact, these numbers are an underestimate because they're based on timber."

"I don't understand," Bulla said.

"I suppose you've never been to Judaea, senator. There's little wood where we're going. A fair bit of tamarisk but not much else. This fort will have to be stone. Fortunately, the Judaeans are excellent masons."

Bulla turned away, clearly sobered by all this.

Sabinus motioned to two of the servants. They went into the kitchen and each returned with a large pan of tyropatina, a delicious honey-sweetened egg custard sprinkled lightly with black pepper.

"We deserve a treat," Sabinus said.

"I'll accept your advice," Bulla said to Rufio. "Tell me what message I should carry back to Agrippa."

"Tell him that Marcus Aemilius Sabinus, Legate of the Twenty-fifth Legion, has graciously agreed to cull the finest stallions from his herd and send them to Judaea for the greater glory of Rome. And that tribune Ulpius Crus will lead them there with honor."

Crus smiled but said nothing.

"And you?" Bulla said. "Shall I tell Agrippa of you?"

"My name will be lost, but the glory of Rome will not. Nothing else matters."

6

THE ARMY IS SCRUPULOUS IN CHOOSING THOSE IT ADMITS TO TOIL AND DANGER, BUT A NOBLE MIND IS FREE TO ALL.

SENECA

Flavia released the bow string and it snapped forward, the arrow slicing the air to the cloth on the center of the hay bale. She allowed no time to gloat but drew another from her quiver, nocked it, and sent it to join the first. Five more in quick succession she launched at the fist-sized red rag a hundred feet away. All seven clustered there, silent witnesses to her frightening skill.

For a few moments she stared fiercely at the target, so powerful was the concentration that infused her once her fingers closed around her bow. Finally, taking a few deep breaths, she regained her calmer self.

With her black tunic and brown wool trousers, she warmed quickly in the morning sun. The snow soaked through her soft leather shoes, but she ignored it. She walked across the muddy space behind her new home and retrieved her arrows. Then she resumed her place and began again.

For an hour without a break she practiced, her toned young muscles never tiring. Arrow after arrow she unleashed at the red scrap, soon as tattered as a windswept spider web.

She knew not what dangers they might face in that far off desert land, but of one thing she was certain—any enemies who dared to threaten her man did so at their peril.

"May I make a suggestion?" Crus took the bronze stylus from Flavia's hand.

He reversed the tool and, bending over the table, used the flat back end to smooth away a word inscribed on the wax tablet. Then he rewrote it.

"There. Pull the letters in closer together. You're making the words too difficult to read by spreading the letters out so much."

"Thank you."

"May I read it?"

She handed him the tablet.

When he had finished, he stared down into those guileless eyes.

"All of this is yours?"

"Yes."

"This is very eloquent."

"I've been speaking Latin since I was a girl, but now Rufio is teaching me to write it. I can speak Greek, too."

"I didn't know that."

"Soldiers taught me when I was a little girl. Men who had fought in the East. One of them had even served with the great Pompeius."

"Why did they teach you?"

"I was a quick learner."

"But why did they even begin?"

"I was different than the other girls. I liked the things boys liked. Riding and swimming and hunting. The soldiers were amazed at that. One of them even called me Artemis. She's the Greek goddess of the hunt."

"Yes, I know."

"They competed with each other about who could teach me the most. Some of them knew several languages. I absorbed everything like a dry cloth in the rain."

"You've been very fortunate."

"And when I began to . . . change . . . physically . . . they were my protectors. If a boy looked at me improperly, a vinestick lashed out. Those men might have been lusty with their women, but they were gentle guardians to me."

"I've learned that honor can be found in the most unlikely places. And among the most unlikely men."

"I miss them very much. Most of them are retired now. Some are dead. I adored them." She lowered her eyes, and suddenly she looked even younger than her two decades. "I loved those gray-haired men in the special way that only a young girl can."

"May I sit?"

"Is it proper for a noble Roman to be alone with another man's woman?"

"Definitely *not* proper. Which is why I'm safe—Rufio would never expect it."

The corners of her eyes narrowed in a smile. "You may be seated."

The comfortable sitting room was decorated more in Flavia's style than in Neko's eastern tastes. Colorful Sequani blankets hung from the walls, and a large deer pelt covered the center of the floor.

"I won't interrupt you for long. I have a question and then I'll go. Rufio and I are going to be spending much time together. I need to understand him better, and I suspect no one comprehends him better than you."

"Yes?"

"There's one thing that'll tell me more about him than anything else. What does he value most in life? Other than you, I mean."

"His honor," she said without hesitation.

A smile warmed Crus's face, and he stared away toward the open window behind Flavia. "The answer I'd hoped for." He looked back at her, a dark silhouette in front of the blue sky beyond. "Thank you."

"One thing more," she said, as he was about to rise. "After his honor, the thing he cherishes most is the greatness of Rome. It fills him until he overflows with it. He'd walk through a sheet of flame to protect the spirit of Rome."

"I understand."

"I couldn't grasp this at first. There's no word in Sequani for patriotism. The idea doesn't exist. We're loyal to our chieftains. No one or nothing beyond that. But when I met Rufio, I had to learn a new word. Love of a city—or of an ideal that gave rise to that city. I'm still trying to understand it. Rufio is helping me. I honor my people with all my spirit, but I know that Rufio's love for the fire of Rome gives him a greatness no Sequani has ever had."

"Flavia the Beautiful, you're the luckiest woman in the world."

"Yes."

He stood up. "May the gods keep you safe." He paused as his gaze fell on the tablet before her on the table. "Why don't you begin an ephemeris?"

"What's that?"

"A daily commentary. A record of events and thoughts and feelings. I'm going to keep one."

"I've never heard of that kind of thing."

"It would be good practice, good for your writing." He lowered his voice. "And when you choose not to speak to anyone else, you can whisper to it in the dark and it will always listen."

"I can always confide in my Rufio."

Crus smiled. "Of course. But even goddesses occasionally hug a silent secret to their breasts."

7

GRAVER DANGERS AWAIT.

VIRGIL

"I've never seen you yawn so early in the evening," Valerius said when Metellus covered his mouth with a hand.

"Calpurnia," the signifer answered through another yawn. "I've met my equal."

"I always thought Roman soldiers were insatiable," Crus said.

"Insensible is a better word," Rufio added and put cups onto the small table he had set up in his office in front of the lamplit bust of Caesar.

Neko came in with a pitcher of wine and filled the cups and then withdrew to the shadows.

"I don't know any other men with whom I'd rather share the dangers of the decadent East," Rufio said without preliminaries and sat down. "And if Minerva is with us, we'll return to see another Gallic snowfall."

He looked around the table. All were suddenly serious, empty of any illusions about the challenge confronting them.

"We'll leave in three weeks, on the kalends," Rufio said. "Train the men like fanatics until then. No letup. I want them as keen as falcons. They can rest during the voyage. We'll go down to Massilia and board ship there for Ostia. Understood?"

"Yes," Valerius said. "How much of our own equipment will we take?"

"Everything we'd need for a field camp but not a stick more. Make sure every soldier brings at least one pair of leather bracae. We might be doing some riding. And some wooden swords for drilling. We won't have an armorer out there, so we cannot afford to damage our blades during practice. And bring a carnyx. One never knows. We'll buy pack mules here in Aquabona and sell them when we reach Massilia. Impress on the men how important it is to watch over their gear. In the East, theft isn't a crime, it's a religion."

"I know I'm a tyro in all this," Crus said, "but I don't understand why we don't begin as soon as possible."

"We *are* starting as soon as possible," Metellus answered. "The sailing season—the safe sailing season anyway—doesn't open up until May."

"We'll spend about a week in Italy," Rufio went on. "The men can have leave to go to Rome or stay in Ostia, whatever they want. We're going to need an engineer, and I know one who retired last year from the Second Legion in Spain. He lives in Ostia."

"And our centurion's charms will seduce him back under the yoke?" Metellus said with that look of skeptical bemusement that delighted or infuriated all who knew him.

"He doesn't save all his spells for Flavia," Valerius said.

Rufio sighed. "My trials are many with officers like these," he said to Crus.

The tribune laughed. "I hope my colleagues in the senate someday are as frank with me as your men are with you."

"No chance of that," Rufio said and took a sip of wine. "We'll get passage on some of the coastal boats going from Ostia to Puteoli, where the grain ships dock. Ostia doesn't have a deep-water harbor, so we won't find any there. We'll have to go down to Puteoli to get one or two of the big corbitas to take us to Egypt. A good master will catch the Etesian winds and we should be in Alexandria within two weeks, less if he's especially good."

"I had no idea we could get there so quickly," Crus said.

"At Alexandria, we'll find a vessel to take us to Herod's paradise."

All were quiet with their own thoughts for a while until Crus broke the silence.

"What do you know about these Nabataeans threatening Herod in the south?"

"No Nabataeans are threatening Herod," Rufio said.

"My uncle was lying?"

"The senator is an ignorant man."

When Rufio did not continue, Crus said, "Now isn't the time to be reticent."

"The Judaeans and the Nabataeans do fight occasionally, that's true. And there have been a few Nabataean kings who were aggressive. But they pose no threat to Herod's domain. They're not a warlike people. One of the most unusual things about them is that they treat their women well. Very few peoples in the East do that. Women have high status. Not up there with Roman women, but very high by the standards out there—if you can call them standards. The Nabataeans' ruler is a wise and humane king named Obodas."

"What are they then?" Valerius asked.

"Some raise sheep and camels, but most of their riches come by transporting spices and frankincense up from Qana by camel caravan to Gaza. They've acquired staggering wealth just from this. They have a magnificent city with buildings carved out of solid rock. The Greeks call it Petra."

"I remember some old veterans from Egypt calling the Nabataeans pirates," Metellus said.

"There's truth to that," Rufio answered. "The Egyptians started competing with them by shipping spices and incense up the Red Sea. The Nabataeans were afraid the overland trade would dry up. Their survival depended on that caravan route, so they put to the water to punch a few holes in Egyptians hulls and disrupt the sea trade."

"Then they do fight if they're provoked," Crus said.

"Oh, yes. And they're very skillful on both horse and camel. Some Romans came back after they saw them on camels and said they had no horses, but that's nonsense. They have excellent mounts."

"Are they fighters like the Judaeans?" Valerius asked.

"Herod attacked them about sixteen or seventeen years ago. That was when Cleopatra had her claws into Antonius. She wanted Judaea and Nabataea for herself. She tried to goad Antonius into swallowing up Nabataea, but he resisted her—probably the only time he ever did that. So the Egyptian whore enticed him into getting Herod to attack them under some pretext. She probably hoped the turmoil would cause upheavals in both kingdoms and Antonius would have to step in. But she was no strategist. The Nabataeans shredded Herod's army in Auranitis. The Judaeans limped away and Herod had to beg for peace. Later, he did defeat the Nabataeans near Philadelphia, but to this day he loathes them for shaming him."

"Then we shouldn't underestimate their fighting ability," Valerius said.

"Absolutely not. Sometimes they've resisted us, sometimes not. Occasionally they form alliances with the Parthians, and sometimes they fight them. It depends on circumstances. They're very clever in judging what's to their advantage. And they're a tough people—rugged like the desert they live in. They were nomads once, long ago. They know the drifting sands like you know these barracks. Their skill in crossing that wasteland seems like magic. They've dug huge underground cisterns all across the wilderness. They fill them with rain water or spring water that they channel to them in secret aqueducts. The openings of the cisterns are concealed and only they know the locations."

"Very shrewd," Crus said.

"Their power goes beyond shrewdness. Besides their own language, they speak Aramaic and usually Greek. Many of them speak Latin, too. And their physical endurance defies any kind of rational reckoning. It makes them masters of that desolation. They're as dark and hard as volcanic rock. The Greeks and Judaeans call them Arabs."

Neko came in with a late evening treat.

"By the gods, that smells good," Crus said.

Neko stepped up to the table with a freshly baked loaf of bread, wrapped in a towel and still steaming.

Valerius broke it open, and they all indulged like carefree bachelors at a late night party, rather than soldiers of Caesar planning a journey to a hostile land.

"Neko, you're a treasure," Crus said.

"I have friends among the bakers," he answered with a smile and refilled their cups and withdrew.

"What about the Judaeans?" Valerius said to Rufio.

"An interesting people but very difficult to deal with. They'll be one of our biggest problems. Just when you think you've reached them on some sensible level, they start appealing to their god and invoking their lunatic prophets, and good sense dies in its cradle."

"God?" Crus said. "Only one?"

"That's more than enough," Rufio answered.

"What is he called?" Crus asked.

Rufio laughed. "He has more names than I do. I'm not sure, but I think his official name sounds something like Yahweh. But nobody is allowed to use it except priests in their temple. And I'm not certain even they use it anymore. The common people call him Adonai instead. That means Lord. Evidently that doesn't insult him. But they use that name only when they pray. They say that if they use it outside of prayer, that offends him, too."

"He's a petulant sort," Crus said.

"So their common word for him is HaShem. That means The Name. That's the one they can use in conversation."

"So that's the one we'll hear?" Crus asked.

"No, because they don't speak Hebrew anymore except in prayer."

Crus laughed. "You're not making all of this up are you?"

"I'm not that clever."

"Well," Crus said, "it's been my experience that people who are always worried about giving offense—whether it's to a man or to a god—are also the people most likely to *take* offense."

Rufio smiled. "Welcome to Judaea."

"Then what *do* they call him?" Valerius asked.

"Elah," Rufio said. "It's the Aramaic word for The Awesome One."

"Are we finished now?" Crus said, smiling and shaking his head."

"You have to understand that the Judaeans don't practice a religion, they marinate in it. Even a peasant can quote pages of their holy writings. And they're superstitious to the point of madness. But they can also be as hardheaded as Sicilians. Very practical and sharp when they choose to be. No race on earth values learning more than they do. They use it as cleverly as Hercules uses his lion skin."

"As protection, you mean?" Metellus asked.

"For protection and wealth. Dump ten people of ten different races onto a couple of bare hectares, and the Judaean will always end up the most prosperous. While the other nine are still trying to figure out how to dig a latrine, the Judaean will already own the land and be selling them a hole to piss in. He's smart, he knows mathematics like a Greek, and he works as hard as an ox at a millstone. And he still takes one day in seven to rest and worship his god."

"No wonder they have so many enemies," Crus said. "Envy is a poisonous cup."

"They're some of the strangest people you'll ever meet—very easy to admire but not always easy to like."

"If they're as keen as a dagger," Valerius said, "why do they do others' bidding rather than the reverse?"

"Because they have a toxic flaw," Rufio said. "They battle among themselves. Every time a conquering army has stepped on their throat, it's because they were already bled white by fratricide. It's endless. They take a twisted pleasure in arguing about meaningless things. If you ever hear them bickering about some trivial point of politics or philosophy or some idiotic food law, you'll think you're in a room full of madmen."

"Can they fight on the battlefield?" Valerius asked.

"When they're willing to obey their commanders—which isn't often. An individual Judaean can be one of the most formidable people you'll ever know. But if you have thirty Judaeans, you have fifty opinions and a civil war."

"What about their army?" Crus asked.

"Small by our standards, but still a good size for a little kingdom. About fifteen thousand infantry and maybe four or five thousand cavalry."

"That's a high proportion of horsemen," Crus said in surprise.

"You'll see that often in the East."

"Well equipped?" Valerius asked.

"Their weapons and equipment are essentially the same as ours. And they're fairly skilled at using them."

"How loyal?" Metellus asked.

"At one time, they were the spine of Herod's kingdom. They swore a sacramentum directly to him. But things have changed. Now he has Greeks and other foreigners in his army. They're loyal because they're paid well, but the Judaeans . . . They still make up the bulk of the army, but they've wearied of Herod's whims and follies. They're not to be trusted."

"By Herod or by us?" Crus asked.

"Yes," Rufio said with a cold smile.

"Yet you admire them nonetheless," Crus said. "It's in every inflection of your voice."

"They're the most astounding race in an astounding land."

"But?" Crus asked.

"But they'll never achieve the greatness they should. Their self-destructiveness dooms them. That's why Judaea will always be the flagstone under the feet of every marching army in the East."

The cold wind bit into the flesh of anyone foolish enough to stand against it. Senator Bulla pulled up the hood of his cloak and stared off from the eastern wall parapet into the darkness beyond the ditches.

"Look out there," Rufio said.

"I cannot see much."

"You can feel it." He pointed toward the threatening wilderness shielded by night.

A sliver of moon allowed them to make out only the most ominous shapes.

"The Germans are out there," Rufio went on. "Always hungry, always ready, never resting. Feel it now, so you can carry it back with you."

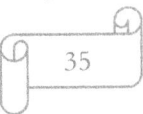

He turned and looked at Bulla in the bleak moonlight.

"Why have you brought me here, centurion?"

"So you can sense what these men sense every day of their lives. So you can know what these men face for the glory of Rome."

Bulla gazed back into the dark. "I do know—now. I didn't until I came here. I'm not a foolish fat man, regardless of what you might think."

"Your nephew is a brave man. I know that because he's afraid now. You're wise enough to know that bravery isn't the absence of fear—it's the conquest of fear."

"Yes."

"He could have chosen other routes to advancement, but he chose this. Remember this cold night when balmy Italian breezes fill your nostrils."

"This might surprise you, but I will."

"And don't forget it when your head touches the pillow. When you close your eyes without worry because these men stand between you and savage races full of envy and hate."

Bulla peered at him through the gloom. "You're not what I expected."

"I'm never what anyone expected."

"I care about my nephew very much."

"I know that."

"Bring him back to me."

"I'll do what I can."

"I know. And I'll honor you for that." He smiled. "So tell me, what was it like to hunt lions with the King of Judaea?"

"I don't know."

"You lied? No, I don't believe it."

"I never said I hunted lions with Herod. I said he asked me to."

"You turned him down?" Bulla asked, laughing in disbelief.

"I was the last one in line when he moved down the rank. All the other soldiers were almost drooling after the honor. When he put the question to me, I said, 'My lord, when I kill, it is not for pleasure but for Rome.' He stared at me with those fearsome eyes—eyes that had felt so much pain and inflicted so much pain. Then I saw what I thought was the ghost of a smile, and he turned and left, followed by his parasites. I never saw him again."

8

GREAT THINGS ARE NOT ACCOMPLISHED WITHOUT DANGER.

TERENTIUS

"Caesar thanks you for volunteering for this noble task!" Crus boomed from the makeshift wooden tribunal.

The Second Cohort exploded in laughter. The voices of almost five hundred men rolled out from the muddy training ground and across the Gallic countryside.

Crus knew that only one of them had volunteered. The other five centurions and the men of the six centuries would now march with that centurion to the edges of the Empire.

Even more astounding, they would willingly go with Crus. He could hardly believe it. A year earlier, they had sneered at him, when they thought of him at all. Now they would follow him across a wasteland. The greed and hatred of a dead German barbarian had altered much in the tribune's world, and he thanked the gods for it.

These men had changed as well. Crus gazed at them with affection and pride. Last year, they were unknown soldiers toiling in a distant outpost. Now they were the heroes of what was being called the battle of Scorpion Hill. An obscure Greek writer had jolted the people of the Tiber. Not just in the Senate, but in the taverns and byways his stunning story of the Twenty-fifth Legion was everyone's favorite topic. In his ancestors' tongue, Diocles of Rome had written a searing tale of valor and horror such as no one had read since Polybius. In the basilicas of the Forum, Sabinus, the young commander, was being touted for higher offices, though he seemed indifferent to the acclaim. Recruitment to the legions had jumped. Schoolboys spoke of the gallant Macer, struck down in battle. Of Probus—the Rock they called him—solid as Egyptian granite at the center of the battle line. Most of all, they chattered about a man who had requested that Diocles refer to him simply as "a centurion of the Second Cohort," but the obstinate Greek had refused. Now in the alleys of Rome and in the fields of Latium, boys competed with each other to play the role of Rufio. The centurion himself received letters from aspiring soldiers and—according to Flavia—shockingly explicit erotic proposals from women eager to share themselves, much to the amazement of Rufio and the amusement of Flavia.

"Judaea is our ally," Crus shouted to his men. "It guards our eastern gate. Wolves are sniffing there. The men of the Second Cohort hurry east now to prove that when our friend is threatened, *we* are threatened. And to show the wolves that they are not wolves at all—just toothless dogs when faced with the iron might of Rome."

The men roared.

"One thing more," Crus said. "You may have heard that Herod is a savage tyrant. Or half-mad with disease. No matter. We care not for his quirks. Mad beast or not, he's on a Roman chain, and there he will remain." Crus paused, and then said, "All right, you gentle souls, now you know where I stand. Tomorrow we face the inferno."

9

NOW I KNOW WHAT LOVE COULD BE.

VIRGIL

I have performed brave deeds. I am not a silly little girl who would try to impress men by pretending I am weak. But there is one thing I do fear, and that is the displeasure of the man I love. So before beginning this thing called an ephemeris, I told him. At that moment I felt like a blushing child, rather than the woman who ignites him. I feared he would think I was keeping secrets. Oh, how much I have to learn. He smiled at me with pride and got me all the writing materials I need. Papyrus sheets are rare outside the fort. He gave me more than I could carry. And pens and ink. I told my dearest Vara and she was stunned. She said that no Sequani man would approve of this private chamber of the spirit. Even her beloved Adiatorix would scowl at such a notion. I am very young and I have not known many men, but I am old enough to know that Rufio is like none of them. So many are just jealous boys. Rufio's trust in me is so great it overwhelms me. And my love for him makes me feel I am about to burst.

"Dead?" Rufio said in surprise.
"Yes, centurion. Last spring."
The look of loss in the servant's eyes revealed the effect the departed woman still had in this stricken house.
"Please come in for refreshment," the young man said.
"Why won't you tell me where your master is? Do I have to search all of Ostia?"

"I truly don't know. You may try the popina near the temple of Diana."

"This early in the morning? Is he drinking too much again?"

The servant was silent.

"Tell him I'll be back." Rufio handed him a sestertius. "You're a loyal servant. Bellator is a fortunate man."

Rufio turned and walked away from the door.

The villa of Titus Manlius Bellator spread out from a small rise overlooking the sea. Behind the house, a pine woodland would grace the villa with the sweetest of scents when the onshore breeze began blowing in the evening. Rufio smiled at the memory of his old friend. For all his gruffness, Bellator had always had a softness for animals. The woods offered shelter to the deer and squirrels and rabbits he would surely sneak out to feed early in the morning.

Rufio turned toward the coast and sucked in the luscious smell of the sea. He knew if there was one way he was a typical Roman it was that he cared little for traveling by sea but loved gazing at it and inhaling its essence.

Bellator had a spot here to be envied by an Asiatic monarch, but now Aurelia was dead, and his aromatic villa had become a reeking necropolis.

Rufio walked down the road toward the center of town. For the first time in more than three years, his feet became dusty with Italian soil. He thought he had not missed Italy. Now he knew he had been wrong. And of the dozens of raucous ports he had sampled in his career, none did he enjoy more than Ostia. He inhaled deeply again and strolled out onto the Decumanus, the east-west road that traversed the city. From here he entered the core of the great pulsing organ that pumped food into the body of Rome.

Carts and wagons heavy with Egyptian wheat creaked along the massive basalt cobblestones of the Decumanus. Unlike Rome, where most wheeled traffic was forbidden during daylight to reduce congestion, Ostia exulted in its daytime commerce. The gray cobbles bore deep grooves ground into them by the relentless roll of iron-rimmed wheels. Foot travelers darted in and out of the flow with the nimbleness of butterflies fluttering among flowers. Faces of merchants and sailors from countless lands challenged even the cosmopolitan Rufio to identify their place of birth. It was as if Neptune had cupped a hand and swept it across the sea and dropped them here to give Ostia a vibrancy and texture unique in all of Italy.

Rufio bought two salted fish from a boy selling them out of a sack on his back and then made his way east. Women of several races lolled in the shade of balconies jutting from apartment buildings. Unlike most ports he had known, Ostia sported relatively few prostitutes, but these doubtful maidens gave him looks that needed no translation.

He turned left off the Decumanus and walked past a field recently cleared and where a foundation was now being laid, possibly for a theater, from the shape of it. He continued north and stepped into the welcome shade of a vine-covered portico fronting an open square of offices. In the center of the square rose a temple to Ceres, the goddess to whom the grain merchants headquartered here made special obeisance.

An intricate mosaic formed the pavement in front of one of the offices. Two black tile ships contrasted with the white background. A gangplank linked the vessels, and a man was passing from one ship to the other with an amphora hoisted to one shoulder. Rufio had found what he was seeking, and he went inside.

He was quickly disappointed.

"They all left on last night's tide," said the harried clerk to Rufio from behind the counter where he seemed to be conducting four conversations simultaneously with four impatient customers. "There aren't any ships the size you need."

"What size would that be?" said a voice from behind Rufio.

He turned to see a man looking at him from the doorway.

"How big a ship do you have?"

"You didn't answer my question, soldier."

Rufio smiled. He was wearing his usual bright blue tunic with a simple belt and no weapon, but this seaman saw beyond that.

"A full cohort."

The gray-haired sailor scratched a cheek beneath a beard of silver wire. "And are you a generous man?"

"I trade in Caesar's silver."

"Ceres smiles on both of us. Let's talk and eat."

Fortunatus evidently felt that humility had no place in the world of the purveyor of fine food and wine. The pavement in front of his tiny tavern advertised his name in bold black and white mosaic, along with a figure of a cup and an invitation to come in and have a drink.

The soldier and the seaman sat at a small table inside and shared some spring water and some cool white wine from the Alban Hills. At other tables, Neptune's slice of the human race carried on around them.

"Call me Salario."

"You're joking," Rufio said with a laugh.

"No."

"All right, Salty. Quintus Rufio. Twenty-fifth Legion."

"Where are you headed?"

"Judaea."

Salario winced. "Why?"

"The will of Caesar."

"Rufio . . . ? Haven't I heard of you?"

"How big a ship do you have?"

"A corbita."

"Full size?" he asked in surprise. "Here?"

"Anchored far out. I can carry a thousand men."

"I don't understand. I've never seen one at Ostia before."

"I just purchased it here from one of the shipping companies. We leave soon to buy Egyptian grain to feed the hungry mouths of Rome. You can help defray the cost of the voyage. We can catch the Etesians and go straight to Alexandria."

"Originally I thought I'd have to get a corbita at Puteoli."

"Now you can skip that. I can be ready in five days."

"I need a week."

"Done."

"We haven't talked about a price yet."

"No landsman has ever been clever enough to cheat a seaman. And besides"—a grin creased the wind-seared face that was as leathery as dried venison—"I know honest eyes."

Rufio smiled.

"I've never been swindled by a soldier. I don't expect to be shorted now by the man who led the right wing at Scorpion Hill."

Rufio sighed but said nothing.

Salario sipped his wine. "Do you know why I like Ostia so much?"

"I think you're going to tell me whether I ask you to or not."

"The exotic women. Gauls and Africans and Spaniards. They pass through here from all over the empire." He was gazing past Rufio's left shoulder. "That might be the most beautiful creature I've ever seen in my life."

Rufio turned and looked at the woman coming through the doorway.

"Don't you agree?" Salario asked.

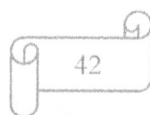

"How do I know? I don't know how many women you've seen."

"It doesn't matter. Look at her. I'd like to perch her on my rod until it weeps no more."

"Before you do, caress the cute little leaf-shaped mole behind her right knee."

Salario squinted at him as if he were speaking a foreign tongue.

"Try it," Rufio said. "It always makes her giggle like a child tickled with a feather."

Suddenly Salario looked like someone had flung scalding water into his face.

"I'm so sorry." Even his brown skin could not conceal the blush burning through. "I feel like a fool with three heads. Please forgive me."

Flavia saw Rufio and smiled and rushed over, followed by Neko.

She wore a black tunic ending at mid-thigh and bunched at the waist by a belt holding a Roman soldier's dagger at her right hip. The black leather bracer on her left wrist and the bronze torque around her right biceps finished off the outfit with the flourish of some mysterious outland. She strode into the room with those long and powerful legs, and every male present suddenly looked as if now he could die a happy man.

"One week from today at the shipping office," Salario said to Rufio and rose from the stool and hurried toward the back door.

"What happened?" Flavia asked when she reached Rufio. She brushed some windblown hairs away from her eyes and stared after the retreating seaman. "That's the first time a man has ever run from the sight of me."

"He embarrassed himself with an impure thought."

"I see." A slow smile, wise beyond its years, warmed her eyes as she watched him go.

"Do you know you're irresistible when you smile like that?"

She looked down at him, her smile deepening. "Yes."

Rufio gestured and she and Neko sat down. He pushed the pitcher of wine toward them and gave Flavia his cup and handed Salario's to Neko.

"Neko has been wonderful," Flavia said excitedly. "He's taken me on a tour of the city. The shops and the baths and the markets, and we fed deer in the pine woods and ate smoked fish by the sea"—she was almost breathless now—"and we saw Numidian jugglers and Persian magicians and . . . and just everything."

Rufio smiled at Neko. "I owe my steward much."

"Flavia is a student all teachers would envy."

"What pine woods?" Rufio asked Neko. "Near Bellator's?"

"Yes. A vacant villa close by."

"Aurelia is dead."

That startled Neko. "The world will mourn her."

"And Bellator is drinking again." He turned to Flavia. "My engineer."

"He needed her," Neko said. "She was the gentle and correcting hand."

"Will he not go with us then?" Flavia asked.

"I haven't found him yet." He looked at Neko. "We have a ship to take us from here all the way to Alexandria. Buy the provisions and have them ready in a week. Don't be frugal. Cheeses, cured meats, dried fruits—I want the best for the men. And all the wormwood wine you can find." He pulled off his bronze and cornelian signet ring. "Use this if anyone questions you."

A sly smile narrowed Neko's eyes. "I'll tell any skeptical trader that the silver is Caesar's and is backed by the word of Rufio of Scorpion Hill."

"Stop it. Where's Paki?"

"Reclining in the cart outside. Serene as a queen."

"Keep her with you. Flavia and I are going up to Rome."

10

HE DENIES ANY PORTS ARE OPEN.

LIVIUS

Crus stood on the stone dock and supervised the loading of food. A half-dozen single-sailed boats, each about forty-five feet long, bobbed on the swell and creaked as the goods were transferred to them. The bow or stern of each boat was attached by a line to a mooring ring of carved volcanic rock jutting out from the dock. The tufa rings stopped the boats from smashing sideways into the pier.

Neko sat on a box and used a bigger crate for a desk and tallied everything with fanatical Egyptian precision. An endless line of wagons rattled toward the dock from the east.

"I've never seen one of those before," Metellus said, staring out toward the deeper water where the grain ship was anchored. "It's a monster."

"We certainly won't run out of food when we fill its belly," Crus said.

"Tribune, why don't you go up to Rome? I'll stay here and handle this."

Crus smiled. "I will when—."

Hoofbeats interrupted him. Valerius was hurrying down the road toward them on horseback.

"Found him!" the optio shouted and pulled up in front of the dock.

Crus looked back at Metellus. "I'll go once I've done this."

The popina they were seeking was near the center of the city not far from the temple of Diana. Like many taverns, this one formed the ground floor of an apartment building. Over the entrance, brick arches reinforced by travertine brackets supported a balcony where lodgers could enjoy balmy evening breezes.

Several idlers sat on a pair of stone benches on either side of the doorway. Crus and Valerius passed them and entered the cool interior. To the left, just inside the entrance, squatted a massive chest-high counter faced with gray marble slabs, perhaps reclaimed from some demolished building. From here the tavern keeper doled out his wares. A couple of basins in an arched opening below the counter top were filled with water for washing dishes. Behind this counter were some shelves holding bread and a variety of fruits and vegetables.

Crus and Valerius went further inside. More marble shelving against a freestanding wall in the center held extra loaves and fruits. Above these and barely visible in the dimness hung a painting of grapes and radishes and olives, in case anyone was unsure what other delicacies were for sale.

Crus looked around. Opposite the entrance was another doorway on the south side of the tavern. Beyond this spread a sunny courtyard with mosaic paving and a fountain and stone benches for customers who preferred taking their refreshment outdoors.

"Over there," Valerius said as he came up beside him.

In the shadows, near a wall separating the central room from what appeared to be a kitchen, a man of about fifty sat alone at a small table. A pitcher and cup were set before him, and he seemed to be staring into eternity.

"Centurion Bellator," Crus said when he went over to him.

The man looked up. "Yes."

"I'll join you." Crus grabbed a stool and sat opposite him.

Valerius took a position behind his tribune and stood in silence.

"Ulpius Crus. Twenty-fifth Legion."

"Should I be impressed?"

Crus decided to ignore that. "Your old friend Rufio is looking for you."

"I know. Why?"

Bellator's round face was creased by a thousand suns, but the real decay lurked in his eyes, bleary and dull from wine and despair.

"The Second Cohort travels to the East to build a fort in Judaea. You're an engineer. We need one."

"I'm a drunkard."

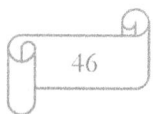

"I figured that out when I smelled the cheap wine."

"You're mistaken. It's very expensive wine."

"On the voyage from Massilia, Rufio told me how you once fought back to back outside a brothel in Antioch. How you had to drag two of your drunken men out and how in the moonlight you were attacked by a half-dozen Syrian thieves. And how you stood with your backs to each other and took them on and pounded them down."

"Eight thieves it was," Bellator said with the hint of a smile at the ancient memory.

"Your friend needs you again. I need you. And Rome needs you."

Bellator took a sip from his cup and gazed into it.

"Well?"

"What would you have me say? The one person who matters to me has escaped this ugly world. I have no fire left."

Crus took a deep breath to calm his impatience. "Do you know the worst thing about a drunk? Not the drink. Not the stench. It's the putrid self-pity."

"Is that so?" he said and took another sip.

"You miserable sot! I cremated *hundreds* last year."

"What's going on there?" the popina owner said and rushed out from behind his counter.

"Stay where you are!" Valerius shouted.

The man stopped so quickly he skidded on the floor tiles.

"Now go about your business." He looked down at Bellator. "The tribune is right. Self-pity smells like vomit."

"Tribune?" He looked at Crus. "Wide stripe?"

"Yes."

"And you?" Bellator asked, looking up. "You're too young to be a centurion."

"Optio."

"You inspire loyalty, tribune. I like that."

"Your men need you," Crus said.

"My men? I'm not a soldier anymore."

"A Roman soldier never stops being one."

Crus was startled to see tears in the old fighter's eyes.

Bellator turned away. "I weep too much these days."

Crus said nothing.

Valerius removed the dagger and scabbard from his belt and laid them on the table next to Bellator's hands. "A gift for your return."

"You insulted me. How do you know I won't stick it in you?"

"I didn't survive ten thousand Germans by not being able to judge men."

Crus stood up. "We leave on the Nones on the evening tide. Fortuna will be with us. Will you?"

Bellator looked down at the dagger in his hands. "Don't tell Quintus you saw me this way. Let me live in his mind as a better memory than this."

He rose and approached Valerius and handed him back the dagger. Then he touched the optio on the left shoulder and stepped around him and went out of the tavern and away.

11

YOUR GLORY AND FAME WILL ENDURE FOREVER.

VIRGIL

Rufio smiled as he watched Flavia stare in wonder. Rare is the moment in any man's life when he can gaze at someone truly awestruck.

"Now you know," he said to his Sequani huntress, "why all call Rome the Head of the World."

The marble buildings of the Forum loomed before them and seemed to roll out eastward to the edge of the earth.

Flavia stood with parted lips and in silence.

To their right towered the Basilica Julia.

"What is that?" Flavia asked.

"Law courts," Rufio said above the noise of the hundreds of people who swarmed throughout the Forum.

Over a dozen columns rose from the north side of the building to support the enormous roof.

Flavia drifted to the marble steps.

"Why are all those people there?" She pointed to the young men lounging around outside the basilica.

"Some are clients waiting for their patrons conducting business inside. Some are just layabouts looking for vice."

At several places along the hundreds of feet of steps, round depressions had been carved directly into the marble in regular patterns. At each set of markings, two players were pushing pebbles around the different spots. Flavia pointed to them and looked questioningly at Rufio.

"Game boards they chiseled there to pass the time. It's called latrunculi. A strategy game."

"Do you mean war?"

"In a sense."

"Do you play it?"

"Better than these wastrels."

Flavia smiled and looked to the opposite side of the Forum.

"The Curia," Rufio said. "Where the Senate meets."

"Those doors are big enough to admit the gods."

"The senators wouldn't disagree."

"And that?" She gestured to the right of the Curia.

"The Basilica Aemilia."

She wandered down toward the elegant shops on the ground floor of the basilica.

Rufio hoisted to his right shoulder the sack holding their change of clothes and followed her. So enraptured was she that she never noticed the commotion she was causing. This forest creature with the well filled out green tunic and the black leather trousers was drawing the attention of hundreds of pairs of eyes.

Rufio bought some dried figs from a fruit seller, and Flavia chewed on them absently as she took in the wonders about her.

"This way," he said, and they approached a magnificent marble temple in the center of the Forum. A semi-circular alcove had been fashioned into the base of it at ground level. A white marble altar filled the niche. "Look back that way."

She turned and faced the direction from which they had come.

"That's the rostra," he said, pointing to a raised stone platform decorated with the prows of old ships sticking out of it. "Antonius gave his eulogy there over the body of Caesar. The people were so overcome with grief they seized Caesar's body and cremated him right in the Forum." He turned around and pointed to the altar. "Here."

She stepped back as if she feared to stand on sacred ground.

"It was here," he said, "that Caesar rose to the heavens."

"From this altar?"

"Oh, no. There was no altar then. No temple. Augustus built them later to Caesar's memory. People tore off parts of their clothes here to feed the pyre. They went mad with anguish over the fallen man."

Flavia stared at the altar and then reached out and took Rufio's left hand and squeezed it.

"You are his heir, my love. No, don't say anything." She turned and looked back toward the basilicas. A warm afternoon breeze blew down between the buildings and fluttered the hair hanging halfway down her back. "This is all because of you. You and Valerius and Metellus and thousands of others."

Rufio remained silent.

"All the freedoms these people have. All the pleasures. Even those lying about on the steps over there and looking for young boys to fondle. Yes, I know the type—don't be shocked. All are free because of you. And here you are in their midst and they don't even know it. Well, I know it, and I don't care what any of these blind men think. After all, I'm only a barbarian."

She slid her right arm around his neck and kissed him as passionately as if they were alone in their bed.

Several boys nearby whooped when they saw it, and dozens of older men stared in disbelief.

Flavia smiled her devastating smile. "Let them burst with envy."

Rufio took a moment to catch his breath. "All right, my untamed one, give me your dagger now. We don't want to be sporting any weapons where we're going."

She removed the sheath and dagger from her belt and handed it to him.

He tucked it into the clothes sack. "This way."

They went around the clusters of people and past the south side of Caesar's temple and through the arch of Augustus.

"Why is that one so small?" Flavia pointed to a circular temple just beyond the arch.

"Yes, it's small but none is more important. That's the temple of Vesta. She's the goddess of the hearth. Her flame burns there continually. It's the fire of Rome itself. The virgins vowed to her service live there. They must never allow the flame to go out."

"There's something I don't understand. Where are all the soldiers?"

"What soldiers?"

"The legionaries."

"There aren't any legionaries in Rome. Not on duty anyway. It's illegal for a commander to lead his troops within the city limits."

"But what about Augustus?"

"What about him?"

"Who protects him?"

"He has some praetorian guards."

"That's enough?"

"Yes." He pointed past the temple of Vesta. "That hill is the Palatinum. He lives there. We're going to climb it."

"To see Augustus?" she asked in amazement.

Rufio laughed. "No, I think he's too busy to chat with us today. The south summit of the hill is a great vantage point. Come on. I'm going to show you something you'll remember for the rest of your life."

12

HOWEVER BRIEF LIFE IS, IT IS LONG ENOUGH FOR LIVING WELL.

CICERO

The trusting squirrel sat on Bellator's left knee and took a piece of apple from his fingers. Her swollen nipples showed that she had little ones waiting, but the milk maker needed nourishment. Every day she looked for her friend here in the cool woods. With the guilelessness of animals everywhere, she always expected he would be here. And he always was.

Bellator smiled at her. With her hanging teats, she represented more than motherhood. She symbolized tomorrow. She embodied hope.

Sated now, she lay splayed on his leg and rested her chin on his knee.

"All right, mother, they're waiting." He reached down and she let him scratch behind her head. Then she was scurrying off toward a tall pine known only to her, where her babies huddled in a hollow and waited impatiently.

"You're losing your edge, centurion," said a voice from behind him. "Letting someone come up on you unaware."

"No, I'm not," Bellator answered without turning around. "I heard you. But whatever you're doing isn't as important as what I'm doing." He looked around. "And you are?"

"Metellus. Second Cohort, Twenty-five Rapax."

Bellator pointed to the bed of dead pine needles all around him. "Have a seat in my throne room."

Metellus sat opposite him and folded his forearms across his knees.

"Well?" Bellator said. "Did you come here to stare?"

"You don't look like you're drunk. But from the way you're shaking, I'd say your body is screaming for the grape."

"So?"

"You're trying to give it up, aren't you?"

"The only thing I've ever given up is life."

"A minute ago you sat here nurturing it."

Bellator said nothing.

"Let's talk about the man I follow in battle. Will you do that?"

"Talk."

"He isn't just some officer. You know that. He's a leader like no other I've ever known. And what I owe him is beyond comprehension. I owe him my life and the life of the woman I love and the little girl I'm rearing as my own. It's important you understand that."

"All right."

"Sometimes he's like a father to me. Sometimes a tyrannical older brother. In rare moments, even like a mother. I don't pretend to understand him completely. Or even half. But I'd rip my heart out of my chest and give it to him if he asked me for it."

"Real leadership has a mystical power that defies understanding. Now you've learned that."

Metellus laughed. "Now you've learned that. That's a line Rufio uses."

"I know."

"Will you join us?"

"Why is it important to you?"

"It's important to *him*. He values your abilities."

"He doesn't need them. I've never seen a problem Rufio couldn't bite in half and swallow. He's the most intuitive soldier alive. I don't know where he gets it. Whether it's a natural talent or an acquired skill. Or simply a gift from Mars."

"I doubt if even he knows."

"But you must have seen it. If you or I walk onto a patch of ground, we see a patch of ground. Rufio sees a battlefield. Instantly. Without thought. We see grass and hills. He sees the clash of armies— battle lines and anchoring points and ballista positions. It's like a child staring at the clouds and suddenly seeing a horse or a butterfly. Rufio glances at a swath of turf and immediately sees places to charge from or pivot or turn a flank. Trust me, signifer, he doesn't need Bellator."

"Then do it for friendship. I'm asking you to reach back and find within yourself the strength to give him what he's asking for."

Bellator smiled. "The love of one soldier for another is something no civilian can ever comprehend."

Metellus remained quiet.

"Have you ever been to northern Italy, soldier? There's a town there named Julia Augusta. Before that it was just called Julia, after Caesar's clan. He named it that to honor the soldiers from there who helped him conquer Gaul. Originally it was called Parmula. It's in the hills." He stretched out and leaned back on one elbow and stared off into the woods. "The farmers produce a special kind of ham there. Unique in all the Empire. They feed the hogs whey left over from cheese making. They mix in grains, too, but it's mostly the whey. It produces the sweetest ham on earth. The farmers don't slaughter the hogs until they're the biggest they can get. That's when the meat is densest and the most flavorful. But they don't cook the hams or smoke them. They salt them and air cure them. They hang them in their farmhouses with the windows open and they wait. They swear the special sweet air in that region is responsible for the flavor of their hams. Maybe they're right." Bellator brought his gaze back to Metellus. "Are you hungry yet?"

"Are you joking? I'm already tasting those hams."

"No you're not. You have no idea. The farmers let the hams hang for over a year. They check them continually. And when they're ready, it's as if Jupiter has brought forth a new creation." Bellator paused, then said, "The hams of Parmula are the favorite food of Quintus Flavius Rufio. When we went off to Syria together, we brought two dozen with us. Can you imagine that?"

Metellus smiled. "Go on."

"They don't spoil, so they're perfect for the desert. We doled out slices to our friends like slabs of gold. But we didn't have any wine good enough to set off a Parmula ham. Have you ever drunk Syrian wine? Sheep piss. Then we heard of a centurion from another cohort who had his own private wine stock. He'd brought it all the way from Etruria. Even stored it in a cave to keep it cool. Now we had our plan." He laughed. "We were young and had the arrogance of young men. We didn't try to buy some of his wine—we seduced him with the ham! Syrian lamb was no competition. After you've been in the East a while, the allure of lamb runs its course. Soon just the smell of it makes you want to vomit. We knew the centurion could never resist the Italian hog. So now we had all the good wine we could drink." Bellator sat up, but he stared beyond Metellus at a distant memory.

"Tell me the rest," Metellus said.

"One spring evening, Quintus and I were lying on the edge of a dry wash outside the fort. We were eating ham and drinking Etrurian wine and gazing at the stars. Except for my times with my wife, there was no other moment in my life like that night. Two friends quiet and happy in a perfect world. I've been thinking about that night often lately—and long before you and your arrogant tribune rose like serpents from a hole to annoy me. Rufio will tell you he hates the desert. He does not. The only people who hate the desert are those who have never seen it. He yearns for it still. Do you know that?"

"Why?"

"For its precision and its purity. So when he was posted elsewhere and had to leave it, he left it like a rejected lover. But he never hated it, no matter what he says now. He hated only its absence. The loss of its cutting beauty. And I'm as certain as I can be that he thinks as often as I do of that night along the wash. Ham and wine and a soft breeze and two good comrades under the desert stars."

Bellator stood up slowly and stretched his aging joints. "Come to my home, Metellus of Twenty-five Rapax, and let me feed you now."

13

A WOMAN IS ALWAYS FICKLE AND CHANGEABLE.

VIRGIL

The huge ellipse of the Circus Maximus shook with a titanic roar when the chariots burst from the starting gates. The entire Palatinum vibrated beneath Flavia's feet in the fury of the crowd's excitement. At the summit of the hill, she gazed down in stupefaction at a spectacle incomprehensible to someone reared in a hut in the wilderness of Gaul.

A dozen four-horse chariots thundered along the track. Tens of thousands of fans waved ribbons of red or white to match the tunic colors of their favorites. Out of the gate, each charioteer stayed in his own chalk-lined lane. The drivers were tearing through the sand toward a perpendicular white stripe that cut across the arena at the beginning of the central barrier. When the first three drivers reached it, they seemed to explode out of the pack. Now they could abandon their lanes and bolt toward the inner edge, the shortest route around the track.

"Oh!" Flavia shrieked and grabbed Rufio's arm when the four dozen horses dashed across the break-line and converged on the prized inner lane. By a mixture of magic and skill, none of them crashed.

"Look at the horses!" Flavia shouted. "They're magnificent!"

Two whites and a red had pulled from the pack by the time they approached the three enormous cones at the end of the central barrier. Cut from volcanic stone and decorated with sheets of bronze, the triple posts marked the far turn.

"No!" Flavia screamed. "They're going to crash!"

All three chariots sailed into the turn at impossible speeds. In what was nothing more than a controlled skid, each chariot swung wildly around the pivot point and seemed headed for the mouth of

Hell. The red hit a bump in the track and the feather-light leather and wooden vehicle left the ground. It smashed back down hard. The driver lost control of the reins, but the four straps had been looped and knotted around his waist, and he soon regained command.

"I can't watch," Flavia said and jerked her head away.

Rufio smiled. "Have you ever seen such horses as these?"

She could not resist and turned back.

The three in the lead had widened the distance from the other nine. They raced to the near turn and the end of the first lap.

"How many times around?" Flavia shouted.

"Seven."

"I can't bear it," she said but could not pull her eyes away.

The red and the two whites swept around the three towering cones at the near turn and roared into the second lap.

Flavia dug her fingers into Rufio's right arm and was still gripping him by the time the charioteers had made five more circuits.

Flavia's chest was heaving now, as if she were running with the horses.

"Look!" she yelled when the red driver and his four stunning black steeds broke from the two whites and tore toward the finish. The horses glistened in the sunlight and every shiny muscle seemed to crackle with lightning.

"Go!" she shouted when the red raced to victory.

The cheers of his fans shook the walls of the entire valley.

Flavia leaned against Rufio. She was as limp as if she had run the seven courses herself.

"There's some talk of increasing the number of color teams," Rufio said. "Adding greens and blues. But it hasn't happened yet."

"What is that channel for?" she asked when she had regained her breath. She pointed to the ten-foot wide water canal running around the edge of the track.

"To keep wild animals from jumping into the seats. Sometimes beast hunts are staged here."

"Are there more races today?"

"Oh, yes. A full tablet is about two dozen. When we come back from Judaea, I'm going to give the men a month's leave. You and I will stay in Rome. We'll come to the races so often even the horses will recognize us."

Flavia smiled. "You know how much I love them."

"We'll see them close, touch them and smell them. And we'll walk the track and even meet some of the charioteers."

"Could we do that? Are they famous?"

"Very famous. Most of them are slaves, and many are rich. They'll buy their freedom someday. I know the driver who won today. He's a German. He belongs to the household of a senator I know. The senator's son served as a military tribune with me in Spain." He turned and pointed across the circus to the hill opposite. "That's where we're going now. The Aventinus."

She did not follow his gaze but stared into his eyes.

"What is it?" he said.

"I'm afraid."

"Of what?"

She looked away.

"Flavia...."

She turned back to him. "Your sister."

"Why?"

"A young woman has a special tie with her older brother. Especially when the parents are gone."

He smiled indulgently. "You're being childish now."

"I'm not a child! And don't say it!"

He took her hands in his. "What's wrong?"

"I'm an intruder. I've come between the two of you. I'm afraid she'll hate me."

"How could the sister I love hate the woman I adore?"

Flavia slipped her arms around him and pressed the side of her face against his chest. "I'm so scared."

Rufio and Flavia stood in the shadow of the colonnaded portico forming the perimeter of the garden. Street noises drifted in faintly over the roof, but all was cool and quiet in this central refuge.

Flavia's eyes were fixed on the woman sitting on the edge of the gurgling fountain. She was gathering a bunch of flowers of every imaginable color plucked from the shrubs around her. The sun coming in over the roof just caught her chestnut hair and ignited its auburn highlights, but one of the two Italian cypresses at the far end of the garden dropped its shadow across her face, so Flavia could not make out her features.

"Who was at the door, Demetrius?" the woman said without looking up.

Rufio strode out of the shadow of the portico. "Hello, Puppy."

The woman snapped her head around. Her sharp intake of breath made her sound as if she were choking. She stood up and stepped into the sun, the stems crushed in her hand.

Now it was Flavia's turn to gasp. This had to be the most striking woman in Rome.

The woman came toward Rufio with a look of such longing it seemed to Flavia almost an expression of anguish. Her lower lip trembled like a child's, and the blossoms slipped from her grasp. Almost as tall as her brother, she reached out and ran the tips of all ten fingers over his face, as if she were blind and this were the only way to sense his presence.

He curled his arm around her and pulled her in. She kissed both of his cheeks repeatedly and then went limp, resting her face on his shoulder and moaning with the sweet release of answered prayers.

Flavia was more frightened than ever.

The woman spoke softly to Rufio, and Flavia heard him say, "She's here."

He turned to her in the shadows. "Flavia, meet Flavia."

She stepped out into the sunshine.

Rufio's sister released him reluctantly and approached her. She stopped six feet away.

"By the love of Venus," she said to her brother as she gazed at his stunning Sequani huntress. "You didn't exaggerate."

Flavia remained silent.

"Come here," his sister commanded.

Flavia obeyed and the woman gripped her hands.

"My name is Flavia, too, but my friends like to call me Rosa"—she swept her arm around the garden—"because of all the flowers."

"Yes," Flavia whispered.

"Thank you for bringing my brother back to me." She released Flavia's hands but slid her arms around her shoulders and drew her close. Her slate blue eyes, so like Rufio's, were just inches away. "Thank you."

Flavia nodded.

"I know why you're afraid," she said so softly only Flavia could hear. Her eyes were as wise as Rufio's own. "You need not be. We're sisters now."

Flavia burst out crying and pressed her face against Rosa's breasts and soaked her pale blue stola with her tears.

"I know, I know," Rosa said, caressing Flavia's hair and rocking her gently. "It's all right."

"I was so scared," Flavia managed to say at last.

Rosa smiled and brushed Flavia's tears away with her fingers. "I know. But we're not competitors. Don't ever think that."

"I've never been in love before," Flavia said so low that Rufio could not hear. "Sometimes it frightens me."

"Then I'll show you how to tame this rogue," Rosa said with a mischievous smile. "I did it long ago."

Flavia laughed through her tears.

"And that's something a wife should know how to do."

Flavia gave her a puzzled look. Surely she knew that soldiers were not permitted to marry?

"Oh, don't concern yourself with that," Rosa said in an uncanny reading of her thoughts. "Forget Augustus's nonsense. In Rufio's letters to me, he has always called you his wife."

Flavia's lips parted and she looked over at Rufio, but failed to produce any words.

Rosa smiled and tenderly brushed one of Flavia's cheeks with her thumb, as Rufio himself was in the habit of doing. "The gods alone choose what unions to bless. And Victoria has always loved her Rufio."

"Optio Marcellus, stand straight and report!"

The thirteen-year-old boy smiled at his uncle. "All is well on the Aventinus, centurion."

Rufio laughed and hooked an arm around the boy.

Two female servants were laying out a feast on the travertine table in the garden, and Demetrius was lighting lanterns against the dusk.

Rosa supervised everything with the hawk-like eye of the Roman matron.

"Have you met Flavia?" Rufio asked his nephew.

Marcellus turned around.

Flavia was coming out from the house into the failing light of the garden. She had washed her face and combed her hair and the sight of her almost killed the boy at the door of manhood.

Rufio's eyes smiled. Flavia's barbarously clad figure probably presented Marcellus's imagination with more forbidden beauty than he had ever seen in his life. Rufio could actually hear him swallow as she approached.

"Marcellus, this is my wife, Flavia."

Marcellus nodded and managed to mumble something.

"Dinner," Rosa said and the reunited family indulged in the most joyous of Italian rituals, the communal consumption of food.

The travelers were ravenous, but Marcellus seemed to have misplaced his appetite, though not his ability to sneak glances at the woman with pink skin set off by hair as black as a raven's wing.

Rosa and Rufio smiled at each other when they caught Marcellus staring.

After all were sated, Rufio and Rosa left the table and walked arm-in-arm across the garden. They drifted to the edge of the lantern light, and Rosa rested against her brother.

"I've missed you so," she said.

Rufio kissed the top of her head.

"You're not going to retire now, are you?" she asked.

"No."

"I'm glad. Civilian life is not the life for you. I was worried when you told me you were leaving the army."

"After what happened in Spain, I almost did."

"Augustus needs you out there at the edge. What changed your mind?"

"Neko."

Rosa smiled. "Is he well? I like him so much."

"Very well. He stabilizes my life."

"And Flavia?"

"She inflames it."

"You rogue! How many hearts have you broken across the Empire?"

"Not one. You know that."

"Yes," she said softly. "I was just teasing."

"I've always had an impossible standard for women. They had to be at least half as grand as you."

"I'm so happy you found Flavia. Your wild woman is far more formidable than I could hope to be."

"Every woman has her own unique grandeur." Without warning, he grabbed her and squeezed her tightly. "By the gods, Puppy, I'm so lucky. Just knowing you were here held me together in Spain."

"I'm always with you, no matter how far away you are."

He pressed his lips into her hair. After a few moments, he released her and said, "You've done wonderfully with Marcellus."

"He's a fine boy."

"Is Demetrius an adequate tutor?"

"He's excellent. They get along well together. . . ." Her voice trailed off.

"But . . . ?"

"Marcellus is lonely. He wishes you were closer."

"So do I."

"He has friends—good ones. But he's smarter than they are and more sensitive." She smiled. "As his uncle was at that age. He wants so much to be the head of the household, but he can barely walk across the room without bumping into things."

"That'll soon pass."

"The girls are already eyeing him."

"He has his mother's looks."

"But girls just dazzle him. He told me once how much he wished Julia had lived."

"Julia? Why did he say that?"

"He wishes she were here to guide him. To explain all those mysterious female ways. A boy his age certainly cannot speak with his mother."

Rufio looked across the garden. Flavia and Marcellus were deep in conversation. His stare of adolescent hunger had vanished. Replacing it was a look of awe rare in a male of thirteen, or of twenty-five, or of fifty.

They were too far away for Rufio to make out Flavia's words, but her tone was clear. It was gentle but serious, as if she were speaking not to a child but to an adult who could understand adult realities.

"She certainly has the way about her," Rosa said.

"Oh, yes," Rufio said with a smile. "She has the way."

"Do you understand now?" Flavia asked. "Staring flatters a woman, but it also troubles her."

"I understand," Marcellus said, averting his eyes.

"Admire her, but do it gently. Your gaze should be like a ray of sun across a beautiful lake. Not burning through her but glancing off her and making her even more beautiful by the light from your eyes."

Marcellus violated her rule at once and stared at her in worship. Finally, he said, "I wish you could stay longer."

"I wish that, too."

"I don't have anyone to tell me about these things. My father died when I was a baby and my mother . . ."

"Is your mother."

He nodded.

Flavia placed her right hand on his left one. "I know." She could feel him tremble.

He looked around and saw his mother and Rufio going into the house.

"May I tell you a secret?" he asked.

"Yes."

"I miss my sister very much."

"I didn't know you had a sister."

"She died when she was a baby. Five years before I was born."

"Before? Then how can you miss her?"

"I think about her. When I'm confused. I wish I had her here to teach me."

"What about your friends?"

He laughed. "They're as confused as I am."

"Then why don't you ask me?"

He pulled his hand out from under hers. He looked terrified.

"Are you afraid of me?"

He nodded.

"Why?"

Even in the dim light his blush was obvious.

"Why, Marcellus?"

"My friends and I . . . we talk about you."

"About *me*?"

"Yes. About Flavia of the Sequani."

"I don't understand."

"We read about you in Diocles' book. We've tried to imagine what you were like."

Flavia could see his guilt torturing him. Clearly "what you were like" meant more than fantasizing about the color of her hair.

"Stay here!" she said and grabbed his wrist and pulled him back as he tried to leave.

Embarrassment filled his eyes, but Flavia struggled to keep from smiling. Some imaginings those must have been!

"My friends are tired of hearing me boast about how great my uncle is. I know they envy me. They'd rather talk. . ."

"About girls?"

"You. They said that no woman could ever do the things Diocles said Flavia had done. Or be as beautiful as he said you were."

"Obviously I am not."

"Oh, yes you are," he said without shame.

"When Rufio and I return from Judaea, we're going to stay with you for a while." She smiled at him with the mischievous eyes of a forest sprite. "You can introduce me to your friends. We'll let them decide what's true."

"I will!" he said.

"Until then I want you to think about something." Her tone was serious now. "I could never be your sister, but I can be your friend. Write to me in Gaul. Send your letters to the Twenty-fifth Legion. I'll get them. We can discuss the dark forests where women keep their secrets. And no one else on earth need know."

Marcellus seemed incapable of speech.

"Two things more. Continue to boast about your uncle to your friends. If they object, do it twice as much. They'll respect you more if you defy them than if you give in."

"I promise I will."

Flavia extinguished the lamp on the table next to them. Now they were graced only by moonlight.

"What's the second thing?" Marcellus asked.

Flavia gazed at him with the womanly compassion all adolescent boys deserve. Like a Gallic goddess, she knew she could exalt him or shatter him in an instant. With eyelids half-lowered and concealing her mystery, she leaned forward and pressed her lips sensuously to his cheek. She lingered there for an endless delicious moment and then whispered, "Tell your envious friends that you have shared a kiss with Flavia of the Sequani."

She stood up and stared down at him.

Intoxicated, he seemed barely able to breathe.

Flavia smiled and laid her right hand on his head in a special blessing. Then she turned and strode off into the darkness.

14

WE WILL NEVER CONQUER DANGER WITHOUT DANGER.

PUBLILIUS SYRUS

"I've never liked traveling by sea," Rufio said, staring at the vast blue expanse. "But I like being near it. Looking at it, smelling it. Listening to the shore birds."

Crus smiled but said nothing as they stood together at the dock.

"On the way down from the city, Flavia told me how much she enjoyed Rome. But I know where her heart is. It's here, in Ostia. She's captivated by it. Who wouldn't be?"

"You could retire here someday. It has the sea, as well as those exotic flavors you've developed a taste for."

"I've thought about it."

"You should."

Rufio's eyes bored into those of the tribune. "You wouldn't have another motive, would you?"

"What could that be?"

"Well, by then you'll be a politician in the city. Perhaps you'll want a battle-scarred old soldier on hand to steady your judgment. To tame the wilder flights of folly favored by young politicians."

"Never entered my mind."

"Now how are you going to be an office seeker when you still haven't learned how to lie?"

Crus burst out laughing. "I can never deceive you, even when I really try."

"Only beautiful women have done that. And very few of those."

"Yes, I'd like you near. I want Lucia to know you. And my children and grandchildren."

Rufio gazed out across the water. "There are many wars to fight before that." The humor in his eyes had vanished like an ocean mist.

"I know."

"Barbarians clawing at the edge. I won't sheath my sword until the last of them sinks into the blackest waters of Acheron."

Crus turned and stared out to the horizon. "I told Lucia I might not return."

"That was very brave."

"Not as brave as she. Tears filled her eyes, but she wouldn't weep. She's a true Roman. Not a decadent Neapolitan like I."

"I'd like to meet her."

"Do you know why I didn't ask you to?" He turned back to Rufio. "Because I knew you'd look into her eyes and promise to bring me back safely. No man—not even you—should have to make that pledge."

Rufio remained silent.

"I want us to go back to her together when this is done. We'll shake the dust of Judaea off our feet and I'll place her hand in yours and she can thank you."

"How do you know I'll survive?"

"You?" Crus said with a laugh. "You always survive."

"The Fates can be malignant."

"Yes, but you needn't worry. Victoria guards you with a lover's passion. She'd storm the halls of Jupiter himself if he dared even to consider letting you fall. She'll never leave your side."

Rufio's left thumb idly caressed the cornelian stone of his signet ring.

"That's why I plan to stand beside you in battle. Not because you're so tough, but because I know that in her eagerness to protect you, Victoria will also shield the finest cohort in the Roman army."

Rufio laughed.

"And," Crus went on, "to answer the question you're too kind to ask—no, I'm not afraid." He placed his right hand on Rufio's left shoulder. "How could I be, with men such as these under my command?"

Rufio turned toward the clatter of wagons coming down toward the dock. The earliest arrivals were approaching.

"Your men are always the first risers," Crus said.

"People waste too much of their lives in bed. I've trained my century not to."

"I saw Salario at dawn. He wants to leave on the evening tide."

"We'll be ready."

By late afternoon, most of the equipment and supplies had been ferried to the big corbita anchored far off. Salario prowled the dock and shouted orders with the authority of a battlefield commander. A wide-brimmed straw hat shaded the taut ox hide of his face, but no one needed to see his eyes. His sharp voice startled even the gulls, birds accustomed to commotion.

Rufio sat on a coil of rope and watched Metellus rattle toward him in a heavily laden wagon. The signifer sported the bemused look that had so often infuriated Diocles, but that Rufio found as reassuring as Valerius's unselfconscious valor.

Rufio went up to the wagon. A bronze helmet lay on the seat beside Metellus.

"A gift for you," Metellus said. "I was told to deliver it myself."

Rufio hefted it, a battered relic from a dozen campaigns. He smiled as he ran his fingers over it. "See this?" He pointed to a deep dent across the left brow. "A smelly Syrian bandit did that. His blade would have cut through the bronze had it not been for a black-haired young optio who partially blocked it. And then spilled the Syrian's entrails onto the desert sand."

"He said that maybe it would protect you the way you had protected him that day."

"What's all that?" Rufio pointed to the back of the wagon.

"More gifts." Metellus whipped off the cloth covering.

"I don't believe it!" Rufio said with the smile of vanished youth.

The wagon was filled with Parmula hams.

"He said you'll have to supply your own Etrurian wine."

Rufio touched one of the hams encased in netting, and then without another word turned and walked off toward the edge of the dock. He sat back down on the rope coil and smiled to himself as years of his past life rolled across his mind.

Metellus came over and sat on the stone dock beside him.

"I tried," the signifer said.

"I know."

"I'm certain he wanted to come. I'm just as sure he didn't want you to see him as a lesser man."

"A drunken soldier is better than most of the civilians I've known. And a half-broken Bellator is better than all of them."

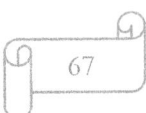

"He's ashamed."

"He always trusted me before. I wish he could do it again."

"I think he does. He doesn't trust himself."

Rufio looked back toward the land as the cool air caressed his face. "The onshore breeze is starting. This is my favorite time of day."

He stood up and walked away with a stride that told Metellus not to follow.

15

HE WHO AIMS TO REACH THE GOAL FIRST BEARS AND DOES MANY THINGS.

HORACE

"One hundred and eighty feet," Salario said in answer to the tribune's question about the length of the ship. "Almost fifty at the beam."

Crus gazed forward from the stern. Most of the men of the Second Cohort were aboard now and claiming deck space. The hold was usually given over entirely to cargo, so all the sailors and passengers slept on deck. The single deck cabin near the stern was shared by Salario and his sailing master. From the farthest part of the rear deck rose a great gilded goose head.

Crus strolled forward. The huge square mainsail loomed above him at mid-deck. Furled now, it would soon be dropped to gather in the winds that would carry them to the East. Above it rose a triangular topsail for snatching any helpful wayward breezes high up. A small squaresail at the bow helped to maneuver the sea-going monster.

"Careful with that!" boomed a voice from amidships.

Crus saw Bellator standing on deck and directing a half-dozen sailors struggling with amphoras.

"Wine is the blood of Jupiter," he shouted at them. "Spill it and die."

"Now isn't that a sight?" Rufio said, coming up behind Crus.

Bellator hefted his gear onto his shoulder and approached the tribune and centurion.

"I have a few months to waste," he said and dropped his equipment at his feet.

Crus turned to Rufio. The centurion's face was as hard as a baked tile.

"Do you expect a trumpet blast in welcome?" he said to the engineer. "Find some deck space and see me when I'm not busy."

Rufio brushed past him and called out to Valerius on the crowded foredeck.

"That's what I've always yearned for in him," Bellator said. "His tenderness."

"Welcome," Crus said.

"Rome called. I'm here."

"And the tavern incident?"

"Don't apologize."

"I have no intention of doing so."

"Good. It's unworthy of a patrician. Let's move on."

"We've moved."

Bellator turned to the sun dropping toward its nightly dip in the sea. "I like embarking on the evening tide. The cool night wind always brings adventure."

"Find a place. We'll talk later."

Crus joined Rufio forward.

The soldiers had set out their equipment and other belongings as neatly as if the deck were the ground of a marching camp.

"I was going to pitch the tents," Rufio said. "It's not uncommon for passengers to do that—but Salario doesn't want all those holes in his deck. We'll pray for fair weather."

Crus noticed that several of the men already looked pale just from the gentle pitching of the ship at anchor.

"Time to bring out the wormwood wine?"

"Yes," Rufio said, looking at the pasty faces. "It won't settle every stomach, but it'll help."

"What's your measure of Salario?"

"He seems as honest as any of these water rats."

"But as a sailor?"

"It won't matter much. His gubernator is the real sailing master. He'll tuck us in the arms of the Etesians if he's any good. That's him over there."

A tall man, as lean as leather, shouted orders and curses from amidships.

"The sailors look like they want to kill him," Crus said.

"Maybe they will someday. Seamen are a sour lot. I wouldn't trust them to carry a dead dog."

Crus smiled. "I noticed we're riding low in the water. Didn't Salario say he had no cargo?"

"He found some at the last minute. The crew of the ship that was supposed to take it rioted over something. The idiots almost burned down their own vessel. The traders were happy to find Salario."

"I'm sure he squeezed every coin out of them."

"Until they yelped. We're standing above nine thousand amphoras of olive oil and wine."

"Well, we won't go dry," Crus said with a smile.

"Salario gets double payment—our passage and the cost of shipping the cargo. I think he can spare a cup or two for the fighting men of Rome."

Salario seems like a nice man. He is not an Italian but a Greek freedman who works for a rich man in Neapolis. He offered me his cabin for the entire voyage, but I sleep only next to my Rufio. I am writing this before the sun goes down on the evening we are leaving. Some of the soldiers are already seasick even though we are still at anchor. I am not surprised. The smell of wet wood and musty cloth gags me. The swaying of the ship makes me feel as if my meal wants to jump out of my belly. The sun is very low and I am having difficulty seeing well enough to write. Salario is about to sacrifice a chicken to ensure that the portents are good. I am certain he hopes they are. He is eager to sail.

"It's good to be at sea again," Bellator said as the corbita plowed through the darkness. "Nothing more purifying than the salt air."

"Mmmmm," Rufio murmured.

"You don't agree?"

"You know I don't agree. I'd rather have dirt under my feet."

"Even the sand of Judaea?"

Rufio laughed. "Even Judaea."

The two men stood alone at the bow and let the onrushing night wind buffet their faces.

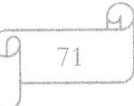

"Why did you change your mind?"

"Metellus. He made my self-pity seem so vile I couldn't stand the sight of myself. I thought a sea breeze and a desert baking could scour me clean."

Rufio leaned sideways against the rail. "He's one of my best officers."

"The smartest, too, I'll wager."

"In some ways, in others not. He's keen to the follies of men."

"And on the battlefield?"

"As brave as Scipio. But so is Valerius. And my optio is sharper in the ways of soldiering. He can size up terrain or whip together a battle line with hardly a thought. So they complement each other."

"Fortunate for you."

"Fortuna had nothing to do with it."

"Victoria?"

"Of course."

"We're going to need all the help she wants to give us."

Rufio turned and stared ahead into the blackness. "I know." He sighed. "Judaea. Jupiter's joke on the human race."

16

EQUALS MOST EASILY CONGREGATE WITH EQUALS.

CICERO

Life aboard this ship is strange. The sailors are hard men, but it is not the hardness of soldiers. They seem to be castoffs of the most frightful kind. Many are runaway slaves who have been caught and branded on the face, only to escape again. They know and resent the fact that they have no standing among people of the land. The work here is brutal and dangerous and only the desperate would choose it. They hate the soldiers, who are paid better and eat better. Salario provides us no food, only water, so we have brought our own. The seamen eat their morsels and scowl at us. The soldiers do not notice. To them the sailors are as invisible as fleas on a dog.

The crew are harsh to each other. They rarely use real names. They call each other by cruel nicknames that point to some physical deformity. I have heard crewmen called Limper, Blinky, and Stump. There is one boy of about eighteen who has had a terrible infection in his face. It left a deep hole. Other sailors callously call him Pus. There is even one who is called One Ball, though how anyone can vouch for that I cannot guess.

"So that's it," Crus said, finishing up a summary of the few crumbs of information provided by Bulla.

The five other centurions of the Second Cohort had joined Rufio and Valerius and Bellator. They sat in a small circle on the foredeck.

"Agrippa didn't even hint where he wanted the fort built?" Bellator asked.

"In the south," Crus said.

"That's like saying, 'Somewhere on earth.'"

"There's been bandit activity south of a place called Hebron. In some town near the edge of the wilderness. Agrippa thinks the bandits might actually be Parthians probing."

"Is it near that stinking toxic sea?" Bellator asked, turning to Rufio.

"Not too far from it," the centurion said.

Bellator squinted into the afternoon sun as if he suddenly resented its rays. "The armpit of the world."

"It has its own beauty," Rufio said.

"Can we build a fort there?" Crus asked.

"If we can find water and materials," Bellator said. "We'll have to scout the area."

"We'll need Herod's blessing in any case," Rufio said. "We'll stop in Jerusalem and ask him for his suggestions."

"The king himself?" Valerius asked in surprise.

"Certainly," Rufio said. "He's from the area south of there called Idumaea."

"That should be entertaining," Bellator said. "Annoy the old bastard right in his own lair."

"Why not?" Rufio smiled. "He's going to resent us anyway. Let's give him reason."

After the meeting ended, Rufio watched Bellator drift away by himself. Rufio gave him a few minutes of privacy and then joined him amidships. Bellator had the look Rufio had not seen in years. The engineer leaned against the rail and stared toward the setting sun, but Rufio knew his mind was focused inward. Bellator was always happiest when taunted by a challenge. Now he was invigorated. He even looked younger, though the wet air had aggravated an old injury and his limp had returned.

"What do you think?" Rufio asked.

"It's a problem with a hundred mysteries. The terrain, the enemy, water, materials."

"And Herod."

"Oh, yes. That old wolf isn't going to want us there."

"But he won't defy Rome."

Bellator smiled. "It'll be nice to watch him have to swallow sand for once."

"Herod is supposed to supply us with troops."

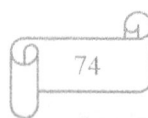

"Why?"

"If a major Parthian force sweeps out of the desert, we'll need cavalry."

"I have no confidence in Judaeans."

"They're very tough. You know that."

"They fight like Gauls. They ignore their commanders all the time. Even in battle."

"If they desert, they'll do so only once."

"How do you know that?"

"Because if they challenge the authority of Rome, I'll hunt them down and kill them."

Bellator nodded and turned back to the sea. "Tell me about Crus."

"He fought with valor along the Rhenus."

"So did thousands of others. Tell me more."

Rufio smiled. He loved Bellator's cranky persistence. When he wanted to know something, he was as relentless as an insect boring through wood.

"He has potential he doesn't even know he has."

"Brave?"

"Without question."

"Honorable?"

"As you."

"Well, I don't know I'd consider that a sweetener."

"True enough, you bitter weed."

Bellator burst out laughing. "Oh, Quintus, where have all the years gone?"

"To the service of Rome."

"Amazing that we should be sailing together again. A pair of old dock rats escaping the rancid shore."

"The gods have their ways."

"I think not. They abandoned me long ago."

"Don't even consider that possibility," Rufio said.

"We cannot relive our youth."

"We should never even try."

"Do you regret anything?" Bellator asked.

"Only folly."

Bellator gazed at the water. Suddenly he lost the energy he had just a moment before. His eyes looked weary and forlorn. "When I was young, I had hoped to do great things. Now?" He seemed to sag a bit inside his own flesh. "Now, I'll be happy simply to die without dishonor."

Few human experiences are more soothing than a peaceful evening on a peaceful sea. Flavia stood at the bow and let the cool breeze caress her. She turned and saw Neko straightening up Rufio's gear in the area on the deck where he slept. She waved to get his attention and then gestured for him to come to her.

Neko joined her at the front of the ship.

"Be with me for a while?" she asked.

The Egyptian bowed slightly. "Your desire is my desire."

She pointed to a spot on the deck. He dropped down and she sat opposite.

"Can you tell me about Spain?"

"I don't understand your question."

"What Rufio suffered there."

"Many trials. Many sufferings."

"I mean a suffering of the heart."

"Ah, yes."

"There was a woman. I know that."

"Yes."

"And she died."

"Yes."

"Did he love her?"

"No."

Flavia gazed into the dark-skinned face that seemed incapable of deceit.

"No," Neko said again. "As far as I know, he has never loved any woman but you."

"Then why did he suffer so?"

"He was at the edge of love. The way a sailor stands on the shore of the sea before embarking on a sunny day. And then a terrible storm erupts and lightning flashes and his ship capsizes and all are drowned."

"Oh, Neko . . . Tell me."

"She was a Cantabri woman. A widow with a baby boy. A spark had flashed between Rufio and her. And that spark has flashed rarely in Rufio's life. But a fever struck her down. The baby, too. He died first, though she did not know it. When she was burning up on her deathbed, she asked Rufio about her boy. Rufio lied and said he was well. She asked Rufio to rear him to manhood. He promised he would. She smiled and died in his arms. Shortly after that, he volunteered for a dangerous journey and was ambushed and almost died."

Flavia could feel the tears in her eyes and turned away.

"I have never seen Flavia weep. Do not weep now. Rufio would not want it."

She sniffed and ran her hands across her eyebrows and looked back at Neko. "Thank you for telling me."

But Neko did not move. "May I help you now?"

She stared at him uncertainly.

"You may tell me."

She moistened her lips. "I want so much to give him a son."

"Perhaps one day you shall."

"I don't think I can. We have been together many times. But nothing."

Neko remained silent.

"I feel so empty sometimes because of it."

Neko extended his right hand in invitation to her.

She slipped her fingers into his.

"Do not weep for that," he said with a gentleness that could have stilled the sea.

"Why?"

"Rufio does not need a son. I doubt that he would want one. He is unlike other men. He does not desire to live another life through his offspring, as most men do. He has fought and laughed and struggled through far too full a life to want to live another through a son. And think of the boy. Growing up in the shadow of Rufio?" Neko shook his head. "Do not weep for that."

Still holding his right hand, she laid her left hand on both of theirs.

"Thank you, my dear friend," she whispered. "Stay with us always."

"I have no other life. Nor do I want one."

17

WE ARE BETTER ABLE TO WIN WITH PLANNING THAN WITH ANGER.

PUBLILIUS SYRUS

Rufio smiled at Paki. Like all cats, she was impervious to seasickness. When not prowling the hold below for mice, she could often be seen prancing about the deck or curled up with his gear and taking one of the thirty or forty naps she managed to squeeze into a day. At other times, she gazed curiously at the numerous soldiers ejecting their most recent meal over the side of the ship. Now she lay languidly on the centurion's red cloak and was trying to see how long she could make herself with an enormous stretch.

Rufio scratched her under the chin and smiled at her wink of contentment before he went to observe Valerius leading the men in their morning weapons drill.

"How did Arrianus ever meet the height requirement?" Rufio said as he came up beside his optio.

"Isn't it obvious?" Valerius answered with a smile. "A well-placed bribe."

Rufio watched the short but very tough soldier burn through his drill. "He seems especially energetic today."

"He's boiling inside. He lost a senator's ransom in a dice game."

"Again?" Rufio said in exasperation.

"It wasn't the money. Beakless, that rat turd, publicly humiliated him. Just for fun."

"Beakless?"

"The gubernator. Didn't you notice he has a chunk missing from the end of his nose? Bitten off in a fight."

"What did he say?"

"That Arrianus was just an Italian dwarf and could never beat a man of the sea. He did everything he could to goad him. Called him the degenerate spawn of a greasy whore. Of course, Arrianus didn't tell me this. I got it from some of the others."

"These sailors are endearing, aren't they? What did Arrianus do?"

"Nothing."

Rufio would have trusted Valerius with his soul, so the skepticism in the centurion's eyes was out of character.

"On my honor," Valerius said. "He just walked away."

"Why?"

"Because of you."

"Stop feeding me from the end of a pin."

"After what happened at the bath house, he won't disobey you on this again."

Rufio smiled and looked back at Arrianus thrusting and sweating. "He's a good Roman."

Rufio turned away. He saw Salario and Beakless talking in front of Salario's cabin near the stern. The look on Salario's face was not reassuring. Something was amiss.

Beakless left abruptly and disappeared down a hatch into the hold.

"Get the tribune," Rufio said to Valerius. "Ask him to meet me at the stern."

Rufio followed Beakless down a ladder into the dark hold, rank with the reek of mold and rot and stagnant water.

The sailing master seemed to be checking the sturdiness of the racks holding the amphoras.

"Are we expecting trouble?" Rufio asked.

Beakless ignored him and kept at his work.

Rufio sloshed through the black bilge water toward the gubernator.

Finally Beakless turned and straightened up. He was about a half-foot taller than the centurion.

"Tell me about the dice game."

Beakless smiled, proudly displaying five brown teeth. "I won."

"Why did you humiliate my soldier?"

"He's a weakling."

"Mocking a man in front of his comrades is as vile as pissing in his face."

"I know that. You arrogant Romans should learn the feeling of piss. I feel it every day."

"You hate your life?"

"Wouldn't you?"

"Should I weep for you?"

Beakless said nothing.

"I'd never commit that kind of crime," Rufio said. "Never ridicule a man before his men. I wouldn't even do it to you."

Like a scorpion bolt, Rufio's fist drove deep into the gubernator's stomach. Foul breath exploded from his lungs and he buckled like a snapped tree. Three more times Rufio's fist slammed him. Beakless was vomiting now and sank to his knees and finally collapsed into the bilge water.

"Never steal a man's pride," Rufio said with just a hint of exertion. "Even if you hate him. Never."

"Tell him," Rufio heard Crus say to Salario as he joined them in front of the cabin.

"We have trouble," Salario said. "One of my men just told me he overheard someone in a popina in Ostia asking about our cargo."

"Go on."

"I think we're going to be attacked."

"Not pirates?"

"Yes."

"I thought Pompeius wiped them out fifty years ago. Swept the seas with an iron rake."

"He did. But no vermin are ever totally exterminated. There are still some desperate savages who'll kill without a thought."

"We have over four hundred fighting men on this ship," Rufio said in a dismissive tone. "What does it matter?"

"It does matter," Salario said. "A pirate ship is small and fast. They have rowers besides sails. We cannot outrun them. They'll appear on the horizon and stay back to see if we furl our sails in submission. When we do, we'll be helpless. If we don't surrender the vessel, they'll dart in and rip open our belly with the bronze ramming plates on their prow."

"What would they gain by sinking us?" Crus asked.

"They don't have to sink us," Salario said. "They know the threat is enough."

Rufio folded his arms and drifted toward the edge of the deck. He gazed out at the water. His men had finished their weapons drill, so now the only sound was the incessant creaking of the giant corbita. He stared at the sea for several minutes.

"Your gubernator is down in the hold," he said, turning to Salario. "He isn't feeling well. Offer him some wormwood wine and tell him I want to speak with him."

Salario hurried off.

"Have you seen Bellator?" Rufio asked Crus.

The tribune gestured behind him.

Rufio turned and saw the engineer coming aft. The old soldier was as sensitive to trouble as a dog to distant thunder.

"What is it?" Bellator asked.

"There's a pirate ship out there," Rufio said. "It wants our vessel. If we don't submit, it'll split open our bowels and send us to Neptune's maw."

"Submit?" Bellator said with a laugh. "Very entertaining."

"Is there a hidden language you two are speaking?" Crus said. "Isn't this very serious?"

"Of course it's serious," Rufio said. "But we're serious men." He looked at Bellator. "I think we should greet them with a bird."

The engineer's fleshy face broadened in a grin. "A raven?"

"My favorite fowl."

"I'll get together with the ship's carpenter. We can have one in an hour."

"I'll speak with Beakless. It'll need some fancy sailing on his part, but I think he's the man for it."

"He's a surly lout."

"Maybe to you," Rufio said. "But he and I are on the best of terms."

18

OPPORTUNITY IS NOT EASILY GAINED BUT IS EASILY LOST.

PUBLILIUS SYRUS

*P*irates *are coming. The seamen are near panic. They feel helpless. I have never seen such terror in men's eyes. Yet I have no fear. I am surrounded by the bravest men on earth. Any one of them would dash a woman's fear. Hundreds of them make fear impossible.*

I asked Rufio if he had ever seen pirates.

"Only nailed to crosses," he said to me. "We crucified four in Tyrus many years ago. They endured two days pinned to those planks. I wish their agony had lasted a week."

He speaks with such hatred of them it would frighten the dead.

"Without mercy, without honor, without souls," are the words he used to me. "They slaughter with no restraint and die with no shame."

When he speaks of pirates, even the Suebi recede into the background of his hatred.

"You're the key to everything," Rufio said to Beakless. The two of them sat with Crus and Salario in a circle on the deck near the master's cabin. Neko had tapped the Etrurian wine at Bellator's insistence, and now the Egyptian passed around cups of the finest liquid the gods had ever allowed mankind to savor.

"Without your skill," Rufio said to Beakless, "we'll all die a horrible death."

"No finer gubernator sails the Great Sea," Salario said.

"Good." Rufio looked at Beakless's chalky face. "You're as pale as a fish belly. Are you over your illness?"

"Yes."

"Be certain. Only then can we be partners."

"Partners?"

"Men in crisis are always comrades. Minor stomach troubles count for nothing."

The hint of a smile in Rufio's eyes clearly startled Beakless. He was staring with the naked fierceness unique to men of the sea. Yet he could hold it only briefly. Then he, too, smiled back.

"Comrades," Beakless said in tribute to the special bond shared by tough men in a hostile world.

"You have a plan then?" Salario asked.

"Always." Rufio smiled. "Though my plans don't always work. We'll test this one in combat."

"As far as I can see, we're completely at their mercy. And they have none."

"Roman soldiers rely on no one's mercy." He turned back to Beakless. "As soon as their ship appears, furl your sails in surrender. Let them approach. But here's the important part—don't let us drift. Keep a delicate hand on the steering oars. Make sure our ship stays pointed in the direction they're coming from. Can you do that?"

"With my eyes closed and my left big toe on the oar stick."

"Excellent. They have to come up alongside us. Not perpendicular to us."

"I don't know that word," Beakless said.

"This." Rufio made a "T" with his hands. "They must come up along our beam, not cross our bow."

"Easily done."

"Then what?" Salario said to Rufio, unable to conceal his skepticism.

"We'll board the ship and take it."

"That simply?"

"Nothing worth doing is simple."

"How will we do it?"

"You won't do it. None of your crew is to fight. The men of the Second Cohort will give them a taste of Roman steel."

"I thought our steel was made by the Celts," Crus said in a gentle barb.

Rufio smiled. "Now why spoil a daring venture with a tiny detail?"

"I've never seen anything like that," Salario said, staring at the massive wooden plank.

"I've never even heard of anything like that," Beakless said.

"Then you've neglected your history," Rufio answered.

The ship's carpenter and two helpers hammered away under the direction of Bellator.

"During the first war with the Carthaginians, those savages were much better seamen than we were." Rufio inspected the carpenters' handiwork as he spoke. "They were as lethal as sea monsters at sending our men to the bottom. But we knew we could face them down, sword to sword. So we turned their deck into a battlefield."

The boarding bridge was about twenty-five feet long and six feet wide. Yet its size was secondary to its strange terminus. Fastened to the end at a right angle was a huge iron spike.

"That's the secret," Rufio said, pointing to the newly sharpened tip gleaming in the sun. "The raven's beak."

Salario examined the bridge more closely.

"We'll hoist it on a mast amidships," Rufio said. "When the pirate ship sails up next to our beam, we'll let it fall. The beak will bite into their deck as deeply as the Kraken's teeth. We'll board the ship and fight on the deck like Scipio's men on the plain of Zama."

"Won't the pirates see the plank?"

"Of course," Rufio said. "But they might as well be blind men trying to read the entrails of sheep. They'll have no idea what they're seeing."

Salario looked up at Rufio and back again at the bridge, then wandered off as though lost in thought.

"He looks ill," Rufio said.

Beakless nodded. "He is. A sickness of the heart."

Rufio waited for him to continue.

"The ship that stalks us—he thinks he knows who the captain is. There are so few pirates left, he's probably right."

"And?"

"An arrogant criminal called One Eye. He captured Salario's son's ship. Tortured all the officers and drank and laughed while he did it. Then he pushed them over the side with the point of his sword. The pirates laughed like fools and watched the men flounder until they sank. They released the rest of the crew on the coast of Africa. A few made it back to Ostia. That's how Salario learned about his son."

Rufio gazed at Salario standing alone at the stern and staring out to sea. Then he turned to Bellator.

"Almost done?

"Close. Then we'll build the mast. We'll put railings on the bridge so nobody slides off. I'm not tempting Fortuna. Nobody has used one of these ravens in two hundred years."

"It's so ancient it's fresh. Like you."

Bellator tried to scowl but failed. "It's like the old days," he said with a grin. "By the gods, Quintus, this feels grand!"

19

ARMS ARE OF SMALL VALUE IF THERE IS NO WISDOM IN THIS COUNTRY.

PUBLILIUS SYRUS

*R*ufio has spoken with the other centurions. They are ready. They respect him very much, though all five are older than he is. Words mean nothing to a centurion. Deeds are all. The flash and polish of fine metal is only that. These men speak with steel. They and their centuries fought like a six-headed beast at the Hill of Scorpions. Nothing can cut that bond.

Crus had just completed making the rounds of the other centuries when he joined Rufio and Metellus at their allotted deck space. Paki sprawled next to them. Wine and hard cheese and smoked fish were laid out on the planks for their evening meal. Valerius was off conducting an equipment inspection.

"Tomorrow?" Crus asked, reaching for the wine.

"Very soon," Rufio said. "They won't delay."

"Captives?" Metellus asked.

"Depends on circumstances. We'll see how many are eager to die like fools." Rufio looked at Crus. The tribune seemed as pensive as an old philosopher as he stared into his cup of wine. "Help Valerius with the inspection," Rufio said to the signifer.

Metellus hurried off to give his friend a hand.

"How do you always know what to do?" Crus asked after Metellus had left.

"It's an illusion I encourage," Rufio said with a laugh.

"I'm serious."

"I have much experience. If you confront a problem a hundred times, it's no magic to be able to solve it the hundred and first."

"You've fought pirates before?"

"No, but others have. I'm familiar with all their accounts."

"Your library you mean?"

"I swim in the seas of history."

"I envy you."

"Don't."

"I want to be able to turn my hand to any problem with solutions flowing from my fingertips."

"That takes decades. And much suffering."

"I'm impatient."

"To suffer?"

Crus set down his cup and stared off into the distance. "Perhaps."

"Then you're heading to the right place. Living in the desert with a pack of Judaeans is more suffering than any man deserves."

Crus smiled. "You always set me at ease. In Gaul. Here at sea. You have a talent."

"Even a two-legged squirrel turns up the occasional nut."

"You like to bat me away like a cat with a kitten." Crus seemed suddenly serious. "Don't do it tonight."

Rufio remained silent.

"There must be principles that guide you."

"What kind of principles?"

"I'm not sure. . . . Lessons from all your experience. And from your readings of Caesar and others."

"Have you read Caesar?"

"Seven times."

"Good. If you retain one-tenth of Caesar's wisdom, you'll be wiser than any man alive."

"But you must have rendered down your own experience into certain essences. Ideas you can share with me."

"Most ideas slip from our grasp unless they've been sanctified with blood."

"I risked my blood along the Rhenus," Crus said with a touch of anger. "You know that."

"Then I guess you're ready."

Crus relented in a smile. "You test everybody, don't you?"

"Test? I'm just a simple soldier."

"Teach me now."

Rufio stood up. "Let's go to the bow. The evening breeze can clear our thoughts."

The soft wind soothed them as they sailed south toward Africa and took in the setting sun off to their right.

"All soldiers who've smelled an enemy's hatred have learned lessons of leadership. Or else they've died on the battlefield. Some have dozens of them. A few have hundreds. How many do you want?"

"You decide."

"For a tribune? Five will be a heavy load. You might have to hold your balls in your hand while you lift."

"I'll take that risk, centurion."

"Good. Five are all you'll need. Master them and you'll master any crisis. Even on the Senate floor."

"Go on."

"The first is the simplest. When a decision is necessary, always make it immediately. Decide at the outset. That's when the greatest number of possibilities exists. As time passes, your options decline fast. Never wait so long that a decision makes itself."

"I understand."

"The second flows from the first. When you make a decision, execute it at once. If you decide something must happen eventually, make it happen immediately."

"But what if you want to think about it a bit?" Crus said. "Maybe try to devise a better plan?"

"That's nothing more than a catastrophe tugging at your sleeve. In a crisis, matters almost always get worse on their own until you intervene. That has to be countered. When a German draws his sword, your slashing with your blade today on the Nones is better than giving him a perfect thrust on the Ides."

Crus looked away toward the orange disc about to slide into the sea. "This isn't as simple as I'd hoped."

"Nothing is as simple as people hope."

Crus turned back to Rufio. "Go on."

"The third is as difficult as bending cold steel. If you decide not to move, you have to portray it as an aggressive act. Your enemy must see it as a taunt. Under no circumstances can he be allowed to think it's timidity or weakness. Even a decision *not* to move forward must be seen as an act of defiance."

"I can't even begin to imagine how to do that."

"Remember when Barovistus murdered the three Roman traders? The legion refused to give battle over that. He knew we weren't afraid. Sabinus threw dirt in his face and he had to swallow it."

"So Barovistus raised the stakes and attacked the Sequani village."

"Yes. By refusing to act, we defied him. He knew it wasn't fear. Our inaction was a challenge and it infuriated him. So we drew *him* out. And then we destroyed him."

"These get harder as we go. I'm happy there are only five."

"I told you—there are hundreds. But five will do."

"Proceed."

"The fourth is a simple one. Never buy the same vineyard twice."

Crus frowned and searched Rufio's eyes for meaning. "Explain."

"When you've smashed your enemy, never pull back. Never let him regroup and retake the field. If you have to spill your men's blood twice for the same soil, you insult the gods who protect you and betray the men who serve you. Victoria will spurn you and your men will loathe you. Then you have no choice but to fall on your sword."

"Oh, yes," Crus said with a sigh. "Such a very simple principle."

"I've saved the most vital for last."

"I don't doubt it."

"Even if you forget the first four, remember this one. It's more important than all the others combined."

"Tell me."

"Chisel this into your soul: Authority is never something you're given—you have to take it."

Crus gazed in silence at Rufio, who had embodied that principle in his frightening decision to pivot the entire right wing of the legion at the Hill of Scorpions. And with it, annihilate the Suebi horde.

"Thank you," Crus said and laid his right hand on Rufio's left shoulder. "I fear I was never meant to be a soldier."

"None of us can truly know what the gods intend for us."

"I thank them that you are here."

Rufio said nothing.

Crus turned away and gazed out to sea. "I just wish I could have your confidence."

Rufio smiled. "You're too young for that. It takes many years."

"Of fighting?"

"Of fighting. And of living."

"Philosophers talk about everything except what's important," Crus said with a touch of annoyance. "Why can't they talk about that?"

"I don't understand. About what?"

"About confidence. About where it comes from. Or even what it is."

"You should never ask a philosopher that."

"Then whom should I ask?"

"Isn't it obvious? A soldier."

He turned back from the sea. "All right, I'm asking."

"Tribune, confidence is the plainest and calmest thing in the world. And the rarest...."

"And what is it?"

"Confidence is simply knowing that you're capable of dealing with the unthinkable."

Crus stared at him in silence for a long time.

"Speak to the men now," Rufio said at last.

Crus looked alarmed. "I haven't prepared anything."

"That's the perfect time. Speak from the soul."

"Our task is simple," Crus said to the men of the Second Cohort. "Destroy these pirates."

Awash in moonlight, the soldiers sat in neat ranks and files on the deck.

"If we don't surrender, they'll sink this vessel. Romans don't surrender to thieves. Show them that the reach of Rome is greater than they can comprehend. A single cohort adrift in a ship on the Great Sea is still the arm of Caesar. Flex the muscles of that arm and sweep these vermin from the earth." Crus looked at Rufio. "Centurion!"

Rufio rose from the first rank and stood before his men, while Crus stepped to the side.

"Expect them tomorrow," Rufio said. "I know your centurions have explained our tactics to you. Just consider the deck of the enemy ship another battlefield. Fight as you would on land. I'll lead the first and third centuries across. Tribune Crus will follow with the second and fourth in reserve. The fifth and sixth will guard this vessel. Spare any man who submits, and kill any leaders you see. They'll be dressed no differently than their men, so cut down anyone who even looks like he might be giving a command. Sleep well and remember that for them it will be their last sleep before they're swallowed by the waters of Acheron."

Flavia stood with Rufio by Salario's deck cabin near the stern.

"Salario offered us the use of his quarters for the night," Rufio said.

"Do you want to?"

"No."

She slid her arms around him. "Neither do I. Just hold me."

He kissed her on top of her head. "I don't have to tell you to stay on this ship tomorrow, do I? I have enough warriors."

She nestled her head in the hollow of his shoulder. "Have I ever disobeyed you?"

"Yes."

He could feel her shake with a soft laugh.

"I promise."

"Look at me."

She gazed up at him.

He pressed his lips to each of her eyebrows.

"I love when you do that," she said dreamily.

He smiled. "I know."

20

HE WHO SPARES THE WICKED HARMS THE RIGHTEOUS.

PUBLILIUS SYRUS

"Ship!" one of the lookouts shouted.

The first pink light of a misty dawn was just now sliding across the sea.

Already in full armor, Rufio ran to the stern. Beakless was manning the steering oars, and Crus arrived next to them in an instant.

"A bireme," Rufio said. "I'll wager it's one of our wrecks that's been refitted."

"Look how fast she moves," Crus said. "She'll be on us quickly."

"It's time." Rufio turned and rejoined his men.

Having been up since an hour before dawn, the soldiers of the Second Cohort had already eaten their breakfast of wheat porridge and dried fruits and were now pulling on their mail loricas. The sword and dagger belts followed, and then the bronze helmets.

Rufio took his place at the head of them.

"You know the plan," he said without preliminaries. "As usual, there are only three things to do. Remember your training, follow your centurions, and look to your comrades. Victory will follow." He smiled at the men who were now as much a part of him as his own skeleton. "And remember, I am with you always."

The pride and the loyalty he saw in the eyes fixed on him would have made Caesar weep.

"Ready now," he said, and then hurried back to the stern.

Flavia and Salario had joined Crus there.

"They're close enough," Salario said. "They know we see them. Time to furl."

He gave the order and the sails were raised.

The naturally sluggish corbita slowed like a dying fish.

Rufio turned to his men. They were lying on their bellies on the deck with their shields beside them. From the smaller and lower pirate ship, the soldiers would be invisible. The high gunwales of the corbita added further to their concealment. The five other centurions posed in full view, as arrogant as statues on plinths. Rufio had positioned them that way not only to taunt but to baffle. Six men defending a corbita seemed an absurdity. Rufio wanted to hear the pirates laugh.

"It's him," Salario said with the cold loathing of a man watching a spectre rise from the ashes.

"Who?" Rufio asked.

"One Eye. Look at the oars. They're painted silver. Only he does that, the pompous swine." He turned to the centurion. "I want his head."

"I'll ask him for it," Rufio said and rushed off to Bellator amidships.

"Ready," the engineer said.

The immense railed plank loomed straight above them. Attached to the mast by a rope and pulley, it awaited its moment to sink its single fang into the spine of the enemy.

Rufio looked astern. The pirate vessel was only about a quarter mile off. Its two banks of rowers propelled it toward them with the speed of a water insect skimming the surface.

"Positions," Rufio ordered.

His five centurions stood against the gunwale near the raven.

The corbita seemed to be drifting, but Beakless was cleverly steering it so its port side ran parallel to the closing ship.

The pirates approached without caution, as if they had been ordered to be fools.

Salario came up and stood next to Rufio along the port beam.

"There he is," the master said.

A man of no more than thirty, missing his left eye and his left ear, stood grinning near the bow.

"He doesn't even have a weapon," Rufio said.

"He's accustomed to submission."

Dozens of pirates lined the rail. A few held a dagger or a sword, but most appeared unarmed. Their vessel slid up slowly beside the corbita. Some of the pirates were pointing at the half-dozen centurions and laughing. A few stared up at the raven in confusion and perhaps even alarm.

"Do you know the most fascinating thing about the Gauls?" Rufio asked.

"Gauls?" Salario stared in surprise at the centurion speaking about people who were hundreds of miles away, and doing so as calmly as if he were discussing a philosophical problem in his study, not facing a ship manned by ruthless killers.

"Yes," Rufio said. "They're the toughest fighters in the world, but they always lose in the end. Why is that? Because ferocity — even Gallic ferocity — is never a match for seasoned troops."

He spun around to Bellator.

"Now!"

Like a bolt from Zeus, the raven's beak crashed to the deck with the boom of a thunderclap. Three pirates went down beneath it. Two were crushed to nothing. The third, still alive, had been pierced by the iron spike and wriggled hopelessly like a speared fish.

Rufio sprang to the head of the gangway, his two centuries right behind him. Cheered by the priceless advantage of attacking from a greater height, they rolled down Bellator's bridge with the force of an avalanche.

The pirates scattered and scrambled for weapons.

In what seemed like only seconds, Rufio and his two centuries stood amidships on the pirate vessel. He pivoted to the left toward the bow, and Crus rushed behind with his own centuries and swept toward the stern. Already the pirates had been split in two.

A toothless pirate slashed at Rufio with a rusty blade. The centurion knocked it aside with his shield and thrust his sword deep into the man's stomach. He deflated like a collapsed bladder, and Rufio kicked him aside.

The front rank drove forward, smashing and stabbing the bewildered pirates. To Rufio's left, Arrianus took a terrible toll of the sea bandits, and Rufio felt safe in focusing on the killers before him.

Shieldless and with no training worthy of the name, the pirates were lost. The Romans slew them like blind rats trapped in a hole.

A dark-skinned thief slashed at Rufio with a cavalry sword, but the bronze edge of his shield deflected it. Rufio thrust his sword into the gaping armpit. The steel sank as easily as hot metal into soft grease, and the dark man dropped with a thud.

"Rufio!" he heard Metellus shout above the banging and screaming.

He looked to the bow and saw One Eye igniting bundles of rags. Dozens of pirates blocked the way to their leader.

"Get him!" Rufio yelled, but there was no way to reach him.

The pirate chief had already tossed several flaming bundles onto the corbita, and the seamen were trying to put them out.

"That madman is going to burn us all alive," Arrianus shouted.

Alone at the bow, One Eye readied another fiery bundle. The soldiers struggling to reach him might as well have been a hundred miles away.

An arrow tore into One Eye's throat and a second ripped through his chest and drove him to the deck.

Rufio spun to the left.

Flavia stood atop the roof of Salario's cabin and nocked a third arrow and let it fly. Then a fourth and a fifth. One by one she took down her foes. They wailed and fell before the Sequani huntress unleashing the full fury of her savage race.

And now the pirates lost their minds. Battered and slashed and stabbed, and now pierced from above, they climbed over the corpses of their friends and bolted to the rail. They dropped their weapons and jumped over the side in the final madness of the doomed.

Rufio turned toward the stern. Hardly a pirate remained alive. Crus and his men had laid waste without mercy the other half of the pirate crew. The Romans leaned on their shields and paused for breath as the few surviving thieves groaned on the bloody deck before them.

"Rufio! Look!" Valerius yelled and pointed into the water.

Rufio ran to the rail.

The pirates were floundering.

"Most of them can't even swim," Valerius said in amazement.

They flopped around, desperately trying to keep themselves afloat. Dozens of them looked up at Rufio with the bulging eyes of terrified children in a nightmare.

Where were the ruthless killers now? Soon they would all be gone.

"Get lines to those men!" Rufio boomed.

The startled soldiers flipped ropes over the side and were soon fishing them out. Several of them threw themselves at Rufio's feet and hugged his legs, but he stepped away from their obeisance.

"No need," he said to Arrianus, who had run up with twine to bind them. "They're now the most loyal subjects of the Empire." He turned to his centurions. "Secure the ship."

Crus joined him at the bow, and soon Salario strode the deck of what the previous day had been the terror of the waves.

"On your knees," Rufio said to the hundred or so wet wretches shivering before him. He turned to Crus. "The men?"

"Not even a wound."

Rufio smiled and looked back at the pirates. His smile vanished.

"You have one chance. Serve this ship. When we reach Egypt, the master will decide your fate, so serve him well. If even one of you steals so much as a crumb out of a rat's mouth, all will go over the side that day." He looked at Crus. "Orders, tribune?"

Without hesitation, Crus seized the authority.

"Strip this vessel of anything of value and distribute it among Salario's crew. Then burn the ship so it's not a menace to navigation." He turned to the soldiers standing in ranks behind him.

Rufio watched him closely. He hoped the tribune would not be effusive. Flattery rarely worked with fighting men.

Crus looked from left to right, and then said, in an almost casual voice, "Well done, but next time could you make it a little bit quicker?"

The soldiers roared with laughter.

Crus turned to Salario. "Have you a word for my men?"

The master stepped forward. "As of this moment, I'm buying the cargo of wine. Today we'll feast and drink to the health of Caesar!"

The men cheered.

Crus raised a hand and they quieted. "After you're finished your work, clean your equipment and ready it for inspection. Then offer a prayer to Minerva for guiding your hands this day. And when you've made the proper thanksgiving, we'll gorge together like decadent Greeks!"

The men laughed even more loudly than before and banged their shields in unison on the deck.

Rufio smiled to himself and then turned back to the corbita. Flavia still stood on the roof of the cabin. He raised the point of his sword to salute her. She jumped down and ran to meet him.

21

I FEAR GREEKS EVEN WHEN THEY ARE BEARING GIFTS.

VIRGIL

Bellator was regaling the Second Cohort with tales from his youth, when Rufio noticed Crus standing alone on the foredeck. The moonlight glinted off the sword belt and dagger that he had not bothered to remove.

Flavia followed Rufio's gaze. "I'll bring him some refreshment," she said and stood up and refilled her cup with wine.

"That's not it," Rufio said. He pressed her back down with two fingers on her shoulder. "Stay here."

Crus must have heard Rufio's hobnails against the deck, but he continued staring south into the blackness.

"That was a fine act you put on," Rufio said. "About feasting."

"I'm not hungry."

"I know why."

Crus turned to face him. "Do you?"

"Today was the first day you ever felt another man's hot blood on your hand."

He looked away. "Yes."

"It's not like reading Homer, is it?"

"No."

"Good. If you told me it was, I'd know you'd gone mad."

"How can you ever get accustomed to this?"

"To killing?"

"Yes."

" 'Accustomed' is the wrong word."

"Then what's the right word?"

Rufio hesitated. "I don't believe there is one."

"Then how do you endure it."

"We endure what we must endure."

"The feelings I have now. . . They're . . . I can't even describe them."

"Do you really believe you need to describe them? To me?"

Crus sighed. "No."

"Elation. Even euphoria. Then revulsion, then almost a feeling of disbelief. After that, a heavy, nauseated deadness and a desire that this day come to an end. And, finally, a haunting fear that it never will."

"Oh, no," Crus said with a groan. "Stop looking into my soul."

Rufio remained silent.

"Have you ever pissed yourself in battle?"

"Four or five times."

Crus looked at him sharply. "Don't lie to me."

"I've never lied to you."

"I'm so thirsty now," Crus said. "I cannot get enough water."

"That's common." Rufio knew that after-battle discussions were vital. They exposed tactical mistakes, and also they enhanced a soldier's confidence by shining a lamp onto his skills. More importantly, they helped him to face his private horrors. Rufio realized long ago that terrible experiences were tacky as fish glue. They always stuck. The fools were those who denied this and continually pulled them off, ripping away pieces of the soul every time. The wise soldier was he who examined these experiences, accepted them, and then wove them onto his spirit like a section of new garment. Only when they had become a permanent part of his character did they lose their power to torment. Now they could protect and instruct, rather than horrify and corrode.

"The first one I killed I'll never forget," Crus said. "He was no more than twenty. The older pirates pushed him forward to take the onslaught. He came at me with a rusty blade. It was pathetic. I sank my sword into his stomach. It went in so easily I wasn't sure I'd actually done it. His mouth opened and I think he groaned, but I'm not certain. Everything was so quiet. I couldn't even hear the men fighting beside me. I couldn't see them either. I couldn't see anything. Only this boy's face. His legs turned to mud and he began to sink. He looked so sad. He reached out and tried to grab the front of my lorica. It's weird, but *that* I could hear. I can hear it still — his fingernails scraping against the mail. Then he went down. I swear, I almost saw the life escape from his mouth like a vapor. I moved on and we finished our business. Afterward I went back to look at him. His eyes had never closed. His lips were still parted. I was stunned to see that I'd stabbed him four times. I have no memory of that. We threw him over the side like trash. Someone who'd once been a laughing baby at his mother's breast."

Rufio let him wallow in his emotions for a bit, then said, "Look at me, tribune."

Crus turned around.

"Consider this. When I face an enemy on the battlefield, I don't pause to weep that he might have a wife who will mourn his fall. Or children who will go hungry. Or aging parents who will die bitter and alone. Do you understand?"

"I understand."

"I don't have the luxury to recall the verses of Roman poets singing of the virtues of the colorful barbarians. Their quaint ways and homespun customs. What do those Romans know? Bloodless parasites who rarely venture outside their own villas. Whose idea of barbarism is an undercooked game bird. When a savage three feet away from me draws his sword, I see someone who wants to shatter and burn all I hold dear. All that Rome is. All she'll ever be." He paused, then said, "I'm not reluctant to destroy him. I hunger to destroy him."

Crus turned away from his centurion.

"Sometimes . . . sometimes you frighten me more than the enemy does."

"If you're frightened of me, you're frightened of life."

"You have a rather grand view of yourself, don't you?"

"I'm just a simple soldier."

"That's all?"

"No more."

"You're batting me away again, centurion. I don't believe you mean that."

"You're traveling from Gaul to Egypt to the East—and it's all Roman. *That's* the grandeur. The centuries and cohorts that make it possible. That's where the greatness lies."

"And you?"

"I'm just one of thousands. It's the totality. These soldiers with their courage and their skills and their honor. Their ferocity, too. It's the legions that are the true pride of Rome. The glory of the human race."

"May I ask you something very personal?"

"You're my superior."

"I'm just a man."

Rufio smiled. "Please ask whatever you like."

"How many have you killed? Do you know?"

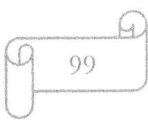

"I keep no tally. Though others do."

"Very many?"

"Oh, yes."

"More than ten?"

"Many more."

Crus looked away. "Do you know what bothers me the most?"

"Yes."

He quickly turned back. "You do?"

"Of course."

"What?"

"You fear that you'll dream about it."

"Will I?"

"Times beyond counting."

Crus sighed and gazed back at the black water.

"Killings never go away," Rufio said. "They burn your soul like a hot iron. One or a hundred—they sear forever. Now you've learned that."

"That's not acceptable," Crus shouted with the patrician arrogance Rufio had not heard in many weeks. "I reject that."

"No one can reject reality and still hold onto his sanity. But you have to learn that a killing is not your enemy."

"It certainly isn't my friend."

"No, but it can be your ally. Use it."

"How? To haunt the night?"

"To teach you. There's no sterner tutor than the hand of death."

"What can stabbing a man possibly teach me?"

"The value of what you have. The slashing sword of a hateful man tells you instantly that most of what you thought you cared about is meaningless. Those great villas you build in your mind. The mansions of power and wealth. You know now they're just structures of nothingness. Walls built of wind."

Crus was about to say something but turned away.

"Go on," Rufio said.

"Do you know what I thought about right after the battle?"

"Of course I do. Lucia."

"I'd have given everything I own just to hold her for a moment."

"At the end of every fight, after I've accounted for my men, I always experience the same thing—the smell of the flowers Flavia crushes in her hair."

Crus stared at Rufio for a moment, then said, "Help me not to lose my mind here."

"Mind? You're a tribune. I've never known one who *had* a mind."

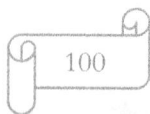

Crus laughed and laid a hand on the centurion's left shoulder.

Rufio smiled with him. The centurion knew that humor—especially the blackest humor—was the essential caustic for dissolving the bloody crusts of the battlefield.

"We'll work on it together," Rufio said with the reassurance of an older brother.

Flavia came up with two cups of wine.

"Thank you," Crus said.

Rufio smiled his thanks with his eyes, and she left as quietly as she had arrived.

The two men sipped their wine in silence. Crus gazed ahead into the night, while Rufio was soothed by the pleasant monotony of the creaking of the great vessel as it sailed on.

"I want to visit Alexander's tomb when we reach Egypt," Crus said.

"Good. Every soldier should."

"Well, finally we agree on something. I admire him as much as you do. I—why are you laughing?"

"As much as I do?"

"Yes."

"I despise him."

Crus hesitated. "Are you testing me again?"

"No."

"Then why . . ."

"Because he was despicable."

"You don't think he was brilliant?"

"I didn't say that. He's part of that great trio with Hannibal and Caesar. No one has ever had a greater military mind, and he was brave to the point of folly. A more audacious commander never walked the earth. But as a man, he was nothing. His life was obsessed with a single empty idea—conquest without purpose and without end. He liked to pretend he was spreading Greek culture, but he was no more civilized than a gutter rat. The Macedonian slaughterer would have laughed at the idea of morals. He wouldn't have recognized Greek culture if he fell into it up to his neck."

"Your views certainly aren't typical of most soldiers I've known."

"Should I apologize?" Rufio said with a laugh. "Hannibal was a barbarian of sorts, but he had his code. Some of it was the hatred of Rome, but that's just part of the sweep of history. And Caesar pardoned every vile traitor who had schemed against him. Alexander? At the height of his power and fame, he brought false charges against some of his finest commanders. The little Macedonian savage was afraid that these poor dedicated soldiers might try to steal some of his glory. So he accused them of treason and had them killed."

"But his brilliance was—."

"Irrelevant. It was a natural talent. Do you admire a beautiful woman just because she's beautiful? She didn't have anything to do with it. It's what she is inside that matters. And of what use were his talents? Destruction on a scale never seen before or since. And as soon as he died, the whole rotten edifice came crashing down. A miserable, twisted butcher. He lived in a frenzy of death and died in a drunken stupor."

Rufio finished his wine and threw the cup over the side, as if the entire conversation had soured him.

"And yet Caesar killed many," Crus said.

"Caesar did things we wouldn't confide to our little daughters in their bedtime stories. But he towers over everyone. He had his codes, though sometimes they seem elusive to us. Alexander was a moral dwarf. If you remember only one thing, remember this—Caesar forgave his enemies, Alexander killed his friends."

22

EITHER I WILL FIND A WAY OR I WILL MAKE ONE.

ROMAN SAYING

Flavia and Neko picked their way quietly around the sleeping soldiers. The centurions were already moving about the deck. It seemed to Flavia that even when centurions slept, they were at least half awake.

Neko held Flavia's right hand to guide her step in the darkness. She was as sure-footed as a doe on a rocky slope, but she allowed Neko to think he was helping her.

When they reached the foredeck, Neko pointed south.

"Look out there and see something you have never seen before and will never see again."

Hundreds of stars flickered in the sky, but there was nothing new in that.

"I don't see it," Flavia said.

"Yes, you do. Look at that large star straight ahead."

She peered into the distance. "It looks yellow. Why is that?"

"Because that star was not made by the gods. It's made by men."

"You're teasing me. Men cannot make a star."

"And yet they have."

She looked again. "What is it, Neko? Tell me."

"It is one of the most magnificent creations in all the world—the Pharos, the great lighthouse of Alexandria."

Flavia continued staring. "What is it for?"

"A tremendous beacon that shines night and day to warn sailors they are approaching the reef that girds Alexandria. It glows from a limestone tower over three hundred feet high."

"How is that possible? How can they keep a fire burning on a tower that touches the sky?"

"They cannot. The fire burns deep in the tower's bowels at the base. Massive mirrors of polished bronze—so big they would shame the Titans—snare the light and reflect it outward for all to see."

Flavia averted her eyes and glanced down at her hands on the rail. "I feel so small."

"No, do not feel that way."

She looked up at the Egyptian. "What is a woman on horseback along the Rhenus compared to something like that?"

"And yet that woman shook the core of the toughest man I know. And rescued his spirit when the wounds of life had almost destroyed his fire."

"Could I really have done that? Or is this all just a dream?"

"Self-doubt from Flavia? It does not adorn you favorably. Cast it off."

"I think it's the strange humors given off by the sea. They're beginning to poison my judgment."

"Of course they are. That is why all seamen are half-mad."

"Will you take me to see the Pharos when we land?"

"Yes. And the Canopic Way with its shops and entertainments. Rufio will be busy. He has given me the privilege of showing you the land of my birth."

"That will be an honor."

Alexandria had been built on a great land spit running parallel to the coast northwest of the Nile delta. Off the northern shore of the city, the lighthouse island, also called Pharos like the structure itself, was connected to the city by an immense causeway the Greeks had named the Heptastadion. This split the coast in two and created a pair of ports, the Great Port to the east and the Port of Good Return to the west.

Rufio sat outside a small tavern near the southern end of the causeway and gazed in admiration, as he always had, at the Pharos. The lower portion, more than two-thirds of its height, was rectangular, the middle section an octagon, and the top a cupola surmounted by a colossal bronze of Zeus.

Behind him sprawled the Canopic Way. A hundred feet wide, it stretched for three miles east and west from the Gate of the Sun to the Gate of the Moon. Its colonnades broke up the street into countless arcades offering every temptation to corrupt the soul of man.

A cool offshore breeze took the edge off the late morning sun. Rufio sipped the superb Alexandrian wine. How absurd that he and his men had almost been sent to the bottom of the sea for a cargo of wine, when the Alexandrians had long ago mastered the mysteries of the grape. Oil, too, had been part of the load, and another oddity. The olives of Egypt were so fine that oil had once been a royal monopoly of the Ptolemies. Rufio took another sip and gave up on the puzzle. Egyptian tastes had always baffled him.

"Alone in a city of so many?" Salario said and sat down beside him on the stone bench in the shade.

"My men are working off their urges. Flavia is exploring the city with Neko, and the tribune is trying to find us passage to Judaea."

"No luck yet, I assume."

"Fortuna toys with us."

"Good. I will take you to Judaea."

Startled, Rufio searched the master's eyes.

"Why?"

"You saved my life and my cargo and my crew. I'm not known as a generous man—ask my crew—but I *am* known as a fair man. I have a debt of honor. Now I will pay it."

To Rufio, the refusal of a gift was the greatest insult imaginable. "Rome accepts. Thank you."

"And I'll return the money you paid for passage here. You'll need it in Judaea."

"I'll personally see to it that the Vestals offer a prayer for you."

Salario went and got a cup of wine and rejoined Rufio on the bench. They sat in silence for a long time, though they constantly brushed away the street vendors hovering like flies around honey.

"Have you been here before?" Salario asked.

"Oh, yes. I was posted to Egypt long ago. Alexandria is one of the sweetest experiences of a lifetime. I wish I had a month to renew her acquaintance." He sipped his wine. "Perhaps another day."

Salario set his cup down on the bench. "I need to ask you something."

Rufio nodded.

"Your men . . . how long have they served with you?"

"About a year."

"Did you train them?"

"Some of them."

"The way they respond to you . . . I've never seen anything like that before."

"They're Roman soldiers," Rufio said, as if that should be explanation enough.

"It's that simple?"

"There's nothing simple about it."

"That's what I mean. They cannot be typical."

"Well, no centurion thinks his men are typical."

"You're avoiding the question."

"I don't believe you've asked it yet."

"My crew obeys me because they fear me and my officers and because they dread not being paid. Why do your men obey you so quickly and so well?"

"Ah," Rufio said, laughing. "Now I understand. You want me to give you the secret of command."

Salario turned away. "I suppose I do," he said, embarrassment in his voice. He looked back at Rufio. "What I saw on that ship looked like magic."

"Not magic. Divinity. The Roman soldier is the physical presence of the mind of Mars."

"No, no—no philosophical smoke. Give me a real answer."

Rufio eyed the old sailor with admiration. There was no putting him off.

"There are reasons beyond counting why a soldier obeys his commander."

"But there must be some essence. Some core."

"There is."

"Share it with me."

"The first reason is fear—but not fear of me. My men obey me because they fear my disapproval. My scorn."

"But why would that matter?"

"Because of who I am. Because of what they perceive me to be."

"It's that powerful?"

"Yes. And it matters not if that perception is true or false. It matters only that it's real."

Salario smiled. "And is it true? In your case, I mean."

"It's not appropriate for me to judge myself."

"Now that surprises me. You don't strike me as a humble man. Or a blushing virgin."

"I'm not. But I have my code."

Salario leaned forward, his forearms on his knees, and gazed out toward the Pharos.

"Why the sigh of despair?" Rufio asked.

"None of my crews will ever respect me like that."

Rufio said nothing.

"Is there any other reason?" Salario asked.

"Yes. It grows like a branch out of the trunk of the first. It's more subtle. A tender shoot instead of tough and hardened bark. But its roots are deep and its life is long."

"Can you explain it to this old salt?"

"I'm tired of wine." He set down his cup. "How about some spring water?"

"I'll get it." Salario went into the tavern and came back with a clay pitcher and two cups.

"That's better," Rufio said after a sip.

"Now what about this delicate tendril?"

Rufio leaned back against the cool stone wall of the tavern.

"Most civilians have no idea what makes a soldier—or a legion. They think it's training or courage or toughness. Those things are important but not important enough. They're like armor. They protect the soldier, but they don't make the soldier. More than any single thing, it's honor that thickens the blood of the legion. The problem is that even most centurions don't comprehend this. Don't blame yourself if you don't understand it either."

A smile creased the sailor's face. "I'm not sure if you're being kind to me or harsh."

"I'm being honest."

"Go on."

"We spend endless hours trying to instill loyalty in our soldiers. Tales of heroism from ages past. Sacred oaths. The glories of Rome. All these things work, but only partly. Most centurions are not Homer. They shouldn't pretend to be. The secret—and it isn't really a secret if you just think about it—is that honor and loyalty move on two ladders."

Rufio paused to allow that to penetrate.

"Continue."

"Most centurions are obsessed with training their troops to be loyal to *them*. To the legion, to Rome. Many of them forget that *they* have to be loyal to their men."

"You're losing me. Come about. One of us is off course."

"It's you, Salty. What the best centurions know is that loyalty has to run up the ladder but also *down* the ladder. Even a dog in the street doesn't expect a kick for no reason and needs a pat on the head. Rare is the centurion who remembers this. Rarer still is the one who practices it."

"So you're talking about rewards?"

"Tear your mind away from silver for a minute."

Salario looked irritated. "I apologize for being so mercenary."

"It's not your fault. It's your business. What I'm talking about is more vital than money or privileges. What do you think is the most difficult thing for new troops to endure?"

"The physical training, I'd guess. The pain. The exhaustion."

Rufio smiled. "Everyone thinks that, but it's wrong. Homesickness and loneliness are the biggest threats to the cohesion of the century. Certain recruits deal with that better than others, but some soldiers it just crushes. Too many centurions are indifferent to it. They're too concerned about showing obedience to the tribunes or licking a legate's ass."

"And you're not?"

"Ask my commander. Those centurions forget about loyalty to the men below them. The officers above you change all the time. And often they're more concerned about their political careers than with the woes of their cohorts. And even if they stay at their post for a while, they can change their attitude toward you. But your men are always your men. That never changes. There's nothing more important for a soldier to know than that when he's at his saddest and loneliest he can reach out in the dark and his centurion will be there."

"But you're just talking about recruits. That doesn't apply to veterans."

"It does. But I have to approach them differently. My men must be sure that I'll stand like Hector between them and any danger. It doesn't matter if it's a vicious tribune or a screaming German. My toughest men rest their heads on their pillows at night in the absolute certainty that I'll hold my ground before them—even if a Suebi splits me open and my intestines are spilling out onto the ground."

Salario laid a hand on Rufio's right forearm. "Whatever Caesar pays you, I doubt that it's enough."

"It's more than I have time to spend."

"I cannot imagine being so popular with my men."

"I'm not. Not in the way you mean. There are times during training when some of my soldiers would like to pick up a rock and crush my face with it. I accept that. Secretly yearning to smash your centurion's face is a time honored privilege. But I'm certain beyond doubt that if I asked them to, every one of them would plunge into the rivers of Hell for me."

Salario smiled and held up his cup of water. "To Rome."

"To Rome."

Both men stared out at the twin harbors busy with boats large and small.

"I love Egypt," Rufio said. "It's like being present at the creation of man. A great civilization glowed here when Romans were scrambling like animals for scraps on the bank of the Tiber. It was a sad day when the Macedonians overran this land."

"And Judaea?"

"It's a cauldron."

"Where to you want me to take you?"

"Caesarea. My men need a treat. I want them to see Herod's masterpiece. They deserve that much."

"You sound troubled."

"Centurions are always troubled."

"Why?"

Rufio laughed. "In general or now?"

"Now."

"Soldiers like to control as many things as possible in a hostile land. Their survival pivots on it. In Judaea we'll control almost nothing. We have vague orders. A brutal climate. Ugly terrain. Uncertain supplies. A half-barbarian king who doesn't want us there and would rather hear that we drowned enroute. And the surliest people on earth."

"I suppose I should be grateful I've had few dealings with them."

"Thank whatever gods you pray to."

"Surely your natural charm will seduce them."

Rufio narrowed his eyes in mock anger.

"Ah, the centurion's glare. I had better keep my hand on my dagger."

"Spend a month with Judaeans and you'll weep for deliverance. They're the most backward looking people on earth."

Salario frowned. "What do you mean?"

"They don't simply live in the past—that would be stupid enough. They *relive* the past with every breath. The problem with people like that is they never forget a slight. Wounds stay open and fester forever."

"But what does that matter? I don't see how that can pitch your vessel into the waves."

"When Pompeius conquered Judaea because it was a weak and unstable mess, he didn't use the lightest touch. Pompeius was a great commander, but he was blind to tact. He pranced into Jerusalem and rode his horse right up the steps of their temple and into the sanctuary itself. He profaned their holiest shrine. That was decades ago. To the Judaeans, it happened this morning just after breakfast." He shook his head in disgust. "A thousand years from now, they'll still be wailing about Pompeius's horse."

Salario laughed until he almost fell off the bench. "All this makes being a ship's master seem like a child's game. What happens when we arrive in Caesarea and the Judaeans see your men disembarking? Won't they think they're being invaded again?"

"Herod is supposed to have soldiers there to meet us." Rufio stood up and stretched. "Fine troops, no doubt," he said sarcastically. "I'm sure they'll be the burnished blade of Judaean manhood."

I was standing near Salario's cabin and watching the crew load supplies when I overheard Salario arguing in the cabin with Rufio. Salario was furious. Rufio was not. I could tell by his voice. He sounded amused.

Salario said, "All of it? You gave them all the money I returned to you?"

"Every sestertius."

"Why?"

"They deserve it. They're a good crew. A gift from Rome."

"Now I know why Beakless was grinning and why twenty-three of those drowning pirates begged me to take them on as crewmen."

"You should thank me."

"But it was my money! You could never have given it to them if I hadn't returned it."

"You're a generous ship's master."

"But you get all the credit!"

"Rome is generous." I could hear the smile in Rufio's voice when he said, "And Rome is also wise."

23

HE WORKS SO ENERGETICALLY THAT HE ACCOMPLISHES MANY THINGS.

ROMAN SAYING

"That's incredible!" Valerius said, taking in the sweep of the gleaming harbor.

Rufio smiled and leaned against the gunwale of the ship. "Welcome to Caesarea."

"Desert barbarians built this?" Metellus asked in disbelief.

"Oh, no. This is far beyond them. It isn't even a Jewish city, though there's a small outpost of them on the northern edge."

"Who built it—Herod?" Metellus asked.

"He's one of the great builders of the world," Rufio said. "Take a big sip of this sweet drink. You won't taste its like again in this sour land."

With no natural bay to help him, the Judaean king had flung a massive artificial harbor a half-mile out from shore to sea. Bright stone breakwaters topped with at least a dozen towers enclosed entering ships in a great protective rectangle. Outside the opening at the northwestern corner, twin pylons flanked the entrance. A trio of columns on each supported colossal statues.

"Who are they?" Valerius asked, pointing to the sculptures.

"Neko!" Rufio shouted.

As always, the Egyptian appeared with the speed and silence of a mist.

"Those bronzes," Rufio said.

"Augustus's family," Neko answered.

"And another Pharos," Valerius said as he gazed at the looming lighthouse to the right of the harbor's entrance.

"Never dare to call it that," Neko said. "Herod has named it the Drusion, after Augustus's stepson. The entire harbor is named Sebastos, which is what the Greeks call Augustus."

"Is that a Roman temple beyond the harbor?" Metellus asked.

"To Augustus himself," Neko said.

"Remember one thing about Herod," Rufio said. "He always knows which way the dice roll."

"Are the breakwaters limestone?" Metellus asked. "It doesn't seem possible."

"It isn't," Rufio answered. "Only the facings are limestone. The cores are concrete. Herod imported Italian materials and Roman engineers. They built titanic forms and hauled them out to the water and poured the concrete there."

"That's amazing," Valerius said. "Who set the forms onto the sea bed?"

"Divers from Capri specially trained for it. The soldiers call them 'Urinators' because of all the pissing they do after being up and down in the water so much."

"The city doesn't look finished," Metellus said as he stared off at the bright half-moon of buildings nestled against the edge of the water.

"Not yet," Neko answered. "A few more years. But the storehouses are full." He gestured to several dozen large buildings with orange tile vaults at the southwestern edge of the city abutting the sea. "And Herod knows how to please his subjects when it suits him. Look there."

To the south of the city an enormous theater glistened in the morning sun.

"And there."

A half-built amphitheater for combats and games was rising to the northeast.

Metellus laughed. "He has Roman tastes."

"Herod has long found it difficult to be a Jew," Neko said. "And even more agonizing to be the *king* of the Jews. But, then, ruling Jews has always been a universal torment."

"It's time to get the men ready to disembark," Rufio said. "I want all weapons except daggers packed away. All armor, too. I don't want there to be the slightest chance of giving offense to these people."

Neko smiled and turned away.

"What our Egyptian scholar means by that look is that it's impossible to deal with Jews and *not* give offense. But they're a minority here. We'll do our best to keep below the ridgeline. No need to flaunt our power by throwing a Roman silhouette against the sun."

"I haven't seen the tribune this morning," Valerius said.

"He's already ashore smoothing our way," Rufio answered.

"Alone?" Metellus asked.

"Such was his wish, but I advised him to take Bellator with him."

"And our plan now?" Valerius asked. "Can you share that?"

"Let's eat."

Rufio joined his troops camped on the deck and sat with them. Breakfast was being prepared, and Arrianus handed him a bowl of steaming porridge and dried fruits. Most soldiers tightened like twisted twine when approached by their centurion. Rufio's men always relaxed. Subtle it was, this easing of the spirit. Only the most astute observer, or the most experienced, could have noticed it. Yet it was as vital to their wellbeing as the daggers on their hips. Rufio relished the effect his silent reassurance had on his men. It was one of his greatest gifts to them.

"I want our men to enjoy the pleasures of the city," Rufio said to his two officers. "But I don't want to billet them there. That's like grinding a stone against a stone. Too much friction. We'll camp outside the town."

"We're not going south immediately?" Metellus asked.

"We have to wait for Herod's escort," Valerius said.

"Whether they're here yet or not doesn't matter," Rufio said. "Men who've been posted along the Rhenus cannot just march off toward the Judaean wasteland. Troops who've been caressed by Gallic breezes need to get accustomed to this furnace. Why are you grinning?"

Valerius tried to stifle his smile. "In Gaul, I've been caressed by more than breezes."

"He's not talking about your own hand," Metellus said.

"Nor am I, you dead stoat," Valerius shot back. "I mean that out here I'm going to miss those delicate Sequani fingers with the softest touch."

Rufio looked up and beyond Valerius.

The optio turned on his haunches.

Flavia stood behind him with a cup of water for Rufio.

Valerius flushed as red as a Roman cloak.

Flavia leaned forward and handed the cup to Rufio. As she did, her face was only a few inches from the optio's.

"You are a fortunate man," she said to him. The blue fire in her eyes could have melted metal. Then with the hint of a smile and an eyebrow arched toward Rufio, she whispered, "But not nearly as fortunate as he."

She straightened up and strode away from the gathering of men.

"By the gods!" Metellus said with a laugh.

Valerius suddenly found a reason to examine his fingernails.

"Now about the climate . . ." Metellus said, plucking his friend off the hot rock.

"Ideally we'd need about six weeks," Rufio said. "We don't have that much time, so I'll give the men three."

"Will the Judaean commander know our destination?" Valerius asked.

"He'd better," Rufio said. "My guess is that it'll be somewhere southeast of Jerusalem. According to the senator, Parthian bands have swung up around the bottom of the Salt Sea. Probing actions."

"To what purpose?" Metellus asked.

"Probably to cause unrest and give encouragement to Herod's enemies. Judaean enemies I mean. In his court. Even in his own family. Herod sees plots in every corner. Some of them might even be real."

"And an internal upheaval will weaken the kingdom," Valerius said.

"Like an earthquake. Parthian horsemen are always most lethal when riding among shifting sands."

The six centurions sat in a circle on the foredeck with Crus and Bellator.

"We're set," Crus said. "The Judaean troops are here, so there should be no trouble with the populace. Two hundred and fifty cavalrymen. They should . . . centurion?"

Rufio's smile had startled the tribune.

"A comment?" Crus said.

"Two hundred fifty? Are they escorting *us*, or are we escorting *them*?"

"Don't worry," Bellator said. "They're picked men. The commander is a seasoned soldier. Hard as Roman pavement."

"We'll camp here for three weeks," Crus went on. "Then we'll move south. Instruct your men that while we're in Caesarea, we have to be as pure as Vestals. A watchful eye glowers on us all." He looked at Rufio. "The king is here."

"Herod here to bless the soldiers of Rome?" Rufio said. "A rare treat awaits. The desert lion himself."

"I doubt a blessing is what he's pondering," Crus said.

Rufio smiled but said nothing.

"One thing more," Crus said to his centurions. "Never was I prouder to be your tribune than at the Hill of Scorpions. And then in the fight with the pirates. But this is something special. A hideous land, no friends, no real allies. A ruthless enemy. No other army would even consider doing what we're about to do. And no other cohort on earth would dare attempt it." Crus stood up. "Each of you is a pillar supporting the power of Rome—and its honor. Minerva stands by our side with her unsheathed sword. May she protect us all."

The tribune turned and walked away.

Rufio smiled. Crus was learning that if confidence was the blade of command, brevity was its whetstone.

After the centurions dispersed, Rufio joined his century. Metellus was down on one knee and packing his gear when Rufio touched him on a shoulder.

The signifer turned and stood up.

"A delicate task for you," Rufio said. "I cannot overrule the tribune, so I need your discretion."

Metellus gave him that ironic look. "I'm as discreet as a virgin surrounded by four walls."

"Circulate among the centurions and let them know that the men won't be troubled by me if they acquaint themselves with the local beauties. But quietly—no typical Italian flourishes."

"I understand."

"And there's one exception—no Jewish women. Their men will crush the women's heads with stones for even the suspicion of dishonor. We're Romans, not barbarians. We don't need any dead girls on our conscience."

"A voyage to remember," Salario said, staring out to sea with his back to Rufio.

"Every voyage is, don't you think?" Rufio said.

The men of the Second Cohort had assembled on deck and were waiting for the small boats to ferry them ashore. They joked among themselves but stood as orderly as if they were about to march toward the Rhenus.

Salario turned around. "It was a fateful day when we met in that shipping office. A Greek sailor and a Roman soldier."

Rufio smiled. "Who would have dreamed it?"

"The gods have their ways I suppose."

"I've often questioned their wisdom," Rufio said, "but never their sense of humor."

"When will you return?"

"To Ostia?"

"Yes."

"Toward the end of summer. Our labors should be finished by then. If not, it will take better men than we are."

"There *are* no better men than you."

Rufio remained silent.

"How will you return?" Salario asked.

"Not really a concern at the moment."

"Nor will it be. I'll be here then to take your cohort home."

Rufio's surprise always took the form of a frown. Now the grooves in his brow looked like they had been cut with a knife.

"And I'll do it on my silver," Salario said.

Again Rufio was stunned. "Rome is grateful."

"Wherever the men of Rufio's legion need to venture, the ships of Salario will be there to take them. On my honor."

"Thank you, Salty."

For a moment, the old sailor's eyes softened. "Now go teach these Judaeans about the nature of strength. And about the power of Rome." He turned and stared back again out to sea. "Farewell, my friend. I will miss you."

24

THE NATION THAT MAKES A GREAT DISTINCTION BETWEEN ITS SCHOLARS AND ITS WARRIORS WILL HAVE ITS THINKING DONE BY COWARDS AND ITS FIGHTING DONE BY FOOLS.

THUCYDIDES

I must have eight or nine hours of sleep every night to be refreshed, but Rufio needs far less. Yet never does he let me go to bed alone. There are times, though, when I wake up in the dark and he is gone. A lamp burns in another room, and I go to see and peer from the doorway. He is digging deeply into a book. It might be a history by a Greek or an obscure traveler's tale about some far-off and mysterious land. He is voracious about the methods of war of other peoples and relentless pursuing the ways of living of other men. Often Neko will be there. He has an even greater knowledge of Rufio's library than Rufio does. He is at hand to point out some forgotten text, or to prepare a warm drink for his master on a cold night.

Some centurions from other cohorts make jokes about Rufio among themselves. They are always careful to be out of hearing range when they do, but I have overheard them in the village. They call him "The Philosopher" because of his appetite for books. One evening at supper in his quarters at the fort, I was startled to hear him mention it in passing. I had no idea he was aware of this. I was even more shocked when he laughed about it. He took a sip of wine and said that those who ridicule learning in soldiers merely display their ignorance and their envy. He told me that no one can confront others in battle unless he knows what drives them – their hungers and needs and, most of all, their fears. He said that unless one knows what lusts inflame the centaur, and what horrors terrify his soul, one can never face his charge. The student of war, he told me, must first of all be a student of men. All wisdom flows from that. Then he said something that affected me so deeply I chiseled it *into my memory forever. He smiled at me in that protective way he sometimes does and said, "So I allow other centurions to have their private laugh and gamble their pay away and roll and sweat with dishonored women. Meanwhile, Neko warms me a cup of wine and sleepy Flavia peeks at me from the shadows while I seek the knowledge that will ensure the survival of my men. And because of that, I'll die not on some muddy field but in my bed. When I close my eyes for the final time, I'll smile because I'll know the borders of Rome are secure, and those I love are safe at last."*

In a move so outrageous that even Rufio had to laugh to himself at his own audacity, the Second Cohort marched inland and built a fortified camp in a field about a mile southeast of the theater. With the speed of the hand of Caesar, the Romans went to work, and ditch and mound and caltrops appeared as if they had condensed out of the morning mist. Rufio knew from experience that people from hot climates were always slow off the mark, when they chose to respond at all. Before most inhabitants were aware of the Roman ship in the harbor, neat rows of goatskin tents arose within a fortified perimeter on the soil of the kingdom of Herod.

As with every other place Rufio had been, the children were the first to notice. The Romans watched the clumps of boys forming outside the camp. Rufio knew that their looks of wonder were due at least in part to the efficiency and speed of what they were seeing. Very different indeed from the behavior of desultory troops of uncertain loyalty to a half-mad king.

The centurions inspected the perimeter inside and out, posted sentries, and checked the gateway. The tesserarii distributed the watchword, and the Rhenus soldiers, cloaked now against the sun, awaited the Judaean commander.

Rufio and Neko were sorting some scrolls on a table dominated by Paki in the centurion's tent when Crus entered with a Judaean soldier.

Already this was a bad sign. The commander was snubbing them. The soldier he had sent in his place, though impressively outfitted with a white tunic and Roman equipment, was younger than Valerius.

"Centurion Quintus Flavius Rufio," Crus said. "Matthias bar Jacob, soldier in command."

Rufio looked at Crus in surprise, and then made a mental note to ram a foot between Bellator's butt cheeks.

Obviously reading his thoughts, Crus tried to suppress a smile.

"Commander," Rufio said. "How may I address you?"

"Matthias."

"I am Rufio. Thank you for offering escort to my men."

"My duty to my king." Matthias's Latin was excellent, but the half-heartedness of his tone was not reassuring. Worse, Rufio wondered how a battle cry could be raised by a man who could barely raise a beard.

"We have a labor ahead of us," Rufio said. "Let's lead your men and mine in a way that makes it a memorable one."

Matthias smiled but, it seemed to Rufio, not just in pleasure but in relief. With the lightest touch, the Roman had swept aside political concerns and ethnic rivalries. Now there were just two groups of men sworn to the brotherhood of arms.

"The king commands your presence tomorrow morning," Matthias said.

"All of us?" Crus asked.

"Just the tribune and his senior centurion. Herod is uncomfortable near armed men unsworn to him."

"Will you accompany us?" Crus asked.

"I have not been commanded."

"I insist," Crus said. "The three of us will go together."

"At your command, tribune."

Rufio enjoyed the look of satisfaction on Crus's face. The tribune was learning quickly. He had not waited for authority—he had taken it.

"Neko," Rufio said.

The Egyptian came forward and gestured to a table at the far side of the tent. Bowls of dried fruits, plates of salted meats, and a new wineskin covered the table.

To the Romans, this was a modest outlay, but the Judaean stared at it in surprise. It was clear that Herod was not overfeeding his men.

"I must rejoin my troops," Matthias said. "I'll return early in the morning and we'll see Herod together."

"Until tomorrow then," Crus said.

Rufio nodded, and the Judaean was gone.

"Read the entrails for me," Crus said, pointing to the doorway of the tent.

The two men went outside and strolled around the camp.

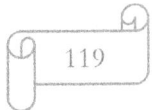

"I see some of my young self in him. Proud, a bit uncertain, green as new pine, and swamped by an almost boundless ignorance."

Crus laughed.

"But tender shoots can be toughened," Rufio said. "And ignorance is easily cured."

"Battle worthy?"

"I doubt he ever drew blood, except when shaving. Probably why he stopped trying."

"It must be a terrible strain trying to produce that stubble."

As they walked along, Rufio laid a hand on Arrianus's shoulder as he was down on one knee and tossing stones from the area in front of his tent.

The soldier smiled as the two officers moved on.

"Matthias seemed surprised that we were cordial," Crus said.

"Caesarea might look like a Greek city, but Herod doesn't want his people corrupted by idiotic ideas of freedom."

"You think the Judaeans were told to stand clear of us?"

"I'm certain of it."

"Tomorrow should be interesting. Do you think Herod will remember you?"

"No chance of that. May I give you some advice?"

"Of course."

"Honor him as if he were your own king. But if he tries any nonsense, stand fast. Augustus admires the way the old rogue can control these Judaeans. Who else on earth could? But if he ever insulted a tribune of Rome, Augustus would crush him like a bug."

"You lying dog! Hard as Roman pavement!"

Bellator burst out laughing as he came out of his tent. He threw a small sack to Rufio.

"Let's walk," Bellator said.

They left the camp, and Rufio pulled several slices of Parmula ham from the sack and handed the remainder to Bellator.

The sun was low and the onshore breeze had picked up. They wandered toward the northeast where the Judaeans had pitched their camp against a low hill.

"It's a blessing from Fortuna that the winter rains are done," Bellator said, taking in the tents thrown up haphazardly along the bottom of the rise. "But a spring storm will flood them out in ten minutes."

"These aren't the legions of Hannibal."

"What's next?" Bellator asked.

"Train lightly and get accustomed to the climate. Have you spoken to the Judaean commander?"

"Crus did the talking."

"He was so uneasy when we met that he forgot to tell me where we're headed."

"Does it matter? Soldiers are never sent where it's pleasant."

"Unless they're posted to Gaul," Rufio said.

"Well, of course," Bellator said with a laugh. "Land of warriors and wild women. And air so sweet it's as if it's been washed with blossoms and honey."

"You're quite the poet. Perhaps you'd like to drink again of the Gallic dew."

"Oh, no. Don't even try."

"Sabinus doesn't need another engineer, but he'll always find space for an experienced decurion."

"I don't ride horses anymore. You know that."

"I know that Titus Bellator is an important enough man to be allowed the privilege of changing his mind."

"It was long ago. My hip hurts too much for me to ride. Horses and I have parted ways."

"No, no, I know better. When you bleed, it smells like hay."

Hoofbeats distracted them.

"We have a visitor," Bellator said as he peered through the half-light at a rider approaching from the north. "I can't make him out."

"Hannibal."

Matthias pulled up in front of them. "There's something I forgot to tell you earlier. You should know it before we see the king tomorrow. Herod has spread the story that you're here at his request, not by your demand."

"And how do you know we're not?" Rufio asked.

Matthias smiled. "I know Herod well enough to know the truth."

"I see. We'll keep his story intact. Our task is not to shame the King of Judaea."

Matthias seemed surprised at this delicate touch from the veteran Roman soldier.

"But thank you for warning me," Rufio went on. "May I give you a bit of advice?"

"Yes...."

"Never address a senior officer from horseback. Always approach him on level ground."

Stunned by this gentle rebuke, Matthias seemed embarrassed — and angry at his embarrassment.

"Yes, centurion," he said crisply.

"I'll see you in the morning."

The Judaean reined about and rode back to his men.

Bellator handed back the sack of ham, and Rufio saw that he was grinning.

"What is it?" Rufio said.

"You like that boy, don't you?"

"He has potential."

"If he has too much, Herod will kill him before he's thirty."

"This is a savage land," Rufio said in an exasperated tone that acknowledged the wisdom of his friend.

25

WE OWE THE GREATEST RESPECT TO A CHILD.

ROMAN SAYING

A lush dawn on the edge of the sea drowned the senses like nothing else on earth. Crus relished every breath. The cool wet air tinged with brine could wash clean, at least for a moment, all the iniquities of man.

Though light had barely begun seeping over the horizon, the men of the Second Cohort were already dressed and fed and performing routine checks of their equipment. Crus saw Rufio. He was wearing a new bright blue tunic and standing near his tent at the end of the line of tents of the First Century.

"Centurion!" Crus said and walked toward him.

"Tribune."

"I've made a decision. Herod will wait. We'll see him tomorrow, not today."

Rufio gave him a puzzled look but said nothing.

"I decided last night," Crus went on. "'Herod commands our presence' is not an expression that pleases me. The King of the Judaeans can bite on marble. Herod commands nothing. Herod awaits the pleasure of Rome."

Rufio smiled like a father whose son had just won his first fistfight. "I'll tell Matthias."

"No, I will. You take the day off. I also want two centuries to have leave to go into the city. You pick which ones. Every fourth day I want two centuries to have leave. Four centuries will stay in camp at all times."

Valerius had come up behind Rufio and stood there quietly.

"Valerius, I want you to tell the other optios that I hold them responsible for the behavior of their men."

"Yes, tribune."

"Any breakdown in discipline and I'll have their balls on a pilum."

"Even though they're being as pure as Vestals?"

"Don't be silly."

Valerius smiled.

"Go now."

Valerius turned and was gone.

"Questions?" Crus asked.

"None," Rufio said.

"I'll stay in camp. You go into the city. I assume Herod built some baths. Relax there. Or take a plunge in the surf. There's nothing better than salt water to scrape away the dead skin of the soul."

"My soul is too scarred for that."

"You surprise me. I thought you were somebody who could recover from anything."

"Oh, yes, that's Rufio. The iron man."

"You take too much on yourself. The sun rises whether you will it to or not."

"I had an idea last night...."

"Go on," Crus said, annoyed once again at making no advance against Rufio's perimeter.

"There's no reason the men should walk all those miles south. We have enough silver to buy horses. All my men are horse trained. Even the worst of them are adequate, and the best are excellent."

"Sounds sensible. Can we get horses here?"

"There might be a Nabataean horse trader or two in the area. And I do have the day off."

"That was for you to relax."

"I'm never as relaxed as when I'm tending to the needs of my men."

"Rufio, do you always have to be the perfect officer? Isn't it possible for you just once to be a fool?"

Crus regretted that as soon as he said it. He had meant to annoy Rufio, but now his centurion simply looked sad.

"If you . . ." Rufio stopped. "May I go?"

"The day is yours."

Rufio was about ten feet away when he paused and turned around.

"If you knew how often I've been a fool. . ."

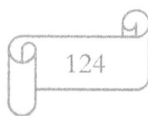

Stunned, Crus remained silent.

"What you see — what my men see — it's only what I want you to see."

Suddenly Rufio seemed older and more tired than Crus had ever seen him.

"Every man has a tomb of his own dead dreams within him. But mine isn't some little ossuary — it's a necropolis. I walk its dank streets every night of my life."

Crust just stared at him.

"And that Sequani huntress grabbed my hand and pulled me back. Just as I was about to slip away into the underworld of dead men's bones."

"I'm sorry. I didn't —."

"And if I seem arrogant to you, it's because I have a belief in my own powers. But it isn't arrogance. It isn't even pride. It's just simple recognition. And if I act like I'm perfect, it's an illusion I nurture to encourage my men and confound my enemies. But don't think for an instant that the sheen of my armor is the essence of my soul."

Crus was about to speak to comfort his friend, but Rufio held up a hand.

"Think twice before you peer down the dark alleys of the city of the dead."

Then he turned and walked away.

At last Crus had penetrated the perimeter. And now he felt like a criminal.

Though born in Rome, Rufio was not a city man. His sister had always teased him about it. Noise, above all, annoyed him like a dry summer wind. So he ignored the fleshpots of Caesarea and skirted the city.

The roads to Herod's showpiece were clogged with traders of every race in the East. Most rode wagons, and an occasional string of camels went by. Rufio stopped a craggy-faced rug merchant atop an oxcart groaning under the weight of his wares.

"Any horse traders about?" Rufio asked.

"In the Field of Beasts," he said and pointed east of the city.

"Thank you. The blessings of your gods on you and your family."

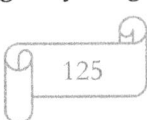

The man gestured in acknowledgement and his cart creaked on.

The Field of Beasts was easy to find. The reek of manure was thick enough to coat the tongue. Several small strings of horses were staked out, but it was the large herd that caught Rufio's eye. Over two hundred magnificent Arabians were enclosed in a huge pen made of posts with a single rope line stretched between them. Some strips of white cloth had been tied to the cord and fluttered in the breeze. It was a clever way to control a large number of horses with minimum manpower. The rope ran about chest high to the horses—high enough to inhibit jumping and low enough to discourage going underneath. A lone tent had been pitched at the edge of the pen.

Rufio approached the grazing herd but saw no one about. An unguarded herd was a risky proposition in this land of thieves. One of the sections of rope had fallen off a post and offered an escape route. Rufio decided to do a good deed.

"May I give you a cool drink?"

Still down on the ground, Rufio turned on one knee.

A girl of about ten smiled at him. He had never before been startled by a child, but for a moment he just stared at the girl. Her eyes, as blue as the surface of the sea, cast their light far more deeply into him than most would ever have dared. And yet she was unafraid of anything she saw there. He felt like he could not move. Even stranger, he did not want to move. Heavy, dreamy lids half-hid her eyes, but still they held him. Most striking was her hair. Not the usual wispy tendrils of the prepubescent girl, but a grown woman's mane. Thick as a forest, but yellow and wild, a golden jungle that made her head seem big for her body. Her lithe frame was as thin as a blade and draped in a black caftan.

"Yes, I'll take some water."

Still smiling, she handed him the cup.

"What's your name," he asked and took a sip.

"Morlana."

He returned the cup to her. "Mine is Rufio."

"You've met my decurion," a Roman voice said from beyond her.

Rufio looked up. A man of about fifty and thick as a pillar strode toward them. Rufio knew instantly that he had once been a soldier.

"Now I know why she speaks Latin so well," Rufio said, standing up.

"Decimus Mallius."

"Rufio. Twenty-fifth Legion."

"Well, I've been retired for years, but if my memory isn't entirely dry-rotted, the Twenty-fifth is in Gaul."

"Rome is wherever a legionary rests his head."

"Good answer!" he said with a laugh. "Are you here with a vexillation?"

"One cohort."

He whistled softly. "Brave men among all these jackals. Why are you here?"

"Not something I can discuss at the moment. Why are *you* here?"

"I served in Syria with III Gallica. Decided to retire and live with the Judaeans."

"I thought they were jackals."

"Oh, no, not them. The rest. Steal the wax out of your ears."

Rufio glanced at Morlana. She was staring at him and he smiled at her. She smiled and averted her eyes.

"Interested in some horses?"

"If the price is sweet. Are they green?"

"No, much better than that. Each one is married to bridle and saddle. I've tried out each one myself."

"Very thorough."

"I want happy return buyers, not angry riders with broken collar bones."

"Sex?"

"Mostly stallions. A few geldings. The Nabataeans prefer to ride mares. They cull the studs."

"Are the geldings healed?"

"They were trimmed in the winter, when the flies are scarce. How many do you want?"

"All of them."

He laughed again. "Don't tease a tired old soldier."

"In fact, I need more than you have. I want to mount the entire cohort."

"My partner will be here soon with at least another three hundred."

"How soon?"

"This is the desert. Time has no meaning to these people."

"If he arrives before we leave, I'll take them all. The silver is at hand."

Mallius slid an arm around this daughter. "Sweetheart, let's share our tent with this good man."

With hardly enough light left to see, Flavia hurried through the camp to the centurion's tent. Inside, Rufio sat in near darkness in a wicker chair he had bought in the city. The tiniest of lamps burned weakly on a table behind his right elbow. He seemed not so much a man as a forbidding silhouette carved from the darkness.

"What's wrong?" Flavia asked.

"What do you mean?" were the words that slid out of the shadows.

"The tribune told me you weren't well. That he upset you this morning and you haven't been well since then."

"Crus? How could he upset me? What are you talking about?"

"I don't know. How could I know?"

"Come here."

She stepped next to his chair and he slipped an arm around her waist and pulled her close.

"I've had a terrible day."

She dropped to the ground next to him and leaned against his legs. She still could barely make him out in the darkness.

"Tell me what happened," she asked.

"The most amazing thing. And the most terrible thing. And they were both the same thing."

She kissed his knee and rubbed it gently as a signal for him to continue.

He told her about looking for a horse trader and finding Mallius and making the deal. Then he told her about Morlana.

"I cannot get that little girl out of my mind."

Flavia encouraged him with her silence.

"She was so open and confident. She came right up to me without hesitation."

"You were with children the first time I saw you."

"This was different. It usually takes a while. People have feared me all my life. Some say it's my stare. Children or adults—it doesn't matter. But this child came up to my door and knocked, and I opened it without a second thought. Now I cannot stop thinking about her. I close my eyes and I see her face. And I don't know why."

"Do you need to know?"

"YES!" he shouted.

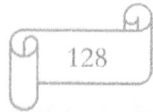

"Perhaps she's a special little girl," Flavia said gently, undeterred by his anger.

"I saw her gazing at me many times while I spoke with her father. She was so trusting. Unafraid. I wanted to reach out and cup her chin and caress her cheek."

"With your thumb. The way you do with me."

"After I finished negotiating with Mallius for the horses, she wouldn't stop asking me questions. About Gaul, about Rome, whether I had any children, how my dagger was made. She was insatiable."

"I was right. She's a special girl."

"Mallius had some business in the city, but it was clear she didn't want to go. She was having too much fun with this warrior from a strange land. She asked her father if she could stay with me while he was in the city. He didn't even hesitate to say yes."

"He's a wise man."

"He trusted a near-stranger with his beautiful child. I spent all day with her. She pummeled me with questions. Everything you can imagine."

Flavia smiled.

"She was tireless. She loved to talk about animals. When I described the horses in the great circus in Rome, she actually gasped. She said she wanted to see that more than anything."

Rufio paused, and Flavia allowed the quiet and the dark to soothe him.

"About halfway through the day, I said to her—jokingly—that I'd never gone to all this trouble for a child before. Without an instant's hesitation, she grinned and said, 'Well, you're doing a good job!' I burst out laughing."

Flavia squeezed his knee.

"I couldn't bear the thought of the day ending. Finally when Mallius came back, it was time for me to go. I was about to leave when Morlana lunged at me and threw her arms around me. She hugged me so tightly I could feel every rib in her lean little body. And I stood there like a fool. I was afraid to touch her. My arms just hung there. I looked past her and saw Mallius smiling. So finally I curled my arms around her. She hugged me even more tightly. Without thought, I pressed my lips against those golden waves of hair."

Flavia leaned her face against his thigh. "You're a very different man than most people see."

"Finally she eased up a bit but still held me. I asked her if she would come to see me. She looked up at me but seemed too filled with emotion to speak. She just nodded. Never have I left the presence of a child and felt the pang I felt today."

Flavia waited, but he seemed finished.

"You're not telling me everything. You said that something about this was terrible. What?"

"The beauty of it was terrible." His voice was unsteady.

"I don't understand."

"All my life I've fought. I've always chosen the line of greatest resistance. I've raced around the Empire and smashed back the barbarians. Laid roads and built towns. Battled the enemies of Rome. I've asked for nothing in return except for a place to lay my head...."

"That's one of the reasons I love you so much."

"But I've never created life. Mallius created something precious. In an almost offhand way. Today I saw the road I chose not to take. All my triumphs—what are they compared to a trusting little girl throwing her arms around me?"

"We can have children, my love."

"No, no, it's too late for that. Too late for me. I've made my choices."

"They were for the good of your men. For the glory of Rome."

"I know. Yet my victories seem like a passing breeze compared to a ten-year-old girl who didn't exist for me one day ago."

Flavia longed to comfort him, but she did not know how.

"I don't understand this!" Rufio said.

"Some things cannot be understood. They can only be felt."

She reached up in the dark and touched his face.

"Keep these things locked in your heart," he whispered. He sounded drained.

"I will. Forever."

26

COMMON DANGER BRINGS FORTH HARMONY.

ROMAN SAYING

"No, I've foresworn the grape," Bellator said.

Mallius's daughter retreated with the cup and returned it to the tent.

"Shall we inspect the horseflesh?" Mallius asked.

"Let's do it now."

They climbed over the rope and walked out toward the herd.

"I thought the centurion was pleased with the purchase."

"He is," Bellator said. "But I was a cavalryman in my infancy, so I thought I'd pass my hand over a few flanks."

Bellator heard running behind him, and he turned and saw the little girl hurrying to keep up. She looked around eagerly as if she were expecting someone.

The crisp morning breeze had invigorated the horses, and they snorted and twitched with all the vibrancy of their desert race.

"Well, I commend Rufio and I commend you," Bellator said, taking in the Arabs. "A wise purchase indeed. I don't think I have to finger any teeth today."

"Thank you."

"What about tack?"

"There are several honest makers here in Caesarea. I've already made arrangements for a fair price for you. I keep them fat the two or three times a year I bring horses up here. They deal honestly with me."

"I want four-horned saddles."

"You'll have them."

"You'll pardon me," Bellator said and sat down on the grass. "I have an old injury that this wet air is torturing."

"Is that why you no longer ride?" Mallius said, sitting down across from him.

"It splays my hips too much."

The girl was still standing and searching the distance beyond Bellator.

"Morlana," Mallius said and pointed to the ground.

She immediately sat beside him but was as restless as a filly.

"Do you work for the Nabataeans then?" Bellator asked.

"I work for myself. The Nabataeans don't care to associate with the Judaeans, so I buy the horses and resell them for a fair profit."

"How do you get them here? Where are your helpers? Besides Morlana, I mean."

"I hire them when I begin and dismiss them when we arrive here."

Morlana touched her father's sleeve. He turned and she leaned forward and whispered something.

"It's not polite to whisper in front of a guest," Mallius said.

"That's all right," Bellator said with a smile when he saw her redden.

Mallius placed a comforting hand over hers and looked back at Bellator. "We were wondering if the centurion is going to join us."

"No, he has business with the king."

"Herod?" Mallius said in surprise.

"Yes."

The disappointment on Morlana's face spoke with the eloquence of a tragic ode. Bellator was always amused at how young girls never felt anything halfway.

"He must be an important man," Mallius said.

"He's an unknown soldier from a frontier outpost. Or at least he was unknown until this year."

Mallius turned to his daughter. "Maybe we'll see him again before we leave."

"Where is home?" Bellator asked.

"A village near the Salt Sea."

"That's a long way to travel alone. What about bandits?"

"They're an endless worry in Judaea. And they're merciless. But there are fortified inns along the way. We'll stay there at night."

Bellator glanced at the fidgety girl who probably had little excitement in her life. And who, apparently, had taken a fancy to a stern-faced soldier from the wilderness of Gaul.

"Why not travel with us?" Bellator said. "No place on earth is safer than in the midst of the Second Cohort."

Morlana's eyes widened and she looked up at her father.

"Where are you headed?" Mallius said.

"Same direction."

"Then we shall."

"Oh, daddy," Morlana said and threw her arms around her father's neck and kissed him on the cheek.

"Perhaps you can repay us," Bellator said. "You understand the Nabataeans. The tribune will want to talk with you. He has a commission from Caesar on grave matters."

"I asked Rufio about it, but he was a tight as a murex."

"On his own, he's daring to the point of folly, but he's very cautious with the lives of his men."

"I'll give whatever advice I have. And I can tell you at the outset that you needn't fear the Nabataeans. But the Parthians are another animal entirely."

"As we suspected."

"When do you leave?"

"A few weeks. Why not join our camp now? We have only one pretty face at the moment." He gazed at Morlana. "It would be much nicer to have two."

She blushed and smiled and squeezed her father's arm.

Crus and Rufio followed Matthias down a narrow palace entryway guarded by four soldiers with swords on their hips. The three visitors were ordered to leave their daggers. One of the guards then escorted them through a doorway to the left. Off to the right stretched a bank of rooms, and Rufio could smell steam and fresh water emanating from them. There must have been a bathhouse in the palace. Roman tastes indeed.

To the left, the three men entered an open air forecourt similar to the one in the Principia at the fort, though smaller. At the opposite side, a doorway opened to the throne room. Guards were posted there as well.

Long like a Roman basilica but narrower, the reception hall of the king was paved in white mosaic. Twin rows of magnificent columns of pink Egyptian granite topped with Corinthian capitals performed Atlas's task of supporting the roof. Bucolic garden frescoes in the

Roman style adorned the plastered walls. Yet they were oddly sterile. Neither man nor beast nor fowl dared enter these silent gardens, in deference to the bizarre Jewish proscription of animate images of any kind.

At the end of the hall loomed the man who had summoned them. The three men strode with measured respect down the long room between rows of guards. About thirty feet from the throne, three soldiers stopped them and one searched Matthias for weapons. The guard declined to inspect the Romans, and all three were now allowed to pass.

In a chair carved from cedar on a raised marble slab sat the man of legend. He wore a white tunic and pants trimmed with gold, with a half-cloak of red around his shoulders. The most hated and feared ruler in the entire East gazed at them in silence. Forever watched by Romans, smothered by sycophants, badgered by fools, betrayed by his own blood—now he was confronted by two specimens of that relentless race to whom he owed his throne, and who never let him forget it.

Herod was shorter than Rufio remembered. Stouter as well. Silver streaked his black hair and thick beard. His brow seemed heavier than it did years ago, as if now he had to make an effort to keep it from falling. He was clearly past his prime. Yet the fearsome eyes remained. It was as if some capricious god had melded the eyes of a Greek philosopher with those of a caged lion. Hopeful for honesty and expecting treachery, those eyes now burned into the Romans.

"The people of Judaea welcome our Roman friends," Herod said in a powerful voice that rumbled down the throne room. His Latin was excellent in both enunciation and intonation.

Crus stepped forward. "Caesar sends his greetings with those of the Senate and the people of Rome."

"Approach," Herod said in a softer voice.

Crus closed to within comfortable speaking distance.

"You are the tribune of whom Matthias spoke."

It was not a question so much as a pronouncement.

"Ulpius Crus."

"A political soldier then."

"I am."

"Tested in battle?"

"If ten thousand Germans can test."

The wrinkles deepened at the corners of Herod's eyes. "Well said."

"We offer our skills at locking the bolt on Judaea's southern gate."

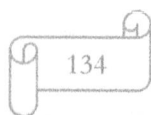

"The people of Judaea accept with gratitude. We will grant all the assistance you require."

"Caesar has always praised the generosity of the King of Judaea."

"Caesar's tribune is wise in the ways of men," Herod said. "He will sprint like a gazelle through the halls of power."

Crus inclined his head forward in a small bow.

"And this man?" Herod's gaze slid past Crus's right shoulder.

"The commander of Caesar's cohort," Crus said. "Quintus Flavius Rufio."

"Approach."

Rufio stepped beside Crus.

Herod nodded to the tribune, and he returned to where he had stood before.

"You are the true soldier," Herod said with satisfaction. "The centurion." His voice was so low only Rufio could hear.

"One of many whose cause is the will of Caesar."

Herod examined Rufio's face as searchingly as one poring over the map to a secret city.

"You have been to Judaea before?"

"Only as a traveler, my lord. I was posted to one of the Syrian legions. But that was long ago."

"And how few centuries there are to make up a man's life."

Unsure of the king's meaning, Rufio remained silent.

"Our friend Matthias tells the king that the Second Cohort are picked men. The pride of a Gallic legion. You may wonder how so young a man can know that, but he is not the fool so many of my soldiers are."

"Matthias is generous in his judgment."

"He is fair."

"May I ask the king a question?"

"You may."

"Matthias is fair, and yet he is searched. Is that customary?"

"Everyone is searched," Herod said with what appeared to be genuine sadness. He seemed weary now and lapsed into the singular pronoun. "If I could, I would search even the people in my dreams."

Rufio knew he might never feel it again, but at this moment he felt a great sorrow for the aging tyrant.

"Leadership is a terrible trial," Rufio said. "Few know that."

The camaraderie of shared pain shot energy back into Herod's eyes. "There are those who envy a king." He roared the most ferocious laugh Rufio had ever heard. "It is like envying being burned alive."

Almost imperceptibly, the king relaxed a bit in his cedar chair. He seemed oddly at ease with this foreign warrior.

"And how does Caesar's centurion command the loyalty of his fine troops?"

Herod seemed genuinely to want to know.

"I have never done that, my lord. Their loyalty is not commanded. It is freely given."

"Ah, that is a sacred thing. A treasure even a king can envy."

"My men are my life."

For the first and only time, Herod's gaze softened. Almost affectionately, he smiled at the younger man. Yet it was also the expression of one who clearly saw the end of the road ahead. Then he stood up.

"At our age, we must nap in the middle of the day. How sad that is. Have you ever slept with a dagger on your pillow?"

"I have, my lord."

"Then you know that is not sleep at all. I will pray to Elah to bring me rest, but I fear He stopped hearing me long ago."

Herod seemed reluctant to leave, but he turned away. A few feet from the throne, he paused and looked back. He stared at Rufio even more deeply.

"Have you ever hunted lions, centurion?"

"No, my lord."

"Not even once? In Syria?"

"No, my lord."

Herod nodded in acceptance of that and went off to the horrible sleep that could not refresh.

27

IT IS A COMMON MISTAKE IN GOING TO WAR TO BEGIN AT THE WRONG END, TO ACT FIRST AND WAIT FOR DISASTERS TO DISCUSS THE MATTER.

THUCYDIDES

The blue seas and the white towers and the ships from all nations splashed a stunning vision before the three officers.

"This is a marvelous place," Crus said, sitting down at the stone table outside the tavern at the edge of the dock. He looked around for Mallius.

"I prefer a popina in Ostia," Rufio said. He turned and held his cup of wine toward Matthias. "What pig's bladder did they squeeze this out of?"

"It's Syrian," he said.

"No, I've had Syrian swill. This is some Judaean poisoner's elixir."

"Well, wine aside, Caesarea is magnificent," Crus said.

"Herod has many talents," Rufio said, "and none greater than his genius for building. Yet the Jews hate him." He looked at Matthias. "Don't you?"

"Like poison."

"Why?" Crus asked.

"Reasons beyond counting," Matthias answered.

"A child's reply," Rufio said with a dismissive wave of his hand.

"He's a cruel man," Matthias said.

Rufio laughed. "Name a single Jewish king who was not."

"David was a man of God. He—."

"David? Didn't he win his bride by presenting the old king with a bushel of Philistine foreskins?"

Matthias hesitated. "It wasn't a bushel."

"Ah," Rufio said. "My mistake."

"Herod is obsessed with plots. He's half-mad with them."

"And he isn't justified in that, is he?" Rufio said. "Surrounded by jackals and sucked dry by leeches—odd that he should search the shadows for traitors. Especially since his father was murdered by one. Odder still that he should find them."

"You don't understand."

"I understand more than you think. You hate the king because Judaeans have always hated their kings—no exceptions."

Matthias turned away and gazed out toward the water.

Rufio looked at Crus, and the tribune smiled.

"They hate him," Rufio went on, "because he treats them with arrogance and contempt."

Matthias looked back at Rufio. "Yes."

"And why?" Rufio asked. "Because he's restored your greatness, made you a power again, built grand cities all across this land. And he's asked for only a single thing in return. Just one—gratitude. And you've never given it."

"We'd be better if we were rid of him."

"So you don't deny ingratitude?" Crus said.

"No," Rufio answered for Matthias. "Do you know why? Because Judaeans never show gratitude to anybody."

"How can you say that?" Matthias asked.

"I've read some of your holy writings. How many times have you abandoned your god? He's been very generous to you, but you always turn away."

Rufio waited for a response, but Matthias said nothing.

"How often has your god had to lash you back into line? He's used many scourges—Egyptians, Assyrians, Babylonians. Now it's us. I give you my word, Matthias, if the Judaeans revolt against Herod or one of his sons, they'll see Hell before they'll see light again. If Judaea causes chaos out here, we'll smash it down into the sand so hard it won't draw a breath again for a thousand years."

"Three fine soldiers!" Bellator boomed. "A sight to make the Parthians tremble."

"Did you recommend this place?" Rufio asked, holding up his cup.

"I must have my little joke," Bellator said, laughing as he approached. Mallius was by his side.

After the proper introductions, the five men sat together at the stone table but avoided the wine.

"Thank you for the fair dealing," Crus said to Mallius. "You've eased our burden."

"It's my special pride to serve the legions once more."

"Bellator says you want to enlighten us," Crus said.

"About the foe you might face," Mallius said.

"And who hides among the sands?" Crus asked.

"Fear no Nabataeans. Their blades have no thirst for Roman blood. They are peaceful men."

"Very well."

"It's the Parthians who rattle the hinges on the door."

"Are you certain?" Rufio asked.

"Beyond question."

"Tell us why," Crus said.

"Phraates is full of hate."

"Their king." Crus said.

"Yes. The peace he made with Augustus a few years ago settled nothing. When Phraates agreed to return the standards taken from the legions slaughtered at Carrhae, Augustus celebrated it. Gloated over it even. Had it put on coins. That ate a hole in Phraates' stomach."

"And . . . ?" Bellator said.

"He wants the Romans out. He knows he cannot do that directly, so he'll try to humiliate them by upending the Judaean kingdom. And he'll happily pick up any pieces that tumble his way."

Rufio looked Matthias in the eye and then turned to Mallius. "How?"

"Get the Jews fighting among themselves — they do that naturally anyway. Cause chaos and upheaval. He wants to make the Romans' experience in the East so sour that just the smell of hummus will make them vomit for centuries."

"Do you mean an invasion?" Matthias asked.

"Oh, no. Phraates fears the Syrian legions. But successful attacks on villages in the south could cause a revolt. You don't love Herod and he knows it."

"How can you be sure of this?" Matthias asked.

"I've seen some of the raiders the Judaeans have killed. They're Parthians."

"Maybe they were bandits," Matthias said.

"True, there are Parthian cast-offs who've become bandits, but these were soldiers."

"And what of Phraates himself?" Crus asked.

"Cunning and brutal. He murdered his father and his brothers and seized the throne."

"What about his troops?" Rufio asked, impatient to get to the battleground.

"I've seen only horse archers. And they're very difficult to defeat. They ride Turanian horses. You can never get Parthians by the throat. They're slippery as snakes in a bucket of slime."

"Tell me about the horses," Rufio said.

"Turanians are slightly taller and longer than the Arab. Thinner, too. They're very lean. They're just as fast as Arabians and about as hardy. They can walk for hours without tiring, just like the Arab. They don't have the beautiful mane the Arab has, but some of them have an amazing sheen to their coats. Not every Turanian has it, but the ones that do are stunning."

"Are they as intelligent as Arabians?" Rufio asked.

"That I don't know." He smiled. "But what horse is?"

"What about the heavy cavalry with the ten-foot lances?" Bellator asked. "They helped smash Crassus."

"They did, but there are very few of them. The heavy horsemen are strictly the nobles. They're the only ones who can afford the armor and weapons. The Parthians don't have a standing army in the Roman sense. If Phraates wants to field a large force, he has to petition the nobles for their troops."

"Have you seen any of these cavalry?" Rufio asked.

"No, and I doubt you will either. Phraates would never be able to entice his nobles into a Judaean adventure. They'd stand up to him. The mounted archers are another matter. They come from the less wealthy classes and they'll fight for plunder."

"Would they dare attack Romans?" Bellator asked.

"They have before," Mallius said.

"How many can we expect?" Crus asked.

"Probably not many. Phraates wouldn't risk a full-scale war. But all in the East fear the Parthian bowmen."

"No troops are unbeatable," Rufio said with annoyance. "You've been too long away from Romans."

"Perhaps," Mallius said. "But you've dressed enough wounds to know that confidence is not always a virtue."

"And you're old enough to know that the lack of confidence is always a vice."

"I didn't come here to argue," Mallius said. "Only to inform."

"Then inform us how best to face the Parthians," Crus said.

Mallius looked at Rufio.

"Seize the bit," Rufio said with an expansive gesture. "Don't be inhibited by me."

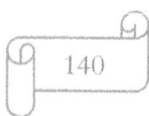

"Infantry won't beat them," Mallius said. "The Parthian horsemen will simply stay out of reach. If you had mounted archers, they could inflict pain on them if they're as good as the Parthian riders, but they never are. So you have a dilemma. Foot soldiers can hurt them but they cannot catch them, and horse archers can catch them but most aren't skilled enough to hurt them."

"You're not helping me here," Crus said with impatience.

Mallius looked at Rufio. "There's only one option left."

"Heavy cavalry," the centurion said. "Caesar learned from Crassus's mistake of not having enough cavalry. He planned a very different campaign than the one Crassus devised. My father told me that if Caesar hadn't been murdered, he would have moved East with ten thousand cavalry."

"Yes," Mallius said. "That the archers truly fear. Men who can race them down and strike them down. Provided there aren't any of their own heavy cavalry to protect them."

"We have our own cavalry," Crus said. "Matthias and his—."

"Us?" Matthias said.

"Aren't you?" Rufio asked.

"We're bowmen."

"Jewish horse archers?" Rufio said. "Whoever heard of such a thing?"

"We do have some. We have a colony up in Batanea. It's called Bathyra. We have about five hundred horse archers there. Good ones. Herod found them so impressive that he decided to create more."

"You and your men?"

"Yes." He looked embarrassed. "Except we haven't been trained yet."

Rufio looked at Bellator in frustration.

"These are deep waters," Bellator said.

Rufio turned away. "And how I hate the sea."

Rufio strolled along the dock and watched boatmen of many lands haul their cargoes ashore. He heard the cadence of a strong stride behind him and recognized Crus's gait.

"Centurion!"

Rufio turned around.

The tribune came up to him. "What's wrong?"

"What isn't? You heard Mallius. We don't—."

"No, not that. Why are you so irritable today?"

"Am I?"

"Don't sneer at my good sense."

Rufio turned and squinted out toward the horizon. "I ache."

Crus was quiet.

"Is that enough?" Rufio asked.

"Yes."

Rufio laughed wearily. "No it isn't. You want more. I was thinking about a little girl."

Crus stared at him in confusion.

"I baffle you, don't I?"

"Endlessly."

"Let's head back to camp."

The shadows lengthening across the dock made a tired man even slower.

"I wish we'd thought to bring horses," Crus said. "I feel like I have lead in my legs."

Rufio gestured with his chin past Crus's shoulder.

The tribune turned around. In the distance he saw Valerius on horseback leading two more Arabian mounts.

"I knew we wouldn't want to walk back."

Crus laughed. "I have to learn to think three steps ahead. Like my centurions."

"It's just habit."

"Speaking of which . . . ."

"Yes?"

"Mallius's dilemma. Can we find a solution? You were very quiet after he left."

"There's a *potential* solution."

"It must be well hidden, because I don't see a trace of one."

"It rests with Bellator. Let's bathe and eat and rest and meet in my tent in a few hours."

Valerius came up with the horses.

"Don't I have the best optio in all the legions?" Rufio said with a smile.

"Sorry it took me so long. I tried to cut through the small forum east of here but I couldn't get through. There was a huge crowd."

"A bit late in the day for that," Rufio said.

"Everybody wanted to see what was happening. These desert women are insane. Somebody in the mob told me that a woman had just cut off a man's ear. Right there in the middle of the forum."

"What?" Rufio said.

"That's what he claimed."

Rufio sprang toward his horse.

"What's wrong?" Crus said.

"It's Flavia!" Rufio shouted and gripped the horse's mane and sailed into the saddle.

"How do you know that?"

"Who else would it be?" he yelled and galloped away.

28

NECESSITY KNOWS NOTHING ELSE BUT VICTORY.

PUBLILIUS SYRUS

An hour earlier, Flavia had stood with parted lips at the edge of The Field of Beasts.

"What kind of creature can that be? Is it crippled?"

Morlana giggled. "It's supposed to be that way."

"No, it must have some disease. Look at that twisted spine."

"That's fat," Morlana said, still laughing.

"For what?"

"There isn't much food and water where it lives. It's called a camel."

"It's going to give me nightmares. Why is it spitting at that man?"

"Camels are mean."

"I could never have dreamed of an animal like that." She looked at Morlana and laughed. "And I've had some scary dreams!"

Morlana smiled back and slid a hand into Flavia's. The little girl seemed so hungry for affection.

"Your laugh reminds me of my mother's," Morlana said.

"If you look like her, she must be a beautiful woman."

Morlana's smile melted. "She died last year. She was bitten by a viper."

Flavia squeezed her hand.

"But I have her eyes and hair," Morlana said.

"You must attract stares here. There cannot be many blondes in Judaea."

"And not many Suebi either!"

Stunned, Flavia was speechless for a moment. "You're Suebian?"

"My mother was born near the Rhenus. I even know her

language." She smiled and said in Sequani, "And I can speak your language, too!"

Impulsively, Flavia hugged her. "We'll have great fun together." She pulled up the hood on Morlana's brown cloak. "The sun is getting high."

Flavia pulled up her own red hood.

"Why are you staring?" Morlana asked.

"Am I?" Flavia knew she was, but how could she tell her why? How could she explain to her the gods' own irony of a man who had slain countless Suebi and yet who was now held in thrall by a little Suebi girl who had done absolutely nothing except smile into his eyes?

"What would you like to do today while your father is doing man things?"

"Just see the city. I don't have any money, though."

Flavia smiled. "We have the purse of Caesar at our command. Today whatever you like is yours."

Morlana threw her arms around Flavia and squeezed.

Flavia knew gratitude was one of the sweetest emotions in children, but the expression of it was rare. She hugged back this uncommon little girl.

As Neko had toured Flavia around Ostia and Alexandria, now she and Morlana explored Caesarea together. Much newer than Ostia, Caesarea had not yet developed the texture of a seasoned port. Yet it was trying. Awash in colorful characters whose nationalities could barely even be guessed, Caesarea promised to become one of the most dynamic ports in the East.

After several hours of strolling and eating and drinking, during which Morlana talked endlessly about every topic imaginable, they came to rest at a small forum at the eastern side of the city.

"My feet hurt," Flavia said, and the wanderers sat on the steps of a basilica near the edge of the forum.

"Flavia . . . ?"

For the first time all day, Morlana seemed hesitant.

"Yes?"

"Does Rufio not like me?"

"What?" Flavia said in surprise. "Why would you believe such a thing?"

"When I came out of my tent this morning, Rufio was near. He was talking to one of his men. He barely looked at me."

Flavia reached out and took both of Morlana's hands in hers.

"He likes you very much. More than he can express. But those feelings are new to him. He's never had children of his own."

"But why wouldn't he look at me?"

"You touch him in a special way. It makes him uneasy. Even a soldier can be frightened by something he doesn't understand."

"But I'm just a girl."

"He's confused by feelings he's never had."

"I cannot stop thinking about him," she said with a look that begged for understanding. "I talk about him to my father all the time."

"How does your father feel about that?"

"He's happy for me."

Flavia smiled.

"I love my father, but Rufio is different. He's like . . . I don't know . . . an uncle . . . no, I don't know."

"Don't try to describe him. I gave up long ago."

"He never criticized me. We spent all day together that first day. He never told me I had to act like a sweet little girl."

"I think he's likes you just as you are."

"Then I'll never change!" she said with a smile. "I know I talk too much, but he never stopped me. He was so nice to me for no reason."

"What do you mean no reason?"

"I'm a foreigner here. The Judaeans are never friendly to me."

"Well, he's an Italian and Italians are different."

Flavia took the hem of her cloak and wiped some fruit from the edge of Morlana's mouth. She had to be the sloppiest eater in the world. Before Flavia dropped her cloak, Morlana spotted her dagger. She looked as if she were about to speak, but then said nothing.

"Shall we go soon?" Flavia asked. "Are you rested?"

"Yes. Will you come with us to Hezrail?"

"Where is that?"

"Our village. Near the Salt Sea."

"We're headed in that direction. We're going to build a fort down there. Maybe we can spend time together."

"That will be fun!"

"I know you can ride, but have you ever shot a bow?"

"You're teasing. Girls don't shoot bows."

"Sequani girls do. I'll teach you. And then when you're good enough, I'll show you how to shoot from horseback."

"Oh, Flavia!"

"I wasn't much older than you when I learned. But you have to promise me something first."

"I will."

"You must promise never to say I did it for no reason—because you *are* the reason."

"I promise!"

"Now let's go see those men who are special to us."

The crowds in the forum had started thinning out as the sun had begun its descent. Even the loungers and vice peddlers decided to move on. Yet the three young men in the street ahead stopped when they saw Flavia and Morlana. The popina behind them had probably just fortified them with the courage of Bacchus.

"Flavia," Morlana said, and touched her sleeve.

"I see them," she said but did not slow down.

One of them, evidently the leader, swaggered toward them. The other two followed.

Flavia pulled back her hood to improve her field of vision.

"Look at that black mane!" the one up front said.

Bare-headed women were rare in a culture where repression and shame were enshrined as virtues.

"They think you're a . . . that you're a bad woman," Morlana whispered.

"No they don't. They're just treating me like one."

Many of the men leaving the forum had paused. They smiled now with the prospect of a bit of excitement.

The three men, only a few years older than Flavia, strolled forward with the arrogance of half-drunks the world over.

Flavia stopped and Morlana drew close to her. The forum crowd, neither more nor less vulgar than any crowd anywhere, had boxed them in, by accident rather than by design.

The three men were closing the distance.

Morlana squeezed Flavia's right wrist. "Flavia, we have to leave."

Flavia turned and looked down at her. She pushed back Morlana's hood and ran a hand over her hair.

"You wouldn't have me run, would you, Morlana?" she said gently.

The fearlessness in Flavia's eyes banished Morlana's terror in an instant. She reached up and squeezed Flavia's fingers.

"Let's show them that Sequani and Suebi women run from no one," Flavia said. "Least of all these gutter dogs."

"Yes," Morlana whispered.

"Stand aside!" Flavia shouted to the leader.

Not an unattractive young man, he stopped and laughed almost pleasantly. "Only for someone better."

"They stand before you."

"Where?" he said mockingly. "I see only undraped women unattached to men. Give us some fun and we'll give you some coin."

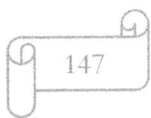

"We're not unclean women," Morlana said.

"A spirited one, that little blonde," he answered with a laugh and approached Flavia.

With the force of an iron ram, Flavia's fist smashed into the center of his face. He dropped like a collapsed roof. His head hit a paving stone with a crack. He groaned, and blood gushed from his crushed nose.

The second man charged with more valor than wisdom. Flavia's right foot slammed into his testicles. So sharp was the sound of the impact that several men in the crowd yelped as loudly as the victim. Gasping, he pawed at Flavia as he fell on top of her. She pushed him aside and jumped to her feet.

"No!" came a scream from across the forum.

The third man had grabbed Morlana and dragged her off, perhaps as a hostage against Flavia's wrath. Morlana's fists pounded his face. He struck her across the cheek but still she flailed at him. He wrenched her right arm behind her back and she wailed in pain.

And then something in Flavia snapped. The little girl's cry of agony obliterated everything—all but the predator and her prey. It was no mate of a Roman soldier who stood in the midst of a crowd in a half-Greek city. Untouched by the hand of civilization, here was a feral creature, implacable in the fury of the forest gods flooding her soul. The forum had vanished. It was now a darkened wood empty of sound. Flavia pulled off her cloak and flung it aside. She began her run slowly, almost casually, the terrible daughter of a barbarous race glaring at the object of her rage. Not a man present dared to warn the unsuspecting victim. And then she was upon him. Like a forest cat, she leaped onto his back and brought him down. Her left arm hooking around his throat, she felt nothing and heard nothing as he fell backward atop her. He reached back and tried to claw her face, but her dagger was in her hand. She slashed upward and flicked his right ear from his head as if it were a leaf. She heard him shriek, but from far off, as though in a valley on the other side of the world. Still he struggled to tear her face with his fingers, and then his other ear flew off to join the first, never to return. Flavia thrust the point of her dagger against his throat.

"Beg for mercy, you stinking dog!" she whistled through her teeth. "Beg now or I'll kill you where you lie!"

"Please, no more!" he screamed.

She slid out from under him and sprang to her feet.

He turned over onto his hands and knees, blood pouring from both sides of his head.

She raised her right foot and, in the ultimate gesture of contempt, pushed it against the side of his face until he toppled to the stones in the final pathetic humiliation.

Flavia swept around and searched the forum. She smiled as Morlana bounded toward her and leaped into her arms.

29

WHO ASKS TIMIDLY COURTS DENIAL.

SENECA

Rufio raced through the mob. The crowd scattered like dry leaves as his horse burst into the forum. Valerius dashed in behind and swept the perimeter like the good soldier he was. Crus galloped in at the rear and covered Rufio's back.

The three maimed men still moaned on the paving stones, and Rufio snatched up the scene in a single glance.

"Look!" Morlana yelled, pointing toward Rufio and pulling Flavia along with her.

Flavia smiled and released the little girl's hand.

Morlana sprinted toward the centurion.

Rufio reached down and scooped her up behind him onto his horse. He gazed again at the stricken men and then at Flavia. She was a windstorm loosed by inscrutable gods and sweeping across the land. One could stand off and admire the beauty of this natural wonder, but only madmen would attempt to bar her path.

Valerius called to her and she gripped his left hand and glided up onto the back of his mount.

Then the three horsemen wheeled and quit the forum at a gallop, leaving the dazed crowd to nurse the follies of drunken man.

"They gave me no quarter, so I —."

Rufio held up his hand, and Flavia stopped.

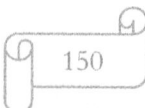

"I asked for no explanation last night, and I need none now. Just keep it in that Sequani mind that this is a difficult charge we have from Caesar." He crossed the tent to his table and picked up a cup of wine and handed it to her. "So while we're in Caesarea, no more lopped appendages falling to the ground."

"He deserved it."

"What drunks deserve is not the concern of Rome."

"Morlana adores you."

"Adoration doesn't suit me," he said, sitting down at his table and looking through some documents that Paki was reluctant to relinquish as a bed.

"You don't mind mine."

No answer came.

"She's hurt by your indifference."

"Indifference?" Rufio said, looking around.

"That's how she understands it."

"She told you that?"

"The conversations of women are not for the ears of men."

"To a woman with a dagger, even the ears of men are not for the ears of men."

"Just trust my judgment."

"Why should I do that?"

"Because I am Sequani."

He extended his left arm.

She came over and sat on his lap, and he pulled her in tight.

"Some men think if they love younger women, they'll retain their youth. They're wrong."

"What do you mean?"

"You age a man a decade in a day."

She nestled her head against his shoulder. "Then we'll age together."

"Centurion!" Bellator's voice boomed from outside the tent.

"He never rests," Rufio said with a sigh.

"You've given him a new life."

"No, I just opened the latch on the gate to it. He walked through on his own." Rufio nudged her gently and she got up from his lap. "He's like those horses he loves. You cannot force them to do anything, but if you encourage them they'll do everything."

Rufio crossed the tent and stepped out into the sunlight. Bellator was pacing, despite his limp. Rufio stepped past him. His men were tending to their soldierly tasks in a camp as neat and orderly as the fort along the Rhenus.

"This is where it pays," Rufio said, folding his arms across his chest and smiling. "A year ago, many of them wanted to smash my face with a wicker shield. And now?"

"Such love," Bellator said with a laugh.

"No, not love. This cuts deeper."

"And do you have a name for it?"

"No one does. But it's as piercing as light reflected from a rare stone. And as incorruptible as bindings of bronze."

"Many would just call it training."

"Then they're fools. Hannibal's men were trained. But his soldiers didn't have it. They fought for pay. They were all mercenaries from foreign lands. It was Hannibal's greatness that he could forge a mess like that into one of the most magnificent armies that every marched. But if you murder the paymaster, you murder the army." Rufio wandered forward and watched two of his centuries grunting through their afternoon weapons drill. "I've fought in many lands beside many men. But no soldier—not one—ever stood by me in battle for a couple of hundred denarii a year."

Bellator remained quiet.

"It's something that impels a man to risk his life for men he didn't know not so long ago. And to follow a leader into a hostile land full of ungrateful people to serve a Caesar most of them will never see. And there isn't even a term for that."

"You're wrong."

Rufio turned toward his old friend.

"There *is* a name for it." Bellator had never looked more serious. "The spirit of Rome—and it has no equal."

Rufio smiled and gazed back at his soldiers. "By all the gods at once, I'm proud of these men."

"The little girl's father is looking for you."

Rufio turned, but Bellator was speaking to Flavia as she came out of the tent.

"Where is he?" she asked.

"Tending the horses."

She hurried off.

"Speaking of horses . . . ." Bellator said.

"Yes?"

"We have training to do."

"I know."

Rufio strolled down a row of tents with his arms folded.

"Remember my bad hip," Bellator said, struggling to keep up.

"You whine like a Greek."

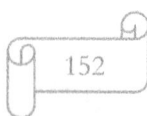

Rufio pulled two camp stools from the tent shared by Valerius and Metellus and set them near the triangles of pila and shields propped at the front.

"Rest your decaying carcass."

Bellator eased himself down. "We have to train horses and we have to train men. Which do you prefer?"

"Did I miss the transfer of command?"

Bellator gave him a puzzled look.

"Has Crus abdicated his authority to you?" Rufio asked.

"You and I know horses and horsemen better than he does. We'll save him the effort."

"He's a young man in his first command. Even if the decision is really ours, he has to make it. For his own good."

"All right, but let's discuss it here first. How skilled are your men on horseback?"

"All are adequate, and a few are excellent."

"I should have known."

"I trained my own century last year. My centurions did the same with the rest of the cohort."

"We have to go beyond crude skills, but we cannot expect too much. We don't have the time."

"Agreed. Do you think it can be done?"

"I do," Bellator said.

"And the horses?"

"The same problem. We have to train them, but nothing too complex. Time is our enemy."

"Have you looked over the herd?"

"I have."

"And the verdict?"

"Much better than average."

"I'd expect no less from Arabians."

"I culled twenty-three. Most for bad feet—some battered hoofs, a diseased ranula here and there. A few had capped hocks. Those will heal, but I don't want to wait. Four I pulled for temperament. They seemed suitable for nothing so much as kicking jackals to death."

"Hold onto all of them."

"Why waste forage on horses we don't want?"

"Indulge my whims." Rufio stood and took a long, slow breath of the damp air blowing in from the sea. He folded his arms and walked down the tent line a dozen or so paces. "And the instructors?" he asked without turning around.

"A cavalry officer should train the men. For their own safety."

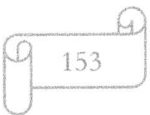

Rufio looked back at Bellator. "And the horses?"

"They should be guided by a man who can interpret the mysteries of their souls—but since I'll be busy, we'll have to look elsewhere."

Rufio laughed. "You broken down old manure shoveler."

"No foot soldier I know has the feel for horses you do. And I know no other callus-footed infantryman who has his own copy of Xenophon's treatise on horses. That Numidian stud of yours—what's his name?—he'd dance on a knife edge at your wish."

"Cormagnus."

"If Big Heart can do it, then I see no reason why these horses cannot. All are already saddle mounts. They know the commands."

"But they aren't warhorses."

"That's why they have to breathe in the martial vapors of a man of war. So they don't die a hideous death in these baking sands."

The tribune's tent was larger and more elaborate than Crus would have wanted, but Rufio had advised that it was necessary not simply to be the commander but to look like the commander.

All six centurions sat on one side of the table along with Bellator. The tribune sat alone on the other side.

"And you're certain this can be done?" Crus asked.

"As certain as anyone can be when dealing with animals and men," Bellator said. "Rufio tells me his soldiers are able horsemen, though maybe a bit out of practice. If I had to train mounted archers, we wouldn't have time. It's too complex. But becoming a cavalryman isn't as complicated. That doesn't mean it's easy, but the maneuvers are few and fairly simple. It's courage and stamina on horseback that will rule this battlefield."

"And the mounts?" Crus said to Rufio.

"These are very fine horses. The problem is that they're Arabians—and Arabians always think they're smarter than men. The trick is to bend their will without poisoning their spirit."

Crus smiled at his favorite centurion. "You sound almost mystical."

"Well, no one who works with animals should ever be considered normal. And horse trainers are out on the fringe even there."

Crus laughed. "And you can do this?"

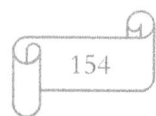

"In Egypt I trained many Numidians. For my own pleasure.'

"Are they like Arabians?"

"Very similar. And all my centurions are skilled riders. Some of my other officers, too. And Flavia is half horse herself. We can master this task."

"Excellent. Let it be the will of Caesar."

Crus held Bellator and Rufio back after the other centurions had filed out.

"Why do I think you two had decided this before you ever entered my tent?" His voice was as cold as chilled steel.

Caught off guard, both men waited for him to continue.

"Decisions are made by the tribune, not by centurions. Nor — may the gods help us — by an engineer." He glared at Bellator. "You're more experienced than I, but never think — not for an instant — that you're any smarter. Now get on with it."

"Tribune!" Bellator said and left the tent.

Crus turned toward Rufio, but his expression eased into the hint of a smile. "Lesson learned. Dismissed."

30

IT IS A BAD PLAN THAT CANNOT BE CHANGED.

PUBLILIUS SYRUS

The late morning sun bleached an expanse of empty land beyond the Roman camp.

"What do you think?" Rufio asked.

Bellator dropped to one knee and examined the ground. "Possibly. It looks flat enough and not too hard." He pounded the earth with his right hand and then sifted some soil through his fingers. "If it were harder, the horses would get aching shoulders and sore tendons. Any softer and they'd get muscle strains. This is as good as we're likely to find."

"And these horses are already accustomed to this."

"That helps." Bellator stood up. "We'll need a gyrus. About a hundred feet or so in diameter. I want solid fencing to keep out distractions."

"What about the parade ground? I'm assuming about two hectares."

Bellator smiled. "See? You do know more about this than you let on. Two hectares should be fine. Have the men comb the ground as fanatically as if they were looking for lice. I want as many stones as possible cleared off. Horses with torn tendons are just leopard meat."

"How many animals do you think we can train at the outset?"

"Fifty is plenty to work with right now, even with several good men—and a good woman. Do you think you'll need more?"

"You know the answer to that," Rufio said. "Soldiers always need more. We'll try to get seventy ready. Charges, sudden stops, back-ups, pivots on the hindquarter. Four or five maneuvers are all we can hope for. There's no time for anything more."

Dressed in a white caftan and holding a small water flask, Morlana stood by herself at the edge of the rope horse pen.

"Why are you out here alone?"

She spun around.

Rufio smiled as she ran toward him. But she stopped abruptly, as though unsure what to do next.

"I need a strator."

She looked confused.

"You."

Her lips parted, but she just stared at him.

"Well?"

"How can I take care of your horses? I'm just a girl."

"It isn't age, it's character. I never misread a woman's eyes."

She seemed overwhelmed and gazed at him in wonder.

"How long have you been riding?"

"I've always ridden."

Probably she could scarcely remember a time when she had not.

"That's what I mean."

"My mother taught me."

"The Suebi are natural riders. You could glide out among that herd with more confidence than any of my men. And no doubt with more skill, too."

She giggled.

You're still too young and trusting to be afraid, he thought. And he adored her for it.

"Do you want the job?"

"Yes!"

He extended his right arm and she slipped her hand into the grip of his calloused fingers. He had forgotten how delicate a little girl's hand was, how fragile.

"I haven't seen you around the camp today," he said.

"I don't want to be a pest." Her blue eyes looked up at him in the desperate hope that she was not.

"Oh, Morlana." He slipped his left arm around her shoulders and pulled her in for a hug.

"Rufio?"

"Yes?"

"I love Flavia. Is that all right?"

He leaned back a bit and looked into her questioning eyes. "Of course it's all right. Why would you ask that?"

"Because she belongs to you."

He laughed. "Flavia belongs only to herself. But she shares herself with those she loves."

Morlana pressed her head against Rufio's ribs. Her silent tears wet his blue tunic.

"Why are you crying?"

"Because I'm silly."

"Sit."

She dropped down to the ground, and he pulled his scabbard out of the way and sat across from her.

"I'm going to tell you a very special secret."

Her eyes focused intently and her lips pressed together.

"The day we first met was not a good one for me," he said. "That night, in my tent, I felt a terrible pain."

She seemed troubled by this incomprehensible revelation.

"I knew I'd never have a daughter like the little girl I'd just met. And I couldn't bear it."

Her lower lip fluttered, and her eyes moistened again and reddened in an instant. She reached out and he took her thin fingers in his.

"Please stay with us in Judaea," she said.

He rested his thumb as delicately as a butterfly against the back of her hand. "I know only this—the gods didn't bring me thousands of miles only to dash a gray-haired man's heart against the rocks."

Her eyes searched his as she yearned to understand.

"The gods have their ways," he said. "And even they have their longings and their dreams."

Footsteps behind caused him to look over his shoulder.

"This seems serious," Mallius said as he approached.

Morlana pulled her hand from Rufio's.

"I just hired a strator."

"They come no better," Mallius said and sat beside his daughter. "So tell me—why are you going to build a fort at Hezrail?"

"Who says we are?"

"Morlana."

"I guess military secrets died with the conquest of Gaul," Rufio said, trying to conceal his annoyance. "I cannot discuss it."

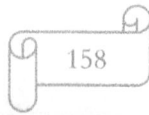

"You misunderstand. I'm not asking about the fort. I mean why at Hezrail. There's already a fort there."

"What?!"

"About a mile southeast of the village. Pompeius's men built it years ago. There was some disturbance in the south and he sent a vexillation to flash some Roman steel. They'd barely finished the fort when he pulled them. The unrest had evaporated as fast as a desert rain, and he had pressing matters elsewhere."

"Mallius, if you were prettier, I'd kiss you. This saves us much time—time to work with the horses and the men."

"You'll just have to sweep it out. It's stone and looks as good as the year it was built. There's probably only a rat's nest here and there. And maybe a leopard dozing in the shadows. But that's it."

"Thank you for clarifying this," Rufio said to Morlana in a tone no different than if she were one of his own officers. "This helps us very much."

She glowed.

Mallius reached across and placed her right hand back into Rufio's. "It's all right," he said with a smile and got up and walked out among the horses.

"Welcome to the Roman army," Rufio said.

She grinned and squeezed his fingers as tightly as she could.

31

LOVE IS THE SAME IN ALL.

VIRGIL

*T*his day I learned, more forcefully than ever, the hideous weight of command. And the crushing effect it can have even on the most extraordinary of men. I have never seen Rufio so angry at me as today. Occasionally I have annoyed him with womanly whims, but today he glared at me in fury. I was very frightened. I know he would never hurt me, but I was terrified by the fire of his rage. No woman likes to be seared by that – or be the cause of it in the man she loves.

He refused to speak until we were out of the hearing of everyone. He led me to a low hill overlooking the field where the horses were penned. When he turned and faced me, my mouth became as dry as the soil under my feet.

"Have you never heard of military secrets?!" he almost shouted.

I could not speak.

"We're not some roving band of Gallic barbarians flushing out game. We're a Roman cohort."

"I don't understand," I said, and I could hear my voice cracking.

"The fort! You talk about that with people as if you're discussing the weather?"

"But I –."

"And with a ten year old girl?!"

My tongue refused to work.

"Anything you learn stays locked in you. I have over four hundred men to keep alive. And they have parents and sisters and brothers and sweethearts. Will you write the letters if they're cut down in an ambush because of a careless remark?"

Now I was furious – at myself. I knew he was right. But I was far too proud to admit it. So we just stared at each other in blind anger. Finally he expelled a breath in disgust and walked away.

"Centurion!"

I had never called him that. He spun toward me. Now I was frightened again, but not for the same reason. His anger had vanished. I thought I saw pain in his eyes. My addressing him in such a way cut him. That a man so tough could be hurt by the single cold word of a young woman seemed incredible. At that instant I saw, I think for the first time, the terrible loneliness of his life. And its brutal burdens. He has only three solaces — the ferocious valor and loyalty of Valerius and Metellus, the love and wisdom of Neko, and me.

"You're as taut as a bowstring," I said. "Even the greatest archer knows that sometimes he must unstring his bow."

"A luxury denied to a centurion."

He said the last word as coldly as I had hurled it at him.

"If an ignorant Sequani woman may say so to the great Roman soldier, it's an indulgence he cannot afford to deny himself."

"Finally we agree. 'Ignorant' is the proper term."

I wanted to slap his face. I spat my words at him. "Maybe the centurion can find sweeter release in the arms of those women who write letters to him. The ones who are so eager to describe the width of their thighs."

It was an awful thing to say, and I immediately hated myself.

"Perhaps," he said with an exhaustion that scared me. It seemed as if it was the last word he would ever speak in this life. Then he turned and walked away.

"My love." My voice sounded like a croak, and my eyes were already hot and wet.

He looked back over his shoulder, and I was on him in an instant.

"Don't ever turn from me." I felt the tears running down my cheeks and hugged him so hard I hurt my own muscles.

Then I could have sung to the stars, because he gave me his eye smile. "I suppose I'm a poor imitation of Atlas."

"Who is that?"

"The god who holds up the world."

"You hold up your men every day."

He leaned forward and kissed me on both of my eyebrows. Then he slid the side of his face against mine.

"By the gods, I love your scent," he whispered.

"I'll hold you up forever."

Never would Crus have thought that the sight of a fortified camp would thrill him. In Rome, wealthy men began wheezing and folding in on themselves as they were sapped by the very pleasures they sought to stave off their own spiritual depletion. The army was a contrary world. Here the simplest undertakings conferred the sweetest delight. This small camp—orderly and sanitary and patrolled by determined and audacious men—offered him more joy than all the salacious alleys of the Suburra.

Crus strolled down the streets of the camp and chatted with the men. Asked them about the food, the taste of the water, about any health problems. Encouraged them to share their concerns—and even jokes about their officers. They were all at ease in the relaxed informality between officers and men that Caesar had enshrined in his legions a generation earlier. They clearly enjoyed the interplay with their tribune. He had become like them, leaner, darker from the sun, a bit more wrinkled. When Crus took his proper place in the Senate in a few years, these men knew he would be no flaccid place holder, overfed on sweet cakes and flattery. He would be a toned soldier who would cross the Forum to the Curia with a confidence few men ever have. More importantly, Crus knew this, too. A year ago, he had been just a strip of raw doeskin. But since then he had been through life's tannery. He was becoming as taut as the belt supporting the dagger on his hip. And he relished every bit of torment that had done this. Most of all, he relished these men. Within their flesh they carried, sometimes with a sigh and a groan, the wisdom of the battlefield. In this school, wiser than the Greek Stoa, Crus had learned a primal truth. Suffering, even anguish, and the silent endurance of both were among life's greatest goods. He knew many in Rome who said they could not believe in the gods because even cruel gods would never allow so much agony. The fools. Pain was one of the gods' finest gifts, for it made men men. And he knew that it had lashed him into becoming far more than he could ever have hoped to be. To these soldiers, he was the leader, but to him they were his teachers. As he stood at the edge of the camp, he smiled and thanked the gods for these rough tutors—smart and maddening and vulgar and magnificent.

"Metellus!"

The signifer emerging from his tent hurried forward at the tribune's command.

"Find Rufio and tell him to assemble the other centurions. Bellator as well. We'll meet in my tent immediately."

"Yes, tribune." And Metellus was off.

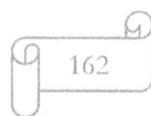

When the centurions and Bellator took their places at the long table in the tent, Crus saw that some were still sweaty from conducting weapons drills. All the centurions in Rufio's cohort kept an eye on the skills of their men by wielding blades at their sides a few times a week, rather than always delegating it to their optios.

"We'll tempt the Fates," Crus said, when all had sat down. "We'll move south now. The men seem to have gotten accustomed to the climate very quickly. We'll exploit that. Since we have to train the men, we'll train them where they'll fight—not near damp ocean breezes. We—."

A frowning centurion raised a hand, apparently to object.

"I know you agree with me," Crus said, cutting him off. "No need to make public affirmation." His eyes swept the table. "Two days. Questions?"

There was silence.

"Prepare."

Rufio remained when the others had left.

"You know you're pushing these men. . . ." Rufio's tone was neutral.

"Yes. It's good for them."

"I agree."

"What's our greatest concern?" Crus asked.

"Water, especially for the horses. And forage."

"Suggestions?"

"I've already plotted our route with Mallius. He knows every spring and oasis and blade of grass. He had to in order to get his horses here."

"And the Judaean soldiers? Will they be ready?"

"They're always happiest to put distance between themselves and Herod. When they're not scheming to overthrow him. They'd be ready in an hour if you told them to."

"Your concerns?"

Rufio smiled. "Only one. That Diocles isn't with us to write it all down. I think this desert adventure would make quite a tale."

32

THE NOBLE ANIMAL . . . WHAT A SPIRIT AND WHAT METTLE. HOW PROUDLY HE BEARS HIMSELF. A JOY AT ONCE—AND YET WHAT A TERROR TO BEHOLD.

XENOPHON

Away from the camp, on the opposite side of a ridge near a small spring, Rufio worked a dapple gray gelding through some maneuvers. He had learned long ago never to trust a horse trader—even a former soldier—so he had picked a horse at random to test. Like all Arabians, this one crackled with spirit, and Rufio felt waves of barely controlled energy rippling between his legs.

The horse was taut and spry and quick off the mark, so Rufio cantered him in a wide circle to soften him and bank some of his fire. After about ten times around, he rolled the horse back in the opposite direction and was surprised and pleased to feel him change leads on the fly at the rider's command. A horse leading with the wrong foot in a turn was awkward and uncomfortable to ride and a danger in battle. Ten more circles and then ten the other way, and always the horse glided into the proper lead on Rufio's leg commands. He took the horse down to a trot to cool him off. A few circles at the trot and Rufio brought him to a halt. He pivoted the horse on the forehand, and the animal rolled as smoothly as if he were on wheels. Yet when Rufio signaled with his heel for the horse to turn on the hindquarter, the animal behaved as if he knew nothing about it. Rufio knew it was common for Arabians to try to outthink their riders and suddenly play the moron to avoid a task they did not like. With two thirds of the weight normally on the front legs, the shifting of some of it to the hindquarter and then the swinging of the front-end bulk was not the most comfortable maneuver for horses and many of them fought it.

Rufio backed him up instantly. Not three feet or ten, but fully thirty feet he pulled him back, making him submit to what he hated. No horse in the wild will ever back up of his own accord, so such an act of dominance told this steed at once that here was an animal even smarter and tougher than an Arabian.

Miraculously, the horse suddenly regained his memory and, at Rufio's command, turned on the forehand as if he had invented the movement. After five more repetitions, Rufio let him relax, and he spoke to the horse softly and scratched his withers. Then he dismounted and led him to the spring.

"May I get you a cool drink?"

Rufio turned around, and he saw Morlana bounding toward him.

"Where have I heard that before?" he said as she raced up to him and gave him a bone crushing hug.

"You haven't abandoned your post, have you?" he asked seriously.

"My father is with the horses."

She took him by the hand and led him to the shade of an acacia, where they sat together and she smiled into his eyes. There seemed to be nothing she wanted or needed, other than to be with him. Again he found it inexplicable, but he thanked the gods for it.

"Why do you wear that blue tunic?" she asked.

"Because my men are less likely to obey me if I give an order naked."

"No, no," she said, giggling and blushing as red as Caesar's robe. "I mean why do you wear blue when your men wear white?"

"So I'll stand out. A leader should always stand apart from his men. And I like blue."

"But doesn't that bother them?"

"Bother?"

"Yes. Making yourself special."

"It doesn't matter if it bothers them."

She seemed puzzled. "Don't you want to be loved by your soldiers?"

"No centurion is loved."

"Then how can you lead them?"

Rufio smiled and took her hand. He traced his forefinger along the lines in her palm and out to the tips of her fingers, and then curled them closed and held them.

"We save our love for others," he said.

She still seemed confused.

"The finest commander is the one who enjoys being liked but doesn't care if he's disliked."

He could see her working to absorb that.

"I give my men what they need to survive. Sometimes they hate it. Sometimes they think they even hate me." He decided to relent a little to make her feel better. "Someday they'll care. When they're old men sitting around their firesides with their grandchildren and I'm long gone. They'll love me then. That'll do."

That seemed to soothe her enough. Her expression eased.

"You look tired," she said.

"It's the heat. At my age, it takes longer to get used to it."

"Why don't you have a nap?"

"Out here? It isn't safe to do that. A Roman soldier never sleeps where there's no sentry."

"I can guard you."

The innocence and faith in her eyes could have made an iron ingot weep.

"All right," he said and pulled his dagger from its sheath and handed it to her hilt first.

"You can rest now," she said, smiling. "I won't leave you."

I have never seen Matthias as happy as he is now. The Judaean soldiers hate and fear their king. They long to be far from him.

Today I was standing by the horse herd and watching Morlana instruct the two boys she hired to help her. It was fun to see this girl take command, something very rare in this land. Matthias came up beside me and offered me some water. I could see he was uncomfortable. Judaean men rarely speak with women in public except to give them an order or a rebuke. He certainly would never have spoken with me if any of his men had been nearby. I think he had come to see the horses but was now uneasy ignoring me. My status baffles him. He does not know how to react to a Sequani woman.

He asked me about Rufio, about his battles and his campaigns. I was stunned to learn that Matthias has been a soldier for only seven months. I was even more surprised that he told me this. Rufio says that I draw out honesty in men. I do not know why.

It is easy to see that Matthias is looking to Rufio as a model. I notice that he watches Rufio's bearing and gestures, perhaps even listens to the inflection of his voice. He obviously hungers to be a good leader, but he has little to guide him. And Herod has no desire that any of his commanders be too strong or too skilled.

Then Matthias told me a story, and I was shocked at the nakedness with which he expressed himself. One day Rufio was conducting the morning weapons drill. I believe he had given Valerius leave to go into the city for the day. Matthias and all his men were standing nearby and watching. Matthias admitted to me that none of his men had much training with swords, and they were trying to absorb as much as they could by just observing. A poor way of learning any skill. There must have been something in their look that caught Rufio's eye. Metellus happened to be riding by and Rufio gestured to him. Just a tiny movement, a flick of the wrist, but Metellus is one of the quickest men in the cohort. He rode over and told Matthias to have his men join the group for practice. As they did, Rufio barely acknowledged them, and that is what affected Matthias so deeply. No blaring trumpets, no particular notice at all. As if it were the most natural thing for these poor tyros to take their place on the training ground beside the Roman professionals. I could see by the intensity in Matthias's eyes that Rufio had cemented his loyalty forever.

Whether or not Rufio realized this, I cannot say. He is so natural at leading that I am not sure if even he is aware of it. Centurions are tough and fair — most of the time anyway. But they are often harsh, like one of those savage four-pronged bits some brutal riders use on their horses. Rufio, though, leads his men like a great horseman rides his stallion — delicate with the reins, subtle with his heels, until the horse and the man seem to be thinking with a single mind.

Of course, Rufio can be just as severe as any other centurion in the legion. One afternoon he gave Valerius such a verbal thrashing in his tent that I expected Mars himself to intervene. The optio had overslept after a night of indulgence in Caesarea and had missed the morning parade. When I saw him come out of Rufio's tent, he looked like he would rather have been pummeled with a vinestick than have endured what he just had. He was bleeding from invisible wounds.

I have always liked Valerius very much, so I decided to interfere where I had no right interfering. I went into the tent. Rufio was sitting at his table writing something.

"May I speak with you?" I asked him.

He looked up.

"Sometimes even Valerius doesn't know when you're simply playing the role of the heartless centurion."

"It isn't important for him to know," he said with indifference and went back to writing. Then he paused and looked up again and gave me that devastating eye smile. "It's only important for *me* to know."

We laughed together, and I knew the wayward wolf cub had been forgiven the moment he had left the tent.

Afterward, I felt the need for solitude to help me comprehend all that I was learning in this mysterious land. I went riding on my chestnut stallion and stayed out the rest of the day, with no one to intrude on my private spirit. The sun was dropping when we climbed a rocky slope. These Arabian horses are as sure-footed as squirrels in a tree. I stopped for one last look at a day that, like all others, would never return.

Below me, near a spring where his horse was drinking, Rufio was sitting back against an acacia, that strange tree of these dry lands. Morlana was curled up against him, her head resting in the hollow of his shoulder. She was sound asleep. Rufio's dagger lay on the ground beside her. He was gazing down at her, and on his face was a look of such peace as perhaps he has never had before in this life. This was my Rufio, the authentic and secret Rufio. And he was mine alone. Then I had to smile, for he was more than that. He was this little girl's, too.

33

CALL IT NATURE, FATE, FORTUNE. ALL THESE ARE THE NAMES OF THE ONE AND SELFSAME GOD.

SENECA

Two dozen heavy wagons had been lined up in the Via Decumana of the camp for the tribune's inspection.

"I prowled the docks and warehouses all day," Bellator said. "Matthias helped me. He's a good man. I don't trust this barren land to provide us with enough forage, so I plan to bring my own. Mostly I wanted medica. And I—."

"Medica?" Crus said.

"A type of grass. It was originally grown by the Medes on the plains west of the Tigris. It's the best available. The Parthians still use it for their great Nisaean chargers. I found a whole shipload destined for the chariot horses of Rome. A generous bribe rectified that folly."

"Well done," Crus said with a smile.

"I also laid up a supply of hard feed—horse barley, some wheat, some horse beans. We have to be careful with it, though. With the medica, too, for that matter. These Arabian horses can survive on beetle husks and tree bark, so we cannot give them too rich of a diet. It'll affect the tissues in their feet and they'll go lame."

"I'll make sure the men are careful."

"We'll use this feed just as a supplement when necessary."

"Thank you for going to all this trouble. It was a sad day for the army when you left it."

"Well, a man can leave the army, but the army never leaves the man."

Crus turned away and stared down the long avenue of tents. "I often wonder if it will ever leave me."

"Why should it?"

"Because I'm not a real soldier."

"What?!"

"I'm a politician."

Bellator stepped around Crus and stood in front of him. "A soldier is a man who practices soldiering. What do you think this is? A pleasure trip? We're not snuggled around a fireside in a cozy inn while the wind howls outside. This is a field camp surrounded by hostile people on the edge of a wasteland. If that isn't soldiering, then I'm the queen of the Amazons."

Crus could not help laughing. "The Bellator mold was used only once and then tossed away."

"Mold? Oh, no. I was carved—chiseled by the gods out of dry horse shit."

Still laughing, Crus turned as Rufio rode up.

"Has either of you seen Flavia?"

"She's out riding with Morlana," Bellator said.

Rufio shook his head helplessly. "It's too late in the day for rides."

"Is she armed?" Crus asked.

"Flavia is always armed."

"Don't worry," Bellator said. "Those two females are far more formidable than any nocturnal creatures they're likely to meet."

Rufio rode off without another word.

"He was more relaxed before," Crus said. "Before he had the pains of love."

"Yes, but it *is* a sweet ache. The sweetest there is."

"Will you teach me to shoot soon?" Morlana asked eagerly, pointing to Flavia's bow.

"Soon, little one. There's only about a half-hour of light left. We'll have to start back."

"Can we see one more sunset? They're so pretty here."

Mounted on a sleek black gelding, Morlana presented a dashing figure of a young horsewoman in the gathering twilight. She wore a bright blue cloak similar in color to Rufio's tunic. Flavia wondered where Morlana's father had found it. The hood was pushed back now, and the evening breezes fluttered her wild yellow mane out behind her.

Flavia knew they were running out of time, but how could she say no to someone whose affection tumbled out of her eyes as freely as a rolling river?

Flavia looked around. "Let's climb that hill."

She urged her stallion toward the eastern slope, and Morlana's nimble horse hurried along behind.

When Flavia reached the summit, she silently thanked Morlana, for she would remember this moment forever.

Off to the right, the sun was dropping to the horizon. Yellow only at its center, the sun cast a pale pink wash that darkened into lavender as it seeped and deepened across the night sky.

The valley below belonged to a different world than any Flavia had ever known. The bleached out sands of the day had been swept away by an especially creative god. In their place he had strewn soil and rocks of the deepest blue. A vast sand seascape had replaced the entire earth. Thirsty clumps of stunted trees, greenish black in the dying light, sank roots near dry washes, relics of the winter rains. Several trees would never bloom again. With twisted twin trunks, they strained toward the heavens. All was futile. It was as if giant corpses had been entombed beneath the dark sands, the only evidence now these bleak limbs clawing upward like the skeletal arms of dead men.

Across the valley, the ground rose gradually to a sharp ridge at least fifty feet high. Split and chipped like a battered knife edge, the purple blade would soon shield the valley from the last of the failing light.

"Remember this moment," Flavia whispered to herself. "Remember it always."

Her stallion's ears cocked forward, and he was instantly alert.

On the slope below them, a small rise blocked their view of the nearest part of the valley.

Without speaking, Flavia signaled to Morlana to follow her. They descended the bank together, their horses silent in the soft sand. Without pausing at the bottom, they climbed the low ridge and peered into the nearest quarter of the valley.

A herd of several hundred horses grazed on the clusters of tough grasses fighting for life around the edges of the washes. But the humans were now Flavia's concern.

Three men knelt on the ground with their hands bound behind their backs. Three others armed with daggers stood over them. A fourth lay dead nearby. Even at this distance, Flavia could tell from their tone that they were taunting the doomed men. The bound captive in the middle looked older than the other two. Perhaps he was their

father. His robe had been shredded and pulled down, and he was naked to the waist.

"What's all over that man?" Morlana whispered.

Black streaks marked his upper body, but Flavia knew the color was an illusion of the twilight.

"Blood," Flavia said. "They're torturing him."

"Why?"

"They're bandits. It looks like he got one of them before they overpowered him. They're killers. They attacked at dusk because they knew these men would be tired. And it would be difficult to see in the half-light."

The older man hurled a curse of defiance at his executioners. The words were indistinct, but the tone was clear.

Morlana's sharp intake of breath startled Flavia.

"What is it?"

"I know him!"

"Who is he?"

"Haritat!"

Morlana said nothing else, as if that alone had been enough.

"Tell me," Flavia said.

"He's a great man. A great leader. He raises horses. He's my father's partner. He's my friend."

"A Nabataean?"

"Yes."

Flavia looked back across the valley. "Those are the horses for the Romans then?"

"Yes, yes. Oh, Flavia, we have to get help."

"Those men are about to die." Flavia's voice was as calm as an Appian tomb. She looked back at Morlana. "There's no time to get the soldiers. The gods have cast these dice." She dismounted. "If I fall, tell Rufio I died with honor."

Morlana stared at her with horror and awe.

Flavia made sure her arrows were loose in her quiver.

"Are you going to shoot them?"

"I could only get one before the others would use the Nabataeans as shields."

She took her bow off her shoulder and held it in her left hand. Gripping the reins in her right, she began walking down the slope.

"What goes on here?" she shouted in Greek.

She had no desire to come up on them suddenly. She knew that criminals were always cowards, and startled bandits were especially dangerous.

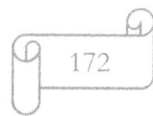

"A trade," one of them said with a laugh and in a strange accent.

"May I participate?" She crossed the ground between them.

"What do you have to offer?"

"Much." She stopped about twenty feet away.

The half-stripped Nabataean gazed up at her. He might have been forty-five or fifty-five. His age was as indeterminate as desert rock, and yet he seemed as old as the memory of time. From his dark face thrust a fierce hooked nose, sharp enough to split granite. Every crease in his skin plunged as deeply as a crevasse.

"You're Haritat, are you not?" she asked. "The horse trader?"

"I am." The voice rumbled like desert thunder.

"The lying son of a lying race," Flavia spat at him. "You've cheated me before."

It was clear that his wise eyes saw something amiss, but he knew not what.

Flavia looked up at the three bandits. Each stood to the rear of one of the Nabataeans. The one behind Haritat was obviously the leader. He swaggered while standing still.

"I need a new mount," Flavia said to him and let her horse's reins slip from her fingers.

"What can you give us?"

The falling sun highlighted her beautifully muscled arms and the powerful legs below her short green tunic. The bronze torque on her biceps gleamed in the last rays of pink light.

"What you'd like the most."

"What are your terms?"

Flavia laughed to distract them from the fact that she was sliding her left leg slowly forward and imperceptibly cocking her hips to the right. "Give me three new mounts," she said in a voice dripping with sin. "And I'll let each of you mount *me* three times."

The leader burst out laughing.

With a lightning arc of her wrist, Flavia plucked an arrow from her quiver and launched it straight through the laughing mouth. It tore through his skull and flew out into the desert beyond, and he collapsed like dust.

The two others, stunned, stood as motionless as rotted trees. In less than a breath, a "twang-ffft, twang-ffft" sliced the air and arrows ripped through each of their throats, and they gurgled and crumpled to the earth.

She sprang like a deer between the Nabataeans. One of the bandits was twitching and moaning. She nocked an arrow and sank it into his chest, and his spasms flickered and went out. The other still lived, gagging on his own blood. She strode over to him. He raised a begging hand in a plea for mercy. She glared down at him and drove a shaft into the center of his forehead.

The amazed Nabataeans pushed themselves to their feet.

Flavia pulled her dagger and cut their bonds.

Haritat looked around for others, but saw no one.

"You are alone?"

"I am Flavia of the Sequani. I ride with the Romans." She raised a hand to signal. "Romans always ride with reserves."

Morlana raced down the hill.

"Haritat!" she shouted.

"Golden One?" he said in disbelief.

She slid from her horse and ran over to him. She pulled off her cloak and used it to dab his wounds.

"You work wonders, Flavia of the Sequani," Haritat said.

Flavia stepped forward, and for the first time in the history of eternity a Sequani huntress and a Suebi child and an Arab chieftain smiled together in the purple desert night.

34

FROM THE CLAWS, INFER THE LION.

ROMAN SAYING

Flavia and Morlana sat on the ground in the black goat-hair tent of Haritat. Multi-colored carpets formed the floor, and lamps flickering from bronze stands cast a lambent glow around the interior. The sheep fat burning in the lamps added its thick feral scent to the exotic ceremonials.

The Nabataean, flanked by his two sons, offered them each the customary bowl of ewe's milk. Morlana sipped it eagerly, but Flavia struggled to get it down.

Crus and Rufio stood in silence about five paces to the rear, while Mallius waited off to the left.

Rufio absorbed every detail, for he wanted to lock in the memory of this night.

"For the Golden One," Haritat said and approached Morlana and handed her a curved dagger in a bronze sheath. "For valor in battle."

She took it reverently.

"You may expose the blade," he said, bestowing on her a rare honor within the confines of his tent.

Her thin fingers gripped the black horn handle and pulled the blade partly from its metal sheath.

"Thank you," she said softly.

Haritat nodded and gave her the vaguest hint of a paternal smile. Then he looked at Rufio.

"May I reward your woman?"

"You may."

Haritat extended his right arm, and the son to his right passed him an exquisite recurved bow.

"For the archer," Haritat said.

Flavia took it and studied it with the curiosity of a hide merchant examining a rare pelt.

"This is new to you?" Haritat asked.

"Yes," she said with a hushed respect.

"Along this side, under the leather, is dried gazelle tendon. It resists pulling, so when you draw, you amass great power." He ran a dark finger down the other side of the wood. "These are plates of buffalo horn. They fight compression, so your draw is producing even more force. Nothing can withstand it."

"I honor you," she said, and then slid her fingers along the strange looking red string.

"You have never seen this?" Haritat asked.

"Never."

"It is a mysterious substance. As tough and magical as if one were able to spin from bronze. It is made from the cocoons of caterpillars in a far off land. It is called silk."

Haritat flicked a wrist at his other son, and the young man left the tent.

"I have never received such a gift," she said.

"No," Haritat answered, and when he smiled, it was as if the earth itself had cracked. "That is not the gift. It is merely a tool for the huntress."

She looked at him in confusion.

He gazed beyond her. "Here is your gift."

She turned around.

The son was leading a magnificent Arabian mare into the center of the tent. So bright a gray was she that she was almost white. She seemed to draw in and reflect every particle of starlight shining outside the tent at this moment.

The young man handed the blue and red beaded lead to Flavia.

The mare lowered her head, and Flavia stroked her face. Wide in the forehead, the mare had a large brain lurking behind those dark brown eyes, knowing and serene as a desert queen. Her jaw, too, was deep and wide, but her throat was gracefully curved and slender. Her cheeks were as hard-edged as Haritat's, but they were dusted with fine hairs as soft as the silken bowstring. Her near-white forelock hung two-thirds of the way down her gently concave face. But again to her eyes Flavia was drawn. The light hairs surrounding them were so tiny and spare that the dark skin showed beneath, reminding Flavia at once of the shadow-eyed beauties of Alexandria. The mare's muzzle, too, was dark and soft and seemed to have been created solely to invite a woman's caress.

Flavia turned to Haritat. "Thank you," she whispered, as a pair of tears slid down her cheeks. "I will call her Artemis."

"Those cannot be what they seem," Haritat said. "Not from so valiant a warrior. They must simply be the first drops of the early morning dew."

He gestured to the men, and they sat up close next to Morlana and Flavia.

"This is a night worth remembering in a life worth remembering," Haritat said.

Rufio was surprised at how light the Nabataeans traveled. With no slaves at hand to serve, Haritat's sons offered hard goat cheese, flat bread, and dates mixed with sheep butter.

While everyone ate, Rufio observed his host. Haritat's lava-dark face was an inverted pyramid with a drooping black moustache streaked with gray. A sharp beard as pointed as a knife tip jutted from his chin. The creases fanning out from his greenish-brown eyes might have been the remains of humorous fireside tales, or the relics of great pain. Both were possible in this harsh land. A black caftan covered his lean body, and he wore a white head-cloth. A curved dagger in a red sash nestled against the left side of his waist.

Haritat invited all to share his tents for the evening, but responsibilities at camp made everyone decline. When it was time to go, Haritat focused his gaze on Rufio.

"I will speak with the centurion, if it is his pleasure."

Even the sons left the tent, but not before bringing in camel saddles and propping pillows against them so the two men could recline at leisure.

"You are the fighting man," Haritat said, leaning back on one elbow. It was not a question but a statement.

"I am."

"The tribune is your leader."

"He is."

Rufio knew that for Nabataeans the posing of questions to a stranger was a great impoliteness. So they tended to throw out remarks and wait for affirmation or denial.

"He is young enough to be your son."

"Almost."

"I do not understand the Roman system."

"Many have not. They're all dead now."

The eye creases tightened. "I sense a rebuke."

Rufio let that one hang there.

"You have lived in the desert before," Haritat said in a lighter tone.

"How do you know?"

"Romans have heavy feet and stiff backs. But you tread lightly within my tent so as not to disturb the rugs. And you sit directly upon the earth with ease and grace. These are a desert dweller's traits."

"I served in one of the legions in Syria."

"Ah, the Syrians. A dull race."

Rufio remained silent.

"May I pose a question to my guest?"

"As many as will please you."

"Why has Rome come to the land of Herod the Mad?"

"It's the will of Dushara."

That startled him. "You know our Holy One?"

"All who walk the East do well to pay homage to the Sun God of the Nabataeans," Rufio said, slipping seamlessly into Aramaic. "I could not have come all this distance through many dangers in defiance of his will. His care must be upon me."

Haritat stared at him but there was no rudeness in it. Simply a fierce desire to understand this outlander.

"Many have crashed through these lands," Haritat said. "Hard feet and minds no more supple than cracked sheepskins. They knew not our tongue or our gods or our passions. They conquered, but they did not vanquish. And they have all fallen away. But you . . . you know our great God and you tell me this in a language as foreign to you as the desert stars." He took a deep breath and let it out with the settled relief of someone who has satisfied himself at last. "You are a dangerous man."

Rufio said nothing.

"And always you call us Nabataeans rather than Arabs."

"I know you prefer it."

"Arav is a Hebrew word for desert, so that is what they call us, but it has no meaning for us. Arabayah is a Persian word. The Persians are dogs."

"And the Parthians?" Rufio asked.

"The offspring of Persians mated with vipers."

"You bear them no love then?"

"As much as I love a scorpion swimming in my cup of milk."

"We're here to stop them. Will you fight by them, by us, or by no one?"

"Are they coming?"

"You tell me."

"I cannot say," Haritat answered. "There are always rumors."

"Confirm them or dispel them."

"Why cannot the Judaeans crush the scorpions?"

"Herod is in decline. His health is failing."

"Yes, I know."

"And Augustus has little trust in the ability of his sons."

"A wise man, Sebastos."

"A Roman cohort in the south will be like a string of camel bells across the gate," Rufio said. "The slightest touch and they'll ring all the way back to Rome."

"A cohort will not deter them."

"Not a cohort—the threat of Rome."

"They sense upheaval in this kingdom. They wait for a sandstorm to disorient their prey."

"I know that. That's why we're here."

"It is a mad task you have—to threaten with a handful of nothing."

"A Roman cohort is worth a thousand Parthians."

For the first time this night, Haritat laughed. "Confidence is hardly a dry well with you."

"I'm an oasis of arrogance,' Rufio said, laughing with him.

"Seek no recruits among our people. We have no love for Herod."

"It was never my intention to do so."

"We have chosen peaceful commerce instead of the glories of the blade." His dark eyes gazed out over the twin cliffs of his cheekbones. "Unless we are roused."

"That is an ornament then?" Rufio pointed to the long straight sword, sheathed in wood and leopard skin, lying by him on the carpet.

"No."

"Mallius has told me tales about your youth. How you slew Egyptians beyond number in battles on sea and land."

"Mallius exaggerates."

"About the number who fell?"

"About my youth." Haritat rose. "May Dushara guard your rest tonight."

Rufio stood, and in Latin he said, "And may Victoria enfold you within her wings."

Haritat smiled. "Ah, yes. You are a *very* dangerous man."

35

NOTHING IS GREAT UNLESS IT IS GOOD.

ROMAN SAYING

*W*e have begun moving south. How I wish Diocles were here to record this. Never has there been so odd an army out here. A mounted Roman cohort flanked by Judaean cavalry, along with a retired soldier and his daughter and a family of Nabataean horse traders.

We avoid the towns the way clever ferrets are wary of snare traps. Yet our dust is visible from miles off, and the children often come out to watch. Occasionally the adults do, too. Their look is not pleasant. They are masters of the surly gaze. Many foreigners have ridden through this land, so I suppose people here have much practice displaying a curled lip.

Fortunately, Matthias is skilled at soothing them. He has a calming manner that wafts over them like an evening breeze. He is not a born soldier like Valerius. He has to work hard at that. Matthias is more like a politician. He knows just the right words to smooth the feathers of these angry grouse that come fluttering out of the villages. If ever anyone were capable of encouraging a revolt against Herod, it would be this clever young man.

Haritat is the opposite. He is the great isolate. A peak in the middle of a vast plain. He never speaks unnecessarily. It is as if words are expensive. Or much effort in a land where life itself is an effort. Where every spoken word draws moisture from the body, and only a fool does that without purpose. Yet when he chooses to talk, he is the most vivid speaker I have ever known. When he speaks of himself, it is always as if he is talking about another – a character in some great saga to which he alone can bear witness. He never deals in ideas. He always uses real objects. A courageous man is not brave – he has "the heart of a lion." A traitor is "a viper's spawn." Once when he did not know I was behind him, I heard him say to Rufio that a woman's scent "was the sweetness of lavender after a rain."

The Judaean soldiers stay away from him. Yet they love to tell stories about him. Legends swirl around him like a desert whirlwind. One soldier said that he has eleven wives. Another that he has fathered thirty-seven children. One of the older Judaeans told Rufio that in his youth Haritat had sailed against the Egyptians when they were trying to take over the frankincense trade by sea, and that after he had sent forty Egyptians to the bottom he stopped counting.

One evening all of us were sitting by campfires after our meal, when I dozed off beside Bellator as I was leaning on his shoulder. Suddenly, something jolted me out of my sleep, and I sat straight up with my heart pounding. At first, I could not understand what had woken me. Then an astounding voice, singing some great tragic tale, swept in out of the night, and I realized that is what had roused me. Haritat was standing alone at the edge of the darkness and singing a melancholy epic I could understand not in words but in the fullness and richness of its feelings.

With me he is the model of propriety. Somehow I can always sense when he is nearby, watching over me. But he is not strictly paternal, at least in his thoughts. He is a man like other men, and my beauty attracts him. However, if his desire is intense, so is the fierceness of his rectitude. He never lets his gaze linger on me but he always turns away. I have learned that strong leaders have strong passions, so the effort for him must be immense.

The most frustrating thing about desert travel is the inability to bathe. Sand gets into everything and clings to everything. Bellator said that I should be grateful, because there are places in Judaea where the sand is like powder and is much worse than this. I told Bellator I have no gratitude. I never feel clean, and there is always grit scraping between my teeth. And there is no escape. I think my teeth will be worn down to stumps by the time I return to Gaul.

After an especially long and dusty day, my face must have betrayed this. We were encamped at an oasis that even Mallius had not known before. Haritat signaled to me, and he took me to a smaller pool some distance away.

"You may bathe here," he said. He never asked me if that is what I wanted or if I were willing to do so in his presence. He pulled his sword from the scabbard and laid it on the ground at the edge of the pool. Then he turned around and sat with his back to it and to me.

I disrobed and slid into the water and it was bliss. I was so selfish that for a while I forgot about everything else. Then I realized how difficult this must be for Haritat. A swift glance toward me would have gone unnoticed — or, if seen, would have cost me nothing. Yet he was as immobile as black marble.

I finished quickly and dressed.

"I'm done," I said, but he did not turn around. He reached behind his back for his sword and stood and replaced it in its sheath.

"Let us eat," he said and started back toward camp.

As caring as a father but tormented like a lover, Haritat knows that fate — or Dushara — has decreed he can never be either to me. Yet he chooses not to draw off. He has decided to endure the pain of longing in order to be able to watch over me and protect me. It is a mindless agony, terrible and pointless. And how I admire him for it. At that moment, my affection for him began to blossom like desert chamomile, and I knew it would bloom forever. And I was certain that the image of the flower was one that he would love.

Rufio sat astride his dapple gray gelding and surveyed the arid expanse below.

This was different than the lush river valleys he knew from Italy. Here the brown land spread out like lumpy dough, made so by the dry washes that cut through it at every angle and in no particular pattern. Countless patches of deep green shrubs and a delicate embroidery of yellow and purple flowers showed that the spring sun had not yet unleashed its fury. A few clouds threw grayish blue shadows across the landscape. To the right, low brown hills rose gently, while to the left a high and jagged escarpment scraped the sky on the eastern horizon.

Haritat rode up on his black mare. "This is it. The land is changing."

"I know. I've been here before. Not this valley, but this region."

"There is a village beyond that southern prominence. Mostly shepherds and wool weavers."

"Good. Many of our saddle blankets are already worn. We need more."

The two men gazed in silence for a while.

"That fascinates me," Haritat said after several minutes.

On a flat patch, the Second Cohort was trenching the perimeter of its field camp in the mid-afternoon sun.

"Why?"

"That you take the trouble to do that every day."

"It pays us back."

To save time watering the horses, the men had dismounted, and Mallius and Bellator had led the horses to a spring-fed pool at the southwest edge of the valley. Haritat's sons, eagerly helped by Morlana, rode herd and kept them together.

"I've never seen so many beautiful horses at one time in my life," Rufio said.

Haritat maintained his usual silence until required to break it.

"Romans are harsh to their animals," Rufio said with a hint of bitterness.

"Why?"

"I don't know. But if you said that to a Roman, he wouldn't understand you. It would be like telling him he's being cruel to a cart or a shovel."

"Romans see animals as objects then."

"Yes," Rufio said.

"But not you."

"I'm a Roman, too."

"But not every bird in the flock sings the same song."

It was Rufio's turn to remain silent.

"That cat of yours," Haritat said. "She lives like a queen."

Rufio refused to acknowledge any gentleness in himself, but he unconsciously stroked the withers of his horse. "We could learn much from the Nabataeans."

"Our horses are a gift from Dushara. Our brothers who fly with us on the edge of the wind."

"I envy you—and you won't hear a Roman say that very often."

"Perhaps we can learn something, each from the other."

Rufio turned away from the valley and looked at the hawk-like face next to him. "Perhaps we can." A slow smile softened his eyes.

"Why did you refuse to return to Mallius the horses you found unsuitable?" Haritat asked.

"How do you know that?"

"Bellator."

"I didn't want them sold to some ignorant Caesareans to be beasts of burden. No Arabians deserve that. Not the worst of them. Not even the killers."

Now Haritat smiled, and it was always startling on that lean and forbidding face.

"Speaking of the horses. . . ."

"Yes?" Haritat said.

"I pulled a few at random from the herd and put them through some maneuvers. They seemed already trained."

"I don't understand."

"Certainly all cannot be trained so well."

"Not all, but most. Those we sell them to usually have neither the patience nor the skill. And I don't want my horses to be beaten by fools. So my sons and I train them first."

"But that takes so much time. The three of you must be training constantly."

"I have nineteen sons."

"Oh," Rufio said with a laugh. "My mistake."

"Of course, you might use them for battle, so they will require further work."

"We're fortunate there. Bellator was a decurion in his younger days."

"What is that?"

"A centurion who smells like horse shit."

"Ah," Haritat said, smiling. "What kind of battle do you foresee?"

"If it's only bandits, then skirmishes. If it's fire-hardened Parthians, then this is a serious roll of the dice."

Haritat turned away and looked off toward the valley.

"Do you have an opinion?" Rufio asked.

"I do."

"Will you share it?"

"Bandits there are. That's certain. They've been locusts on the grain throughout Herod's reign. Mostly in the north, but some in the south as well."

"And the Parthians?"

"Unpredictable as a mare in season."

"Predict anyway."

"Rome is an affront to the Parthians."

"What do you think their intentions are?"

"Who can unravel their barbarous minds?"

"Try."

"Possibly to cause enough desert storms to topple Herod. Perhaps just to distract Rome from designs on Parthia itself. Let us be as true as steel here. Twice Rome has marched on Parthia and failed. Out here, if Rome is known for anything, it's relentlessness. The Parthians are like a stallion that has been lashed but not subdued—they never forget their tormentor."

"And their numbers?"

"Whether there are many or few, it matters not. You will die like soft petals in the first hot wind."

Rufio laughed without arrogance.

No corresponding smile came from Haritat. "The Parthians have the cleverness of Greeks and the souls of jackals. Their king is a chattering savage in a gilded robe."

"Rome appreciates your concern," Rufio said.

"You asked for my opinion. . . ."

"I did."

"It is this—go home. Leave these Judaeans to their fate. To fight among themselves until the end of time."

"The tribune has a charge to fulfill."

"Go anyway. Sebastos is merciful."

"My conscience is not."

"There is no glory here."

"There's little glory anywhere."

"Then?" Haritat asked.

"It's already decided. I don't command this cohort. Nor does Crus. Honor commands. It's an order that cannot be revoked."

"Very well," Haritat said, satisfied. "That I understand."

"We'll extend the hand of Rome and dare the Parthians to strike it. If they do, their howls will echo in the streets of Hell and ripple the water of the Euphrates itself. And their chattering king will tremble in his robes."

For the first time, a full throated laugh exploded from Haritat. "You speak like a Nabataean!"

"Must be the bad diet."

At least the Judaeans were trying. They had abandoned their haphazard camping arrangements after being shamed by the Second Cohort's example. Their tent lines were not as straight as the rows of Roman goatskins, but they were a reasonable effort.

The purple twilight cooled the land, and Crus relished the onset of evening. He strolled down the row of tents and saw Matthias giving an order to one of his men. As always, the Judaean soldiers nearby lowered their voices as the Roman passed. Matthias noticed the hushed tones and turned and saw Crus approaching. He offered the tribune a camp stool.

"Thank you," Crus said.

The two of them sat in front of Matthias's tent.

"What do you need?" Crus asked.

"Need?" Matthias looked confused.

"Why did you invite me here? I wore this new red tunic just for the occasion."

Matthias smiled and seemed relieved. "Simply to thank you. For respecting our Sabbath and not demanding we move on our day of rest."

"It's a small matter. And my men need a day off, too."

"No, it's a large matter and we're grateful."

"I assume I'll need the favor of many gods before these days are done. And Rufio tells me that yours has been known to wield a big sword when the mood moves him."

"It's just that I didn't expect it."

Crus was amused. Matthias was attempting to compliment him without risking insulting him at the same time.

"We're not as harsh as our enemies delight in making us out to be," Crus said. "And as for me . . . well, I gave up murdering babies in their beds and devouring the hearts of young virgins years ago."

Matthias laughed and reached for a nearby wineskin. They had no cups, so Crus squirted some of the Judaean poison into his mouth, in the interests of diplomacy.

"When we reach Hezrail, your troops will be in the van," Crus said. "Even though we'll avoid the town for now and go straight out to the fort, I want your men riding in front like Judaean princes."

"That's very kind of you."

"Practical. I don't want my men to go prancing by there like a conquering army."

"I understand."

"Tell me about your skills." Crus handed back the wineskin.

"What do you mean?"

"Fighting skills. I've seen your men training with ours."

"Our skills are not great."

"How many of your men have tasted battle."

Matthias hesitated. "None."

"Have you ever seen the body of a man who had been deliberately killed by another man?"

"No."

"What about training with a bow?"

"We were taught the rudiments. I wouldn't be confident that my men could hit a target beyond thirty feet. Maybe twenty."

"Riding skills?"

"My men are fair riders."

Matthias looked uncomfortable. It was clear to Crus that he was holding something back.

Crus turned away and stared at the escarpment turning violet in the distance. He took a deep breath of the cool air.

"I love the sweetness of the desert blossoms at sundown."

He looked back at Matthias. Though not much older than the Judaean, Crus had aged years in an afternoon on a Gallic battlefield. Now he gazed at Matthias with the gentle reassurance of an older brother.

"Tell me," Crus said.

Matthias licked his lips. "We're archers and we're mounted . . . but we're not mounted archers."

Crus squinted in puzzlement.

"We've had no training on shooting from horseback."

Crus took another deep breath and tried not to show his exasperation.

"We've shot on foot at stationary objects."

At that moment, Crus knew that these tyros would be far more useful as an enemy than as an ally.

"Well, your god must truly be great," Crus said. "It's only through his generosity that this kingdom still stands."

"I'm sorry."

"Why? It's not your fault. Anyway we have someone who can teach you to shoot better than you do. Do you want to learn?"

"Yes! You would do that?"

"Of course."

"Who will teach us? Rufio?"

"Flavia."

Matthias stared at him in revulsion.

"You look like you swallowed a scorpion. She's already begun teaching Morlana the bow."

"A child?"

"Why not? She's a German. They're a race of warriors."

"No Judaean soldiers would ever be taught by a woman."

"Then the Judaean soldiers can be killed by men."

"It doesn't matter. Even if I commanded it, they wouldn't obey."

Crus sighed and stood up. "Then your god had better get a bigger sword. He's going to need it."

36

DO NOT ASK WHAT IS GOING TO HAPPEN TOMORROW.

HORACE

"Bandits?"

"Five," Arrianus said to his centurion.

Rufio gestured to a spot on the ground near him by the campfire.

"Why were you in the village?"

Arrianus sat down close to the warmth of the crackling brush. "Valerius sent me to buy blankets for the horses. A graybeard told me it happened two days ago."

"Anyone killed?"

"Two on the road outside the village."

"Where is your sword?"

Arrianus looked uncomfortable. "In the tent."

"Did you have it with you when you went into the village?"

"No, centurion."

"Do I have to remind you about that?"

"Never again, centurion."

Rufio saw Crus and Matthias passing by in the shadows beyond the firelight.

"Tribune!"

When they came over, Rufio nodded to Arrianus, and the soldier told them what had happened.

"The odd thing is they entered the village, too," Arrianus said. "Attacked some women and hauled off whatever goods they could carry."

"These are serious men," Rufio said. "Bandits almost never leave the rural roads."

"What does it mean?" Crus asked.

"That they're savages!" Matthias said. "We have to get them."

Rufio laid a calming hand on the Judaean's forearm. "It means they believe they have nothing to fear. And they don't. These villagers are helpless out here. They have no weapons. No troops to protect them. No—."

"But *we're* here," Matthias said.

Rufio's eyes drilled the Judaean. "Don't interrupt me again."

"Can we run them to ground?" Crus asked.

"Two days is a huge lead in the desert," Rufio said. "And it was windy yesterday. In this loose soil the trail will be gone. Almost no chance."

"We cannot just abandon these people here," Matthias said.

"They're safe now," Rufio said. "The bird has already been plucked. The bandits are off to hunt fresh game."

"Any idea where?" Crus asked.

"Well, if they're going south, we might eventually make their acquaintance. The fact that they're willing to enter towns means they're very dangerous men."

Crus threw a few scraps of brush onto the fire and stared into the flames. "Nothing is ever simple about a military undertaking, is it? Nothing ever follows a plan."

"Never," Rufio said. "But it's that kind of excitement that appeals to the best of us. It's why very good men like this join the army." He slapped Arrianus on the shoulder. "Isn't that so?"

"Yes, centurion," Arrianus answered with a grin.

"So we do nothing?" Matthias said.

"There's nothing we can do at the moment," Crus answered.

"Then the Roman army isn't what I thought it was," Matthias said.

"What did you expect?" Arrianus asked. "Do you think we're gods?"

"You act like it."

"Easy, soldier," Rufio said.

"I have to see to my men." Matthias got up and walked off into the darkness.

"I think we disillusioned him," Crus said.

"That's all right," Rufio answered. "The young thrive on disillusionment." He turned to Arrianus. "Have you secured the blankets?"

"Not yet."

"Do it now."

"Yes, centurion."

Rufio's eyes smiled at him as he hurried off.

"That little badger is one of your favorites, isn't he?" Crus asked.

"I have no favorites."

"Oh, yes you do."

"He's one of the reasons Augustus can sleep soundly at night."

"He's one of the reasons I can sleep at all," Crus said.

"Regretting your desert adventure already?"

"Oh, no. I wouldn't trade it for all the sin in the Suburra."

"Then what's troubling you? Other than bandits."

Neko came out of Rufio's tent with two large cups of heated wine.

"A man's wealth is measured in the loyalty of his servants," Crus said with a smile and took one of the cups.

The Egyptian nodded.

"Go to bed now," Rufio said.

"I sleep when you sleep. I'll light a lamp for you in case you want to read a bit."

"Take some wine for yourself."

"Thank you." Then he returned to the tent.

"So what is it?" Rufio asked his tribune.

Crus took a long pull at the wine. "It's these Judaeans. I'll never understand them."

"Nobody understands them."

Crus told of his offer to have Flavia teach them the bow.

"Nothing surprising in that," Rufio said. "Here women are meaningless. Outside the house, they're invisible."

"But it goes beyond that," Crus said, refusing to be put off. "The soldiers themselves don't seem to have any more drive than a crippled dog. They go through the motions, but there isn't much spirit to it."

"Matthias got them to drill with us. Believe me, that's a major feat."

"But why is it major? That's my point."

"You want them to be Romans. They'll never be that."

"You lived in the East before. Explain it to me. How can you stop from wanting to strangle them?"

Rufio laughed. "I'm no expert on them. Nobody comprehends Judaeans except Judaeans. And I'm not sure even about that."

"I never knew it got so cold in the desert," Crus said and pulled his red cloak more tightly around his shoulders and took a sip of the warm wine. "Give me what you can."

"You have to understand that none of the Jewish kingdoms has ever been powerful. Not the way you and I understand power. The few times they've been strong it's only been because the surrounding kingdoms have been in decline."

"And?"

"So their focus here is on smaller things. Their villages and their families. What little power they have lives there. You and I would probably call it status rather than power."

"I understand."

"That status is a chest of denarii to them. It's all they have. They cannot afford to let it slip away. And how do you make sure that never happens?"

"You never take chances."

"Exactly. Why should they do that? They have no power in their kingdom and their kingdom has little power in the world. So they take no pride in Herod's achievements. What would it profit them if they did?"

"Very little, I suppose."

"There's no payoff. The stipendium never comes. So they don't think about the glories of Judaea or even about their own future. They live only in the present. And that's shackled to the past. I mentioned this back in Gaul. So they turn inward. Their families and their villages are the only places they have power. Status."

"And risk taking endangers that."

"It has to. We're Romans, so it's hard for us to grasp. We live for risk. Audacity parades across our annals like a marching legion. But not here. Not for these people. Success is defined very simply. And very narrowly. Success isn't the achievement of something. It's the absence of failure."

"You're right. This is incomprehensible to me."

"Daring isn't rewarded here. Caution is. Learning is, too, because that gives them status. Above all, loyalty is. Loyalty to the family and village. But not loyalty to a kingdom that's always changing hands. For all they care, Herod can choke on his own vomit."

"What happens if someone tries to break out of one of these little groups?" Crus asked.

"Leaving is seen as defection. Even betrayal. So he's lashed back in or permanently thrown out. There's no middle ground."

"How joyous."

"If you travel around the Empire, you'll see that there are people who never imagine anything beyond their own country. Who never look past their own borders. The Judaeans never look past their own street. Every gaze is inward, so it's all the more intense. Their constant anxiety about honor and shame and status. Their weird food laws. The obsession with rituals and rules and sin. Their taste for lunatic prophets."

Crus drained the rest of his wine. "How can anyone live that way? Their inner selves must be prisons."

"It's all they know. Even their god has given up on them. I've read some of their holy writings. He never exhorts them to do good. Never. He simply tells them to avoid being bad. I guess at this point he realizes that's all he can hope for."

Crus could not help laughing. "When your god has to resign himself, I think you've reached the end of line."

"Hold onto what you have. Don't worry about adding to it. Just keep a tight grip. That's why you can live your whole life here and never meet a Judaean who made a mistake. Ever. It's not that they're arrogant. It's that they cannot admit error. Not risk what they think is the loss of status that goes with it."

"But Matthias admitted his lack of skills to me."

"He's an exceptional young man. Most Judaeans would rather go to their deaths than confess to incompetence."

"But that would be the ultimate incompetence."

"They'd be dead, so it wouldn't matter."

Crus sighed. "It's all so strange."

"Suppose I sent Valerius and the century out to build a road and they came across a sinkhole. They'd bridge it or build the road around it and keep moving. Do you know what Matthias would do? He'd sit down and discuss it for a day. Maybe send for an engineer. Argue about it some more. Even consult his father if the old man was nearby. Better to take your time than be thought a fool by your men and the local elders and the farmers and the shepherds and the birds in the trees and the grubs under the rocks. And when they were done, they'd have the finest road you ever saw, while an invading horde was gathering on the horizon. And the beautiful paving stones would soon run with the blood of young dead Jews."

"What a waste."

"Like trying to carry ice in a bucket of fire."

"Madness."

"Thank the gods we're different. It's why we span the world and they lord over the scorpions." Rufio finished his wine and stared into the fire. "Because they're so tough and so learned, there's a floor below which they'll never fall. But because they've chained themselves to it, it's a level above which they'll never rise. That's the tragedy of Judaea."

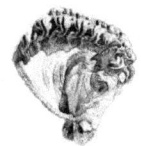

Rufio helped Arrianus distribute the blankets among several wagons. Few techniques of command were simpler and yet more effective than for an officer occasionally to allow his soldiers to hear his grunts of exertion alongside their own.

Rufio had made a crude brushwood torch for illumination.

"Did you know my father raises horses near Venusia?" Arrianus asked.

Rufio hefted a heavy bundle of blankets onto the wagon. "No, I didn't know that."

"I think that's why Valerius sent me to the village. And why your strator hired me."

"Morlana?" Rufio said in surprise.

"She told me she'd share her pay with me if I helped her with the horses."

Rufio shook his head and laughed to himself.

"I took her to the village with me," Arrianus said. "A lively little filly, that one. I named her Twitchy. She loved that."

"It fits."

"She talks about you constantly."

"All young girls talk constantly." He continued tying up bundles of blankets.

"Not like that. If she had a statue of you, she'd burn incense in front of it every night. She thinks you're a mixture of Apollo and Hercules."

"And did you correct that folly?"

"Who am I to take an axe to a young girl's dreams?"

Rufio laughed and tossed a heavy bundle into Arrianus's arms.

"Mallius is a sensible old soldier," Arrianus said and threw the blankets into the wagon. "But I don't see much of him in her."

"I suspect she's really the mare's filly."

"Who is she?" Arrianus asked.

"She's dead. She was a Suebi."

"And her daughter worships my centurion," Arrianus said with a sly smile barely visible in the torchlight. "The gods are wicked, don't you think?"

"Sometimes. But kind, too. Sometimes very kind." Rufio threw the last bundle into the wagon and turned to Arrianus. "Watch her for me when I'm not nearby. Mallius lost his edge long ago. I won't command you. I ask it as a favor."

"I will."

"No one is safe in this land. Not even a child."

37

REMEMBER THAT YOU ARE AN ACTOR IN A PLAY, THE CHARACTER OF WHICH IS DETERMINED BY THE PLAYWRIGHT.... THIS IS YOUR BUSINESS, TO PLAY ADMIRABLY THE ROLE ASSIGNED TO YOU. HOWEVER, THE SELECTION OF THAT ROLE IS ANOTHER'S.

EPICTETUS

*H*ezrail lies before us. About fifty houses of mud brick with roofs piled with soil in conical mounds. Walls of field stones without mortar divide the patches of land. Sheep are everywhere on the low hillsides. It is amazing that they can thrive on so little. Half-wild dogs wander about but seem not to bother the sheep, at least not in daylight. Bellator told me that the Jews do not keep dogs as pets the way Romans do. So these animals just search for scraps and carrion. They are white and black or white and brown and less than half the size of a wolf. Bellator said that they are called the Dogs of the Canaanites, after the people who lived here before the Jews. We are now at the edge of the great Judaean Desert. Yet people and their beasts survive. It is astounding. A magnificent desolation extends beyond Hezrail. There is nothing more than scrub there. Shade for serpents and scorpions. Golden hills and enormous flats all bare of life stretch seemingly to the limits of the earth. Bellator calls it an endless and terrifying nothingness. He says that south of here is a vast toxic sea. Nothing grows in it, nothing swims in it. I cannot imagine such a thing. No living creature can withstand its depths. Mallius refers to it as the pitiless stomach of Hell.

    Yet Hezrail has been spared that. There is actually some green here. Haritat told me that several springs quench the thirst of these people and their sheep and goats, with enough water left for them to grow olives and grapes and a few other things. He said that springs like that are rare in this region, *which is probably why the Romans built their fort here. But we are near the bounds of human endurance, according to my Nabataean friend. Only nomads venture further, and they are always careful to follow the path of the seasonal rains.*

Everything is different here, even one's scent. I rubbed my face with my arm and noticed my skin smelled strange. I looked up and saw Haritat smiling at me. He said that outlanders are always surprised at the magic played on their bodies by the desert air. He then pointed to my arm. There was blood on it from my nose. He told me to smear a little bit of sheep butter onto my nostrils until I got accustomed to the dry air. The thought of that gagged me, so I used olive oil instead and it worked very well.

I am writing this during a pause for rest. We are about to leave now. We will go around the village and ride straight to the fort.

Crus raised a hand to stop the mounted column atop a low rise.

Rufio smiled. The fort stood as silent and strong as the year it had been built decades ago. It was a miniature of the fort at Aquabona but, instead of turf, limestone rose here with shameless Roman arrogance in the middle of oblivion. Sand had blown up against the outer walls, and all was still.

Crus waved the column forward. Matthias rode next to Rufio.

"It's bigger than I expected," Crus said.

"It looks like it can hold two full cohorts," Rufio answered. "We'll have plenty of space."

"But none for the horses," Matthias said.

Rufio looked down the Via Praetoria, but there was no trace of paddocks or stables. "We'll build pens in the shade of the northern wall and buy some homespun from the villagers to make awnings." He turned and gestured to Bellator, who rode up with Haritat and Mallius beside him. "I want a pair of trenches around the fort, except for the north wall," he told the engineer. "Typical fashion. No flourishes."

"We'll begin tomorrow," Bellator said.

"Centurion." Haritat pointed through the open gateway.

Rufio saw some wild greenery deep in the fort along the Via Praetoria.

"They built around a spring," Haritat said. "Smart men, those Romans."

"As I recall, there's another spring just east of the fort," Mallius said.

Crus turned to Matthias. "Tomorrow go back to Hezrail and talk with the village elders. Tell them why we're here. Feel free to say you're in command if it'll make matters easier. Hire some laborers at a good wage to help us clean up." He looked over at Rufio.

"About fifty," Rufio said.

"You have your charge," Crus said to the Judaean.

"Yes, tribune."

Crus deferred to his centurion.

"We'll build a marching camp near the other spring," Rufio said. "We'll live under leather as briefly as possible. I want the men inside within a week."

"We can do it," Bellator said.

"And you?" Rufio asked, looking at Haritat.

"I return to my people. A village east of here."

"Will you come back to help us with the training?" Crus asked.

"Will Romans be trained by a Nabataean?" Haritat said in surprise.

"My men obey the will of Caesar," Rufio answered. "And the tribune embodies that will in this place."

"Then I will return."

Early morning in the desert was always like the birth of a new earth. Rufio loved the beginning of the day in a marching camp. Though he preferred fort life to camp life, the first hours of the day in a camp were always fresh and crisp and bracing, like the first frost on an alpine slope. The smell of hot porridge and wheat cakes hung over the rows of tents, and the men were already going about their business.

Morlana, dressed in a hooded brown caftan and with the curved dagger struggling to maintain its place on her little girl hip, splashed some water onto her face in front of Mallius's tent. She had obviously been up very early and had already tended to the horses, perhaps with Arrianus helping her.

"Strator!"

She spun around, wide-eyed, like a startled fawn. It was an odd habit, and it bothered Rufio. It seemed as if she had been criticized or scolded so often that when someone called her she always expected the worst.

She smiled when she saw him and ran toward him and gave him a morning hug.

"We have to put some meat on you," he said as he felt her ribs against the inside of his arms.

"I eat a lot," she said, trying to reassure him.

"But maybe not the right foods. New soldiers always gain weight if they're thin and lose weight if they're fat. We'll fill you out before you go home."

That was the wrong thing to say. Her smile collapsed. "But I *am* home."

"I mean in Hezrail."

"No, I want to stay here."

"But that's your home."

"It's not a home. I'm an outsider. The girls are mean to me every day. I want to work for you. Forever."

She was so plaintive, this little blonde stick figure staring up at him. Rufio refused for the moment to dash any more hopes.

"Go get our mounts. I have to inspect the fort."

She smiled and ran off. When she returned very quickly, Rufio suspected she had already had the horses saddled.

They left the camp and rode the short distance to the fort.

Rufio had his horse enter at a slow walk, with Morlana following.

Small animals scurried like fugitives in the long morning shadows as the two riders made their way up the Via Praetoria. Three barracks blocks with tiled roofs flanked the street on each side. Beyond these the Via Principalis bisected the fort, and at the middle of it lay the Principia. The Praetorium sat just off to the right, a smaller and more modest home than many commanders would have preferred. Six more barracks flanked the Via Decumana coming up from the other side of the fort, and some store houses lay at that end as well.

"Rufio . . ." Morlana said in a hesitant voice.

"Speak up."

"Why are there no stables?"

He looked around. "Probably they built some temporary pens outside the fort."

The shrubs he had seen from outside clustered around a disused fountain near the Principia.

"Why is that there?" she asked, pointing to a clear space about fifty feet square just past the fountain.

"Looks like they were going to build a bathhouse but never got to it. We'll unplug that spring and get the fountain working again."

He dismounted and walked over to one of the barracks and peered through the open window. Except for the coating of windblown sand, the fully furnished rooms looked like the soldiers had left ten minutes ago. Nothing ever changed in the desert. The eeriness of it was unsettling. Rufio found it repellent. No advance. Not even decline. Just stasis. An inviolate rigidity locked everything down in a world that could not move. And this weird ossification touched more than solid objects. It was in the soul here, in the blighted yearnings and repressed longings of people as immobile as the pyramids. The baking silence of it had created strange races that defied his comprehension. To Rufio, this land was sealed with something more than dust.

"What are the buildings made of?" Morlana asked. "They're beautiful."

"Limestone. But that's just the facing."

She gave him a puzzled look.

"The cores are rubble and mortar. It's easier and quicker than solid stone."

"It's prettier than mud brick."

Rufio laughed. "Italians are obsessed with how things look. That's why if you ever get to Rome, the boys will tremble when they see you."

She blushed—but she smiled, too.

Rufio mounted his horse. "Time for action."

They rode back. Just outside the camp, Bellator had assembled two centuries to begin the trenching around the fort.

"Have some of them work on the spring," Rufio yelled to his engineer. "Get that fountain working."

"Centurion!"

Rufio rode over to him. "And lay out some plans for a bathhouse. Brick and plaster will do."

"You'll have the plans by tonight."

"How much time to build a small one?"

Bellator thought for a moment. "Forty to fifty thousand hours of work."

"So if I assign three of our centuries and get Matthias to provide an equal amount . . . ?"

"A hundred hours, more or less."

"We can afford that. I want three pipes running from the fountain. One to the bathhouse, one to the latrine, and one out of the fort to the horse pens. Have the men dig a cistern by the horses. We cannot afford to waste this water. Now get one of the optios to supervise these men. They don't need you to teach them how to dig."

"Yes, centurion."

Rufio rode into the camp, with Morlana right behind him like a rear guard.

In front of Crus's tent at the center of the camp, the tribune and Matthias sat talking with an elderly Judaean. Crus did not look happy, and Matthias appeared exasperated.

Rufio pulled up and let Morlana come up beside him.

"Morlana, go tend to the horses. Make sure Arrianus isn't overfeeding them. He's not familiar with Arabians."

She just stared at him.

"What's the matter?"

"I have a present I want to give you," she said. "It's in our house in Hezrail. I'll get it soon."

He reached across and curled a forefinger under her chin. She smiled, and he brushed her cheek with his thumb.

"Go check the horses now."

She gazed at him with more love than he knew he could ever deserve, and then she rode off, the happiest girl in Judaea.

Rufio clicked to his horse and casually trotted over to the three men.

"My senior centurion," Crus said to the graybeard.

The Judaean stood up and turned around.

Rufio dismounted and approached.

"This is Simon," Matthias said.

"Quintus Rufio." He grabbed a camp stool and sat down, and Simon resumed his eat.

About sixty, the old man had a crease in his face for every crisis in the history of the kingdom. He conveyed the look of someone who had seen as much as any man can, and perhaps more than most men should.

"Simon takes no delight in our presence here," Crus said with barely controlled frustration. "Nor do the people of Hezrail."

"I see," Rufio said.

Simon stared calmly at Rufio.

"No laborers for us," Matthias said. "He claims all are occupied."

"Then he lies," Rufio said, looking at Simon. "Does Elah not forbid the telling of lies? Or do I misread your holy texts?"

Startled, Simon said, "No Roman knows our sacred writings."

"Look at me," Rufio commanded.

Simon's eyes peered uncertainly into his.

"Do you think I'm just any Roman?"

Simon hesitated.

"Do you?"

"Perhaps not."

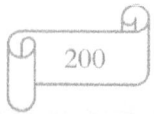

"Don't worry," Crus said. "We're not going to press any of your people into service. We're not brutes—regardless of what you've been told."

"We trust no foreigners."

"You don't even trust each other," Rufio said with contempt.

"Our ways are our ways. And we leave our doors unbarred to no Romans. We have heard the commanders of Roman legions speak promises before. And such promises are always followed by more Roman legions."

"We're here to help," Crus said.

"You're Romans. You're here to help yourselves."

"There are men out there who'd be happy to crush this kingdom like an ant hill," Rufio said.

"Yes, I know. Parthians and others."

"You've seen Parthians?" Matthias asked.

"I have. But we do not fear them. We fear only our God."

"He's the least of your worries," Rufio said.

"We're at peace with Him."

Rufio waved that aside. "A rare moment in the tale of your people."

"If the Parthians sweep in from the desert, you'll all fall before them," Crus said.

"Prostituting ourselves to you first will not lighten that pain."

"Enough!" Matthias said. "Are you mad? You're helpless here."

"No one is helpless in the arms of Elah."

Crus stood up. "We didn't expect incense and sacrifices when we rode in here," he said in the tone of a man learning fast and aging fast. "But we expected more than this."

"Then you know not this people," Simon answered. "Our memories are long. Did you know that Pompeius himself rode his—."

"Sweet Venus's tits!" Rufio shouted. "Not again! I don't care if that horse shit in your temple. There are savage men out there eyeing your children in their beds."

"Elah will send protection."

"He *has* sent it," Matthias said. "Men with horses and blades. Spurn them at your peril."

"Perils we understand." Simon turned to Rufio. "Long after the bones of your horses have bleached in the sun, we will still be here."

"Yes," Rufio said in resignation. "Shackled to the floor."

Simon seemed confused. "I don't understand."

"I know," Rufio answered wearily. "That's your folly. And your destiny."

38

HOW MANY ANIMALS HAVE WE COME TO KNOW FOR THE FIRST TIME IN OUR OWN AGE.

SENECA

Rufio's five centurions gathered around a table inside Crus's tent and had their duties assigned to them. Two of the centurions had been optios in other cohorts. Rufio was forever prowling the legion for exceptional men, and when two of his own centurions retired, he had persuaded Sabinus to promote two optios and transfer them to the Second Cohort. Even as a tesserarius in his youth, Rufio had been as deft of hand as a cheating dice player in dealing with his superiors. Of course, Sabinus had probably known he was being worked. Yet the Legate was indulgent to the man who both induced stomach pains in his commander and, paradoxically, brought him peace as well. To the hero of Scorpion Hill, Sabinus was inclined to give much. Though indifferent to acclaim, Rufio was happy to play upon his fame as if it were a musical instrument in order to enhance the quality of his cohort.

Four of his centurions were older than he, one about the same age. Two had served in Egypt, one in Spain, the other two mostly in Gaul. All bore the scars of wounds or injuries or disease. They rippled with the confidence bestowed by years of service in lands where one never slept without a sword to hand. They were seasoned Roman men.

Rufio assigned one century for fort clean up, one for repairs, the three others for new construction within the fort. His own century he reserved for all matters relating to the horses, including the building of pens and training areas, as well as daily care. The soldier who just recently had been sleeping in the snow and gagging on barley Rufio suddenly promoted.

Arrianus laughed, suspecting a joke, but Rufio's eyes were stern.

"Secondarius Equitatum," Rufio said. "You've never heard of it because I just created it. You'll assist Bellator. In a land like this, nothing is more important than our horses. If they die, we die."

"My father would be very proud of this. It would bring tears to his eyes."

"When we leave this cauldron, you can write to him and tell him."

"Thank you, centurion."

Rufio knew that the finest soldiers were invariably the ones who thought for themselves and who, in their youth, picked their way around orders as if they were avoiding pointed metal lilies in the ditch of a fort. Ultimately such men made the best leaders. The idiocy was that they were rarely allowed to be. They were quashed by older men who preferred geldings to studs. But not in the Second Cohort. Here the rampant stallions were permitted to kick and bite all they wanted. An occasional stick across the withers brought them into line. Rufio knew he had now found another to join Valerius and Metellus. Stomach pains were worth it.

"What is that?" Flavia asked, staring at a structure such as she had never seen before.

"A round training pen for the horses," Bellator said. "It's called a gyrus."

"Why are the walls so high?"

"To keep the horses from getting distracted.

She walked over and examined the boards and iron. "This is from the wagons, isn't it?"

"We dismantled about half of them. Training starts tomorrow."

"But why make it round? Wouldn't it be easier to make it square?"

"It would, but round is better. No corners for reluctant animals to try to flee to."

"Such a simple idea," she said with a smile. "Why did the Sequani never think of that?"

"Well, don't give us the credit. It was invented long ago by the Lapithae."

She turned and looked at him. "I've never heard of them."

"A legendary race of great horsemen from the mountains of Thessaly in Greece. They're famous for having battled and beaten the Centaurs."

"Who are they?"

"A race of beings who are half man and half horse."

Flavia laughed. "You're teasing me."

But Bellator did not smile. "I've seen many bizarre things emerge from Greece."

"But that cannot be. Can it?"

He pointed to a shady spot against the pen wall. Flavia sat and he sat down beside her.

"Our philosophers claim such a thing is impossible," Bellator said.

"But you don't believe them?"

"Never trust a man who is certain. He simply hasn't lived long enough. As for philosophers, the only thing certain about them is the mildew in their moldy brains."

She smiled. "Why are you so shy with your opinions?"

"Natural reticence."

She laughed and touched one of his meaty hands. "I'm glad you're here."

"I'd rather be here than dining with Jupiter."

"But half man and half horse!" she said, unable to get the image out of her mind. "It makes me shiver."

"And they're mad with lust and all forms of debauchery. One was even responsible for the death of Hercules."

"But where could such creatures come from?"

"Centaurus was the deformed son of Apollo. He ran with the horses of Magnesia and mated with the mares and gave rise to the centaurs."

Despite the late morning warmth, Flavia felt chilly and wrapped her arms around herself. "You like to shock me, don't you?"

"Sometimes. But I'm not trying to now."

She saw the seriousness in his eyes.

"Of one thing we can be sure," he said. "If at this moment on the slopes of Thessaly herds of centaurs are running through darkened woods, they care nothing for philosophers who scoff at their existence."

Flavia leaned her head back against the planks and closed her eyes. Thrilled and appalled, she could not let go of that frightening vision. Finally she stood up. She touched Bellator on a shoulder and walked away with troubled eyes.

To Rufio, the desert at night was a pulsing threat. He stood just behind the trench line of the camp and gazed into the eastern blackness. Sounds raced undistorted through desert air. Distance did not matter. On this still night, he was certain he could have heard someone cough in the ruins of Babylon.

Yet, oddly, raids were still possible. If the wind were blowing away from camp, the danger increased. Without leaves to rustle or twigs to snap, this wasteland offered few warnings to the unwary. It was no accident that the Nabataeans preferred mares, animals quieter in ambush than stallions or geldings. And if the raiders rode camels, prepare for the worst, for those strange beasts seemed to walk on the wind.

Rufio toured the perimeter and satisfied himself that all was secure. Nonetheless, he would be happier when his men were sleeping behind walls.

Rufio's tent was a cozy respite from the anxieties of command. Neko had several lamps burning and had set out a pitcher of water along with a plate of cured olives and slices of Parmula ham. He had placed them on the little table where Rufio always kept a single lamp and his small red porphyry statue of Victoria. Long into the night, Rufio would often sit there, pondering the lessons of the day. Neko knew this was his master's sacred place, and the Egyptian always treated it with reverence.

Rufio smiled at Neko dozing in a chair and pulled off his sword and dagger belts. Flavia was long asleep at the far end of the tent, where Neko had made a partition with a wool blanket to give the sleeping area some privacy.

The metallic clatter of the weapons belts woke Neko, who jumped up with a start. The centurion signaled to him to be quiet and to go off to bed in the small adjoining tent.

Rufio stood for a moment in the center of the tent and stretched and breathed deeply. Then he sat down by Victoria and sought her counsel.

Crus inspected the gyrus as well as the training arena being constructed beyond it. The men's progress was amazing. Soon both enclosures would be completed. He noticed Flavia and Morlana outside the far end of the big rectangular arena. Morlana was launching arrows with startling skill at a red rag attached to a hay bale. Occasionally Flavia would correct the girl's stance or posture. The young woman's patience never waned.

Crus wondered if Lucia would ever present him with a daughter. All good Roman men wanted sons, and so did he. Yet the gaze of love of a young girl toward her father could cast a light across the blackest night. Crus understood Rufio's longing. He was certain that Morlana would plead with Mallius to take her to Rome with the cohort when this was done. Rufio and Flavia had become the extended family she had never had. But unless Rufio retired, he and Flavia would eventually return to Gaul. That, Crus was certain, would break the little girl's heart.

Neko seemed always to be busy on behalf of his master. So Flavia was surprised when she pulled back the tent flap to see him in Rufio's wicker chair. A bronze lamp burned next to the statue of Victoria. Neko sat beside the table with his eyes closed and his hands in his lap. He did not seem to be asleep. A look of serene contemplation bathed his features. When a cool evening breeze blew in and touched him, he turned and saw Flavia.

"Sit back down, Neko."

"Not while you stand."

"Neko . . ."

"The centurion will be here soon. Time for me to prepare a refreshment and to lay out a reading or two for him for the night."

She crossed the interior of the tent. "He's meeting with the tribune and the other centurions. They're discussing Parthians. I'm expecting a long night."

She took a chair from beside the big table at the far side of the tent and set it across from the other one.

"Spend time with me, Neko. I need your knowledge and your learning."

Neko was the only man she knew who could settle into a chair as silently as a folded piece of cloth.

"Have you ever heard of centaurs?"

"Yes."

"Do they exist?"

"I cannot answer that. I've not been everywhere."

"I mean *can* they exist?"

"Philosophers say no."

"What do you say?"

"I say that the word impossible should never pass a wise man's lips."

She looked away and stared idly at the wick burning in the bronze next to the little red statue.

"Did you know that there is a race of lizards in which there are no males?" Neko asked.

She turned back to him.

"All females," he said. "They always have fertile eggs inside them. They lay them and the babies hatch out. No males needed. A race of virgins!"

She managed a smile. "How dull."

"Who could believe such a thing exists? But it does."

She traced a forefinger along the edge of the table but said nothing.

"Why this concern about centaurs?"

"I don't know. But it bothers me. The fact that there could be such creatures."

"Some of them are archers, as you are. Wouldn't it be marvelous to see one?"

"Not the way Bellator describes them."

"Ah, the old horseman. Best to treat with a skeptical ear anything you hear from that tale spinner."

"The thought of them makes me restless."

"Perhaps someday you and Rufio and I can go to Mount Pelion in Thessaly and see for ourselves."

She stared at him in horror. "Are you serious?"

"Oh, perhaps half-serious. Rufio and I have been there. Not to the mount itself, but we passed through Thessaly several years ago."

"Oh, why didn't you climb the mount and see?"

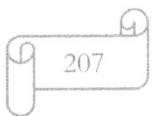

Neko smiled. "Why indeed. I suppose we should have."

"It's the mixture of intelligence and passions that frightens me. And brute power. And then put a weapon into that creature's hand. I know it sounds silly, but it makes me . . . I don't know."

"There are men like that, too."

"Yes," she said softly.

"Is that what bothers you? Does that mixture seem familiar to you?"

"No!" she shouted and jumped up. "Don't say such a thing!"

Neko was imperturbable. "Please sit as a favor to me."

She did so.

"Bellator was selective in his narrative. He left out someone—the greatest of the centaurs. Not descended from the twisted freak Centaurus, but the son of Kronos the titan, the father of Zeus."

"Who is Zeus?"

"The king of the Greek gods."

"Please tell me more."

"Kronos transformed himself into a stallion when he seduced Philyra. She bore the most magnificent centaur of all—Chiron. Noble and wise, he tutored Achilles himself on horsemanship, as well as the arts of the bow and the ways of war. But also the secrets of healing and the glories of music. He could play the lyre like no other. Temperate yet fierce. Gentle but fearless."

"That *is* like someone I know."

"Chiron was the sole centaur who was immortal. But in a terrible mishap he was accidentally wounded by Hercules with an arrow dipped in the blood of the Lernaean Hydra. The agony was unending. Chiron begged Zeus to take away his immortality. Zeus allowed Chiron to die and then hurled him up into the heavens, and the noble archer is now that great constellation of stars whose arrow forever guides sailors on their way."

"I've seen those stars!" She leaned forward and touched Neko's right hand. "That's a wonderful story. Thank you. I don't know what's wrong with me today. All these powerful men on horseback everywhere must be overwhelming me. I think the desert air is affecting my mind."

Neko rose and went to prepare for Rufio's return.

"One thing more," he said, turning back to Flavia. "Some claim that Zeus allows Chiron to return to earth on rare occasions. To intervene for those he favors."

Flavia just stared at him.

Neko smiled. "A comforting thought, perhaps, for the impetuous archer from Gaul. She might be wise to seek his guidance."

Then the Egyptian went back to his duties.

Thank you, my friend, Flavia whispered in her heart. *I love you.*

She went outside and gazed at the heavens. There he was, spread across the blackness, the archer in all his eternal magnificence. Vast, remote, bow drawn in silent unending power.

Flavia dropped to her knees and lowered her head and prayed.

Rufio was looking over the horse paddocks in the mid-morning sun when he saw Crus approaching.

"When was the last time you were inside the fort?" Crus said.

"Three days ago."

"Inspect it now."

It seemed an odd order at this moment. Rufio searched his face for meaning, but it was blank. "Yes, tribune."

Rufio walked to the fort. The ditches had been completed, and awnings had been erected over the guard towers to shield the soldiers from the sun.

He went through the gateway. Stunned, he shook his head and laughed.

The interior of the fort glittered. Judaean soldiers were everywhere along with the Romans, cleaning and repairing.

Rufio made his way down the Via Praetoria. He heard the water from the fountain before he saw it. Yet the most astounding sight was the mud brick bathhouse with the exterior already half up. Matthias stood there directing the construction. He clutched what appeared to be a set of drawings, probably from Bellator.

Hoofbeats behind Rufio caused him to turn. Crus rode up grinning.

"So what do you make of that?" the tribune said and slid from his horse.

"A good man leading other good men. I told you—you underestimated him."

"I did." Crus said. "What do you think moved them to do this?"

"What always moves Judaeans? Shame. We should go into Hezrail and find Simon and kiss him on both cheeks. That dried up old stick embarrassed these men into this."

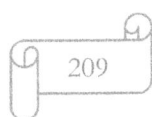

Crus laughed. "Maybe we should get him to sneer at a few more of our requests. Even throw a rock or two at us."

Rufio looked at Matthias pouring sweat. "I've seen many satisfying things throughout this Empire, but nothing quite like that." He folded his arms and smiled. "For once, I'm watching a proud young Jew bury Pompeius's horse."

Bellator made his way outside the fort along the north wall. The shade pens for the horses were almost completed. Beyond them lay a fenced arena that could hold at least fifty horses at a time and was big enough to allow them to run and roll and simply be happy being horses.

Arrianus saw Bellator approaching and signaled to his men to take a rest in the shade.

"Fine work," Bellator said.

"We'll have the horses off the picket lines and in here by tomorrow."

"How are they after the journey?"

"Lean but in good condition."

"How many feedings a day?"

"Three."

"Excellent. Waterings?"

"Three."

Bellator walked down the line and inspected the pens and their homespun awnings. He liked what he saw.

Arrianus came up behind. "Do you think Rufio would let us bring some of the horses back with us?"

"To Gaul?" Bellator said in surprise.

"There's space enough on the ship for some of them."

"Well, *that* would improve the breed up there!" Bellator said, laughing. "I'll speak with the centurion."

"Thank you."

"Pull up a rock," Bellator said when they had reached a shady corner at the end.

Arrianus moved his sword out of the way and sat on a flat stone.

Bellator sat on the round.

"When I was in Syria long ago, I noticed that the horses in one of the other turmae looked better than mine. I've always doted on my horses, so that bothered me. Their decurion was a good man, but no better than I, and—."

"Who could be better than Bellator?"

He gave Arrianus a mock, narrow-eyed glare. "I should be wary of you."

"Just a simple soldier."

"Where have I heard that before? In any case, I was concerned about my horses. After a long ride or a hard patrol, they never recovered as fast as the horses in that other turma. Yet all the horses were getting the same feed twice a day. It didn't make sense. Almost as an afterthought, I asked the other decurion how many waterings he did. Two. I was watering three times a day because of the heat. And I was proud of it, too, because it took more time and work." He paused.

"And that was the only difference? Less water for the other horses?"

"Yes."

"And they did better? In a desert? That's not possible."

"That's what I said. So I divided my horses into two groups. Two waterings for one, three for the other. What do you think I found?"

"I'm not . . ."

"The horses that were watered twice improved. The ones watered three times a day couldn't compare in terms of their condition."

"How can that be? What did you do?"

"I decided to act like a Greek and do an experiment. I kept them in two groups and measured the water I gave them, and then every night I measured what was left. A horse needs about ten congii of water even when it's doing nothing. If it's working hard or the climate is hot and dry, it can need up to fifteen congii. And when I measured the water, I found out that I'd been right all along."

Arrianus searched Bellator's eyes for meaning. "I don't understand."

"The horses that drank the most water did best."

"But you said—." Suddenly he burst out laughing.

"Do you see it?"

"The horses watered twice a day actually drank more."

"Much more. I should have seen it from the start but didn't. It happens to soldiers out here all the time. They collapse because they don't drink enough water. Are they stupid?"

"I hope not."

"Of course they're not. People aren't desert animals. They don't know how much they need to drink. Same with horses. They're grassland animals. Casual drinkers, like people. In the desert, you have to force yourself to drink more than you think you need. Have you ever watched camels at a well? You can see them swell like wineskins. Those miserable bastards know how to drink."

"So the trick with horses in the desert is to make sure they're really thirsty?"

"It's the only way to get them to drink enough to stay healthy out here." Bellator stood up and smiled. "So skip the midday watering. The one exception is when you work them hard in the morning. Then a light watering at midday. Otherwise only two."

"I'll do that. Has anyone ever figured out how long they can survive with no water at all?"

Bellator turned and gazed at the horses like a loving father. "No one has to figure it. Too many of us have seen it. After one day, they're suffering very much. By the second day, they're in agony. They don't have much longer to live. Some horses have actually survived over three days without water, but that's very rare. Usually by the middle of the third day, they just lie down and wait for the end. Seeing that is like watching a helpless child looking you in the eye as it gives up all hope and dies. In a world of heartbreak, it's the saddest sight of all."

39

CONCEDE NOT TO EVILS BUT FACE THEM BOLDLY WITH THAT WHICH FORTUNE ALLOWS YOU.

VIRGIL

Rufio was happy to be out from under leather. No soldier enjoys sleeping in a tent when he can have a roof.

He stepped out of his new quarters in the fort and into the cool midnight air and savored his favorite time of the day. Desert blossoms scented the breeze, although the coming heat would soon burn them away for another season.

He walked down the Via Principalis and was surprised to see Matthias speaking with the guards at the gate.

"I couldn't sleep," Matthias said half-apologetically to Rufio. "I decided to check on the horses."

"Let's walk together."

"You couldn't sleep either?" Matthias asked as they strolled toward the horse pens.

Rufio smiled. "I could sleep on a knife edge. But it's such a squandering of time. The night refreshes me."

"Truly?"

"When I was young . . . well, let's say my youth had many trials. Many pains. My only comfort was to stay up later than everyone else and go out and draw peace and strength from the quiet and the darkness."

Matthias turned toward him. "I envy that."

"If you work at it, it'll come."

Their sandals made little sound as they approached the paddocks. Yet when they were still at least a hundred feet away, a soldier snapped, "Augustus!"

"Sleeps well," Rufio answered.

The soldier had been resting on a small camp chair but now stood as straight as a pilum stuck into the ground.

"Report."

"All quiet, centurion."

"Good. Sit."

Rufio and Matthias moved on.

"I've never seen that before," Matthias said.

"What?"

"A seated guard."

"Two out of three are seated. The others patrol on foot."

"Aren't you afraid they'll fall asleep?"

"An officer is *always* afraid his men will fall asleep."

They came upon more sitting guards and three on foot patrol. Rufio spoke with each of them. None of them appeared to feel that Rufio was checking up on them. He simply seemed concerned about their welfare.

Rufio walked along the rows of pens. Several horses came over, and he stroked their faces affectionately.

"When I was a young soldier in Gaul long ago, we were out one night in a marching camp. We were moving on the next day, so that night we let the horses roam the camp at will. I woke up in the middle of the night, and just outside our tent I could hear a horse softly cropping the grass. It was the sweetest and most innocent and most soothing sound I'd ever heard in my life."

Matthias smiled. "Why didn't you become a cavalryman?"

Rufio used his fingers to brush the forelock of a light gray mare who had come over to greet him. "My talents lie elsewhere." He massaged her behind the ears. "I envy these Nabataeans. They live for the horse."

"I suppose I envy them a little, too."

"I've never heard a Judaean say that before."

"We're so practical. The Nabataeans are mystical—especially with the horse."

"Maybe you could teach each other."

"Do you think that's possible?"

"Like Roman engineers teaching Greek philosophers. Something for both."

"I'm not that optimistic."

"We're in Judaea. No one is optimistic."

Matthias failed to suppress a bitter laugh. "I know."

"Yet optimism is the only sensible course. Pessimists die a hundred times a day."

"Well, I don't think I'd ever have the optimism to let guards on duty sit down in the middle of the night."

"That's not optimism, that's wisdom."

"I don't understand."

"Guard duty is a soldier's most boring job. And the most exhausting. You know that."

"I do."

"And what's more painful than standing in one place for hours?"

"Nothing."

"So if you demand that, soldiers are always looking for a chance to get around it. To sneak a rest. What good are guards like that?"

"Not good at all."

"But you cannot just have patrolling guards either, because then there are weak spots in your perimeter. A thief or a spy just has to wait for the guard to move on. So instead, you have both fixed sentries and moving ones."

"But aren't the sitting soldiers likely to fall asleep?"

"They could. So you have them alternate with the moving sentries every hour. That way, both groups stay as fresh as possible."

"You make it sound simple."

"Sensible leadership is usually simple."

"But then—."

"I didn't say it was easy. That's different. But it *is* simple. Now you've learned that. The problem is that there are too many men in command who aren't simple. They're just simple-minded."

Matthias turned away and absently stroked the Arab mare. "There's so much to learn."

"You have time. And one thing more—the penalty for falling asleep in the field is death."

"Always?" Matthias said, searching Rufio's face in the moonlight.

"My option."

"Have you done that? Executed someone for sleeping?"

"Go get some rest and let me be alone with the night."

Only those who have lived in the desert know how small a sliver of moon is needed for one to be able to see in the darkness. Rufio easily made his way out toward the gyrus. He walked slowly and just bathed in the cool night air.

The gate of the gyrus was open. He went inside and examined his men's handiwork. How strange this thing must have seemed to the simple villagers here—a Greek invention built by Romans to train Arabian horses in a Judaean desert. He smiled with pride. Who but the men of the Tiber had ever had such audacity?

Hoofbeats were the last thing he expected. Softly they came on, in a gentle trot. The weight of his weapons on his hips reminded him where he was. He looked toward the section of wall opposite the gate. The horseman sounded as if he were approaching from there. Even though the gyrus wall was taller than a horse, a man on horseback could see over it.

Rufio heard the horseman ride up to the wall. His horse could not be seen at all, but the man's head rose above the edge of the gyrus. The moon had slipped below the horizon, so there was nothing to see by but starlight. Rufio could make out nothing of the man's face.

"Should I assume you don't know the watchword?" Rufio asked.

"Augustus," came the reply in a timber rich and deep.

"Sleeps well," Rufio answered, trying to conceal his surprise. "And you are?"

"A friend."

"Romans have no friends in Judaea."

"Prudent. But false. I know you well."

"Show me."

"You are Quintus Flavius Rufio, brother of Rosa, uncle of Marcellus, lover of Flavia, and newfound hero to a lonely little girl."

Rufio felt a chill up his arms and across his neck.

"And now?" the man said.

"Why are you here?"

"To see that your cohort lives to return to Gaul."

"Are you a Roman?"

"Alas, no."

"Then why?"

"Is it not true that so practical a man as Rufio rarely asks why? He asks how."

Rufio felt the chill again.

"Is that not your nature?" the man asked.

"Yes."

"The Parthians will come."

Rufio strained to see his features but it was hopeless. "How do you know?"

"I have rivers of knowledge far beyond the dried up creeks of your ignorance."

He spoke with the mellifluous confidence of a philosopher—or a madman.

"How many?"

"That is yet to be seen. Expect no less than five hundred. Prepare for a *drafsh*."

"Horse archers?"

"Yes."

"Heavy cavalry?"

"No."

"How can you be certain?"

The man just gazed at him over the wall.

"Yes, yes, I know about the cracked streambeds of my folly," Rufio said, "but I have to be sure. If there are heavy cavalry—men with armor and lances—we have to withdraw."

"The nobles will not fight for Phraates' scheme."

"And that scheme is what?"

"To unsettle this kingdom. To rob Augustus of his sleep so that the Princeps has too many worries in this land. Too many to bother with campaigns against Parthia."

"What campaigns?"

"The men of the East have a memory as long as time. They loathe the legions of Rome."

"The Parthians threaten our eastern edge."

"They threaten nothing but your dreams. Phraates knows that your belief in that is enough—enough to threaten *his* sleep, *his* dreams."

"Crassus and Antonius are dead."

"Phraates' memory is not. He was a young man on the throne when Antonius tried to stab Parthia through the heart."

"You sound as if you sympathize with *them*."

"I do. The Romans have tormented them for decades. Twice Rome attacked Parthia without cause and without honor."

"Then why help us?"

"One of your people is my friend."

Now it was Rufio's turn to stare blindly into the darkness. Finally he said, "You'd do all this to save one person?"

"I would. And I am."

Suddenly Rufio felt certain the stranger was about to ride off, and he was desperate to keep him there.

"Have we met?" Rufio asked. "You and I? In Rome? Somewhere in the provinces?"

"We have not. Expect the Parthians in no less than a month and in no more than two."

And then he rode away.

A lamp burned on the rough desk at which a now long-forgotten centurion had once sat. Neko had set out pitchers of wine and water and a cup.

Rufio took off his sword belt and set it aside and then sat down at the desk and stared at nothing. He stood up abruptly to summon Neko, but the Egyptian was already coming in.

"You look chilled," Neko said, ever sensitive to disquiet in his master.

"Yes."

Neko poured some wine and then added some water and handed him the cup.

"How many soldiers in a *drafsh*?"

"One thousand."

"Go to the Praetorium," Rufio said. "Ask the guard to wake the tribune and to ask him if he'll join me for wine. Put on a cloak. It's a cool night."

Neko left and was gone only a few minutes. The tribune was not far behind.

Crus stood in the doorway. "Has there been an eclipse?"

Rufio gave him a puzzled look.

"Otherwise," Crus said, "it's a strangely dark time for a gathering of the wise."

Rufio smiled. "Will you join me?"

Neko got another cup and poured the tribune some wine and mixed in some water.

"Now back to Morpheus," Rufio commanded, and Neko withdrew.

Without preliminaries, Rufio told Crus about the warning from the stranger at the gyrus.

The tribune remained silent for a long time. "Well, what do you make of it?" he said at last.

"I'm completely adrift."

"Odd that he knew of you personally. The private details."

"That's not really a mystery. Flavia talks a lot. But the rest—the Parthian archers, Phraates' plan. Where did he get that?"

"Do you think he's a Parthian traitor? Someone at court?"

"It's possible. And I'd like to know how he got the watchword for the day. He had an odd accent that I couldn't place."

"Maybe an Idumaean?"

"Oh, no. He was too positive and direct. No fatalism or doubts."

"And you couldn't identify his clothes or his horse? A Nisaean charger or a Turanian mount?"

"I saw only his face. And that was as clear as a shadow behind a cloud."

Crus smiled. "You're beginning to speak like Haritat."

"And what's this tale about doing all this to protect the life of a single man? Who? Why? We're talking about the struggle of empires here. What kind of nonsense is this?"

"Do you think he was lying?"

"No, and that's the lunacy of it. It's too ridiculous not to be true. And besides, if he was lying, we should just assume he lied about everything. And we can go back to our beds now and forget about all of it."

"But there's no forgetting in this land, is there?" Crus said, turning and gazing out the open door into the darkness. "Everything is chiseled in desert rock forever."

"No one forgets anything in Judaea."

Crus looked back at Rufio. "It's Bellator, isn't it?"

"It has to be. He's the only one besides me who has spent any time out here."

"But if this stranger is an old comrade of his, you'd think he'd want to come in and see his friend."

"Unless that friend is Bellator. You know him—ornery as a toothless old dog. And like a crippled hound, he creates a strange kind of loyalty. You don't want to be around him—but you don't want to see him beaten to death, either."

"All right," Crus said. "In the morning, we'll speak of Parthians. Cancel weapons drills. Give the men an easy day. Have them dote on their horses. At the third hour we'll meet with all the centurions. And Matthias. Agreed?"

"You don't need to ask me for confirmation."

Crus tried to suppress a smile. "Good." He downed the rest of his wine. "This won't be easy, will it?"

"Very difficult. The Parthians are a lethal foe."

"Fair enough." Crus stood up. "So are we."

Rufio closed the door behind his tribune and turned to see Flavia coming out of their quarters in the back.

"Is everything all right?" she asked.

"Flavia, you simply cannot dress that way here."

She stood there naked, sleepily brushing the hair away from her eyes.

"I'm sorry. Will you come to bed now?"

Rufio just smiled at her. Sometimes he forgot how childlike she was, how utterly without guile and without shame.

Rufio put out the lamp and they went into the bedroom. Small but adequate, it had a bed with a new mattress made of homespun and stuffed with fresh medica by Neko.

Rufio undressed and slid in beside Flavia. She nestled her head in the hollow of his shoulder.

"My love . . . ." she said.

"Mmmm?"

"I don't mean to talk so much. I don't mean to annoy you."

"Annoy me? What—oh. Did you hear our whole conversation?"

"I woke up when the tribune came in."

"You don't annoy me," he said and kissed her on the bridge of her nose. "You could never annoy me."

She breathed deeply with contentment.

"Will you tell Bellator about this stranger?"

"I haven't decided. Maybe later. When we're aboard ship on the way back to Italy."

"But wouldn't he want to know about his friend? Wouldn't it make him happy?"

"Not Bellator. It would make him feel like this whole venture now depended on him. It certainly wouldn't bring him peace. He has an odd streak of melancholy in him. Sometimes he's more like a Judaean than a Roman."

Flavia said no more.

Rufio was on the edge of falling asleep when he felt one of Flavia's fingers sliding back and forth across his chest to get his attention. He squeezed her hip to show her he was listening.

"My love, I've never spoken to anyone about Rosa. Or Marcellus. Ever."

When Rufio finally drifted off, it was into a night of uneasy dreams.

40

IN DIFFICULT AND TENUOUS CIRCUMSTANCES, THE BOLDEST PLANS ARE SAFEST.

LIVIUS

"We're being watched," Rufio said, and I looked around, but it seemed that there was nothing alive on the entire earth. Bellator, Rufio, and I had ridden out of the fort just before sunrise. Now we sat on our horses in the high Judaean hills as the sun turned them to mounds of gold. The long shadows made it difficult to distinguish objects on the ground. I saw no men or mounts anywhere. "You're looking for the wrong thing," Rufio said, reading what was in my mind. "Over there." He pointed with his chin. About two hundred feet to the south, in the shadow of an escarpment, I saw some slight movement, like two small objects caught in the wind. But there was not the slightest breeze. Suddenly I realized that they were two little cats playing together in the shade. And they had spots, something I had never seen on cats. A third quick movement caught their attention, and they lunged at it together. Now what had seemed to be just a mixture of sunlight and shadow against the rock sharpened into a creature I had never seen before. A giant cat, spotted like the two kittens, lay there swishing her tail, and they leaped at its fluffy end as if they were capturing a mouse. In a seemingly lifeless abyss, this was the most beautiful sight one could ever hope to see. Yet she would have been beautiful anywhere. The breeze had begun, but we were upwind, and the horses, who were looking elsewhere, as yet knew nothing of her. The young cats stalked and killed her tail again and again, but the great mother never took her eyes from us. She was the queen of this cruel land, and we remained here unchallenged in her realm only with her permission. I looked at Rufio. "The Jews call her the nemar. That's the Aramaic word. We call her the leopard." I asked him if she would harm us. "Not unless we threaten her cubs. She prefers antelope. And the Dog of the Canaanites is her special delight. Let's leave her now."

But Rufio did not move. Instead he continued gazing at her with a look of such gentleness that even I was startled. I, who know him better than anyone does. It was as if he were watching Paki staring up at him from his desk. Yet I think there might have been something else as well, a reason beyond the pleasing sight of a big kitten lolling in the shade. Here in this land of nothingness, a creature of incomparable majesty thrived. Flourished in an almost casual way, where people, for all their cleverness, could barely cling to life. And she did so while embodying a beauty that was almost incomprehensible.

I am not sure, but I think Rufio's eyes were misty as he turned away. Perhaps it was just from the cutting gust of wind that suddenly blew by.

We rode off toward a shaded mountain pass. In the distance I could see a haze beyond the end of the gorge. The hills began to lose their smoothness and jagged peaks the color of tarnished bronze rose on either side of us. When we came out the other end I must have made a strange sound, because Bellator looked at me and laughed. About two hundred feet below us lay an enormous quiet sea. The gorgeous color was what the Romans sometimes call **aqua marina**. It made no sense to me that Bellator had spoken so harshly of this place. But in a few minutes, I realized why. The silence. No fish broke the water. No birds flew low over the surface. And the surrounding terrain was as bleak as any place untouched by a divine hand. This was a land long abandoned by indifferent gods. Along some of the shoreline, and even out into the shallows as well, what looked like great mounds of snow rose several feet. But they brought no coolness here. Rufio said these were giant crusts of salt. He called them "the bones of the sea."

"One thing more," Rufio said, and we turned into a nearby ravine and rode south. We headed downhill, and by the time we came out of the pass we were at least a hundred feet lower than we had been not long before. "Etch that in your mind and never forget it," Rufio said and pointed to a mountain about five miles away. I saw nothing exceptional about it. We were surrounded by magnificent peaks that were much more impressive. The only distinctive thing was that it was flat on the top. I hardly considered that to be special. I looked back at Rufio. "Your young eyes can see more than they think they see," he said.

I examined it again, and then I realized what I was looking at. "Are those buildings?" I asked, not really believing what I was seeing.

"Herod is the master builder," Rufio said. "Not even traitors can ever take that title from him."

I looked back at the mountain. "But up there? How? Why?"

"To keep enemies at bay," Bellator said. "And to prove he can do anything. It's called Masada."

"He'd be safe up there, wouldn't he?" I said.

Bellator smiled but said nothing.

"Well, wouldn't he?" I asked him. "No army could ever get him there."

Bellator turned to Rufio.

"Look to the right," Rufio said to me. "See that spur of land against the western wall? It would be simple to build a siege ramp there, push a ram up, and knock down the wall." He turned to Bellator. "Two months?"

"At the most," Bellator said. "Six weeks with enough manpower." He turned to me. "Of course, no one could do it but us. So as long as Herod doesn't fight the Romans, he's safe." He laughed good-naturedly. "And the Jews would never be foolish enough to fight us, would they, Quintus?"

I laughed, too, and then something happened that unsettled me for the rest of the day. I expected Rufio to laugh with us at the absurdity of Judaea waging war against the Romans, but he suddenly became serious.

"I don't know," he said, and he seemed very troubled. "I don't know."

He turned his horse around and we followed him, and he did not say another word all the way back to the fort.

"Within one month, the Parthians will be on the move," Crus said. "Our information on this is beyond question."

Crus knew he was exaggerating his own certainty, but this was no time for half measures.

A plate of dried fruits and cups of cool spring water had been set out for the eight men seated around his desk. Early morning sunshine angled in through the open doorway of the Principia.

"We should expect as many as a thousand," Crus went on, "although there might be less. They'll be mounted bowmen. Feared by all." He smiled. "Except by us. Presumably they'll sweep up from around the south edge of the Salt Sea. Villages will fall and this kingdom will rattle. Or so Phraates hopes." Crus took a sip of water. "We're here to stop him."

"Tribune," Bellator said.

"Decurion."

"No heavy cavalry? Can you be sure?"

"Well, as a man I admire once said to me, only fools are sure. But that's my belief."

Crus looked around at the soldiers in front of him. These centurions had the relaxed self-assurance of men who had confronted most things, but also the wise caution of those who knew that no one had seen everything.

He glanced at Matthias. The Judaean seemed uncertain. Not fearful, perhaps, but at sea among these storm-tossed professionals. Crus knew it was unwise for him to feel left out.

"Questions, Matthias? After all, this is your land."

Clearly startled to be asked his views, Matthias hesitated. Then he said, "These are ruthless men, tribune. Skilled men. How will we meet them?"

"With Jewish faith and Roman steel."

Matthias was visibly touched. A few of the centurions laughed, and one slapped the Judaean on the shoulder.

"Not bad, eh?" the centurion said. "We'll get it done."

Matthias smiled. "We'll do our part."

"I know that," Crus said. "Now the question is *how* do we get it done. We have no one to match them as horse archers. Infantry is useless, since the Parthian bowmen will stay hundreds of feet away from a sword thrust. Therefore, we listen to the advice of Mallius and smash them with cavalry."

"But where do we get those?" one of the centurions asked.

"We don't get them," Crus said. "We become them."

The seasoned soldiers stared silently at Crus.

"Rufio. . . ." the tribune said.

"Are you going to tell me," Rufio asked his officers, "that you tender souls cannot manage a brawl on horseback?"

They all laughed.

"Well," one of them said, "now that you phrase it so sweetly."

Rufio laughed with them. "We can do this. I'll explain why." He paused for a moment. "The Parthian archers are not warriors." He let that dangle.

"All right," another of the centurions finally said, "tell us why that is."

"Because they never fight. They stand off and launch arrows into helpless throngs and then flee. They're not fighters. They're butchers. They're not soldiers any more than someone who pisses on a pile of grapes is a winemaker."

"You should be speaking in the Curia," Bellator said, laughing. "Your eloquence is wasted here."

Rufio smiled and went on. "Few things are more dangerous than a swarm of Parthian archers. But they're like locusts—they're dangerous only *in* a swarm. Get in close and you've got them."

A scarred older centurion, with whom Rufio had served beside the great horsemen of Spain, looked concerned.

"What is it, Decius?"

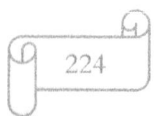

"I thank Mars that you trained all of our century on horses last year, but *fighting* from horseback . . . that's much more."

"It is. But remember that we're not up against Hannibal's cavalry. We're facing riders who fear the blade. When we close with them, we thrust as if we're standing on our own feet. And the horse's four hard feet are more stable than our own two feeble ones."

"Our swords are short for cavalry," Decius said.

"We have what we have."

"Very well."

Decius said no more.

"Today the men can rest," Rufio said. "The next day they begin. Bellator will work with the men, one century at a time. I'll deal with the horses. We have some of the best mounts on earth. Match them with the finest soldiers, and the Parthians will have something to write about in their histories. Those who can write. And those who survive."

Rufio walked by the horse pens and watched his men grooming their mounts and picking their feet and establishing a bond unique in all the world. With Arabian horses that was not easy, insolent half-mad beasts that they were. With an Arab steed, you never issued a command. You made a firm request delicately cloaked with the hint of force. Then you waited an instant—no longer—and allowed him to conclude that your wish was not just truly wise but was really his own idea all along. Then he was yours.

Rufio heard someone running, and he turned to see Arrianus hurrying toward him.

"Mallius is dead."

"From what?" Rufio asked in the blank tone of someone who had seen hundreds fall.

"His horse put its foot wrong and stumbled. Mallius went off. Broke his neck. Gone like a puff of smoke. I was in the village buying some cloth."

"Where's the little girl?"

"I brought her here. She's with Flavia."

"Take someone to Hezrail to get Mallius's body."

"The Jews already put him in the ground."

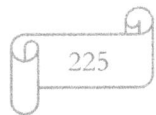

Rufio nodded. "I forgot they buried the dead. Just as well. No need for that child to smell her father's burning corpse. Get a few from our century and collect Mallius's belongings and horses and bring them here. You pick the men."

"They're already on their way to Hezrail."

"Thank you. Well done." Rufio shook his head. "Twenty years in the legions and he goes like that." He took a deep breath and let it out slowly as he turned and gazed at the horses. "Tomorrow we begin training. You're already a horseman, so I want you to help Bellator. Steady the men. I don't want them too eager. You cannot rush things with horses."

"Yes, centurion. I know that."

"Yes, I suppose you do. And don't be formal with me."

"Thank you, Rufio."

"I think that barley put some weight on you. In all the right places."

"Best meal I ever ate."

Rufio stepped past Arrianus and headed back to his quarters.

Neko was seated at Rufio's desk and reading a scroll, no doubt an account of Parthian warfare. He stood up when Rufio entered and he gestured toward the bedroom.

Rufio went in. Morlana and Flavia were sitting on the edge of the bed. Flavia was holding one of Morlana's hands. The front of Flavia's green tunic was soaked.

Morlana's face was the color of goat's milk.

Rufio dropped to one knee in front of her at the side of the bed.

The rims of Morlana's eyes were as red as raw meat. Her lower lip trembled as she looked at him, but she seemed all cried out.

Rufio opened his arms and she reached for him and he pulled her close.

Then the tears came again, and she wept to exhaustion and finally slumped against him.

"I don't know where my daddy is," she struggled to say through her sobs.

"But you do. All Roman soldiers live forever in Paradise. Someday you'll be with him again."

"Are you sure?" she said, her face still flat against his chest.

"Yes."

She squeezed him more tightly. "I'm so afraid. I'm all alone."

"Oh, Morlana," Flavia said. "You'll never be alone."

Morlana turned to Flavia.

"Don't be afraid," Flavia said. "We're with you."

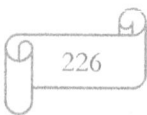

She looked back at Rufio.

"Flavia is right," he said. "You're not alone when you're with the Romans. I need you here. I need my strator."

She seemed shocked. "Do you still want me?"

"Of course I do. These Italian foot soldiers don't know anything about horses. The way to comb out a mane or pick a horse's feet. I need a Suebian horsewoman to show them how."

Tears and a smile flowed across her face together.

Rufio noticed that her right hand was clenched. He stretched out her thin fingers to relax her, and something fell into his hand.

"What's this?"

It was a tiny horse carved from tamarisk, stained dark now from her sweat. She must have been gripping it for hours.

"Your present," she said. "Remember? I was holding it when I saw my father fall."

"I'll keep it forever."

She rested her head back against his chest.

"Flavia is going to take you to the bath house now to get you freshened up. Then we have some work to do this afternoon. I want the horses glowing like Pegasus. I need you to show my men the way."

She looked up, the most fragile and vulnerable creature he had seen since a terrible day over twenty years ago.

"And remember," he said, stroking her hair, "no girl need fear anything when she's in the arms of Rufio."

41

HALF IS DONE WHEN THE BEGINNING IS DONE.

HORACE

The horses had been fed and watered long before sunrise. Now Crus and Bellator watched the men groom their mounts in their pens in the early half-light.

"Give a good soldier a dozen tasks," Bellator said, "and he'll do them well. But he'll complain. Then give him one that involves an animal and he'll change. Soften. I've seen it a hundred times."

Crus continued looking at his men as they went over their animals.

"See how gently they wipe around their horses' eyes?" Bellator said. "How carefully they pick their feet?"

"Rufio says Romans are brutal toward horses."

"That's because he's a sentimentalist about animals. Look at that cat. The Queen of Gaul. And that Numidian stud Cormagnus. He eats better than I do. No soldier can live up to Rufio's standard."

"Even Rufio," Crus said.

"What do you mean?"

"Just a stray thought. Never mind."

"Rufio says that the sound of horses grazing in the night is the sweetest sound there is. He'd rather hear that than a woman's moans."

"Well, I wouldn't go that far," Crus said with a smile. "I've known Flavia too long to believe that."

"All right, maybe I've stumbled out of the arena, but you know what I mean."

Crus gazed back at his soldiers. "They do look like they're enjoying themselves."

"Give a man a beast and you make a better man. He has to look outside himself. Outside of everything he's ever known. And he has to step inside a mind that he realizes he'll never fully understand. And when that mind fires an animal as excitable and mysterious and powerful as a horse—and as spirit-driven as an *Arabian* horse—then you've forged a man like no other."

"And you say that *Rufio* is a sentimentalist."

"He is. I'm a realist."

"Oh. My error."

Objects in the distance beyond Bellator caught Crus's eye. Bellator turned, and they both examined the black figures coming from the east.

"Riders," Bellator said as the men were outlined against the barely lit gray-blue sky.

"I've never seen horses so tall."

"No, you haven't. They're camels."

Crus looked at Bellator and smiled. "Who do you think it is?"

"Haritat. Come back to help us train. As he promised."

Seven riders approached in a "V" with Haritat leading. The camels came on with that uniquely swaying gait that somehow seemed both ungainly and graceful at the same time. The black robes of the riders fluttered majestically in the early morning breeze.

"By Jupiter," Crus said softly, "They're grand. And they know it. I wonder, though, if Haritat is really as fearsome as his legend...."

Bellator began walking toward them. "Let's meet them part of the way. Out of respect."

The two Romans approached with forceful but measured steps, empty of both fawning and insolence.

"I don't understand why they wear such dark clothes in the desert," Crus said.

"It baffles me. But they say it keeps them cooler."

The Romans stopped as the riders came abreast. The three on each side of Haritat swung to the front until all seven stood in a single rank.

The camels dropped to their knees, and the men dismounted.

Haritat stepped forward.

"As I promised," the desert chieftain said.

Crus smiled. "As you did. Thank you."

"These are a few of my sons."

"Rome is honored," Crus said. "And Rome is grateful."

Haritat jerked on his camel's lead and his sons did likewise, and the animals rose with that hideous guttural protest that could easily convince someone that they were being beaten with iron rods.

"Mallius is dead," Crus said as they walked back toward the fort. "He fell off his horse and snapped his neck."

Haritat's face was as emotional as rock. "And the little one?"

"She's with Flavia."

"Wise. I'll speak with her. The comfort of Dushara is a river to the innocent."

As they approached the north wall of the fort, Haritat told his sons to unload the camels. Thick off-white blankets atop the wooden saddles big enough to hold two men softened the journey for the rider. Under the saddles, larger blankets protected the camels. A stunning leopard pelt lay atop the blanket on Haritat's animal. From the front of the frame of everyone's saddle hung a long sheathed sword, and from the back a hornbow in a case and a quiver of arrows.

"The horses look restless today," Crus said.

"It's the camels," Bellator answered. "Horses hate the smell of camels." He turned to Haritat. "I'm surprised you brought them."

"That is precisely why I brought them. The Parthians sometimes use camels to transport their supplies. Our horses must stay accustomed to their scent." To Crus he said, "I would speak with the centurion. With your permission and in your presence."

"I have six centurions."

"The silver one."

"We'll go to the Principia and have some refreshment while the decurion gets Rufio."

"May we perhaps wait until my sons have erected our tents? Sitting in chairs is little more than a taste of Hell. And there is much Hell about—and more coming, do you not agree?"

Rufio and Arrianus walked about the arena among several dozen horses enjoying the freedom of the big enclosure.

"What do you think?" Rufio asked.

"They're ready."

"You're talking about their condition."

"Yes."

"I mean mentally."

Arrianus hesitated. "Well, they're Arabians, so they're all slightly insane. Some more than slightly."

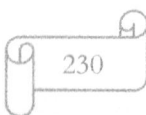

"I want you to cull any you think might be a problem to control."

"I've done that."

"Good. And you're convinced our men are skilled enough? Or will be? Be harsh in your judgment if you have to. I need to know now."

"I'm convinced." Arrianus smiled. "The horses might need a little more persuasion, but that'll come. Haritat has done an amazing amount of work."

Rufio saw Bellator coming toward the arena.

"The Arab and his sons are—."

"Never call him that," Rufio said.

Startled, Bellator stopped short. "They're here."

"I need Valerius and Metellus," Rufio said to Arrianus. "Find them and have them report to the Principia. Then go—."

"The tents are being pitched near the horse pens," Bellator said.

"All right. Then go to Matthias and request his presence with us."

After Arrianus hurried off, Rufio turned to Bellator. "*Arab*? You know better than that."

"Sorry. It's been a tortoise's lifetime since I've been back out here."

On a sudden impulse, Rufio said, "Do you still have any friends here?"

"In Judaea?"

"Yes."

"No. I suppose I never really did. The Jews are too strange. I'm a man of action. The Jews spend too much time thinking and praying."

"That they do."

"And not eating good food. *Is* there such a thing as Jewish food?"

Rufio smiled. "Not that I've noticed."

"What about you? Any old friends in the land of prophets?"

"Just up in Syria."

"Why did you ask anyway?"

"Just wondering."

Valerius and Metellus came running up as Rufio and Bellator reached the large black tent.

"Arrianus is still looking for Matthias," Valerius said.

Metellus, the most fastidious of men, was a bit disheveled, and his tunic was muddy.

"Did you dress for the occasion?" Rufio asked.

"Busy morning," the signifer answered with uncharacteristic brevity.

The four of them went inside.

Crus was already seated on a rug across from Haritat.

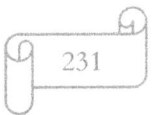

"Welcome." Haritat said."

"My officers, Valerius and Metellus."

"Officers?" Haritat asked.

"This and this," Rufio answered, raising his right hand and then his left.

"I understand. Welcome all."

Cups and pitchers of water had been set out.

"I already told our guest that we're happy at his return," Crus began.

"We're honored," Rufio said.

Haritat poured water into everyone's cup and filled his own last.

"My sons are wise in the ways of horses and schooled in the manners of men. They know that if not for a valiant woman, their father would be gone. They will nourish your men with their knowledge."

"Rome is grateful," Crus said.

"Treat them with forbearance. Tell your men that whenever they are in doubt about a matter, pause for a moment to see if an answer is forthcoming. If not, they may inquire with respect."

"I'll do so," Crus said.

"In the desert, there are fleeting structures of stone. But there are lasting structures of respect. When the greatest carved rock is a fallen ruin, respect remains."

"Very well," Crus answered.

"Tribune?" Rufio said.

Crus nodded.

"My men come from a land called Italy," Rufio said, looking at Haritat. "In that land, people talk without ceasing. They talk until they collapse—or you do. Silence is incomprehensible to them. But when Germans panic, when Greeks falter, when Persians flee, Italians stand fast before the savages of the world. Treat *that* with honor and respect as well."

The creases at the corners of Haritat's eyes deepened in what might have been a smile. "Wisely spoken. An oath of honor, then, among men."

"Agreed," Crus said. "Let's begin."

42

THE GODS HAVE BESTOWED ON MAN THE GIFT OF TEACHING HIS FELLOW MAN BY WORD OF MOUTH WHAT HE SHOULD DO, BUT IT IS OBVIOUS THAT BY WORD OF MOUTH YOU CAN TEACH A HORSE NOTHING.

XENOPHON

Twitchy is what Arrianus calls Morlana, and she smiles or giggles every time he says it. He has been working her at the horse pens as hard as one can work a ten-year-old. He is trying to distract her from her grief. That is always the tough man's way. Naturally he is failing. Sorrow cannot be worked away or wished away. It can only be lived away. I know. I have lost many I have cared for in battles beyond counting.

Better, though, than toil for Morlana are the little gestures of these rough men. The small gifts they give her, the unexpected treats. When I was a girl, I learned that the toughest men have the tenderest hearts, for they alone can afford the risk of having them.

And the most kindly of all is Arrianus. When he is training the men, he has Morlana always at his side on horseback, as if she is his assistant. It makes her glow. This morning he was working with soldiers of the Sixth Century on ways to acquire better balance in the saddle. He had them ride with their reins draped over their horses' necks and their arms extended straight out to their sides. I was amazed at how well they cantered this way. Yet they had no time to congratulate themselves. Arrianus ordered them to stop, and he told Morlana to ride over and place a coin on the back of each man's extended right hand. Then he commanded them to trot. Many riders quickly lost their coins, and it was Morlana's job to retrieve them before they were lost in the dirt. She did this with speed and diligence.

To protect her fair skin from this terrible sun, she was wearing the blue cloak that matched Rufio's tunic. Under it, I knew she had at her waist the dagger that Haritat had grandly given her. She sleeps with it under her pillow every night.

Although I am sure the soldiers were quietly cursing Arrianus during his maddening exercises, I know they got much from them. By the time they were finished, most were able to retain the coin on the backs of their hands while trotting, and some even while they cantered.

Yet Morlana benefited, too, but in a different way. How small a thing it was for this soldier to have a little girl gather up dusty coins. And how thoughtful and caring. When at the end she handed him the sack with the collected coins, she did so with the untainted pride only a child can know. I suspect that Arrianus has a younger sister or two back in Italy. But even if not, he now has one here.

Yet if Arrianus is a brother to Morlana, there is another who is a deity. It unsettles him, I am sure of it, but even gods have their uncertain moments.

Rufio had Neko make another mattress and fit out an empty storeroom as sleeping quarters for him. Morlana sleeps with me, usually with Paki, Rufio's cat, lying curled against her feet. Sometimes I hear Morlana crying softly in the night. Other times I wake up and feel her slumped against me for safety in the dark, and I listen to the soft breathing of her sleep. Once I was startled to see someone staring at us from the shadows in the doorway. Then I realized it was Rufio. He said nothing, so neither did I. In the darkness, he could not see me smile. I wish I could explain to Morlana how truly safe she is. How in the lonely watches of the night the terror of Germania gives up his most precious hours to rise and reassure himself of the comfort of a little German girl. And how her gentle breathing and quiet rest, I think, bring rest to him at last.

"Your horse is *not* your best friend!" Bellator boomed to the troops arrayed before him. He sat astride a chestnut gelding in the center of the big arena. Sixteen soldiers from two tent groups of the Sixth Century sat on their horses facing him in a single rank about ten horse lengths away. Bellator had excused them from wearing their mail armor, but he had insisted on helmets because of questions of balance. It was foolish to get accustomed to riding without one and then have to start all over again with one. By now the men's heads would already be baking inside the bronze.

The remainder of the century sat on the ground outside the arena.

"Do you know who your horses' best friends are?" Bellator went on. "All these other horses." He swept an arm across the arena. "Certainly not you. You're just someone who comes into your horse's life occasionally. As far as he knows, you're just some bum scrounging around the stable. He recognizes no ownership. Maybe you feed and water and groom him, but don't expect him to be grateful. It isn't built into him. He's not a dog. He might learn to respect you and even trust you, but don't consider yourself entitled to that. In some cases—maybe one out of ten—he might even come to like you, to bond with you. If that happens, be grateful. If not, stroke his forehead and thank him anyway for all he *has* given you."

Bellator clicked to his horse, and they began to make a wide circle in the center, as if Bellator were attempting to collect his thoughts, rather than giving a harangue he had tossed off a thousand times.

"Which brings me to another point," the old horseman said as he came back to the middle and faced his men again. "Even though your horse will never be your best friend, you have to be *his*. No herd mate will care about your animal the way you do. When the whole herd panics and bolts, you remain. You tend his wounds, reassure him in doubt, caress him as he dies."

Bellator wiped away the sweat that was running down into his eyes. "All right, relax and take a drink. When you've had enough, take three more swallows."

The men untied the flasks from their belts and did as he ordered.

"One more thing before we get started," Bellator said. "I never want to hear anyone say that his horse made a mistake. Ever. Horses don't make mistakes. Riders do. Who are you to say a horse is wrong? According to what? Your needs? Every horse knows that he's a meal on four legs, and the only power he has is the power to flee. To a horse, everything is a matter of life and death. A horse does what's best for *him*—always. If you want him to do something else, it's up to you to show him the wisdom of it. I don't want to hear anyone whining about his animal. Riders make excuses. Horsemen make tracks. Understood?"

"Understood!" one of the soldiers shouted, and the others joined in.

"A horse is never wrong," Bellator said. "What on earth could he be wrong about? About being human? What does he care? Never forget that *you're* the one who leaped onto *his* back. He didn't leap onto *yours*."

Bellator pointed to one side of the arena. "Fall into line along the rail into one file. Knot your reins. You don't want to lose them in battle. Keep the knot loose, though, and always have your dagger to be able to cut your horse free."

The soldiers took their places along the rail.

"I want three horse lengths between each rider. Start walking, take five strides, then move up into a trot."

After a few moments, most had begun trotting, but a few lagged and the file began to bunch up."

"Is move too hard a word?" Bellator shouted. "It means go! Move!"

The lagging riders clicked to their mounts and then kicked, and suddenly the Arabs recovered their memories on how to trot.

"Don't stop until I tell you."

Arrianus rode up to the gate and came in and closed it without dismounting, a simple task to all who have never tried it.

"What do you think?" Bellator asked as Arrianus took his place beside him.

He studied the riders for a moment. "Too much mouth contact. I'd never give an Arab slack, but all that pulling is going to make hard mouths. Those horses might not stop when they want them to."

"Why are they gripping like that?"

"They're nervous, so they're holding on with their hands instead of their legs."

Bellator smiled. "You have a good eye." He turned back to the riders. "Stop and rest," he shouted.

They obeyed, a little bit sloppily.

"Do you have a suggestion?" Bellator asked his Secondarius.

Arrianus smiled and folded his hands across his saddle between the two front corner pommels.

Bellator returned the smile. "They're going to hate us by the end of the day."

"But they'll love us in their old age."

"You sound like your centurion," Bellator said with a laugh.

"Don't tell him that."

"Attention!" Bellator said to the riders. "Lay your reins down across your horse's neck. Place one hand over the other on your saddle between the horns and move off at a trot. The first soldier who grabs his reins cleans out his whole century's horse pens for a week."

The horses trotted off, and within a few moments three riders were down in the dirt.

"Keep moving!" Bellator said to the soldiers still on their horses. "Forget those men on the ground."

The three riderless horses kept their positions in the file. Without hesitation, the soldiers who had fallen ran to their horses, gripped their manes, and flew up into their saddles.

Bellator snapped around toward Arrianus. "Did Rufio teach them how to mount on the move?"

"He did."

Bellator shook his head. "That silver-haired bastard is wasted in the infantry."

The riders continued trotting.

"What do you think?" Bellator asked.

"Nice balance. Mostly."

"Attention! No, don't look at me. Just listen. When I give you the signal, canter. And no reins!" He paused. "Ready. Go!"

The horses obeyed beautifully, and six riders failed to make it even halfway around the arena before they tumbled.

"That's all right," Bellator said. "No one is hurt. Don't try to remount."

He waited until the remaining riders had cantered twice around the arena and then said, "Drop down to a trot and then stop." He waited a moment. "Good. Drink." He turned to Arrianus. "You, too."

Arrianus took a sip from his flask.

"The desert is a damnable place," Bellator said softly, gazing into the distance at the bleak hills. "You never have only one enemy. You always fight the desert, too."

Arrianus stared off into the Judaean wasteland. "I could never have imagined a place like this."

"Who could? Someone who's never been here could have no idea what the desert is like." He glared off at the vast emptiness around them. "A fierce and terrible thing plotting against your life and your sanity. And here we are—fighting over it."

"Maybe we won't have to."

"Oh, yes we will. Battles are always fought in the most horrible places on earth."

"Then we'll win," Arrianus said with the confidence of a young man on a good horse.

"And do you know what decides it? Not training or valor. Water. Out here it's always about water. We have it and the Parthians won't. Oh, they might locate a spring or a well, but that won't be enough. There are too many men and horses. They don't dare linger out there. They win fast or else they lose."

"Then we just have to hold."

"Just?" Bellator said with a smile. "Yes, just." He gazed back at the lifeless wilderness. "Always . . . it's always about water."

After a short silence, Arrianus said, "Why don't you give your hip a rest? I'll take over."

"Tired of listening to a cynical old man?"

"No," he said sincerely.

"For the next few days, we'll concentrate on teaching them to get and hold a secure seat. Later in the week we'll work on other things."

"Understood."

"I'll be back in a while. Let's try to get through the whole century today."

"We will."

"By the end of the week, I want this cohort to be able to ride without hands and without fear." He looked back at his troops. "I'll stay longer. Let's run them around in the opposite direction."

"Your hip?"

"What does it matter? I have two."

Rufio had ordered that every century take a three-day turn at manning the bath house. The primary tasks were to keep it clean, a job that was second nature to a Roman, and to make sure the furnace was stoked for the caldarium. Paradoxically for the desert, a bit of suffering time in the hot room was somehow the most refreshing.

Rufio lay on the stone table as Neko finished giving him a massage. Rufio had been eating dust in the gyrus all day while running the horses. He needed to see every horse trot and canter at least a few minutes in both directions. He wanted no unsound animals carrying his men into battle. With the help of Haritat and his sons, he had spent a grueling ten hours working his way through about a third of the Roman mounts, and he was happy with what he had seen. Now he needed Neko's ministrations to reinvigorate his body to match his spirits.

Wearing a fresh white tunic, he left the bathhouse and stepped out into the late afternoon sun. He was startled to see some of the people from Hezrail walking up the Via Principalis and escorted by soldiers. They carried baskets or pots, and some were leading goats.

Rufio followed them to the intersection with the Via Praetoria. Then he stood there stunned.

At least a hundred villagers crowded around the front of the Principia. At their head was Simon talking with Crus. Matthias stood slightly to one side and appeared to be mediating.

Rufio managed to get around the noisy knot of people and to reach the front. Crus smiled when he saw him coming and greeted him with an expression of happy bewilderment.

"Tribune?" Rufio said.

"They've brought us gifts," Crus said. "Food, animals. Elah is indeed great."

Rufio looked to Matthias.

"A little girl fell into a well in Hezrail. One of your men lowered himself down and rescued her before she drowned. They want to express their gratitude."

"Who was it?"

"Simon doesn't know," Matthias said.

Rufio gazed out at what he had thought a moment ago was just a mob. Now he saw a grateful gathering of some of the poorest people on earth. They seemed to be carrying all they owned. Rufio knew that he could live a hundred years and still never again be offered half of what there was, let alone all.

"Tribune," Rufio said, "these people eat dog vomit to survive. We should be feeding *them*."

Crus turned to the Judaeans and raised a hand until they got quiet, or at least as quiet as Judaeans could ever get.

"In one hour's time, we'll all feast together at the table of Caesar. Rome will provide the food, because Elah has provided the miracle!"

Stunned at first, the villagers suddenly found their voices, a hundred of them.

"And remember," Rufio shouted to Crus above the crowd, "no ham."

Rufio happened to glance at Matthias. The young soldier was looking at him with the admiration a boy reserves for an older brother.

Rufio winked at him, and Matthias grinned in return.

Rufio returned to the barracks block and went to the quarters shared by Valerius and Metellus. Valerius was off somewhere, but Metellus was seated at a tiny table and working on the century accounts. He stood up when he saw Rufio enter.

Rufio gestured him back down and took a wobbly chair and sat across from him.

"Why was your tunic muddy this morning?"

"I'm sorry. I didn't have time to change it."

"That's not what I asked you."

"There was an incident in Hezrail that I got involved in."

"An accident?"

"It was a small matter."

"Tell me about it."

"I was in the village to buy a few things and saw some boys playing around a well. A little girl ran over—I think one of the boys was her brother—and then she climbed up onto the rock barrier around the well. I was about to tell her to get down when she slipped and fell in. The boys panicked and started screaming. I ran over and cut the well rope and tied it to a rock on the wall and lowered myself down. I scooped her up and had her hold onto my neck and I climbed out. It was all over in a minute or two. I think she got a little bit of water into her lungs, but she's fine. She reminded me so much of my little Kalinda back in Gaul. Sorry about the tunic."

"Forget about the tunic."

"Rufio, why are you asking me about this? It was a small thing."

"Not to the child—or her family."

"Well, if a Roman soldier has to think twice about saving a little girl who's drowning, we might as well roll up the Empire now and be done with it."

Rufio smiled at his signifer. "I should have you posted to the Palatinum to advise the Princeps on dealing with foreign potentates."

Metellus looked baffled.

"Take a walk over to the Principia. Simon wants to see you."

"Simon?"

"The graybeard."

"I have these accounts to—."

"Venus's tits! Forget the accounts." Rufio stood up. "If we send another emissary to Parthia, I think it'll be you."

On the way out, Rufio met Valerius coming in.

"Why didn't you tell me what happened in the village?" Rufio asked.

"What happened in the village?"

"The child in the well."

"It didn't occur to me to tell you. Why would it?"

Rufio just shook his head. "There are about a hundred villagers in the fort. They're going to eat with us. Afterward, I want you to take the First Century and walk with these people to Hezrail. I don't want them to be alone in the dark. Take your horses so you can ride back."

"It'll be done. Why are they all here?"

Rufio smiled and laid a hand on Valerius's shoulder. "To show that it's not time to roll up the Empire just yet."

43

AND THE HOOFS OF THE HORSES AS THEY RUN SHAKE THE CRUMBLING FIELD.

VIRGIL

"What is that?" Flavia said, pointing to the southeast at a line of camels heading northwest.

Morlana set down an armful of bridles near one of the horse pens and came over. "It's called a caravan. Those are Nabataean merchants. They're probably going all the way to Gaza."

"Why did they pass by us? Wouldn't they want to sell things to the soldiers?"

"They probably don't know we're here."

"What are they carrying? Do you know?"

"Different things. Incense. Gems sometimes. Cloth, too, sometimes."

Flavia watched as the camels moved slowly northward. "Would they have silk strings? The kind for my bow?"

"They might. They usually stop near Hezrail. The people in the village come out to trade. They don't have any money, so they trade food for goods."

Flavia smiled at Morlana. "Would you like to go and see?"

"To the caravan?" she asked in surprise.

"It'll be fun. I have Caesar's silver. Maybe we can find some nice things."

Morlana stared off at the caravan. "I'd like to, but I have work."

"I'll help you with it when we get back. Come on!"

Morlana grinned. "I'll tack up the horses!"

The morning sun was still low when they set off. About a mile outside the fort Flavia saw the black silhouette of a man standing to the north. He was staring off into the distance.

"It's Haritat," Morlana said.

"Where's his horse?"

"He likes to walk out alone sometimes."

Flavia wondered if the great isolate turned inward so often because so much of the time he had to gaze outward, to be ever attentive to the welfare of his family and his people. Today he was dressed in black as usual and wore a dark red head-cloth that flowed to his shoulders. Regardless of what others thought, Flavia was certain that this sage of the desert could never be as fierce as they often feared.

Haritat did not turn around, so they rode on.

Some villagers from Hezrail had already arrived at the caravan by the time Flavia and Morlana got there. Many had brought lambs and goats for trade. The merchants had set up their tents and spread out colorful blankets with their wares.

Camels were resting here and there on their bellies, with their legs tucked beneath them in a quiet serenity they rarely showed at other times.

Flavia and Morlana dismounted and led their horses by the reins. Flavia was glad that Haritat had accustomed their animals to the camels so they could walk about without causing a disturbance.

She already knew that she and Morlana were creating enough of a commotion on their own. Unescorted females of any kind were as rare among the Judaeans as were a lovely blonde-haired girl and a beautiful blue-eyed woman riding about in the desert near the Salt Sea. Yet the Nabataean merchants, ever gracious and polite, were careful to say nothing and they gently averted their gaze.

Flavia stopped before a blanket covered with jewelry. She spotted a small silver ring set with a deep blue stone.

"May I?" she asked the handsome middle-aged merchant.

He inclined his head slightly. "With honor."

She picked it up. A galloping horse had been exquisitely carved into the opaque blue gem.

"Does this stone have a name?"

"The Persians call it *lazhward*."

Flavia looked around. "Morlana."

She came over leading the two horses.

Flavia smiled. "See if this fits you."

Morlana took the ring and stared at it as if she were holding a fallen star.

"Slide it on," Flavia said.

It fit her left forefinger.

"Good," Flavia said. "Your other fingers can grow into it."

Morlana dropped the reins and threw her arms around Flavia and squeezed so tightly Flavia could barely breathe.

Flavia opened the little sack on her belt and pulled out a denarius.

"No, Flavia," Morlana said. "That's too much."

But the Sequani barbarian believed bargaining to be beneath her dignity, and she handed the silver coin to the merchant. Then she smiled. "With honor."

The merchant gazed at her as though she were a divine being. "May Dushara cast his glow upon you."

Yelling among the merchants and villagers startled everyone, including the camels.

"Stay here," Flavia said to Morlana and then ran from out of the circle of tents.

A horseman was riding down from the north toward the caravan. Reflexively, Flavia spun to her left and saw two riders galloping in from the west. She turned south and, in a space between the tents and the camels, she saw one more horseman coming hard. The east looked clear.

"Robbers!" someone shouted.

Flavia ran back to Morlana. "Up!" she said, and Morlana grabbed her horse's mane and leaped into the saddle. "Back to the fort! Bring the soldiers!"

Without a word, Morlana turned and raced off.

Flavia grabbed her bow and quiver from her saddle.

"No!" the merchant yelled. "Don't fight back! They'll kill us all!"

Then Flavia saw the last thing on earth she wanted to see. The rider from the north had veered east and was now pursuing Morlana before she could bring help, although he probably had no idea that anything as lethal as a Roman cohort lay beyond the ridge. But Morlana's young black gelding was fleeter than the bandit's depleted desert nag, and Flavia was certain she could outrace him.

Flavia ran back toward Artemis, but the merchant hit her on the side of the jaw to stop her fighting the robbers. She dropped like a stunned bird. Still conscious, she tried to clear her vision, while the merchant hurried off with her horse and bow.

She pushed herself to her feet and saw people everywhere standing as still as dead desert trees. They awaited their fate with the hideous fatalism that so infected this land.

Three bandits rode up to the center of the camp. They wore black robes and head-cloths and had swords hanging from their saddles. Flavia suspected they were Judaeans or Idumaeans.

One of the three robbers gave orders calmly, as if he had done this on a hundred occasions. The merchants brought goods forward and spread them out on a blanket before him, like tribute from a fallen kingdom. Doubtless they, too, had done this many times before.

The bandit leader, a burly scar-faced pirate of about fifty seated on a gray mare, smiled with the relaxed magnanimity he could easily afford.

Hoofbeats from the east drew everyone's attention.

Flavia turned and saw the most horrible sight she had ever seen in her life. Suddenly she wished that she could simply die.

The bandit who had chased Morlana was returning, and in place of his own worn out horse he was riding Morlana's black Arabian.

Flavia felt as if she were about to vomit. She sucked back hard, but that could not stop the tears from burning her eyes at the thought of the beautiful young life that she had helped to destroy.

One of the bandits laughed when he saw his friend returning on Morlana's magnificent mount. He galloped out to meet him with an eerie triumphant cry.

As the two comrades raced toward one another, the one riding out began to slow but the rider coming in did not. With a graceful sweep, a long straight sword appeared in the returning rider's hand, and he pivoted to the other rider's right and slashed down through his skull as if it were a slab of rotten mutton.

Flavia screamed for the first time since she was a child.

Dark red was the head-cloth of this new bandit, not black, one side now tied across his face and revealing only his eyes.

"Haritat!" Flavia yelled in near disbelief.

The chieftain charged down the slope toward the center of the camp.

People scattered everywhere, and the camels' guttural wails of protest shot across the desert.

The three remaining bandits bolted from the ring of tents to give themselves space to maneuver.

Flavia ran into the open, but with only her dagger she could do nothing. Still lightheaded, she dropped to one knee and stared in horror at the terrible and hopeless combat.

The three thieves fanned out and galloped off to meet the doomed madman who dared face them all.

One robber's mount was swifter than the other two, and he pulled away from his friends to cut down the dark invader.

Haritat dashed straight at him.

"No!" Flavia shrieked at what seemed to be the chieftain's suicide.

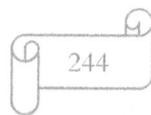

At the instant the thief was upon him, Haritat turned sharply on Morlana's nimble mount, and in a moment he had shot behind the reckless bandit.

The robber pulled violently to the right, and his horse slid and tumbled into the sand as if it had been speared. The rider fell beneath it. Thrashing in terror, the horse scrambled to its feet and bolted away. The half-crushed bandit gagged and choked on blood and struggled to his knees, but Haritat's blade sliced down into his face and ended the horror.

Haritat spun his horse as swiftly as if man and animal were a single being, and now they faced the other two attacking horsemen.

Stunned, the bandits veered, one left and one right, reassessing their tactics against an enemy who had lost his mind.

Suddenly all three riders paused, their snorting horses forming a triangle with Haritat at the top.

The bandit leader, several hundred feet beyond Flavia and to the right, snapped his head toward her. She was the perfect hostage, kneeling as she was in the open, almost daring him. But then he turned away.

Flavia gazed at him in wonder. Brutal thief though he might have been, this man was a warrior, still half-noble in his infamy.

Flavia stood up and tried to push her way past the bewildered camels so she could see, slapping them and yelling to get them out of her way. Four ran off in confusion straight toward the three men locked in a struggle to the death.

The eyes of Haritat swept the field, and then he shouted a word of command to his horse and they streaked off to his right, away from the bandit chief and toward the other robber.

The thief seemed stunned, rigid with fear. Probably he had never been challenged by another armed horseman in his life. In an instant, though, he found his muscles but lost his nerve. He turned and bolted.

Straight toward Flavia he raced. Some of the terrified camels were still bawling in front of her, but the thief was blind to them and to everything but flight. The camels struggled to avoid a collision as they hurried like dazed children out of his path.

Haritat closed with his enemy.

The robber looked over his right shoulder at his relentless pursuer. Then the thief swung to the left, which put Haritat's weapon hand too far away. The desert chieftain dropped his knotted reins onto the horse's neck as casually as if he were on a morning trot, and his sword flew from his right hand to his left as the black Arabian tore up the ground. Abreast of the bandit at last, Haritat slashed sideways into his foe. The bandit's right arm fell away like a chopped branch but Haritat's sword sank even more deeply, halfway into the robber's chest. The bandit plummeted from his horse like a lost soul.

Haritat swung to the north, away from the bandit leader, and then quickly turned east, back toward the fort.

Flavia stared in confusion as Haritat raced up the gentle slope and away.

The bandit leader's horse labored valiantly up the grade in pursuit, but the robber was big and his mount was slow and the distance widened. Soon his animal was winded and failing. In a moment, Haritat would be gone and as safe as he could ever hope to be.

A whirlwind of dust spiraled up around Haritat, and Flavia flinched as she saw it. For an instant there was nothing to see but a great golden cloud, and then, like a launched arrow, the black horse shot back out of the vast vortex of spinning sand swept up by Haritat's pivot. Straight down the grade he charged, the sun now to his rear and the slope falling away before him.

Flavia almost choked as she sucked in air. Before her, two mounted swordsmen hurtled toward each other in a combat without quarter.

The bandit loomed massive and frightening in his saddle as he churned up the slope, but flying toward him was an unstoppable gale.

Morlana's black horse, slick with sweat, glistened like a polished jewel. But this gem was alive, crackling with fire as it thundered down the hill.

Disdaining his reins, Haritat gripped his sword with both hands above his head as he held his seat with only his legs. Like a rippling wave, Haritat's lean and elegant body flowed gracefully in endless and rolling communion with his horse. Many were those who told tales of Haritat, and what he was to each man differed from all others. But Flavia was certain that whatever he was to any and all, he was unquestionably the finest horseman on the face of the earth.

Racing down the incline, Haritat kept to the robber's left to avoid the hand that held the sword. Yet this bandit was wise to the ways of mounted war. He veered to his own left to intersect with Haritat and still slash with his right.

Flavia was unable to breathe. With Haritat scorning his reins, there seemed to be no way to avoid a horrific collision with the bandit's horse or the bandit's blade.

Suddenly Haritat shifted his weight and the black horse stopped. At least twenty feet they slid down the slope, but the magnificent steed retained its footing.

The bandit flew on by, his sword instantly useless as his own horse carried him beyond his enemy.

Still steering with only his legs, Haritat swung around to his right and closed on the robber from behind and to the left.

The bandit's mount struggled on the grade, but the young horse behind him tore up the ground and soon raced alongside the fading animal.

With a mighty slash, Haritat sheared the left side of the bandit's skull from his body, and the chunk of bloody bone and brain flew off into the sand as the husk of the killer fell dead to the earth.

Haritat wheeled about and scanned all directions. Then he sheathed his sword and trotted back to Flavia.

She stared at him in awe.

He slid from the saddle. Covered with dust, he pulled the side of the red head-cloth down from his face and smiled the smile for which so many yearned but so few were blessed to see.

Flavia stepped shakily toward him. "Morlana . . . ." she managed to whisper.

"The Golden One is well."

Flavia slumped against his chest and wept.

"He's an Idumaean," Matthias said, kneeling next to the corpse and examining the face and clothes. He fingered the tip of the arrow protruding from the back of his neck. "Odd . . . ."

Rufio dropped to one knee beside Matthias and then looked questioningly at Haritat.

"This thief was dead before I saw him," Haritat said to Rufio. "He was chasing Morlana when he was shot down by someone here."

"Who could have done it?" Rufio asked.

"I saw no one," Haritat said. "His horse followed Morlana's mount, as running horses will. When she reached me, she shouted to me what had happened and I told her to give me her horse. She took the thief's animal to ride back to the fort to get you and your men."

A rank of ten mounted Roman and Judaean soldiers had lined up off to the side.

Rufio glanced at Flavia and Morlana. Flavia stood behind Morlana with her arms wrapped around the little girl.

Rufio pulled the arrow straight out the back of the robber's neck and wiped it on the dead man's head-cloth. Then he rose to his feet and looked at Haritat. "What I owe you is beyond comprehension."

Haritat was impassive.

"Everything I own is yours," Rufio said. "You have only to ask."

"My entire life has been swords and horses," the chieftain said. "I think Haritat should share his wealth with *you*."

And then the two men smiled slowly into each other's eyes.

44

EITHER FINISH IT OR DO NOT ATTEMPT IT.

ROMAN SAYING

Rufio sat astride his horse near the training ground where Valerius was conducting sword drills in the early morning light. The clever optio had mixed Matthias's men with the Romans so the Jews could learn not only by instruction but by example.

They were progressing quickly, but was that not always the way with Jews? Yet there was so little time. Rufio had no idea what he was going to do with them. Foot soldiers would be lost sheep against the Parthian bowmen. His own men, tested and hardened in a savage battle, had the confidence and mettle to leap into the saddle and be trained by Bellator in the ways of fighting on horseback. But these poor Judaean tyros were too green for that. Their other skills were likewise rudimentary and untried. Certainly by an inspiration from Victoria, Rufio had brought Flavia along, but the Judaeans would have considered it a vile effrontery to be taught archery by a woman, and they would have none of it.

So they seemed prepared for nothing except to be offered as a pauper's sacrifice to a malignant god.

Rufio clicked to his horse and trotted off to the gyrus.

A camel was tethered at either side of the entrance, and three more camels were tied around the outside of the gyrus where they could be smelled by the horses but not seen.

Rufio peered between the gate and the wall and saw Haritat himself working one of the horses with the searing concentration of a Greek geometer. While Rufio waited, two of Haritat's sons walked up with another pair of mounts. Finally, Haritat was satisfied with the chestnut gelding and rested him.

Rufio opened the gate and rode into the gyrus and handed Haritat a water flask.

The Nabataean nodded.

"Would you be willing to help Bellator with the men and leave the horses to your sons? The old stallion doesn't have the stamina he once had."

"I understand."

"Thank you."

"When you train your men, do you handle them gently or harshly?"

Rufio smiled. "Firmly. They don't learn well with coddling — though they might argue otherwise."

"I will work with them."

"My men will profit from a different perspective."

He seemed puzzled by that term. "A word not known to me."

"The angle from which one views things. A Roman cavalryman isn't the same as a desert horseman."

"I see."

Haritat spoke briefly to his sons, and then he and Rufio rode away together.

When they reached the arena, Rufio saw that only Arrianus was there putting the men through their maneuvers.

"The decurion is resting," Arrianus shouted before Rufio could ask. "The heat was affecting him."

Rufio watched his troopers riding the rail of the arena with their arms extended out from their sides and their eyes closed. And why not? Many a horseman in combat had lost his reins and been blinded by the dust of battle.

"You have trained some confident men," Haritat said.

"They were good soldiers before they ever knew me."

Haritat trotted over to the gate. "When you are ready for the next group," he said to Arrianus, "I will take these men to the parade ground."

Arrianus looked to his centurion, and Rufio nodded.

"We will rescue them from the security of the rail," Haritat said. "And then we will teach them to fly."

Morlana came riding up and brought her mount as close to Rufio's side as possible without disturbing his horse.

"Around to the left," Rufio said.

She obeyed, and now the low morning sun hit Rufio, and she could rest in his shadow.

"I believe," Haritat said with the second surprising smile of the morning, "that the Golden One draws from the centurion something more than shade."

Arrianus had finished with his current group of sixteen riders, and they began filing out of the arena.

"Do your men know their right lead from their left?" Haritat asked Rufio. "And how to cue their horse for the lead they want?"

"Yes."

Haritat signaled to the troopers and led them at a trot toward the open parade ground. Rufio and Morlana brought up the rear.

Haritat had the soldiers form a single rank at one edge of the area, and then he trotted off toward the middle of the ground.

"We have a saying," Haritat began in that voice scratched and scored by the churned up sands of a hundred combats. "The breeze that blow's between a horse's ears is the wind of Paradise. No other of Dushara's creatures will sweep you so swiftly from the grasp of death—or so bravely toward it if you so will it. When friends become weak or cowardly or vile, he alone remains. Never will he betray you, abandon you. For a puddle of water and a handful of dry grass and a caress on the brow, he'll carry you across flaming rock to the ends of the earth. He has a heart of sweet myrrh—and hoofs of steel. Thank your gods for it." For a few moments he just gazed at the men while they absorbed that. "Any fool can blunder into battle, and any coward can flee the test. But a man who can strike a blow with force and skill and then retire with speed and grace—that is a man worth fearing. And a horseman worth being." He paused as that penetrated. "Not yet will you work with swords. That will come later. Today you master the most vital skill of all—how to retire from a fallen foe and leave the field or ride to the aid of a comrade."

Rufio watched Haritat closely. He exuded a threatening, half-visible power, like waves of heat rippling off the desert sands.

"Anyone can jerk his reins and hurt his horse and stumble away from an enemy. And fall and be cut like a lamb. Agreed?"

"Agreed," several of the men shouted.

"Instead you will not stagger off but flow away like a drop of oil sliding along a blade. We have little time, so master this or die."

Haritat rode off until he was about a hundred and fifty feet from the rank of riders. He trotted his horse several times in a tight circle and then came back.

"That ring of hoof prints is your goal. You will . . ." He looked across at Rufio. "Your word for the three-beat gallop?"

"Canter," Rufio said.

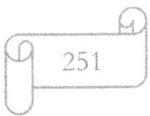

"You will canter to that spot and stop. Do not use your reins to stop. Shift your weight back in your saddle and use a voice command. Then just walk off to right or left to make space for the next rider in line. Keep your sword hand resting on your thigh. Is everyone right-handed? Good. Begin."

They did as he instructed, and every horse but one stopped on a voice command.

"Excellent. Reassemble your rank."

They rode back and lined up again.

"Now for the horseman's art."

Rufio smiled as Haritat paused to increase expectation. He certainly had the master's touch.

"What you will learn now has many names. Some call it the Scythian Spin. Your friends beyond the Tigris insist it is the Parthian Pivot. The name matters not. This time you will roll back to the left. Now—you will canter again to that spot and stop. Pause for an instant to let him bring his hind legs up and get his balance back. If you do not pause briefly, he might just try to scurry off. Not good and not safe. Raise your left hand very slightly and move the reins to the left. Do it just until you can see your horse's left eye—no farther! Imagine you are caressing the cheek of a beautiful woman. Bend your wrist a bit if you have to tighten the left rein. Do *not* pull your right rein across your horse's neck. If you do, you make him drop his shoulder. If he does that, he will not roll straight back but will make a big sweeping turn—and crash into the rider next to you. If he stumbles and falls in battle, the next day you are sweeping the streets of Hell."

Haritat paused and folded his hands across his saddle.

"Simple? Good. At the same time, begin to look to the left. Your horse will see you and feel you. Now he is certain where you want him to go. Your horse will go where you look. Look the wrong way and he will go the wrong way. Shift your weight onto your own left hip. This will cause your horse to shift his weight to his left hind leg, which is what you want for this turn. Move your left leg away from him. With your right heel tap him on the side slightly toward the front. You want his forequarters to pivot, but you need his hindquarters to be tent stakes driven into the ground. Do not kick him—tap him lightly. Pretend you are simply trying to awaken your lover. Again—stop, reins, look, tap, tap, tap. Clear?"

"Clear!" Rufio shouted across the parade ground.

"Now lift your left rein slightly, straighten him out, and push your hands a tiny bit forward toward his ears to give him some slack. If you do not do that, he might hit the bit as he canters off and then refuse to canter the next time you ask. Now ride away. Since the pivot is to the left, take the left lead. Always remember that riding off from a stop is more difficult for the horse than from a walk. So focus your mind. And focus his." Haritat picked up his reins, and the horse cantered away as if he had read his rider's mind.

Haritat rode back and stopped in front of the rank. "It sounds complex. It is not. First rider."

The exercise was not a success. When the horseman pivoted, he jerked the reins too hard. Then as he tried to correct, he overcompensated and the horse took the wrong lead. Fifteen more riders failed with equal skill.

"Haritat lied," the chieftain said. "This cannot be so easy. That is what you are thinking."

The men remained silent.

Haritat gestured to Morlana.

She looked to Rufio.

"Of course," he said.

She rode to the center of the parade ground and stopped beside Haritat. He leaned over and said something in her ear.

She trotted to a place at one end of the rank.

Haritat nodded.

Morlana made a kissing sound to her horse and they cantered away. In little more than a breath, they reached the mark in the sand. The horse stopped and they pivoted with the elegance of dancers and dashed away as though they were racing on air. Her hood blew off and her yellow mane whipped in the wind as she flew back to where she had begun.

Haritat nodded in approval, and Morlana grinned and stroked her horse's neck.

"If the Golden One can do this, why not the men of the Tiber? Shall I have her do it again with her eyes closed? Or shall I get a blind Nabataean and a three-legged horse to show you how men can ride?"

45

THERE IS A GOD INSIDE US.

OVID

Sleep has always been my friend, but last night it taunted me. Morlana was lying beside me at peace, and Paki was sleeping against her. It was very late, but I just stared into the darkness. My mind seemed to be roaring like water falling over a cliff. I rolled onto my side and saw a faint glow coming from the outer room. This was late to be awake even for Rufio. I got out of bed and dressed and went out for the comfort he always gives.

I was startled to see Neko sitting alone at Rufio's desk. I was even more surprised to see the cup of wine beside his hand. He usually reserves wine only for special moments. An arrow lay on the desk in front of him. When he saw me, he immediately stood and found another cup and poured some wine and water for me. After I took it, I told him to sit back down and I got a camp chair and slid it beside the desk.

I love spending time with Neko. I admire his knowledge, but that is a little thing compared to the reassurance I draw from his wisdom. The subtlety of his understanding is always a warm fire on a cold night. And, as Rufio says, Egyptians are the subtlest people in all the East.

"Is something wrong?" I asked him.

Neko smiled, and when he smiles I always feel relieved. "No, something is mystically right."

I smiled back. He enjoys baffling me with his indirect way of speaking.

"Can you share it with me?" I asked.

"I fear you may not yet be prepared," he said.

"Then it's the task of my wise friend to prepare me."

He picked up the arrow from the desk and held it out almost with reverence, and I set down my cup and took it.

"Do you recognize it?" he asked.

"Is this the arrow Rufio pulled out of the thief?"

"It is. Please examine it."

I studied it carefully. The arrowhead had not been cast or hammered from bronze but had been fashioned somehow from a black and shiny material I had never seen before. The edges were extremely sharp and must have sliced through the robber's neck as if they had been passing through nothing stouter than the fleece of a lamb.

"The head baffles you," Neko said. "It is a substance called obsidianus. It is a sturdy glass formed inside the heart of a volcano."

"What is that?" I asked.

"A great mountain that shoots fire."

"I didn't know there were mountains like that."

"Here there are not."

I did not know what to say.

"But the shaft," Neko said. "There lies its secret."

I inspected it and ran my fingers along the surface but found nothing strange about it.

"Ah, my mistress looks and touches but does not see."

"But what is there to see?" I asked.

"The wood."

I still did not understand.

"The shaft is maple," Neko said. "There are no maple trees here. There are no maple trees within hundreds of miles of here."

"Then the man who shot this came from far off?"

"Farther than any man has ever come."

"You're confusing me," I said. "Where do maple trees grow?"

"They flourish in many localities. In many lands. One of the places they grow is in Greece. In Thessaly." Neko's gaze frightened me. "On the slopes of Mount Pelion."

I stared back at him until I realized my hands were trembling. I set the arrow down as though it might burn my fingers.

"No, you must keep it," Neko said. "That lethal dart is not here because of killers and thieves. It is here because of you."

"Another cool evening in the desert," Rufio said and handed Matthias a cup of heated wine.

Neko was looking over some scrolls on Rufio's desk, so the two soldiers went to the small table toward the back of the room. The pair of rough chairs had been softened by rugs Neko had bought in Hezrail.

Rufio pointed to a chair and lit the oil lamp next to the red porphyry statue of Victoria and then sat down.

"How are your men?" Rufio asked in a casual tone.

"Well. Their diet has never been so good. Some are putting on weight."

"Many of them were too thin. We fix things like that."

"Italians know how to eat," Matthias said with a smile.

"It's our alternate religion."

Matthias laughed. "Then you're all very pious."

Rufio sipped his wine. "I have a military problem I'd like you to help me solve."

"Centurion, how could I ever do that?"

"You have ability. And call me Rufio."

"I will."

"You have a quality I noticed at the very beginning . . . ."

"You mean my vast knowledge of tactics?" he said in self-mockery.

"Knowledge?" Rufio said with a snort of contempt. "Knowledge is never something to admire. It's simply an acquisition. Like clothing or horses or weapons. Even fools have knowledge."

"But what can I give you?"

"The best soldiers aren't Aristotle in armor. They don't wrestle with deeper thoughts or subtle ways. The finest warriors don't think more, *but they do pay attention more.*"

Matthias remained quiet.

"You, my friend, pay attention. I've seen it every day since I've known you."

Matthias took a sip of wine and stared off in silence. Finally he said, "I never noticed that in myself."

"It's because you pay attention to everything except yourself. Which is good."

"You flatter me."

"I don't flatter anyone."

"What's the problem you want to solve?"

Rufio glanced at Neko, who was rubbing his eyes.

"Go to bed, weary scholar."

"Yes," he said and began rolling up a scroll.

"Leave it. Time for rest."

"Thank you," Neko said. "May I get you more wine?"

"Sleep."

He bowed gently and went off to bed.

Rufio gazed dreamily at the flame flickering in the clay lamp next to Victoria.

After a long silence, Matthias said, "Rufio . . . ."

"I was just thinking, not dozing. These people out here are so vulnerable. Overripe fruit ready to be knocked off the tree. They have nothing—and yet everybody wants it."

"They can't afford weapons to defend themselves."

"I don't mean that. Their drive is gone. Whatever happened to the spirit of Solomon?"

"You know about Solomon?"

"I read too much."

"Herod outlawed spirit and drive. He's gelded his people to make himself feel safe. But he never feels safe."

"It's one of the saddest things I've ever seen."

"But you're here to protect them."

"No we're not. We're here to shore up the weak flank of an uncertain kingdom. Any protection these people get is just an accident."

"Rufio, you'll never be able to convince me that you ever do *anything* by accident."

He could not help smiling. "Well, perhaps. Now as to this problem, there's a group of soldiers who can ride but have never tasted battle on or even near horses. They carry swords, but they're not really infantry. They can shoot bows, but they have only the most basic skills." Rufio's eyes nailed Matthias to the chair. "What on earth am I to do with them?"

"Allow them to fight with honor."

"How?"

"By using their best skill."

"Which is what?"

"The bow."

"They need more work. Daily practice."

"They'll give it."

"How do I ask for it? These aren't Romans. They're a desert race. Touchy as vipers."

"Let their commander demand it of them for you."

"Will he?"

"I'm certain of it."

Rufio finished his wine. "See what I meant? You've solved it."

Matthias smiled and then ended it with a sigh.

"Tired?"

"Rufio, their commander is worried. I know him well."

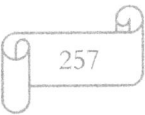

"What worries him?"

"He fears . . . he fears showing fear."

"He won't."

"How do you know that?"

"Trust me."

"I do. . . ."

"But?"

Matthias smiled. "That's not what I thought you'd say."

"What did you expect?"

"I assumed you'd say that everyone is afraid in battle."

"I'd never say that."

"Why not?"

"Because it's ridiculous."

Matthias searched Rufio's eyes. "I don't understand."

"Not every warrior is fearful in battle."

"How can that be true?"

"There are some soldiers who never fear the battlefield. Never."

Rufio went across the room to the brazier, its fire banked now, and took the pitcher of warmed wine next to it. He got the pitcher of water from his desk and mixed the two drinks in his cup and poured some more wine for Matthias as well.

"There are two types of soldiers who are never afraid," Rufio said, sitting back down. "They're rare, but scarcity doesn't mean they don't exist. Any thoughts on who they might be?"

"I'm lost."

"That's all right. You're young. There's still much to learn." He set his cup onto the table. "The first type of soldier who's fearless is the one who believes that, no matter what happens, he won't be killed. And also that he'll survive unhurt."

Matthias looked skeptical. "How can there be anyone like that?"

"Those soldiers are uncommon, but not as uncommon as you think."

"You've known men like that?"

"I have."

"Were any of them ever killed anyway? Despite what they believed?"

"Yes."

"So they were wrong."

"They were wrong—but that doesn't mean all of them were wrong."

Matthias looked off into the shadows. "I can't comprehend that."

"You will."

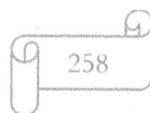

He looked back at Rufio. "What's the other type?"

"The rarest of all. And the opposite of the first. It's the soldier who believes that, regardless of what he does, he's doomed. He's certain he'll be killed in battle. And—."

"But that's not rare at all. There are many—."

"You didn't let me finish. The rare part is that he's resigned himself to it. He's accepted it. So worry and fear are gone. He's calm now and at peace—and so he fights with a serenity denied to normal men. It makes him the most lethal creature on earth. This is a very strange and a very frightening man."

"Men like that exist?"

"They do."

"Have you ever known any?"

"Only four."

"And were they killed as they believed they would be?"

"All four lived to retire. Two have since died. One of the others lives in Spain and one in Rome."

"So they were wrong, too. I mean about being killed."

"They were wrong."

"So you're saying that the bravery of the two bravest kinds of men was based on ignorance."

"I'm not saying that at all. In the first group, some were right."

"The ones who lived."

"Yes."

"But what if it was just chance that they survived?"

"It was not."

"How can anyone be sure?"

"I know." The intensity in Rufio's voice caused Matthias to pull back slightly into his chair.

"I understand," he said softly.

Rufio finished his wine. "We both need sleep."

Matthias stood up.

"Thank you for your help with my problem," Rufio said, standing. "May I make a suggestion?"

"You may."

"Flavia has set up an area to teach Morlana to shoot her bow." He smiled. "It's big enough to share."

"Thank you."

Matthias almost tripped over Flavia, who was sitting on the ground in the darkness outside the entrance.

"I thought you'd gone to bed," Rufio said as she came in and closed the door.

"I was looking at the stars."

She sat in one of the chairs by the little table. "Morlana went to sleep and I stayed with her for a while. But I wasn't tired, so I went outside."

Rufio sat back down.

"Are you going to bed?" Flavia asked.

"Soon."

"Will you stay up with me a little longer?"

"Oh, Flavia, not tonight. . . ."

Her eyelids lowered in a telling look. "Do I tire you, centurion?"

"You'd tire Hercules."

"That's not what I meant," she said, laughing. "I was just teasing."

"I thank Venus for her mercy."

"I heard what you were saying to Matthias and I want to ask you about it."

"It's good you're not a Parthian spy. I should post a sentry by my door."

"Your voice carries like a Sequani spirit."

"What do you want to talk about?"

"You."

"Why?"

"I want to know something."

"Something or everything?"

She reached across and slid her right hand into his. "I want to know all your secrets."

"You already do."

"No, just some. Not all."

"Well, my sentries are napping. What do you need to know?"

"Are you one of those two types of soldiers you described?"

He smiled. "What do you think?"

"Please tell me you're not the second kind. The one who believes he's going to be killed."

"Of course I'm not. How could I be? I could never—what's wrong?"

"I don't know," she said, wiping her eyes. "I just couldn't bear the idea that you felt that way."

"I thought you already knew—I'm the first kind."

"You are?"

"That's why I'm not nearly as brave as you think I am."

"You'll never convince me of that."

"I told you before—I'm going to die in my bed."

"You're certain?"

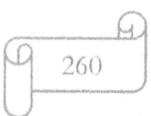

"I'd never lie to you."

"My love, I would so like to be sure."

"You can be," he said and lowered his head toward the red statue on the table beside them.

"Victoria?"

"Yes."

"But how do you know she'll protect you forever?"

"I have faith in her."

Flavia sighed and eased back into her chair. "I wish I could share that feeling."

"Belief isn't a feeling. It's a decision."

Her eyes showed her confusion.

"Faith in something isn't some sort of yearning," he said. "It's not like hunger or thirst—something that just comes. Belief in something is a choice."

"That's all?"

"All? It's much."

"Then how do you do it? How do you believe?"

"You decide to. It's not like mathematics, where you can be sure of the answer. Belief is a risk. It takes courage and it takes will. Believers are brave. It's the skeptics who are cowards."

"Can you teach me?"

"I'm not sure it can be taught."

Rufio draped the rug from his chair across her lap against the chill.

She kissed his hand, and he smiled with his eyes.

"Can you tell me how you began? How you first started to have belief in Victoria?"

He went across the room and put more wood into the brazier and then sat back down with her.

"My mother died when I was very young. I don't think I ever told you that. When she died, my father gave me that statue. It looks as new as last week, but it's very old. He'd carried it everywhere. To battlefields at the edge of the earth. When he handed it to me, he told me to look to Victoria now as my mother. And I have."

"Do you ever doubt?"

"Doubt what? That she's really there?"

"Yes."

"No, I don't. There have been times, though, that I've doubted she was still protecting me. Times on the battlefield that I was certain I was about to be killed. It happened once last year. But that's just human weakness."

"Do you think she was angry at you?"

"For doubting?"

"Yes."

"No," he said, laughing. "Mothers—especially adoptive mothers—are very lenient with their wayward sons. Besides, she's a goddess. She's wise enough to know that belief doesn't mean there's never any doubt. Belief is simply what makes doubt bearable."

"Did you ever see her?" she whispered.

"No, but I've felt her hand on my shoulder and touching my heart."

"How often do you speak to her?"

"I might as well try to count the stars."

"Every day then?"

"Oh, yes. And I draw strength from her, as I do from you."

Flavia pulled up the rug from her lap and around her shoulders and wrapped herself in silence.

After several minutes, Rufio said, "What's wrong, wild woman?"

"I'm just so happy—I don't want this to end."

"Life among sand and scorpions?"

"You know what I mean."

"Who says it has to end?"

"I asked Neko about that once. If he thought we were going to live forever."

"Of course he believes that. He's an Egyptian."

"What about Romans?"

"Depends on the Roman. Plenty of philosophers—."

"Oh, I'm tired of hearing about philosophers. What do you think? Do you think we have a spirit inside us?"

"I do. There's a reason our language has a word for it."

"What do you think will happen?"

"To me? Well, I can tell you what I *hope* will happen when I die. I want to stand before Mars and see him look down and nod at me in satisfaction and say, 'Rufio.' Then he'll smile and say, 'I know you well—Victoria has spoken of you.' And then I'll know I'm in Paradise."

Flavia came over and sat on his lap and rested her head on his shoulder. "You have such beautiful thoughts. And no one knows but I."

He kissed her on the forehead. "Keep them locked away within you."

46

THE SUN SHINES EVEN ON THE WICKED.

SENECA

I noticed that two or three times a week Rufio meets with every tent group of every century. He does this very casually. He visits with them in their barracks or when they are drilling. He jokes with them or just shares some water with them. I believe he enjoys this more than any of his other tasks. He always comes back smiling. I mentioned this once to Neko, and he said that these visits are not casual at all. He said that this is the way Rufio checks on the health of his men. He realizes that soldiers who are ill might hesitate to complain to their centurion, so he just informally stops by to confirm their condition with his own eyes.

Besides this, Rufio has charged each centurion, as well as Matthias, with providing daily medical reports on the men. So far, eleven of them have been overcome by the heat, but they recovered in a few hours. All were Romans. Matthias's men are immune to this cooking pot. They are like Celtic steel, indifferent to the hottest tempering. Rufio was very angry at the men overwhelmed by the heat, especially after Matthias told him that once they had been stricken like that they would be more likely to collapse in the future. Rufio laid into his men with a verbal vinestick about not drinking enough. There have also been seventeen scorpion stings. These are very painful, and some of the men, including Judaeans, suffered from terrible muscle cramps for hours afterward. No one has died, and Matthias told Rufio that it is usually children or old people who are killed by stings, although he has known a few young soldiers who have not survived. Fortunately, there have been no viper bites to the men.

Something that has affected both Romans and Judaeans is the eruption of large boils on their skin, especially on their faces. After a while the flesh looks like it is decaying, and the sores take a very long time to heal. No one knows what causes them. They leave terrible scars, and one can see some old pits in the flesh beneath Matthias's thin beard. The Judaeans refer to these horrible wounds with contempt as "Herod's badges."

Arrianus supplies continual information to Rufio on the condition of the horses. They are much tougher than the men, even Judaean men. The horses' most persistent enemy is the smallest of all. In this arid land, flies are desperate for water, and so they cluster around the horses' eyes to suck out what moisture they can. This can inflame the rims of the horses' eyes and make the animals suffer terribly. Morlana is teaching the soldiers how to make fly fringes to prevent this. These are lengths of yarn or simple strips of cloth that attach to the brow band on the horses' bridles. These fringes allow the horses to see while still keeping the flies off them. The fringes on the horses of the Nabataeans are brightly colored and often have tassels on the ends. Other than some occasional lameness, there has been only one important horse incident. A snake had sought shelter underneath a mound of medica hay in one of the pens, and when a horse came over to eat from the pile the snake struck at him and bit him in the upper lip. In just a few minutes the horse's face swelled to the point where his nostrils sealed and he suffocated.

"I understand the training was excellent yesterday," Crus said, approaching the arena in the early morning half-light.

"Yes, tribune." Arrianus tossed away the stray stones he had picked up in his daily grooming of the surface. "Haritat is a magnificent horseman. He has the mind of a warrior and the heart of a stallion."

"You're beginning to speak as he does," Crus said, laughing.

Arrianus seemed to force a smile.

"If it went so well, though, why were the men so surly last night?"

"You know how soldiers are, tribune."

"I do know. I fought beside them in Gaul. Now tell me what's wrong."

"May we go someplace more private?"

Crus led the way to the gyrus. Arrianus closed the gate behind them and they went over to the plank wall and sat down against it.

"Haritat doesn't know how to speak to Italians, tribune. He has no humor, or else he hides it. Never even a lewd remark to lighten the tension. He's wise but he's harsh—like the land he lives in."

"Do you think he should pamper them?"

"No, I don't mean that. But he should show them some respect. Treat them like comrades. Every man here has fought in at least one bloody campaign. Some have fought in several. Beat them with rods if you need to, but don't speak to them as if they're backward children. Roman soldiers will accept anything except a sneer."

"I understand what you're saying, but those fluffy kittens are going to endure what I order them to endure."

Arrianus's face was blank. "Yes, tribune."

"Did they learn much?"

"They did."

"Then they've done their duty."

"They'll do more than that if . . ."

"If we coddle them?"

Arrianus remained silent.

"Do you think Rufio would treat them any more gently?"

"No, tribune. Did you know that on the day Rufio took command of the cohort he almost choked Valerius to death?"

"You're exaggerating."

"Any man in the cohort can verify it. And then he promoted him to optio. Just a few months ago, he made me sleep outside the fort in the snow—and he fed me barley like an animal. Now I'm in charge of these horses. I had some experience, but Rufio didn't know how much. He didn't care."

"I see."

"I wouldn't have thought that was so smart a year ago, but I do now."

"Why?"

"Because I've lived ten years in the last year."

Crus laughed. "Haven't we all?"

"Tribune, I admire Haritat very much. He's obsessed with horses. But Rufio is obsessed with men. If he needs someone for a specific task, he doesn't write a list of qualifications. He looks into a man's heart and then makes his decision."

"Risky behavior for a commander."

"I know, tribune. Rufio doesn't choose men who are qualified. He qualifies the men he chooses. I've never seen that before. In any centurion. In any man."

Crus smiled. "I guess we can agree that Rufio is not just any man." He stood up. "When I walk out that gate, I'm going to forget this discussion ever took place. You're to do the same."

"Yes, tribune."

"And you're free to tell the men that the tribune said if he suspects any more complaints against Haritat, they won't be eating barley. They'll be eating horse shit."

Crus turned and left the gyrus.

As soon as Rufio washed and dressed every morning, he was out with his horse. Long before his own breakfast, he made sure his gray Arab had been fed and watered.

Rufio knew that skill with horses in a military sense had come late to Italians, which was why the finest Roman cavalry was still comprised of Gauls—and even of some Germans who had been enticed to submit to the terrible yoke of civilized behavior. So Rufio had decided to lead by example and to show his younger men, who someday would be older men instructing *their* younger men, the proper priorities in the life of a military horseman.

Arrianus and Morlana were always on duty even earlier than Rufio, and he checked with them daily on the conditions of the mounts. Any animals that were sore or somehow off were allowed to rest until they recovered their health and their spirit. Rufio and Arrianus taught each of the men how to treat cuts and abrasions on the animals with the same poultices that Rufio's favorite Greek doctor in Gaul had concocted for his soldiers.

"Optio!" Rufio said as Valerius came by the pens with an armful of medica.

"Centurion."

"Let your horse feed for a half-hour and then tack him up. You're taking a day off and riding with me to Hezrail. Tell Metellus he's in command of the century."

Rufio returned to his quarters, where Flavia was filling two water flasks.

"Take four," Rufio said. "And keep your hoods on at the archery field. It's going to be hot today."

"Don't worry," Flavia said with a smile. "I won't let her burn up. I love her as much as you do."

Rufio said nothing.

Flavia laughed softly to herself and turned away to get two more flasks.

"I'm going to Hezrail," Rufio said and took his swordbelt off the desk.

"Alone? I mean other than with Victoria."

"Valerius. And don't forget," he said, tapping the top of his head with two fingers. "Hoods."

The only trail between the fort and Hezrail was the one the troops had made on arrival. Rufio and Valerius eased their horses onto it at a walk. Both men wore white Nabataean head-cloths.

"I think the men were hoping you'd be in the arena with them today," Valerius said.

"Are they weary?"

"Sore and weary."

"I want them trained to the fullest. Haritat is a better horseman than I'll ever be. That dark chieftain nursed at a mare's tit."

"And Bellator is merciless."

"The men of the Second Cohort didn't join the army to find mercy. When it's time for blade work, Bellator will train them. He knows far more about fighting from horseback than I'll ever know. The two old horsemen can train horsemen."

"Is that the only reason?"

"Should I have another?"

Valerius laughed. "You never do anything for a single reason."

Rufio stroked his horse's neck as they walked along. "What's the most important thing about our wooden training swords?"

That clearly caught Valerius off guard. "Our swords?"

"Yes."

"I suppose that they're twice as heavy as our metal swords."

Rufio smiled. "Bellator and Haritat are my wooden swords. After some time with those two fanatics in the arena, the men will think that facing the Parthians is like lying by the sea at Capri."

The two horsemen climbed higher in the low rolling hills. The early sun, still deceptively mild, had transformed the Judaean wilderness into a soft and stunning vision of alluring reddish gold.

"I hate the desert," Rufio said, indifferent to its seductions. "It's not the heat and the snakes and the scorpions. The desert is a death trap for armies."

Rufio scanned the distance for any movement, but all was still.

"Crassus learned that—before the Parthians hacked off his head. Fighting in the sands is like battling on the sea. No matter how many troops you field, you can always be flanked. Especially when your enemy is on horseback."

"But we're on horseback, too," Valerius said.

"The Jews are not."

"What do you mean? Matthias and—."

"Not him. The people in Hezrail. You and I are going there today to tell Simon something no Roman soldier should ever have to tell another man."

Valerius said nothing.

"The irony is that our own men are in a better position than they've ever been. For once, we can vacate the battlefield if we have to. We're outnumbered, but if the Parthians turn our flanks or push us back, we can withdraw to the fort. There we're invulnerable. No cavalry force knows how to lay a siege. Least of all these Parthians. And we have food and water far beyond their means. They'll dry up and crumble while we laugh at them."

"But . . . ?"

"But what about the people of Hezrail? There's never any peace for these Jews. Never."

"I don't understand what you mean. There's peace in Judaea now."

Rufio's laugh was harsh. "Walk the streets of Rome. Or Ostia. That's real peace. This? This isn't peace. This is just the absence of war."

"My wise centurion will have to explain his Greek paradox to his humble optio."

"The Jews' god put them here. *Here*, of all places—at the gateway between the two great halves of the world. Their god should have known more about geography. There can never be true peace here. It's as if two people with equal strength—Augustus and Phraates—are pulling on opposite ends of a rope. Judaea is the midpoint. Perfectly stable, never moving—and taut to the point of agony. Forever."

Rufio took a drink from his flask to wash away the bitter dust.

"Today, I have to tell Simon that I cannot promise we can do anything but watch him and his people die. If a thousand Parthians overwhelm us, if the invincible Romans need to concede the field to their enemies—if we have to let go of the rope—those savages will sweep around the fort and swoop on his helpless people. They have no weapons, no horses. No hope. They'll all fall beneath the arrows of barbarian Asiatics."

"We've been outnumbered before."

"We're *always* outnumbered. But this time there are no reserves. If we have to withdraw, all those people die."

After a long silence, Valerius finally said, "If we weren't here, they would die anyway."

"But we *are* here."

"Isn't a commander's primary responsibility to his men?"

"You're a good soldier, Valerius," Rufio said and stopped his horse and looked across at his optio. "But a Roman's *greatest* responsibility is to his dignity, to his honor—and to the honor of Rome."

"But we're not abandoning that."

"Don't lie to yourself. We're abandoning everything. *Everything*—if we let the little girl drown in the well."

They reached the top of the hill, and below lay the mud and stone village of Hezrail. To Rufio, it might as well have been a plucked game bird waiting for the jackals.

"Rufio." Valerius pointed into the distance beyond the village.

Five horsemen were riding through the valley toward Hezrail.

"Do you think they're from the group that Haritat killed?" Valerius asked.

"I doubt it. Look how badly they sit their mounts. And they look haggard. These are pathetic."

"There's not much for them to take from here," Valerius said. "Lamb. Some water."

Rufio gazed at the riders. "Well, my friend, if they're thirsty, how about if we give them a taste of the Tiber?"

He pointed to a narrow ravine from which they could approach the village unobserved.

"Keep it at a walk," Rufio said as they began their descent.

One of the bandits had already gotten to the village and was shouting orders. His accent sounded Idumaean.

In the early sun, an outcrop at the end of the ravine cast a shadow across the opening.

Rufio and Valerius pulled up and watched from the blue half-light.

The five robbers had dismounted near the well. Four of them had gathered up some simple goods and a few sheep. Old Simon stood between them and a cluster of villagers. Noise behind them caused them to turn, and they saw the fifth thief pulling along two young women toward the pile of pathetic booty.

Rufio saw that the thieves had posted no guards or sentries and seemed as oblivious as scavengers picking over bones. Amateurs.

"They're a haggard lot," Valerius said. "Except for that one."

The youngest thief wore a white, sun-bleached tunic and green trousers with a belt holding a rather feeble looking sword. His long hair was neatly kept by a leather headband. He stood beside a fine chestnut Turanian mare. A hornbow in a camel hide case hung from the saddle.

"Fortuna can be cruel," Rufio said.

"To the Jews?"

"Well, sometimes to them. But today to their enemies." Rufio smiled and looked at Valerius. "Ten-year-old boys are terrible creatures, don't you think? The way they torment young girls with all sorts of pranks. Scaring them for no good reason. I was always good at that." Rufio tightened his fingers around the reins. "Now take a deep seat."

Valerius sank farther down into his saddle and took his reins with both hands.

Without further warning, Rufio let loose a hideous feline shriek that sounded like a cat getting its tail crushed by a wagon wheel. His horse shied sideways, as did Valerius's mount, but the other five horses bolted in terror and streaked off together into the hills.

The Romans shot from the ravine. Without being told, Valerius swung around to the left and hemmed in the bandits from the opposite side.

Rufio closed from the right. Instead of forming a line to confront their enemy, the thieves bunched together. Fools.

The apparent leader, older than the others, pulled a dagger from a belt sheath and held it against Simon's side. The bandit was about forty and still had three or four teeth. He seemed surprised that the Romans failed to realize that the old man and the two women were ready captives.

Rufio walked his horse slowly forward to within a few feet of the leader, and Valerius tightened the ring from the other direction.

More villagers rushed out of their homes at the sound of the commotion.

"Cen—."

"Silence!" Rufio shouted to Simon. "You steal from people as poor as these?" Rufio said to the bandit chief.

"Shall we bargain?" the robber asked with the arrogance of hostage takers everywhere.

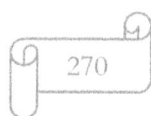

Rufio slid his sword from its scabbard. "With what? What do you have that I could possibly want?"

"Aren't you Romans?"

"We are."

"Then these people are your allies."

"You're not threatening Rome. You're frightening an old man and two girls."

"Let us take food and water, and I'll spare them."

"Any silver in your bags?"

"I'll divide what we have. A fair bargain."

"Simon?" Rufio asked.

The old man looked at the terrified young women. They had wrapped their arms around one another in the only security they could find.

"If they release these girls," Simon said, "let them take the food. I'll go as a hostage. Give them what they want."

"Not what they deserve?" Rufio said.

Rufio thrust his blade into the center of the robber's face and it split like a festered boil. He crumpled with hardly a sound.

The thief beside the women groped for his dagger, but Valerius's sword point sank into the side of his neck. Blood shot from an artery and he fell gurgling and flailing and then lay still.

Rufio slid from his horse. "Weapons."

His voice was gentle and relaxed, and so all the more frightening.

The sword and dagger belts of the three younger men hit the ground.

"You . . ." —Rufio pointed to the bandit wearing the headband— "Go with Valerius and catch the horses. Try to escape and Valerius will ride you down and kill you. The other two of you drag off these creatures and bury them in the desert. Don't defile the village with this offal." Rufio wiped his blade on one of the corpses and sheathed his sword.

By now, most of the villagers not tending their flocks had congregated near the well.

"Thank you," Simon said. He seemed barely able to breathe. "It was good you chose to visit us today."

"Happenstance," Rufio answered as he watched the thieves haul off the two bodies.

"I don't believe in happenstance," Simon said.

"Simon, how many live here?"

"About two hundred."

Rufio gazed at the crowd. A young couple had pushed to the front of the group, and the woman held a little girl in her arms. The child had a fresh bruise on her forehead. She smiled at him and he smiled back.

"If our enemies get past us, we cannot defend this village," Rufio said. "Do your people trust us enough to evacuate to our fort on short notice? We have space, and you'll be safe there."

"After what Metellus did for little Miriam, and after today, I believe they would trust you with anything. The centurion is not a typical Roman, if I may say that."

Rufio glanced again at Miriam and her parents and then looked back at Simon. "Say anything you like, but I'm the most typical Roman you've ever known. No, on second thought, you can't say anything you like. Don't mention Pompeius's horse."

Simon laughed, and it was startling coming from his serious face. "Agreed."

47

AS LONG AS WE ARE AMONG HUMANS, LET US BE HUMANE.

SENECA

"Your prisoner, centurion," Crus said and sat behind Rufio's desk. "Proceed."

Rufio pointed to one of the two camp chairs in front of the desk, and the prisoner sat. Rufio took the other chair.

"Your name."

"Yahlavi," he answered with a tremor in his voice.

"How did you get that?" Rufio gestured to a yellow and purple bruise on his left cheek.

He hesitated. "I fell off my horse."

"A Parthian fell off his horse? Let's understand where we are. I'm going to ask you a few questions. Not very many. I want you to answer truthfully. If you do, you'll be on your way before the sun sets. Your horse is being fed now, and he'll be watered. Then we'll give you some provisions and you'll go. Understand?"

"Yes."

"But if I suspect even a single lie, the conversation is finished. I'll have you nailed to a cross next to your two friends outside Hezrail. They're waiting for you out there in the sun."

Yahlavi stared at him in horror. "You crucified them?"

"No, the day they became bandits they crucified themselves."

Neko came in with a pitcher and some cups.

"But it's a hot day," Rufio said, taking a sip of cool spring water. "They won't suffer up there for long. They'll be dead in two or three hours. If you stand outside the gate, you might be able to hear their moaning on the wind."

Neko handed a cup of water to Yahlavi.

"Some of my men are hacking a couple of tamarisk limbs for you right now," Rufio said. "If you decide to be a fool."

"You're telling me to betray my country."

"You're a deserter," Crus said with contempt. "You've already betrayed your country."

Rufio pointed again to Yahlavi's cheek.

"One of my officers struck me."

"Why?"

"He said I was a poor soldier."

"And then you proved him right by deserting?"

"Yes," he answered so faintly that Rufio could barely hear him.

"Were you with the troops who are coming here?"

"I was."

"Is it a full *drafsh*?"

"More than nine hundred men."

"Any heavy cavalry with lances?" Crus asked.

"None."

"Why not?" Rufio asked.

"The nobles won't bleed for Phraates. They think he's mad."

"And the bowmen?" Rufio said.

"They'll bleed for silver."

"When will they reach Judaea?"

"I don't know."

Rufio stared at him for a moment and then began to stand.

"I swear! I don't know!"

Rufio sat back down. "Who is in command?"

"Durena," he answered, as if that alone were enough.

"Who is that?" Rufio asked.

"One of our finest commanders."

"On a raid like this?" Rufio said. "Why?"

"He is in disgrace. He hopes to redeem himself"

Rufio looked to his Egyptian scholar standing across the room. Neko nodded.

"Is he the one who struck you?" Rufio asked.

"Never. Durena is a good man. A great man. Aridates hit me."

"One of his officers?"

"Yes."

"Why is Durena in disgrace?"

"Because of his greatness. Phraates fears usurpers."

"So he brought false charges?"

"Yes."

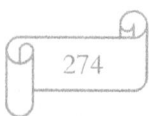

Rufio shook his head and looked at Crus. "It never ends."

"Durena will die even if he wins," Yahlavi said. "Aridates will see to that. We all believe he is Phraates' spy. And his assassin."

"And does Durena suspect this?" Rufio asked.

"Durena knows all."

"And yet he's coming just the same?"

"He's coming."

"Come in," Crus said.

Rufio turned and saw Haritat in the doorway.

"I heard about your captive," Haritat said and entered the office. "Your men are almost finished with his cross."

"You gave your word!" Yahlavi said to Rufio.

Haritat turned to Crus. "May I ask him a question?"

"As many as you like."

Haritat approached the Parthian, and the fear in Yahlavi's eyes turned to terror under the glare of the desert chieftain.

"How many camels?" Haritat asked.

"At least a hundred," Yahlavi answered without hesitation.

Haritat turned to Rufio. "May we speak this evening?"

"Join me then."

After Haritat left, Rufio nodded to Neko and the Egyptian came over and stood before Yahlavi.

"Up," Rufio said.

Yahlavi stood.

"Go with my servant."

Yahlavi looked at Crus but saw no mercy there.

"Go," the tribune said.

Yahlavi stepped uncertainly across the room and through the doorway with Neko behind him.

"I'd say he's too scared to lie," Crus said.

"I agree."

"Where are they going?"

"Neko will give him a meal and then take him to the bathhouse. The people out here simply don't bathe enough."

Crus laughed.

"Except for these Jews," Rufio said. "They're always purifying themselves. All you have to do is look at them cross-eyed and they hurry off to remove the taint with a quick ablution."

Crus laughed even harder. "So did you really have some of your men make a cross for this bandit?"

"Oh, yes. You cannot be subtle with these Asiatics. It's like dealing with petulant children. With a bad temper and shit on their ass."

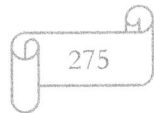

"Ah, I see. And does that apply to Haritat?"

Rufio smiled. "Nothing applies to Haritat."

Crus hesitated and then said, "And what about the other two—the two you had crucified?"

"The centurion doesn't understand the tribune's question."

Crus stared into his eyes for a moment. "Very well. I'll defer to your judgment."

"Thank you."

"Would you like me to join you and Haritat later?"

"I'd be grateful."

Crus stood up. "Until tonight then."

North of the gyrus, one of the countless Judaean hills, barren as a baked skull, rose fifty feet above the surrounding terrain and formed an excellent barrier to absorb ill-shot arrows. Matthias had set up his rows of target hay bales here. By a curious turn of fate, Flavia had chosen an area about twenty feet to the right of it to position a bale for Morlana's archery lesson. Rufio smiled as he stood nearby and watched.

Flavia spoke to Morlana a bit more loudly than necessary, and the still desert air carried each of her wise words of instruction to the Judaean soldiers on her left. Naturally, thought Rufio, they were not listening to this presumptuous female, and a barbarian one at that. Of course, if they happened to overhear her . . . well, that could not be helped.

The Jews were doing well. They had riddled the targets with arrows, and rarely did an arrow fly over a bale and strike the hill beyond. That would be accuracy enough. Matthias's troops would not need to pick out individual targets among the Parthians. Simply shooting into their mass would be lethal.

On the other hand, Morlana seemed unwilling to settle for so little. At a range of about fifty feet, her arrows repeatedly pierced a red cloth not larger than the spread of a man's hand. Rufio was unsure that Mallius would have been proud of her for this achievement. Her father had not seemed to notice her much at all. But Rufio felt a pride in her that he knew he had no right feeling, and even more difficulty explaining.

"Rest and take a drink," Rufio said as he approached her and Flavia.

Morlana grinned as she always did when she saw him. She opened her water flask and offered it to him first.

He took a small sip and handed it back.

"When you're finished here," he said to her, "I want you to go and look after three horses. Arrianus will show you which ones. He's already fed and watered them. Curry them, check their feet, and tack them up."

She looked to Flavia.

"We've had enough for today," Flavia said. "You're a strator first, you know."

Morlana smiled and gestured for Rufio to bend over.

"I love you," she whispered in his ear, and then she ran back to the fort.

"Even the soft words of a little girl travel in the desert," Flavia said with a smile.

"How are your students doing?" he said, ignoring her remark.

"Students?"

"The ones to my back."

"They're excellent. They learn very quickly."

"Jews always do. If they had enough discipline to fit on the head a stylus, they could conquer the world."

"Do you want me to come out here every morning?"

"Yes. Morlana has other duties, but give her at least a half-hour with the bow. She obviously loves it. Do it for her sake." He snapped his head toward the soldiers behind him. "And for theirs."

Rufio walked off, being careful not even to glance in the direction of the Judaeans. He knew that everyone, even allies, needed an occasional rest from the searing gaze of Rome.

"Have you retired?" Rufio asked Bellator standing near the horse pens.

"Ah, can there be no rest for the poor old decurion?"

"You're neither poor nor old," Rufio said as he approached. "Whether or not you're a decurion has always been debatable. Who's with the men?"

"Haritat is working the Second Century in the arena." Bellator leaned against one the rails. "I've never seen them as enthusiastic as they are now."

"What's the exercise?"

Bellator smiled. "The Scythian Spin."

"They're enjoying that?" Rufio said.

"Ever since this morning." Bellator grinned, and it was pleasant to see the old cur smile, although Rufio concealed his feelings with his usual metallic glare.

"I'd heard a rumor that the men were unhappy with Haritat," Rufio said.

"They were."

"Unhappy with what?"

"You know how he his. Wise but harsh."

"That's nothing. They've said it about me many times."

"Oh, no. Never. Wise but hard. Never harsh."

"Stop feeding me with a fingertip. What happened?"

"I spoke to the old rogue about it before the men got there. He seemed stunned—if I can read him at all—and yet he absorbed it well. When the men formed ranks, he rode out in front of them. As best as I can remember, he said something like, 'You are learning well the ways of the desert horse. This should be recognized. I will tell all my warriors that the Parthian Pivot and the Scythian Spin have gone the way of the wind. Now, thanks to the men of the Tiber, the Roman Rollback whips us away from our foes.'"

Rufio laughed. "He's a grand one, isn't he?"

"For a moment, there was total silence. Then Arrianus shouted, 'Haritat!' and the entire century erupted."

Still laughing, Rufio said, "I'll miss that hawk-faced bandit."

"He's one for the ages."

"Have you been working with the wooden swords this week?"

"On horseback?"

"No, on tortoise back."

"I take back what I said. Harsh."

"Swords...."

"Every day I've had the men in the saddle drawing them and moving them around their mounts' sides and necks. Most of the animals have been very good. I had to pull just a few and replace them."

"Are you satisfied that the horses are ready for a real drill?"

"I am."

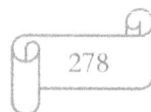

Rufio looked at the sky. "These high clouds are odd for this time of year. We should take advantage of them. The afternoon will be cooler if this overcast stays."

"I'm ready to start the men's sword training."

"Let's start today. Tell Decius to issue the wooden swords to his century after their meal. Rest the men and their horses at midday, and then begin."

After Bellator left, Rufio walked along the row of pens and gave a low whistle. His dapple gray gelding raised his head and ambled over with the leisurely stride that told humans never to get too confident. The horse leaned his head over the rail, and Rufio breathed on the animal's nostrils and stroked his forehead. The horse's eyelids drooped a bit, and he let out the soul-soothing sigh unique to his mysterious race.

"Do you want to go home with me?" Rufio said as he slid his right forefinger beneath the animal's upper lip and rubbed gently back and forth along his gum. "Cormagnus could use a rest. And the grass in Gaul is sweet."

Already many of his men had grown so attached to their horses that they had asked him if they could take them back.

Rufio held a fist in front of his horse's mouth, and the animal began to lick it. After a few sweeps with his soft tongue, the horse got more energetic and starting lipping Rufio's hand, which could be a prelude to a less than pleasant nip.

"You know no biting," Rufio said.

Instantly, the horse stopped and resumed his licking.

"Have you named him?" said a voice behind Rufio.

He turned around. "Good morning, tribune."

"You have a way with them," Crus said and came up and leaned on the rail.

"Perhaps." He reached back for a thought. "The finest horseman I ever knew was a Spaniard. No one rides as well as the Spaniards, except maybe the Numidians. He was an astounding man. I sometimes thought that he ate human food only as a pretense. That in fact he went out secretly at night and grazed in the moonlight...."

Crus smiled.

"He said to me once that only one in every eight or nine horses ever bonds with its owner. And that no man has ever been able to change that number. One out of eight. Written in the stars."

"And was he right?"

"I believe he was. I think that's why we continue to try. To flaunt the will of the gods."

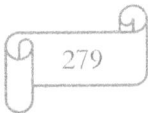

"You've succeeded with this one."

"Do you know how you can be sure your horse has bonded with you? Not when he nickers to you or nuzzles you. That matters, but there's much more. You know you've reached his heart when you do something stupid and he doesn't panic. When, despite your idiocy, he trusts."

Crus gave him a bemused look. "Is this personal testimony?"

"When I was young and serving in Gaul for the first time, I had a wonderful red bay. He was from Spain and smart as Socrates, which caused its share of problems because he was always getting into mischief. I called him Mirus because he was amazing. And he had a sweet soul."

"And how did he show his trust?"

"I'm not the tallest man in the world, so mounting a horse has always been work for me. Sometimes I'd slip back down. Nobody likes to embarrass himself like that. One day when I was tired and sore, I decided to give it an extra effort to make sure I landed squarely in the saddle and didn't look like a fool. I pulled myself up so hard I sailed over the saddle and found myself hanging from the other side. I scrambled to get back up, but I was too far over and just kept flailing. All I could think of was that if my horse bolted, I'd fly off while he was running and break my back. Yet he stood there still as bronze. Here was this imbecile flapping around his off side—behavior that would terrify just about any horse and something he'd probably never experienced before—and yet he never moved. That's a bond. That's trust."

"And did the imbecile climb back on?"

"He fell to the ground like a dropped stone. In the fall, he forgot to let go of the right rein. It pulled the horse backward without warning. That did scare Mirus. Fortunately the rein snapped. As I was on the ground, I could see his feet moving backward next to my face and I realized there was nothing I could do to stop a hoof from slamming down onto my head. But it never did. Mirus was that careful not to step on me. He backed up a few steps and then stopped. Never reared or bolted like so many horses would have. He just stood there by me. Trust again. I got to my knees and looked back at him, and I swear his eyes said, 'Surely we can do better than that.'"

Crus burst out laughing.

"How I loved that horse." Rufio turned back and caressed the lips of the gray Arab. "I see much of those days here again." He rubbed the horse's forehead. "I call him Nimbus, because his coat looks like a storm on the horizon."

The creak of a wagon caused both men to turn around.

Neko drove up with Yahlavi sitting beside him. The Parthian looked clean now but fearful, like a young snake with a newly shed skin but with its head caught under a heel. Neko stopped the wagon beside Rufio and Crus.

"Down," Neko said, and the Parthian jumped off.

Neko threw Yahlavi's weapons onto the ground and handed him a sack. "There's a ham in there and the water flask is full."

Yahlavi stared at him in confusion.

From the opposite end of the row of pens, Morlana came up leading Yahlavi's horse. The Turanian looked magnificent.

She handed Yahlavi the reins. He quickly draped them across the horse's neck and put on his swordbelt and attached his bow and quiver and food sack to the saddle.

Just behind Morlana, Arrianus came from around the end of the pens and led two other horses, with a man walking beside each.

Yahlavi spun toward Rufio in disbelief and then laughed and ran and embraced his two friends.

"I guess I didn't drive the nails deeply enough," the centurion said. "Mount up!"

Without a word, they did.

"Leave Judaea," Rufio said. "Never come back." He turned to Neko. "Go with them to the gate so the guards will let them leave."

Yahlavi just stared at Rufio and then said finally, "You are a man of honor."

"Go!"

Rufio turned away as they rode off, and he began scratching Nimbus behind the ears.

Crus leaned against the rail.

Rufio could feel his gaze. "Tribune?" he said without turning away from his horse.

"Crucified? Hmmm."

Rufio dismissed it with the wave of a hand. "I'm in a mellow mood."

"And those three?"

"Just three young fools. They still have time. I decided to give it to them." He lightly rubbed Nimbus's lips. "The other two were a different matter. They needed killing."

48

I DESPISED HIS HORSES, I DID NOT CAST A GLANCE AT THE MULTITUDE OF HIS MAIL-CLAD WARRIORS.... I PLUNGED INTO HIS MIDST LIKE A FRIGHTFUL JAVELIN.... I MADE THEIR BLOOD RUN DOWN THE RAVINES AND PRECIPICES LIKE A RIVER, DYEING THE PLAIN, COUNTRYSIDE AND HIGHLANDS RED LIKE A ROYAL ROBE.

SARGON II

Crus rode into the arena and up to the rank of horseman assembled in front of Bellator and Decius, their centurion. Two tent groups stood mounted there, while the remainder of the century waited outside the arena. Crus was about to ride to the end of the line when a couple of soldiers made space for him in about the middle of the rank. Crus was holding his wooden sword, as were all the other men.

"The concept is simple," Bellator said. Then he smiled. "Perhaps the execution is less so. We'll see."

Since Decius probably knew little more about fighting from horseback than his men did, Crus suspected that Decius was on his mount beside Bellator as a courtesy to the centurion. The old decurion was very sensitive to the privileges of rank.

"There's one thought I want you to remember," Bellator went on. "Lock this phrase in your mind—*'X' on the horizon*. If you remember that, what you learn today will stay with you forever."

Crus noticed Bellator wince a little bit as he shifted his weight in the saddle.

"There are seven cuts to learn. I won't say 'master' because there's little time, but you'll do fine. First, sit as tall in the saddle as you can. That's not just to give you more height but also more power as you drive the blade down." He raised his training sword. "Upper left to lower right, and then lower right to upper left." He showed them. "That's one side of the 'X'. Now upper right to lower left, and then lower left back to upper right. That's the other side. Simple?"

"A child could do it," Crus said, and the men laughed.

Crus could see Bellator smothering a smile.

"Our tribune honors us today," the decurion said. "Now before you learn what to do with the sword, you have to learn two things you should never do with your horse. These are as important as anything you'll learn from me this day. The first is that you absolutely must not jerk the reins and tighten them at the moment you bring your sword into play. Believe me, you will. Everyone does. You'll do it without thinking. You'll pull those reins tight. Be aware of it and stop it. There are two reasons this is bad. The first is that you'll hurt your horse's mouth, and the second is that you'll slow him or even stop him at the critical moment when you need his forward movement the most. Is that clear?"

"Clear," Crus said.

"No horseman wants to hurt his horse, but there's also a practical reason that this is bad. All of you have enough experience with horses now to know that a horse usually learns good things slowly but bad things fast. Pain is a cruel teacher and a quick one. If you hurt him every time you're about to use your sword, he'll learn that fact after just a few instances of it. Then every time he feels you shift your weight as you're about to cut, he'll slow down or stop to avoid the mouth pain that he's learned will follow. *So don't do it.*"

Bellator paused for effect.

"And the second thing, decurion?" Crus said, impatient to get on with the training.

"I appreciate the tribune's prompting," Bellator said without a trace of sincerity. "The second thing to know is that when you close with your enemy and slash with your sword, very often your horse will veer toward the opposite side, away from the point of contact and what he sees as a possible collision. And sometimes he'll change his gait, too. You've already learned that your horse is much more likely to break his gait on a turn than when running straight. At your moment of greatest danger, the last things you want are your horse changing direction out of your control and also dropping from a canter to a trot. You've gone from a swift and focused mount to a swerving and slowing one. If you don't correct that behavior, your comrades will soon be entombing your urn on the Via Appia."

Bellator looked at Crus.

"Thank you, decurion," the tribune said.

Bellator smiled. "All right, now let me see everyone do both sides of the 'X' — left side, then right. *And easy on the reins!*"

The soldiers, including their tribune, obeyed.

"Slowly," Bellator said. "Speed will come with practice. Again."

They repeated the cuts.

"Very good. Now we'll slice across the horizon." He held his sword out straight. "Blade level with the ground, cut from left to right with your palm down, and then from right to left with your palm up." He paused. "Excellent! What I could have done with you sad foot-sloggers twenty-five years ago!"

With mock respect, one of the soldiers said to the older man, "But, decurion, some of us were still sucking on a tit twenty-five years ago."

The men laughed at their brazen comrade.

"And a good thing that is, soldier," Bellator said seriously. "Because with a face like yours, it's the only tit you'll ever get to suck."

The soldiers roared, and even the victim could not help laughing.

"Seventh cut," Bellator said. "Straight down from top to bottom. Do it cleanly and make me proud."

They did, and Crus could see that he *was* proud.

"Fine. You'll be quicker next time. Questions?"

"Decurion," Crus said, "why not an eighth cut straight up? Why skip that?"

Bellator glared at the men. "Why couldn't one of you dirt kickers think to ask me that? It's a very good question. Does anyone know the answer?"

No one dared reply.

"Because," Bellator said, "it's too weak. Upward cuts are challenging enough at an angle, but cuts *straight* up are even more awkward and difficult for the human arm. So we avoid it."

"Thank you, decurion," Crus said.

"One thing that all of you have noticed is that you're told never to slash on foot but to thrust instead, and yet I just gave you seven different ways to slash on horseback. Do you have any idea why I did that?"

"Because the decurion is confused?" Crus said.

The man exploded in laughter.

Bellator tried to give Crus a stern look, but a smile was seeping through.

"A fair answer," Bellator said. "A better one is that you *can* thrust on horseback, but it's difficult. Especially with a small infantry sword. Also, a slash from atop a horse always has more power than a thrust. You're able to put the most weight behind it because you're coming down rather than trying to push forward." He looked directly at Crus. "Does that make sense, tribune?"

"Like the geometry of Euclid," Crus answered.

"But there's an important difference in executing the thrust. Instead of sitting as tall as you can, I want you to crouch a little bit in the saddle and bend toward the front at the waist. That'll help you drive your blade forward with the most power and accuracy." He turned to Decius. "Centurion."

"All right," Decius said to his men. "Thrust!"

They did, and the phantom Parthians died.

Crus was certain that the real ones would not be so obliging.

"The Parthian bowmen carry no shields," Bellator said. "So they're completely vulnerable to your blades. But you have to hit them fast. It's the middle distance that's the most dangerous for you, because at that range their bows are powerful enough to drive arrows through your mail. But once you close with them, their bows are useless. And always go for the man. Slash his head or pierce his stomach or cut off any limbs within reach. His horse is only a secondary goal. Don't be tempted by the animal's size. If you're unhorsed yourself, go for the rider's legs. Stab the horse in the belly if you have to, but that's your final target, not your first."

Bellator paused while the men absorbed that.

"Decurion . . ." Crus said.

"Tribune."

"What do you do if your enemy is on your left but you're right-handed?"

"Very good question. I forgot to discuss that. If the enemy is on the side opposite your weapon hand, do *not* reach across your horse and try to strike him on that flank. A slash over your horse's neck would be too weak and a thrust would be too short. Unless you're competent fighting with either hand and can switch your weapon to the opposite side—and who is?—bring your sword into play by circling in front of your enemy. If you're right-handed and your enemy is on your left, circle to the left and confront your enemy from your own right. Left-handed soldiers do likewise but from the left."

Crus nodded. "Thank you."

"One thing more," Bellator said. "Success isn't going to hinge on your skill with your blade or on your strength or even your courage.

Victory will be driven by the speed and valor of your mount. And we have the finest and bravest horses on earth. They're ready to ride the storm."

"Is food sacred in Italy?" Haritat asked as he gazed at the table of cured meats and dried fruits that Neko had laid out in Rufio's office.

Rufio smiled and pointed to a chair.

Crus was already seated behind Rufio's desk, and now Bellator, Matthias, and the Nabataean formed a casual half circle on camp chairs in front of it. Rufio sat by the end of the desk to Crus's left.

Neko poured wine for everyone and passed around the food before he withdrew to the shadows.

Ordinarily, Rufio left his front door open, but a hot and wild wind was blowing through the darkness. Desert gales were always ominous. Their erosive effect on men's souls had driven more than one man mad. Rufio pointed to the door, and Neko went over and closed it against the Judaean howl.

"Did the tribune enjoy the training today?" Rufio asked.

Crus looked at him in surprise.

"There are no secrets in a fort," Rufio said.

"I enjoyed it for the first half-hour. After that, my arm seemed to die. But Bellator kept everyone charging and slashing at Decius for about an hour and a half. I'm not sure why, because everyone was accomplishing it fairly well long before that."

"He wasn't doing it for the men," Rufio said. "He was training the horses. Getting them accustomed to the maneuvers and the flailing blades."

"Ah, I hadn't thought of that."

"All right, my friend," Rufio said, turning to Haritat and taking a sip of wine. "Tell us about the camels."

"I'd like to hear that, too," Bellator said. "They're unsettling my horses."

"But not as much as last week, is that not so?" Haritat said. "And even less so as the weeks pass. However, the centurion, I believe, speaks not of the three I brought but of the hundred crossing the desert toward us as we are speaking."

"Yes," Rufio said.

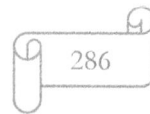

"The camels are the truest arrow in the Parthian quiver," Haritat said.

"Please tell us why," Crus said.

"Fighting in the desert is like fighting on the sea. Everything you need you must carry with you. There is no foraging for supplies or water or food. All must be born on the back and be ready to hand. The Parthians know this. Your failed generals did not."

"Crassus," Crus said.

"And Antonius," Haritat answered. "But at least he survived. Countless hordes have fallen."

"Because of camels?" Bellator asked.

"Do not sneer at our irritable friend," Haritat said. "The Parthians will hide provisions at various points in these wastes in preparation for approaching conflict. No matter the ferocity of the battle, the Parthians will never have to disengage because of lack of arrows or water. They will send a few riders back to these secret caches, where fellow warriors will load whatever they need upon camels and ride them forward. They can do this many times before their supplies are gone. Long before that, their waterless and weaponless enemies will be maggots shriveled on a hot rock."

"Would they do something so elaborate even for a small foray like this?" Crus asked.

"They would do it without even thinking. They would do it in their sleep."

"Is a hundred enough for them?" Rufio asked.

"Fifty would be enough for them," Haritat answered.

"And if you were in our place," Rufio said, "how would you counter them?

One of Haritat's rare smiles brightened the room with its cold light. "If I were in your place, I would pray for a swift and painless death. The only way to deal with them is to encircle them and prevent riders from leaving to retrieve the camels. Or, if that fails, to stop the camel riders from returning and replenishing their troops. But you have not enough men to encircle, is that not so?"

"It is so," Crus said. "So what can you advise us that we haven't thought of?"

"Prayers to Dushara."

"Chief," Bellator said, "you really have to learn to speak your mind instead of always cuddling us with lamb's wool."

Everyone laughed and it broke the tension.

"I brought some camels because your horses need to get accustomed to them."

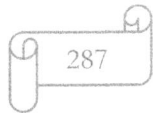

"Because the Parthian camels will get through?" Rufio asked.

"The Parthian camels will get through."

For several minutes the groaning wind outside was the only sound.

"Then it's time to discuss how we move forward," Crus said at last and looked at Rufio.

"Tribune," Haritat said.

Crus turned toward him.

"I agreed to help train your men to ride. I did this not as a favor to the tribune nor as a favor to the centurion. Least of all, did I do it as a favor to Rome. I toil in the sun to repay my debt to the woman who saved my life and allowed me to continue to be a leader to my people. Some time ago I told the centurion that I am not at war with the Parthians and that I will not go to war with the Parthians on Herod's behalf." He stood. "I will be part of no discussion of war plans."

Crus rose, as did Rufio.

"Rome respects your wishes and Rome thanks you for what you've done already," Crus said.

Rufio smiled and nodded at the Nabataean.

"Now I will return to my tent and ask Dushara to grant you greater wisdom than you have so far shown."

He turned with a swish of his robes and was gone.

"Well . . ." Bellator said. "I suppose someday we'll have to teach him to be a bit more to the point."

"I'm not sure I understand what he meant," Crus said.

"To some extent, he sympathizes with the Parthians," Rufio said. "And he thinks we're fools for fighting for the growling Idumaean and his ill-tempered subjects." He looked at Matthias. "Isn't that true?"

The Judaean laughed. "It's true."

"But we're not fighting for Herod," Crus said. "Surely he—."

"Tribune, he does know that," Rufio said. "Part of him anyway. But another part of him considers it folly." He took a sip of wine and stared at the door. "The desert has a short horizon. Survival is a day-by-day struggle in a land where water is scarcer even than human courage. The people out here care little for the sweep of empires."

Obviously sensing a long night, Neko lit more oil lamps.

"So how shall we proceed?" Crus said.

"The weapons training is going well," Bellator answered. "As I expected it to. These men were experienced with their swords long before I met them. All they needed was confidence in the saddle for them to be able to blend riding and cutting." He looked at Rufio. "But individual skill isn't the problem, is it?"

"No." Rufio set down his cup. "Neko, how did our Parthian friend like his tour?"

The Egyptian smiled as he stepped forward. "Impressed, I believe. I walked him around and told him we had a thousand Roman cavalry and five hundred Judaean infantry. The size of the fort helped convince him of that."

"Why should we care that a failed robber thinks we're more powerful than we are?" Crus asked.

"Because," Rufio said, "he's going to return to Durena and tell him what he's learned."

"You think he was a spy?" Crus said in surprise.

"No, I think he's a loyal Parthian who honors his commander. I think he'll go back."

"But how does that help us?" Matthias asked. "Wouldn't it be better for Durena to underestimate us rather than overestimate us?"

"My thoughts as well," Crus said.

Rufio looked at Bellator. "What do you think, you old war dog?"

He smiled. "I think I'm going to agree with what you're about to say."

Rufio turned to Crus. "Some commanders believe it's an advantage if your enemy thinks you're weaker than you are. In that way, you can shock and stun him on the battlefield. There's merit in that. But merit rides many horses, and there's more merit in the reverse. There's an enormous advantage to you if your enemy enters the field uncertain—or even fearful of your strength. You've already begun slowly poisoning his resolve."

"But do you think he'd fear a thousand Romans?"

"Much more than he'd fear only a single cohort. You win the battle not when you've killed the enemy's men but when you've killed the enemy's will. If the commander is ill at ease at the outset, you can be confident that toxin has already started seeping into his troops."

"I wouldn't have thought of that," Crus said.

"When I was your age, or Matthias's, I wouldn't have thought of it either."

"But whether they're unsure or not, there are more of them than there are of us," Crus said.

Rufio looked toward Bellator. "Any thoughts?"

"Only that perhaps Haritat is much wiser than we are."

"Ah, the voice of hope," Rufio said.

Bellator laughed.

Rufio turned back to his tribune. Suddenly, out of nowhere, the thought of Lucia, Crus's sweetheart, came to Rufio's mind. How proud she would be of her man now as he faced an implacable foe in the middle of this godless Hell.

"Rufio?" Crus said.

"Sorry. I was thinking — which is more than this decurion is doing."

"Prudent silence can be powerful," Bellator said.

"It can. But so can an empty well if you fall and hit your skull on the bottom."

Bellator shook his head in mock exasperation. "And I gave up feeding my squirrels for this?"

"All right," Crus said. "How do we face them?"

"My squirrels?"

Rufio saw Neko smile and then retreat to the shadows.

"Neko," Crus said, "get a chair and sit by us. We might need your scholarship." He looked at Rufio. "Take us to the battlefield."

"The first thing we have to do is admit what we *cannot* do. We cannot flank them. We don't have enough troops. We have maneuverability, but no more than the Parthians do. And not nearly enough men. So encircling them is no more possible than capturing the wind." He looked at Bellator. "Agreed?"

"Yes."

"We cannot destroy them, either. Cripple them, yes, but not annihilate them. Again, we don't have enough troops for that."

"Then what *can* we do?" Crus asked.

"What we *must* do is kill enough of them, and do it quickly enough, to cut their arrogance out from under them. More than inflicting blood and death, we have to smash the myth that makes them proud. Only then will they fall."

Silence followed, and then Bellator said, "But *they* have enough men to flank *us*."

Crus looked at Bellator and then at Rufio.

"The aging horseman has a talent for tripping over old manure," Rufio said.

"Then let's ride over it," Crus said.

"The first thing," Rufio went on, "is that we have to start the men on maneuvers outside the arena."

"That was already my plan," Bellator said. "How broad of a file?"

"Four."

"No, not ranks. Files."

"Four — narrow as a knife blade."

"You want columns?" Bellator said in surprise.

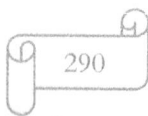

"Ordinary tactics won't work. You know that. Throwing a wall of horses against them would be madness."

"You'll have to explain it to me in more detail than that," Crus said.

"Challenging the Parthians with a broad front is suicide. It just gives them an ideal target. That was the mistake Crassus made with his legions at Carrhae. If you shoot an arrow at a flock of sheep—even sheep with teeth, like the legions--you don't miss. If you shoot it at a sword point, you waste an arrow. I want four files and twenty ranks for each century. We're not going to push them or hammer them. We're going to stab them."

"Have you ever done this before?" Crus asked.

"No," Rufio said. "We're going to use the tactics that Sharrukin used against the Urartians."

Crus looked at Bellator, but even the decurion was lost.

"The king of Assyria over seven hundred years ago," Rufio said. "One of the great conquerors of those times. Savage like all those Assyrian slaughterers, but brilliant with cavalry. *He* knew how to fight in this land. Our Jewish friends call him Sargon. Those old Hebrews got everything right but the name."

"He laid waste everywhere he went," Matthias said.

"Sargon's army overran the ten northern tribes of Israel," Rufio went on. "He claimed to have carted off over twenty-seven thousand captives from Samaria alone."

"And the Urartians?" Crus asked.

"Urartu was a kingdom northeast of Assyria," Rufio said. "A fairly powerful one, too. And a stone in Assyria's hoof. Assyria believed that Urartu was threatening its trade routes, as well as the area where Assyria got its horses. Sargon unleashed a major campaign. It was mountainous country and the conditions were brutal on his troops. They were beaten down by the terrain and the elements. There was even talk of mutiny. When Rusa, the king of Urartu, marched out his troops to give battle, he had every reason to be confident. But he should have known better—he was challenging Assyrians. And Sargon." Rufio took a sip of wine.

Crus smiled. "You like to pause for that special effect, don't you?"

Rufio set down his cup. "The Assyrian conqueror decided to shame his troops and inspire them at the same time. He attacked one wing of Rusa's line on his own with nothing more than his household cavalry. About a thousand men in a single column. Sargon himself led the assault. He—."

"From horseback?" Bellator asked. "The king himself?"

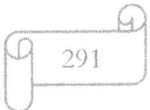

"Probably from a war chariot. That was customary for royalty in those days. The Urartians were stunned. The wing collapsed and the Assyrian infantry took heart and smashed into the Urartian ranks." Rufio sipped his wine. "And the kingdom fell. Because of a thousand cavalry." He cocked an eyebrow at Crus. "Three hundred and fifty years before Alexander was born."

There was silence for a few moments, and then Rufio turned to Bellator. "Have Haritat work more on the Parthian Pivot. I—."

"You mean the Roman Rollback," Bellator said.

Rufio smiled. "Yes. I want that to be perfect. It *has* to be perfect."

"It'll be done."

"And what of *my* men?" Matthias asked. "What do we do?"

"We'll have to think about that some more," Rufio said. "Keep them practicing at the archery field. They looked very good today."

"They're improving," Matthias said.

"Neko," Crus said, "what do your researches tell us about the Parthians' fighting style?"

"Semi-organized," Neko answered. "Like most cavalry. No groups of horseman are ever as sound as a phalanx or a cohort. But that's expected. They make up for that with swiftness. And mobility."

"I see," Crus said.

"And the numbers aren't as bad as they appear." Neko turned to Rufio for permission to continue.

Rufio nodded.

"Romans have been outnumbered much more severely and still prevailed," Neko said. "Remember the Hill of Scorpions."

"I do."

"The most terrible blunder the honorable Crassus made was forming his men into a square," Neko said. "That was disastrous. It allowed the Parthians to shoot at his troops from all directions. The Romans were cut to rags."

"And we're in a better position than Sargon was against Rusa," Rufio said. "There are only about a thousand troops facing us. Sargon had an entire army against him. Our six centuries will take the field in six columns. One column will hit each wing of the Parthian line, and we'll hold four columns in reserve. We'll use converging columns, which Sargon couldn't do because there weren't enough troops in his household cavalry to hit both wings at the same time."

"But how do we stop the Parthians from surrounding us the way they encircled Crassus?" Crus asked.

"We have an advantage Crassus didn't have. His troops were static in a square. Ours are mounted. Wherever the wings of their line can go, we can go. The chaotic swarm of bees will never outrace the hornets. But we probably won't have to worry about a flanking attack anyway, because they don't have heavy cavalry to coddle their delicate heads, as they did at Carrhae. Remember, they have no armor and no shields. Without armored men with lances protecting them, the security of the bowmen lies in their mass and in keeping a safe distance. If their commander is half as clever as Yahlavi said, he won't risk breaking up his troops by a useless attempt at flanking and closing on multiple mounted columns armed with swords."

"What we must be wary of, too," Neko said to the tribune, "is the false retreat. It's one of their favorite tactics and it's killed many Romans. The Parthians used it at Carrhae. The Parthians flee and their enemies pursue what they believe to be terrified horsemen, and then the pursuers are cut off, surrounded, and butchered."

Rufio snapped his head up like a man startled out of a dream. He glanced at Bellator, who had noticed Rufio's reaction and gave him a questioning look. Rufio turned and gazed at Matthias, whose eyes were on Neko.

"Thoughts, centurion?" Crus said.

"I need quiet and darkness to roll these dice around in my head. Allow me a night to think about this."

"Well," Crus said, smiling, "if you can solve this in a single night, I'll buy you a villa at Ostia."

Rufio gestured for Matthias to remain when the others left.

"The wind has died down," Matthias said, staring out into the darkness from the open doorway.

"There's something hideous about desert winds," Rufio said as he joined him at the door. "Cold winds hurt, but these hot gales twist the mind."

Matthias turned and smiled at him. "You Romans are too accustomed to balmy breezes from the sea."

"No, it's not that," Rufio said seriously. "On nights like this, I've seen quiet young men start fights over nothing at all. And tough old centurions weep at some sad song. And drunken soldiers—good men—having competitions about biting the stingers off living scorpions. I hate desert winds."

"Did you volunteer to come out here?"

"This time?"

"Yes."

"I did."

"May I ask why?"

"For a friend."

"Augustus?"

Rufio laughed. "No, not Augustus."

"The tribune then?"

"The tribune."

"He's a fortunate man."

"Well, when he boards ship in Caesarea on his way home—that's when someone can say he's fortunate." Rufio stepped past Matthias and went outside. "Let's walk."

They went slowly in the darkness toward the Via Praetoria. Rufio waved to soldiers at various guard posts as they walked by.

"I know your Sabbath began at sundown," Rufio said. "So I appreciate your attending the meeting."

"Our God is more understanding than many people think."

"Certainly more than ours are."

"Truly? Don't you pray to any of your gods?"

"Only to one."

"And does he not—."

"She."

Rufio's tone was sharp enough to end the discussion.

They reached the fountain near the Principia. It was not actually a fountain at all but really just a glorified spring with a tiny stream of cool water dribbling out. Rufio pointed to the stone bench beside it. Matthias sat and Rufio sat down next to him.

"Matthias, I want to use you and your men as bait."

After a brief hesitation, Matthias said, "So you've rolled the dice in your mind already."

"I'd done that before the tribune left the room, but I wanted to discuss it with you first."

"How would you do it?"

"I haven't worked out any details yet. But I want to use the Parthians' own ruse against them. Draw them in and cut them down. That they'd never expect. Their arrogance is a stone wall—and as blank as their imagination."

"You want to offer Judaean lambs to the Parthian wolves?"

"I do."

"And will the Romans be sheep hounds and protect the helpless flock?"

"Yes. Or die in the effort. You have my word. And that of Rome."

"How will you do it?"

"You and your men will be in the middle of the line—but on foot. Troops on the ground are the most tempting bait there is to Parthian horsemen. You're free to choose the number of ranks you use, but I wouldn't make it more than three deep. In their rush to end everything quickly, at least some of the bowmen will overshoot you and waste their arrows. You'll use our shields, which are bigger and heavier than yours and so a better defense against arrows. Of course, you'll have to set the shields down to use your bows. But at least you can use them during advance or withdrawal. Do you know how to form the turtle?"

"With our shields all around us?"

"Yes."

"We've practiced it a few times."

"You might need it, but let's hope not. When you shoot your arrows at the slavering Asiatics, they'll be massed—you won't miss. But in the beginning, you have to *look* vulnerable. And you have to trust us to make sure you're not."

"Well," Matthias said with a smile, "if there's one thing Judaeans understand, it's how to be vulnerable."

"The Romans will be the Dogs of the Canaanites on your flanks."

Matthias turned toward the fountain. The air passing over the running water cooled the space around both men.

"I hate the desert wind, too," Matthias said. "I've always hated it."

Rufio remained silent.

"The fact that I'm considering agreeing to what you ask says much about you."

"It says nothing about me. It says everything about you. And about the valor of Judaea."

Matthias turned back toward Rufio. "Are you flattering me?"

"Is what I said true?"

"About Judaean valor?"

"Yes."

"It is true."

"Then how can I be flattering?"

Matthias laughed. "I think you belong in your famous Senate. Not out here in angry winds."

Rufio went over to the fountain and cupped his hands and helped himself to some spring water. "Respect your commander. But don't bend your knee to him. That's the road to ruin."

"How do you mean?"

Rufio sat back down. "Many years ago I overheard one of my soldiers say to another, 'What I am in the eyes of Rufio, *that's* what I am as a soldier.' Most centurions would love to hear any of their men say that. But it can be disastrous. A fine soldier becomes a finer soldier if he cares about the opinion of a good commander, but he can't worship it. If he does, he stops thinking for himself. A Greek in a phalanx can afford not to think for himself. A Roman fighting in an open rank cannot."

"Did you correct him?"

"He corrected himself. I found some little infraction of his and punished him severely. Some might say unjustly." Rufio smiled. "That was enough. He had a more realistic view of life after that. And of me."

"Was he a good solider?"

"Oh, yes. He died in Syria of a snake bite. He was twenty-two."

Matthias leaned forward and rested his forearms across his legs and stared at the fountain. "I need to learn more about dealing with my men. That's why I watch you so much."

"I know."

"It's not easy, is it?"

"Commanding men? It's the most difficult thing of all. It should've been the thirteenth labor of Hercules."

"Haritat is very different from you with the troops. They don't seem at ease with him."

"They're not, but that's a problem they have to deal with. I'm not going to hold their hands."

"But you do it differently. I'm not sure exactly how. I'm still trying to figure it out."

"Do you want some help?"

Matthias took his gaze off the fountain and looked at Rufio. "Yes."

"What Haritat does is to find a man's flaws and work on them constantly. To cut them out like pustules under a rusty blade. Most centurions do the same thing. Eventually Haritat gets what he wants, but the surgery has been brutal. His way can be effective, but it works best with inexperienced troops. Men who aren't seasoned enough to resent an insult. With veterans like mine, it causes suppurating sores that take a long time to heal. And it's hard to sit in a saddle on a sore ass."

"But you just said you're willing to criticize a soldier if it's needed."

"Criticizing soldiers isn't the same as chewing on their imperfections. The difference between the two is the difference between a horse and a horsefly. One is powerful and majestic. The other is just a biting bug...."

"Go on."

"If you want to correct a soldier's flaws, don't gnaw at the flaws. Instead, cultivate their opposite. Don't chew on his vices like a rodent. Feed and nourish the contrary quality. That can be slower but the result lasts. Once he's developed that virtue, it'll endure forever. And the vice just withers and dies like a vine without water."

"You make it sound simple."

Rufio smiled. "I make everything sound simple. Of course, that doesn't mean it is."

"Can you give an example that even a poor slave of Herod can understand?"

Rufio thought for a moment. "When I was in Africa, one of my men wanted to learn how to ride. He was actually afraid of horses and wanted to conquer that. He liked horses very much—from a distance. But they intimidated him. He asked one of the decurions to teach him to ride. The decurion was a good horseman, but no philosopher when it came to instruction. My soldier was bucked off during his first ride. Now he was really scared. The decurion ordered him back into the saddle and naturally the horse felt the fear in my soldier's legs. The next ride was a disaster. But the decurion wouldn't relent. He kept telling him not to be afraid, that it was stupid to be afraid, that it was weak to be afraid. Do you think that was effective?"

"No, I don't."

"Of course not. You cannot teach a man to be a horseman by throwing him at a horse. It's like telling a man he can learn to be an armorer by stabbing him with a sword."

"Did he ever learn to ride?"

"Not from that fool. I taught him."

Matthias smiled. "Can you tell me how?"

"I got him a calmer horse—mine, in fact—and the first thing I told him wasn't that if he fell off he had to get back on. I told him that as soon as he came out of the saddle we were done for the day. Now all he could think about was his balance. He didn't want the lesson to end. He desperately wanted to learn. He forgot about all that muscle and bone and impulsive power between his legs. And that was fine because I knew Cormagnus would take care of him. The first lesson lasted over an hour and I taught him how to correct his position the whole time. When we'd finished, he had a fair seat. I praised him like he'd never been praised before. Always end at a moment of success—as you do with horses. In fact, his hands had been terrible. He'd jerked the reins all over the place. But that wasn't the point this day. He'd started out afraid, but I never mentioned fear. I let him overcome his dread by keeping his mind on something else and by helping him cultivate the physical skill that would increase his confidence and drain his fear. I did it by praising the tiniest bit of success. Just as you would with a colt. The issue with the reins could wait."

"Did he learn in the end?"

"Like Perseus on Pegasus."

Matthias smiled. "Where is he now?"

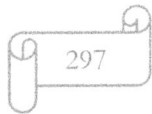

"Spain. Where he awes them. If you can impress the Spaniards with your riding, you can impress the gods."

"Still, it was more difficult than you're making it sound, wasn't it?"

"I'm simplifying the story for one of Herod's slaves."

Matthias laughed.

"First instruct your men, then correct, then exalt—when you've mastered that, you'll know how to train. And to lead."

"Exalt? I don't know that word."

"Toss a hosanna their way now and then."

"I'll remember that."

Rufio remained silent for a long time and then turned and saw that Matthias had been staring at him.

"What is it?" Rufio asked.

"I was just wondering what you'd have been if you hadn't become a soldier."

Rufio swatted that away like a fly. "Don't waste your time with that." He hiked a foot up onto the bench and leaned forward on his knee. "If there's one thing you should learn from all this it's that there are two kinds of leaders in the world—and only two. The first is common, the second as rare as a viper's pity. The first is the cattleman. If he needs to move a herd of oxen, what does he do? He mounts a horse—an animal the oxen fear—and rides behind them and drives them forward. The other type of leader is the horseman. If he wants to move a herd of horses, he mounts a horse like the cattleman does, but this time it's so the other horses *don't* fear him but are comfortable with him. Then he rides to the front of the herd, faces forward and moves off. You *drive* cattle, but you *lead* horses. Now you've learned that. Always be a horseman to your men. And never forget—never—that to lead your men you always have to trust them enough to turn your back to them, face front, and ride off."

"I won't forget."

"For every man who's a true leader, there are a hundred who couldn't lead hogs to slop." Rufio looked away and absently pressed a finger to the little tamarisk horse that hung against his chest beneath his tunic. "Teach men as you would horses. And remember that if you want to train your horse to ride through a storm, always begin on a quiet day. The lightning will come soon enough. And thunder will follow."

49

EXPECTATION ARISING OUT OF HOPE HAS OFTEN DISAPPOINTED THE BRAVE.

LUCIUS ACCIUS

*H*aritat has to leave. One of his many sons rode to the fort late yesterday to tell him that foreign soldiers have been seen near his village and might have discovered one of the Nabataeans' hidden water cisterns in the desert. Rufio believes they are probably Parthian scouts. Haritat must now return to his village in case the strangers are hostile. To Haritat, the wellbeing of his people is everything.

I am going to miss him enormously. In a sense, one cannot be safer than with a Roman cohort, even in a brutal land and with enemy troops riding toward us as I am writing this. Yet Haritat somehow offers a special comfort. I lack the ability to describe it, but by some mysterious magic his presence is a dark protective shade blocking a merciless sun. Now that shield will be gone. I am certain that others will experience his absence as I do.

But there is another loss that I feel, one that I am half afraid to think about. In a soothing way, he is like a father to me, and yet he is not, for there is no blood bond. And that is what scares me. Perhaps no passionate woman deeply in love with her man should have a friend like Haritat, a being of such towering and frightening maleness. There is no barrier of kinship to ensure my honor, no horror at an unthinkable act to make my affection safe, to make it pure. I fear the painful longing that I might feel when he has gone. Not the pain do I fear, but the longing. And my appalling dread that it might somehow be impure. And I tremble at this thought even though I know I will never see him again, for without doubt he will never truly be gone. He will live in my heart forever.

Wearing his mail lorica, Rufio carried one of the Roman shields across the archery field, along with Flavia's hornbow and six bronze-tipped arrows. He propped the shield with a piece of plank about four feet in front of Morlana's practice hay bale and then walked off about twenty-five feet.

He laid down his weapons and stretched his arms and upper body and shook them lightly to loosen them. Then he picked up the bow and one arrow and positioned his feet as he gazed downrange. He had not shot a bow since the previous year, when, before a flickering campfire, he had demonstrated the lethality of Roman rage to three slave traders on the last night of their lives.

He nocked an arrow. Then he drew the bow and aimed it straight with no arc and, like all fine archers, shot without hesitation.

He examined the shield from a distance and did not like what he saw, which was nothing. The two-and-a-half-foot arrow was gone. Shooting two more, he got the same result. He walked down to the shield and looked behind it. All three arrows had pierced the laminated shield completely and lodged in the bale behind it. So much for the vaunted Roman craftsmen.

He walked back a distance of about fifty feet this time and shot the last three arrows. He peered downrange and was gratified that at least he could still see the fletching on the arrows. He went back to the shield and saw that each missile had penetrated all three layers for about ten inches of the shaft length, more than enough to strike a body part taking shelter behind it. He decided that Roman woodworkers needed a lesson in humility.

He removed the three arrows and set the shield aside. Then he took off his mail lorica and subarmalis. Filled with a middle layer of wool and then quilted to keep the stuffing in place, the linen undergarment was now packed by Rufio with hay to create a makeshift dummy. Then he fitted his mail lorica over it and set it atop a bale.

He repeated his six shots, three at each distance, and returned to examine the damage. From twenty-five feet, the arrows had breached the mail fully but the padding only slightly. Rufio decided that this Roman would have bled but probably survived, at least if infection did not set in. From fifty feet, the results were better. Although the arrows still succeeded in driving through the mail, they had not fully pierced the wadding. They would have caused painful bruises but probably little else. The lesson from all this was clear. For the Romans and Judaeans to survive the Parthian bowmen, distance was as critical as steel.

When he had been younger, an extra heavy tunic had been all that Rufio had used to cushion his body from the mail, but those days were over. He now gave his men the option of using a padded subarmalis if they wanted one, and most of them chose to do so. If they decided against it, he removed the choice and, with simple centurion simplicity, commanded them and got what he had intended in the first place. Today's experiments confirmed the wisdom of that. Rufio was certain now that if Macer had been wearing a heavy subarmalis beneath his lorica at Scorpion Hill, he might still be alive.

Rufio rode up to the arena where Bellator was working on some turning maneuvers with Decius's sweating century. Rufio gestured to the centurion, and Decius trotted his horse over to the rail.

Many soldiers had remarked throughout the years on Rufio's skill at concealing his emotions, but sometimes even he had to admit how difficult it was for him to suppress a laugh. Decius mounted on an Arabian looked like nothing so much as a bear riding a squirrel.

"It was an unfortunate day when you decided to be an infantryman," Rufio said. "The cavalry should have been your choice."

Decius looked wary. "And why is that, centurion?"

"Our army would never have had to fight a single battle. Or even draw a weapon. The enemies of Rome would simply have collapsed in laughter."

Decius's face creased in a half-grin. "You're a cruel man, Rufio."

"I need two favors, old friend. I want two patrols eastward every day from now on. One in early morning, one in late afternoon. I'd like your century to handle this."

"It'll be done."

"Four men on each patrol. And no splitting up."

"I understand. And so will they. They're good men."

"I know. The second favor is that I want you to take command if I'm cut down. I've already told the tribune."

"Very well," he said but looked troubled.

"What's wrong? You have more than enough experience to command this cohort."

"It's not that. . . ."

"Well?"

"I've never known you to be a doubter before."

Rufio took a deep breath and let it out slowly. "I'm not, but I have to admit I feel my optimism running off into the sand. And don't repeat that."

"What's the matter?"

"Even I have my bad moments." Rufio folded his hands across his saddle and stared off toward the east. "It looks like the Parthians have found a water supply. We can no longer rely on their breaking off the battle if they run low. And they have a hundred camels to carry that fresh water forward. One of our greatest strengths was that we had unlimited water and they did not. Now that's changed."

Decius shook his head wearily. "It's always about water out here."

"Always."

"Well, there's no need for you to worry. If you skin a toe, Decius will ride into battle and knock those barbarians out of their saddles with giggling fits."

Rufio could not help laughing. "Thank you."

"Even if they don't use up their water, it's possible they could run out of arrows."

"True, but I doubt it. The camels will be carrying those, too." Rufio looked toward the arena. "Tell your men to take a break and take drink. Leave them in Bellator's delicate hands and join us at the parade ground as soon as you can." He touched a heel to Nimbus's side, and the horse pivoted as if on wheels and cantered off.

Rufio's century and the four other centurions were waiting for him at the parade ground. All men wore helmets and full armor and swords and daggers. On the left arm of each soldier was a small cavalry shield borrowed from some of Matthias's men. Because there were about twice as many Romans as Judaeans, only about half of the Romans would have shields in battle. Rufio had instructed the centurions to decide on a way to apportion the shields fairly. As matters turned out, the troops solved the problem themselves. The soldiers with the greatest number of years of service had volunteered to forego their claim on shields in favor of their less experienced comrades.

Rufio rode to the front and asked the centurions to take their place on either side of him.

"All right, centaurs," Rufio said to his men. "Four files and twenty ranks."

They formed a perfect column in just a few moments. Rufio was glad that last year he had taken so much time with their horse training. Some had grumbled at the time about its pointlessness, but Rufio knew that on the frontiers of the Empire nothing was irrelevant.

"Keep your swords in your scabbards. This is strictly horsemanship today. I assume you know how to kill." He nudged Nimbus a few steps forward. "There will be two columns hitting the wings of the Parthian line, with four columns in reserve. On the command, each attacking column will move forward at a canter. A hundred feet from the Parthian line the entire column will slow to a trot except for the first rank. That rank will hit them hard. The soldier on the far right of the rank is in command of the four. I don't care who he is—you're all experienced enough to command a rank. You'll maintain contact with your enemy for no longer than it takes a man to count to fifty. Draw as much blood as you can. If one of you is injured or comes off his horse, the man next to him is *not* to go to his aid. I don't want any holes opening up in the line. The man *behind* him in the next rank will ride forward to help him. After a count of fifty or sixty, the soldier in command on the right will evaluate the situation on the line. If everyone is well and ready to ride, he'll order a rollback—one word, "Roll!" The two soldiers on the left will roll to the left and the two on the right roll to the right. Canter straight to the back of the column and rest. The instant the next rank in line hears the command to roll, it starts cantering forward immediately and takes the previous rank's place and thrusts into the enemy. Questions?"

There were none.

"Since you're not accustomed to fighting from horseback, you're going to get arm weary. With the tactic you're learning today you'll spend more time resting than fighting. The Parthians will get no rest. And remember, once you close with them their bows are useless. They have swords, but they're not swordsmen. If they draw their blades against us, they're just pleading for death." He turned toward his centurions. "You're not going to like this, but I don't want you fighting after the first rollback unless you have to. And I mean *really* have to. Otherwise I want all of you on the right of your century about three ranks back and organizing your men and keeping the files in order. And rushing help to the front rank if it needs it. And making sure the Parthians don't try to flank. I doubt they'll try it because our columns will be too long and too swift, but one never knows. If they try it, pivot as many ranks in that direction as you think you need to and hit them fast and hard. But turn only the minimum number of ranks, and reassemble the column as quickly as you can. Keep your optio at the rear as usual to watch over everything and your signifer with you in case you have to send a message to me or to one of the other centurions."

The expressions on the faces of the centurions showed their displeasure with being left out of most of the fighting.

"Ah, is there anything more lovely than a centurion's grimace?" Rufio said. "Stop scowling. All of you bled enough for Rome on the Rhenus. You have nothing to prove here. I don't want heroes, I want victors. Understood?"

"Yes!" Decius said as he came riding up.

Rufio turned back to his men. "We're going to practice five complete runs. No swords, just movement. The six of us up here will be the enemy. Pretend that you want to kill all these charming centurions." Rufio smiled. "That shouldn't be too challenging to imagine. Hit, roll, hit, roll. After one complete run of all twenty ranks, stop to rest and take a drink. Then we'll do four more. All right, take a drink now and get ready."

Rufio rode past the horse pens and saw Haritat's sons finishing packing their gear. Haritat was down on one knee and speaking with Morlana. Crus was standing off to the left and watching as well. Haritat pushed back Morlana's blue hood and tousled her wild mane. She said something to him and he let loose that great laugh that was so thunderous and so rare. She threw her arms around his neck and held him for a long time. Then she kissed him on a cheek and ran off to her equine charges.

Rufio dismounted and left Nimbus ground tied as he and Crus approached the desert chieftain.

Haritat stood up and faced them.

"Rome is grateful for all you've done," Crus said. "Of course," he continued, smiling, "I know that means nothing to you, but I had to say it."

Haritat gravely inclined his head forward an inch.

"I've already said all I can ever say," Rufio added. "You know my heart."

"I do, and I honor it," he said, staring into Rufio's eyes. "But the appreciation of the centurion or of the tribune or even of Rome itself is of little concern to Haritat."

Rufio noticed that Haritat's gaze had slid past him. He turned around and saw Flavia standing about twenty feet away. She seemed rigid, not her usual relaxed self. Her eyes were already moist. Rufio gestured to her to come forward.

Flavia moved toward them as if her entire body ached. She glanced at Rufio and Crus and then stood before Haritat.

"I've come to say farewell," she said to the Nabataean.

"I thank you. And I am honored." His voice was soft, consoling. "Dushara has led us through many trials, has he not?"

"Yes," she answered faintly.

A pair of tears burned their way out and slid down her face.

Haritat pressed each of his forefingers to her cheeks and glided his fingertips along the two lines of tears and made them vanish. "Merely the first drops of the early morning dew."

Rufio could see her lower lip quivering, and her hands began to tremble. By colossal force of will, she seemed to have rooted herself to the ground.

"Flavia," Rufio said.

She turned to him.

"It's all right."

She stepped hesitantly toward Haritat and he slid both of his hands around the back of her head and drew her to his chest.

What an apparition, Rufio thought, a vision he would never forget. That hawk-like face carved from rock and hided over with dark and drawn leather, and gazing down now at a pink and soft-skinned huntress from a shadowed forest far away.

At last Haritat eased his hands from her hair and Flavia straightened up.

She reached out and touched his left cheek, and Haritat surprised them all by smiling a smile as warm as a glowing blade pulled from a hot forge.

His eyes overflowing with affection, he laid his right hand upon her head in blessing. "Farewell."

He then turned away and rode off into the mists of memory.

50

WHAT SHATTERS OR EXALTS THE STRENGTH OF A SOLDIER IS HIS CAUSE.

PROPERTIUS

The yelling of children made Rufio smile as he leaped onto Nimbus and rode to the training arena. About thirty boys from Hezrail were sitting outside the fence of the arena and shouting and laughing while Bellator and Arrianus worked on rollbacks with the Fourth Century. Like adults everywhere, Rufio was unable to resist the laughter of children and he laughed along with them.

Crus came riding up with a look of bafflement on his face.

"Matthias did his work well," Rufio said. "I told him to promise that any boys who came today and screamed themselves hoarse would get a midday meal and enough food to take home to their families."

"But for what?"

"The Parthians are famous for shouting to unnerve their enemy in battle. And especially their enemy's horses. After a few days of these shrieking bandits, our horses will consider the Parthians little more than mutes."

Crus laughed. "You think of everything, don't you?"

"I wish I could. But this will help. We'll be blowing horns next, because the Parthians love those, too."

Morlana handed out cups of water to the thirsty children so they could continue without searing their throats.

"Decius was looking for you earlier," Crus said.

"I was checking on our Judaean archers."

"I believe he went out on this morning's scouting with his men."

"He's a good Roman. Did they see anything interesting?"

"He said he wanted to follow proper military procedure and speak with you first, but he certainly seemed excited about something."

"Well, Decius is not an excitable man. Do you know where he is?"

"With his horses."

Rufio found Decius at the pens. He and his men were just finishing watering the animals they had ridden on patrol.

Rufio dismounted and walked over to the centurion. "Any Oriental delights to dazzle me with?"

A rare smile lifted Decius's heavy face. "Better than that. You have to see it for yourself."

Rufio grinned. "What a fortunate man I am to have centurions who live to make me happy. Should Matthias see it, too?"

"Yes, he should."

"Get a fresh horse and we'll find him and the tribune and go."

Ten minutes later the four men were riding out of the fort and off to the east.

As they passed at a trot through the already baking Judaean wilderness, the color of the soil began to lighten, and the terrain started flattening out into an uneven plain.

After about two miles of this, Decius pulled up and said, "There."

The earth seemed to drop away, a great gorge opening before them. The chasm was actually a dry riverbed, no doubt flowing with water only during the violent winter rains. It sprawled about a half-mile north to south and slightly less west to east, where it cut through yellow bluffs that rose about two hundred feet in front of the riders, up to the Judaean flatland stretching beyond to infinity.

The creamy hues of the tops of the cliffs faded away toward the bottom of the valley. There the entire surface was an eerie and deathly white.

"It looks like snow," Crus said. "What . . . ?"

"Salt," Rufio answered.

A few valiant acacias were struggling through the lifeless and crusted soil, the trees' distinctive flattened branches spreading out hopefully in a landscape without hope. No birds could be glimpsed, no insects heard. Other than the acacias and a few defiant shrubs, no scrap of life was seen.

Even Rufio, who had witnessed so much in an eventful life, was taken aback. He dismounted and walked toward the edge of the precipice. "By all the gods at once . . . . this has to be the cruelest place on earth." Staring in horror at an expanse of blanched and brackish nothingness that would have caused Jupiter himself to turn away in despair, he said softly, "We've finally reached the end of the world."

The others dismounted and came forward. In the manner of desert warriors everywhere, the four soldiers sat on the ground in the shadows of their horses, animals far tougher than feeble men.

"Did we pass the entrance to this?" Rufio asked Decius.

"About a quarter-mile back."

"Is the entrance wide enough for the entire cohort?"

"It is."

"And that defile to the east — did you explore it?"

"We did. A grade from the plain beyond it leads down it into this dead valley."

"And the slope is big enough for a thousand Parthian horsemen to swoop on our vulnerable Judaean friends?"

Decius smiled. "Yes."

"They could never flank us down there, could they?" Crus said.

"No," Rufio answered. He removed his water flask from his belt and took a long drink. "If we can lure them in. . . ." He smiled. "Which we can."

"I could sting them with my century and then retreat," Decius said. "Use their own tactics against them."

"That won't be necessary," Rufio said.

Matthias turned to Decius. "This is our land. We'll suck them in and strike them down. In that way, your century doesn't have to be worn out before the battle."

Rufio looked at Crus. "If we can challenge them in that abyss — with the walls guarding our left and right elbows — we can take the risk of striking with two columns on each wing rather than one and still hold two in reserve. Nothing could be better than that." He stared across the salt valley to the tableland beyond. "From here, we should be able to make out the Parthian camel riders coming to replenish the troops with water and arrows. The sun will be in our eyes, but we should be able to see well enough. We'll have someone up here with a carnyx to warn us down in the gorge."

"Bellator?" Crus asked.

"It has to be. He's in no condition to ride into battle. But he can blow the carnyx."

"What is that?" Matthias asked.

"A Celtic horn," Rufio said. "Of course, if the Parthians have already taken control of one of those hidden Nabataean cisterns, they might not need the camels. At least for water."

"But for arrows?" Crus said.

"Probably," Rufio answered and took another drink.

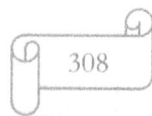

"What about water for *our* mounts?" Decius asked. "We can't just go back to the fort."

"No we cannot," Rufio said. "We're going to tear down the gyrus and make water troughs and fill them up and bring them here with the wagons we have left. We'll leave the wagons here to bring back the wounded and the dead."

"There's one thing I don't understand," Matthias said. "Why would the Parthians be kind enough to do what we want? To pounce on us in this gorge? Even for such tempting prey?"

"Because they cannot afford not to," Rufio said. "They'll come. I'm certain of it. They'll ride straight in and kill us or die."

"Once they're down there, can we try to cut them off at the other entrance to the gorge?" Crus asked. "Trap them and destroy them?"

"No, tribune," Rufio said. "We don't have enough troops to risk that. But it doesn't matter, because even if we fight only to a draw, we win. Unless they smash us, they have to go back in disgrace. Let them go. To Phraates, dead Parthians will be forgotten—he'll make sure of that. But he'll see his own vanquished as nothing more than disgusting worms humiliating him by crawling home in shame."

When the four men returned to the fort, Rufio met with the other centurions and once more discussed the particulars of the battle plan. All were eager. Rufio had decided long ago to have Matthias leave some of his troops back to guard the fort. After traveling so far with his own devoted soldiers, he was not going to leave any Romans out of the fight. Someday these men would have grandchildren who would be eager and proud to know how their grandfathers had fought the barbarian Asiatics in the Judaean wasteland.

Rufio ordered the centurions to give all their men the afternoon off from training and to rest all of them and their horses the following day. Only routine duties would be required, other than the dismantling of the gyrus and the fabrication and the transport of the troughs.

Bellator was less than enthused about the details that Rufio laid before him. His reason, though, was personal rather than tactical. Yet he finally relented, for he knew as well as Rufio that his bad hip prevented him from sharing the battlefield on horseback with his troops.

"Besides," Rufio had said to him, "I want you on the plain above us overseeing everything and signaling if needed. Who else is there?"

Rufio spent the next several hours with the horses. He randomly checked legs and feet and found none wanting. The horses had endured the rigors of training as if they had all been the spawn of Pegasus. Certainly there were more tractable and less arrogant breeds than the Arabian, but he had found none sounder and tougher.

Tack, too, he examined with a searching eye and was pleased with what he found. Arrianus and the young blonde strator had doted on it daily with the diligence of fanatics.

Toward the end of the afternoon, Rufio grabbed an armful of medica and led Nimbus from his pen to the empty parade ground far from everyone. He dropped the hay on the ground and sat beside it, and then leaned back as Nimbus bent down to feed. To Rufio, no cup of Setian wine could be even half as soothing as simply relaxing in the long shadow of one's horse as it grazed contentedly in the failing light.

Running footsteps behind him ended his rest far too soon. He recognized Valerius's crisp trot without even bothering to turn around.

"What is it?" Rufio said with more annoyance than Valerius deserved.

"The cohort has a visitor."

Rufio turned and looked over his left shoulder. Valerius had a bemused expression more appropriate to Metellus than to the usually serious optio.

"And who interrupts the repose of Caesar's soldier?" Rufio asked.

"The centurion has only himself to blame."

"All right," Rufio said. "Who?"

Valerius smiled. "Yahlavi awaits the pleasure of the servant of Caesar."

Rufio laughed and jumped up, startling Nimbus. "Where?"

"The tribune's office."

"Take care of my boy here," Rufio said and handed the horse's lead rope to Valerius.

Yahlavi looked frightened when he turned in his chair and saw Rufio enter Crus's office. He stood up quickly.

"What's wrong, soldier?" Rufio said.

That seemed to relax him a bit. Rufio had never called him that before.

"I was afraid you'd think I'd betrayed your trust," Yahlavi said.

"If you'd not gone back to report to your commander, you'd have betrayed my good judgment."

"You knew I would?"

"I'm a fair judge of men."

Yahlavi smiled. "Thank you, centurion."

"Sit back down," Crus said from behind his desk.

Rufio slid a chair next to the Parthian and sat.

"Yahlavi has come here to warn us," Crus said in a rather buoyant tone.

Everyone was sounding like Metellus today.

"No," Yahlavi said. "Not to warn. To take you to negotiate."

"About what?" Crus asked.

"Your presence here."

"Didn't you tell your commander that it's not negotiable?"

"I did, tribune. But this is Durena."

"What's that to Rome?"

Yahlavi hesitated.

"Well?" Crus said.

"His name should count for much."

"Along the Tiber it counts for nothing."

Yahlavi looked to Rufio for help.

"And do you speak for Durena?" Rufio asked.

"No, centurion. He wants to meet with the tribune personally."

"How benevolent," Rufio said.

"When?" Crus asked.

"As soon as possible. Now."

"Where?"

"Not far. I'll show you. And you have to come unarmed."

"How far is the entire *drafsh*?" Rufio asked.

"At your doorstep."

Rufio smiled. "It's not nice to lie to the man who could have nailed you to a cross. We have patrols out. The whole force cannot be closer than a day's ride. My guess is that it's farther."

Yahlavi looked embarrassed. "I'm a poor deceiver, I know. Two days' ride distant. On my honor."

"Who will be at the meeting?" Crus asked.

"You and the centurion and Durena and Aridates."

"And the tribune's safety?" Rufio asked.

"Promised on Durena's honor."

Crus laughed. "Well, I'm satisfied."

"Draw us a map," Rufio said.

"I'll take you."

"You'll take no one," Rufio said. "You'll stay here as a hostage until the tribune returns to his men."

51

TO FIGHT FOR OUR COUNTRY, FOR OUR CHILDREN, FOR OUR ALTARS, FOR OUR HEARTHS.

SALLUST

Rufio and Crus rode across the desert with the sun at their backs. The arid air always failed to retain even a hint of its ferocity as the day began to wane, and their easy trot was pleasant in the fading light.

They rode along a dry streambed and saw the tracks Yahlavi's horse had made as the Parthian had ridden to the fort.

"Should be soon," Rufio said, and as they turned left through a narrow gorge they saw two men seated on horseback in the deep blue shadows of the ravine and patiently waiting for the coming of Rome.

Rufio and Crus stopped about twenty feet away.

The man on the right was clearly the leader. He reeked of authority and the confidence of command.

"You're supposed to be unarmed," Durena said in a soft voice.

"You're supposed to be in Parthia," Crus answered with the cool assurance bought at great price in the valley of the Rhenus.

Rufio smiled to himself.

"Did not even your Caesar say that it was not the custom of Rome to negotiate with an armed enemy?"

"Caesar is dead," Rufio answered. "He died unarmed."

"Shall we dismount?" Durena slid from his sleek Turanian bay without waiting for a reply.

The Parthian leader was the first to sit, and Aridates sat after him.

Rufio and Crus dismounted and pushed their scabbards out of the way and sat on the ground beside their horses.

"Yahlavi?" Durena asked.

"Probably in the bath house by now," Crus said. "Waiting for our return."

"You Romans and your hostages...." Durena said.

"A practice forced on us," Crus answered.

Rufio was not certain, but Durena might have been the handsomest man he had ever seen in his life. Darker than the few Parthians Rufio had known, Durena would have commanded attention anywhere. He was taller than most Romans and wore an off-white belted tunic and trousers. His neat black hair came down over his ears and was secured by a camel hair headband. He wore no helmet but a simple red cloth cap on the back of his head that came to a soft point at the crown. It gave little protection, but Rufio suspected it was there so his men could see him easily on the battlefield. His moustache and pointed black beard were carefully trimmed. Dark eyes, of indeterminate color in the half-light, missed nothing. Rufio guessed that Durena was about thirty years old. Later Rufio would learn that he was forty-two.

"Feel free to speak," Crus said with an expansive gesture. "I am Crus of the Twenty-fifth Legion."

"Legion?" Durena said. "I was told there was only a cohort."

"Rome spans the world."

"We want—." Aridates began but was silenced by a look from Durena.

Aridates appeared to be about twenty-five and wore the pinched and starved look that so often seemed to adorn the envious and the weak. To Rufio, he had the aspect of a man who would cheerfully throw a sack of kittens into an icy river.

"How may we induce you to go?" Durena asked.

"Go where?" Crus said.

"Back to Rome."

"Rome is anywhere the soldiers of Caesar lay their heads."

"Then how may we rouse you from your slumber?"

Crus smiled. "You have. That's why we're here."

"And this one?" Durena said, looking at Rufio.

Crus turned to Rufio and nodded.

"Rufio," the centurion said.

"The commander...." Durena said.

"The tribune is the commander," Rufio answered.

"I see," Durena said with a knowing look. He turned back to Crus. "Will gold induce you?"

"Don't be foolish."

"Tribune, may I speak?" Rufio said.

Crus nodded. "I'm already growing weary of this."

"We're on a commission from Caesar himself," Rufio said. "You'll have to kill us all—or yield."

"I cannot yield," Durena whispered in a dust-choked voice heavy with the weariness of one who had ridden many hard miles only to end up nowhere.

"There is no glory here," Rufio said, and suddenly he felt an odd compassion for the Parthian warrior.

"*Here?*" Durena said. "There is no glory anywhere."

"Then why . . . ?"

"To regain some of what I've lost."

"Surely a great commander knows that along that road lies madness."

Durena stared into Rufio's eyes and then turned to Crus. "The heart of a poet lurks in this soldier's soul."

Durena rose and took a water flask from his saddle and removed the top and offered the flask to Rufio.

The Roman took it from him and drank.

"Nabataean water," Durena said.

Rufio had a second sip and handed back the flask. "No doubt that's why it's so sweet."

Durena offered it to Crus, who declined, and then then the Parthian sat back down. "What if we simply ride around you? Sweep past your petty cohort and shake this rotten hovel they call Judaea?"

"You'd never do that," Rufio said.

"Why wouldn't we?" Aridates asked.

Rufio ignored him.

"I would like to know," Durena said.

"Because you cannot afford to," Rufio answered. "We can disregard you if we choose, by you cannot close your eyes to us."

"You sound very confident of that."

"I can afford to be. You'd never risk having a Roman cohort at your rear in a hostile land when you knew that the legions from Syria might be coming down to smash into your front. Even this thing"—he pointed to Aridates—"would know that much. Let alone the Parthians' finest commander."

"Then what can we do?" Durena asked.

Rufio was shocked because Durena genuinely seemed to want to know.

"Commander," Rufio said, "it's not our task to tell you what you can do. It's out duty to tell you what you *cannot* do."

The silence seemed to last a week.

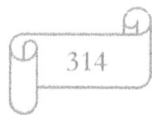

"Besides," Crus said, "Rome has heard a rumor that if you're successful, the toad on the Parthian throne plans to have you struck down and to seize your triumph." He gestured to Aridates.

"Durena," Rufio said, "if you win, you still lose—and if you lose on the battlefield, you lose even more. These Judaeans aren't going to take captives. Herod is pitiless."

"Ah, centurion," he answered with a sigh, "don't you think I know that?"

"Then why are you here?"

A mournful smile drifted across his face. "Where else can a fighting man go?"

"To Rome. Cross the Tiber of your own accord and you'll be treated like a prince. Be dragged there in chains—that's another matter."

"And betray my country?"

"Your country has already betrayed *you*." Rufio glanced at the glaring Aridates. "What about this reptile? Do you dare turn your back on him?"

"I never turn my back. But I must do what I was born to do."

"To kill Judaean children in their beds?"

"I would never do that. But why is the pride of Rome here? You've tormented us for years beyond number. Crassus, Antonius. Anyone who wants to gild his glory by killing Parthians. What good is this wasteland to Rome?"

"We don't want Judaea," Rufio said. "Regardless of what these Judaeans think. Or what you think. Why would we want it? There's nothing here."

"Then why . . . ?"

"Judaea is a buffer. Or a doorway—depending on how one wants to use it. It's always been that between East and West. Rome will tolerate no disturbance here."

"And you care nothing for these Judaeans?"

"I didn't say that. But that's not your concern. Our steel is your concern."

Nimbus shied suddenly and took two quick steps backward.

Rufio looked up and saw an archer standing on the ridge to his right at the top of the gorge.

"There," Crus said.

Another bowman was poised on the opposite crest to the left. Aridates stood.

"A man of honor?" Crus said with contempt to Durena.

"What is this?" Durena demanded of Aridates.

"If we cut off the head, the Roman beast dies," Aridates answered.
"I gave my word."
"To these?"
"To the world."
Rufio began to stand.
"Stay where you are!" Aridates said.
Rufio started measuring distances between himself and the Parthians.
"What about Yahlavi?" Durena said to Aridates.
"Less than nothing."
"They'll kill him."
Aridates smiled. "I'll try not to weep too—."
Rufio lunged at Aridates, but it was pointless. An arrow sheared into the side of Aridates' skull. A pair of screams rocked the ravine, and the two archers from above plunged to the sand a few feet away.
Three men pierced with arrows in the time it took for Crus to leap to his feet beside his centurion.
Sword in hand, Rufio rushed over to Aridates, and Durena stared at him in disbelief.
"You brought archers to ambush us?" the Parthian said.
"No, that's an Eastern ruse." He sheathed his sword. "Ask this corpse." Rufio placed a hob-nailed sandal on Aridates' neck and pulled on the arrow. It slid out of his head with a horrible sucking sound. After examining it, he handed it to Durena. "This isn't Roman."
Durena wiped some of the blood and brain matter from the strange black arrowhead. "What is this?" he said, thumbing the edge.
"Obsidianus," Rufio answered. "Glass from a volcano."
Durena stared at Rufio for several moments. "Who uses missiles like this?"
"Only the gods can say. And they watch over Rome."
Durena looked around at the three broken bodies.
"That is what awaits you," Crus said. "All of you."
Durena turned away from the dead men. "And Yahlavi? Will you kill him now?"
"We'll see you on the field of battle in two days," Crus said.
"Where?"
"A place of our choosing. Find it. We'll be waiting."

52

WHY CHANGE OUR HOME FOR LANDS WARM WITH ANOTHER SUN? WHAT EXILE FROM HIS COUNTRY FINDS THAT HE HAS LEFT HIMSELF ALSO BEHIND?

HORACE

"I'm prepared to die," Yahlavi said in a voice that sounded unprepared.

"Well, you might die," Rufio said, not bothering to look up from his desk as he sorted through some documents. "But it won't be at the tribune's hand. We're keeping you here to spare your life."

Yahlavi seemed stunned.

"In two days, Durena will be dead. There's no reason for you to share his folly."

Yahlavi just stood there.

"I'm busy," Rufio said, finally looking up. "Go!"

A few minutes after he left, Flavia rushed in as Rufio was getting ready to leave to confer with his tribune and the other centurions.

"I heard what happened," she said and ran to him and threw her arms around him in a crushing hug.

"All is well." He pointed to a strange arrow on the desk. "Thank you for your prayers."

"*My* prayers?"

"Oh, yes," he said with a smile. "Who but Flavia has the wiles to summon the Archer of the Night?"

He kissed her on the bridge of her nose and went off into the darkness. When he arrived at Crus's office, the other five centurions were already there. On their behalf, Decius had asked for this meeting with the tribune.

Crus seemed upset. "Sit down, all of you." He pointed to the camp chairs he had positioned in front of his desk.

"Rufio," Decius said as he joined the half circle, "your father fought with Caesar, did he not?"

"He did."

"And did Caesar ever command from the front rank?"

"Like the fool Alexander?"

Decius's meaty face creased in a smile. "Like the fool Alexander."

"No. Not if it wasn't necessary."

Decius turned to Crus with a triumphant look.

"Apparently these brutes fear for my safety," Crus said to Rufio.

"The tribune should be on the high plain with Bellator," Decius said. "From there he can command the entire battlefield with signals and riders." He smiled. "Even troops as brilliant as the soldiers of the Second Cohort need their commander intact."

"He's right," Rufio said to Crus.

The tribune gave him a skeptical glare. "Then why didn't you tell me that?"

"I know my place. This battered old drunkard does not."

Decius laughed.

"It looks unanimous to me," Rufio said, and all the centurions laughed together.

"To command is to fight, tribune," Decius said. "Whether one draws one's sword or not."

Crus remained silent.

"We cannot afford for you to be struck down by a stray arrow," Decius said. "And besides that, after the battle who else can carry our glory to the halls of the Palatinum?"

The centurions rumbled their approval.

Crus stood up, and the soldiers stood as well.

"Thank you," Crus said in a soft voice. "Know this, though—if you fall, I'll fall with you." He seemed to be trying to clear the emotion from his throat. "Now return to your troops. And let me offer a prayer to Minerva for all of you."

The men turned and began leaving.

"You stay," Crus said to Rufio.

When they had gone, Crus gazed at Rufio for a few moments.

"Did you encourage them to do this?"

"No, tribune." He smiled. "But I expected it."

"Then why didn't you simply tell me?"

"I preferred to let these fine men show you what they truly are."

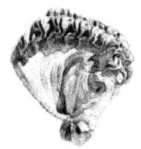

A large fire crackled in the middle of the parade ground, and the centurions and Bellator had gathered on camp chairs on either side of a small table set up in front of it. Most of the century was seated on the ground before them. Crus suspected that only those on guard duty were missing. Off to the right, he could just barely make out Flavia sitting on the ground at the edge of the darkness. Morlana was sitting between her legs, and Flavia's arms were wrapped around her protectively.

Crus stayed at the back in the half-light. Rufio rose from one of the chairs and walked to the center and leaned casually against the table.

"About a year ago, I had to give a talk to my century," Rufio said, folding his arms. "They didn't know me yet, although a few of them already wanted to kill me—Valerius will give you details...."

The troops burst out laughing, none more loudly than Valerius, whom Crus could see sitting in the front rank.

"Diocles made much of my talk in his book, all sorts of literary flourishes, but you know how writers are—always in love with bombast."

"We want Diocles!" one of them yelled, laughing.

"But that was long ago," Rufio went on. "After what we endured together at the Hill of Scorpions, I no longer have to explain to you our role in this life. So no rousing speeches tonight. But I do want to speak briefly about why we're fighting *here*."

He paused, as though gathering his thoughts, although Crus assumed it was more for effect than need.

"No vast army like the German horde is facing us, and we're not an army either, just a cohort. So no book like Diocles' great work will be written of this battle—although I've heard a rumor that some of you are keeping an ephemeris." Rufio peered into the darkness. "If any of you scribes are out there, perhaps you can think about passing your thoughts on to Diocles...."

Crus smiled to himself.

"But what we're about to do is as vital as what we accomplished with blood and blades along the Rhenus. The back doorway of a man's house is nothing. In fact, it's less than nothing, just an empty space. Yet it's the most important part of his home, because that's where the robbers force their way in. Judaea is a worthless mound of rubble—

except it's not. It's a doorway. And the door is weak and the hinge uncertain. So we've come here to show the robbers of the East that anyone who tries to smash the lock at the back of the Empire will bang his face against the might of Rome. The Parthian commander is an intelligent man, if I'm any judge of men, but even he doesn't understand. Do we want Judaea? Of course not." He held out his arms in a plaintive gesture. "What is there to want?"

The men laughed again, but a bit more softly than before.

"We're here at this moment precisely because we *don't* crave this wasteland. Rome wants only that Herod keep it. And that he keeps it safe. And makes sure his troops can keep the door bolted — *and we want them to do it without us.*" He pushed himself away from the table and strode forward into the midst of his men. "Garrisoning Judaea has never been to Augustus's liking and never will be. To him, it's a bitter weed. But if Herod falls, or if his heirs are fools, the legions will have to march back in. And if they do, they might have to boil in this cauldron for another hundred years. It's the fate of the Second Cohort of the Twenty-fifth Legion to make sure that's never necessary. And to do it, we have to show the Parthian bowmen — and everyone else out here — that no matter how much Herod totters, he's our ally. And that because of it, this gate is sealed with Roman steel."

"And show them we will," Valerius said.

"No troops on earth are better matched for this task," Rufio went on. "Of course, the Parthians are more experienced horsemen than you — how could they not be? — but they're lesser fighters." He placed his hands on his hips and swept the men with his gaze. "And because they're Parthians and you're Romans, they're also lesser *men*. May Victoria protect you all."

Only a soft murmuring followed, rather than the raucous cheering that had ended his speech in Gaul the year before. Now there was just quiet and manly acceptance.

"And perhaps one more thing . . . ?" Metellus asked from the front rank.

Rufio smiled. "Yes, and one more thing — I am with you always."

Crus drifted back into the darkness before the soldiers dispersed. He waited until Rufio had time to return to his quarters. Ten minutes later Crus found him sitting silently at his desk and staring at something only he could see.

"We'll have the troughs finished and filled and brought out to the dry river bed tomorrow," Rufio said abruptly, standing as Crus entered. "And I'm going to tell each of the centurions to take his century out tomorrow to show them the battleground. I don't want them surprised by the sight of it the day they have to fight there."

Crus gestured for Rufio to sit back down.

"What's wrong?" Crus asked as he sat across from him.

Rufio looked puzzled. "Do you mean with the world?"

"With you."

He gazed off at a corner of the room and took a deep breath and let it out slowly. "I'm going to do something that I've never done before. Something I've dreaded my whole career." He looked back at Crus. "I'm going to kill a man I don't want to kill."

"I know. I could see it in your eyes."

A harsh laugh slipped out. "I used to be better at masking my feelings."

Crus said nothing.

"It isn't necessary to hate a man to make war on him—but it *is* necessary to hate at least what he stands for." Rufio shook his head helplessly. "Durena stands for valor and he stands for honor."

"He might stand for those things, but he fights for Phraates."

"That's the horror of it. And that's why I have to kill him. But it's an ugly killing all the same."

"He leads a thousand half-mercenaries who want to kick this kingdom off a cliff."

Rufio said nothing.

"And we're not going to let them," Crus said.

"I know. We definitely are not. I've told the other centurions to order their troops to look for the rider with the red cap and strike him down as fast as possible. Those archers won't fight without a leader. Maybe we can end this thing quickly."

53

MANHOOD IS TESTED BY ADVERSITY, AND VALOR CLIMBS UNAFRAID THE ROCKY PATH AND DIFFICULT ASCENT THAT LEADS TO GLORY.

SILIUS ITALICUS

Rufio awoke two hours before dawn and made a point of sharing porridge with some of his troops. By the time he returned to his quarters, Morlana had already gone with Arrianus to the pens to feed the horses, and Flavia was practicing with her bow behind the barracks.

"Barbarian!" he called to her.

She turned and smiled and hurried to him.

He pointed to the ground and they both sat.

"I hope you don't have any thoughts about fighting in this battle..."

"No," she said. "I know that war is for men."

"Good. I have a task for you. I want you to ride to Hezrail and find Simon and tell him to prepare his people to come to the fort early tomorrow. Stay at Morlana's house in Hezrail overnight and ride back with them in the morning. Take Morlana with you. If any of the children are afraid, she can calm them."

Flavia looked hesitant.

"What's wrong?"

"The Judaeans don't deal much with women, do they?"

"No, but I cannot spare a solider to send."

"But how do you know Simon will do what I say? If he'll trust me?"

"It's his choice. I've already spoken with him about it. I don't know if he can read, but I'll also get Matthias to write a note. There's only so much we can do. But don't worry—they'll come."

"Shall we go now?"

"As soon as you can."

"All of you will be gone by the time we get back tomorrow, won't you?"

"Yes."

She turned away and said nothing.

"Don't worry."

She looked back at him. "I won't. At least as not much as I did last year. I know that Victoria watches over you. . . . But this time . . . I don't know. . . . Even she might not be enough."

Rufio smiled. "We have to trust."

"I'll try. I know Morlana does."

"How do you know that?" he asked, laughing.

"She's not worried about you at all—to her, you already *are* a god."

Flavia took his right hand and gestured for him to stand.

"Hold me one more time," she said, slipping her arms around him. "And tell me that you'll hold me again when the battle is done."

Pulling her tightly to him, he pressed his cheek to the side of her face and inhaled her scent and promised that they would be bound together forever. And he hoped that Victoria would forgive him for making a pledge that she alone had the power to fulfill.

By one hour after sunrise, most of the gyrus had been dismantled, and two hours later the first water troughs were ready to be filled and carted away. Rufio praised the Romans and Judaeans working side by side and then rode off.

Nimbus was especially responsive this day. The man and the animal were becoming one. There was still much to be done, but Rufio knew that once the gate had been opened, and only the horse himself could open it, success was certain.

Rufio rode to each of the barracks and checked again on the health of the men. All the centurions assured him that their troops were at their peak.

From beyond the walls toward the parade ground, Rufio could hear hideous sounds only a Celt could love, practice blasts from the big bronze boar's head of the carnyx. Bellator was no Sequani, but at least he had powerful lungs.

As Rufio rode down the Via Praetoria, he realized how much he was going to miss this little fort. Though slight in comparison with the great timber citadel at Aquabona, this gleaming and indestructible stone stronghold in the desert seemed to swagger with a pride of permanence denied to even the vastest structure built from wood.

Rufio noticed that there were few Judaeans about, which was odd since they were supposed to have a day of rest. On an impulse, he rode out to the archery field. There they were, toiling with their bows.

Rufio dismounted and walked over to Matthias at the edge of the field.

"They're doing well," Rufio said.

"I'm proud of them. And they're proud of themselves."

Rufio folded his arms and watched as they unleashed a few more practice flights. "Parthians beware."

Matthias smiled.

"May I offer a suggestion?" Rufio asked.

At one time, that question would have made Matthias look anxious. Now he took it well.

"Yes."

"Give them the day off. They've earned it. And they need one. It's possible to train a soldier too much."

"I don't understand."

"To take him to his peak but then work him harder until he slips over the top and starts sliding down the other side."

"I see. Thank you. We'll rest today."

"And make sure you rest, too."

Matthias pointed to the ground, and they both sat in the shadow of Nimbus. "Thank you for all you've done."

"I did it for Rome."

"Thank you anyway," Matthias said. "I've learned so much."

"Soldiering isn't very difficult. Harder to learn men."

"That's what I meant." He smiled. "You don't take gratitude very well, do you?"

"I do if I'm worthy of it."

"Don't you deserve it from me?"

"I deserve it from Rome."

"And will you get it?"

"I believe so. In an oblique way."

"Oblique?"

"From an angle."

Matthias turned to his men and shouted to them that it was time to stop for the day. Then he just stared at the ground near Nimbus's hoofs.

"I have much to do," Rufio said and rose.

Matthias looked up. "You'll be leaving soon."

"In one way or another. If we're beaten, I'll be dead. If we're victorious, our task will be complete and you'll be taking command. Don't worry. You're ready."

Matthias stood. "I'll pray to Elah for you."

Rufio gripped Nimbus's mane and leaped into the saddle and then smiled at Matthias. "I've heard he wields a big sword. So I'll take it."

Rufio rode out to the horse pens and was surprised to see Crus and Arrianus in what looked like an intense discussion.

Rufio dismounted.

"Join us, centurion," Crus said.

Rufio walked over to where the two men were standing in the shade of a stack of medica. He let Nimbus help himself to the hay.

"Your little strator has been hurt," Crus said in annoyance.

"Morlana?"

"No, I said the little one."

"The tribune is a cruel man," Rufio said.

"Show him," Crus ordered.

Arrianus held out his bruised and swollen right wrist.

"Were you bucked off?" Rufio asked.

He looked embarrassed. "The horse shied and I slid off."

"Is it broken?"

"No," Crus said, "but he can't wield a sword. He was concealing this until I saw him trying to work with only one hand."

"You know better than to hide something like this from me," Rufio said.

"I can't let down my friends."

"Trying to fight with an arm like that *is* letting them down," Crus said.

"Is there a solution?" Rufio asked.

Crus stared at Arrianus. "Is there?"

Arrianus hesitated. "No, tribune."

"That's why you're a soldier and I'm a tribune. Of course there is. I need a rider with me on the ridge if I have to send messages. You're with me until the last Parthian flees or dies."

Arrianus seemed stunned.

"Your grandchildren can thank me when you tell them of this fight," Crus said. "Now get back to your charges."

Arrianus looked at Rufio and smiled.

"Yes, tribune," he said, turning back to Crus. "Thank you."

Crus could not help laughing once Arrianus was out of earshot. "That wild little ferret. There aren't ten senators combined who could make even half of him."

Hoofbeats caused both men to turn and look toward the four horsemen riding in from the desert.

"Decius has gone out with the morning patrol every day," Crus said.

"Well, I certainly didn't order that. He's a good man."

"You fought together in Spain?"

"We served in the same legion but never shared a battlefield."

Decius trotted over on his horse while his soldiers rode into the fort for rest and refreshment. He dismounted as gracefully as a boulder tumbling off a cliff.

"Tribune," Decius said, removing his helmet.

Crus smiled. "You saw something. . . ."

"They're here."

"How far?" Rufio asked.

"We stopped at the rise above the riverbed from Hell and saw their dust on the plain beyond it. About six or seven miles off."

"Did you see any scouts?"

"Three."

"Did they notice you?"

"Oh, yes."

Rufio was surprised by Decius's smile. "And . . . ?"

"We made sure they saw us. We behaved as if we didn't notice them and rode down into the riverbed. I told my men to dismount and to act as if they were measuring out a site for a marching camp. The Parthians are riding back to Durena right now to tell him that the ignorant Romans and the pathetic Judaean doves will be fluttering around in that nest tomorrow."

Rufio laughed. "And helpless before the Parthian hawks that'll come swooping onto us."

"At least that was the idea," Decius said. "They should be waiting for us at the top of the grade and then come charging down into the gorge."

"Excellent." Rufio turned to Crus. "What our clever centurion has done here is use an old stratagem that's always fresh. He's enticing the enemy to do what we want by giving them information that they think is secret and that they believe they've gotten on their own. There's no more effective seduction."

"And because of that they'll do what we need them to do?" Crus asked. "Confront us on the riverbed?"

"This is war, so nothing is certain," Rufio said. "But this is close. They think they're going to trap us. They're not."

"Well done," Crus said to Decius. "If we survive to make it back to Gaul, I'll speak with Sabinus about the appropriate honor."

"Tribune, the only honor I'd like is the privilege of never having to sit in a saddle again."

"Go get some food and drink," Crus said, laughing.

As Decius led his horse back toward the gate, Rufio stared after him. "Where does Augustus find such men?"

"Don't you know?" Crus said. "In the Twenty-fifth Legion, all he has to do is throw a stone and he'll hit one.

Rufio asked me to go to Hezrail to tell Simon that it was time for his people to seek the safety of the fort. I was worried that Simon would not deal with a woman, but he was courteous and kind. He had already prepared the villagers for their short journey, and food and water were quickly gathered. Rufio was right that some of the children were afraid. At least that was true of the girls. The boys considered it all a great adventure. Morlana tried to soothe the girls, but they drew back from her. Though she has spent much of her life here, she is still an outsider, a golden-haired oddity the Judaeans cannot comprehend. Or, at least, that is what they pretend. Mallius made a mistake long ago in bringing his sensitive daughter to this place.

After everything was arranged for the trip back the following morning, we went to Morlana's house, where I made sure she was settled in for the rest of the day. Then I told her something that I had decided during the ride to Hezrail. I explained to her that she had to go back tomorrow with the villagers without me because there was something I had to do. I told her that there was no time for me to give her the details and that she just had to trust me. She gazed at me with that mixture of innocence and intensity that I find so endearing and that makes me love her so. I was surprised that she had no questions but just reached out and kissed me on the cheek and then squeezed me to her. I was happy that she did not question me, because I would have found it difficult to explain to her that I had been riding in the wrong direction.

54

IN NOTHING ARE MEN MORE LIKE GODS THAN IN COMING TO THE RESCUE OF THEIR FELLOW MEN.

CICERO

Two hours before dawn Rufio awoke and cleaned his teeth and washed. While he dressed, Neko prepared a breakfast of wheat porridge and fruit. Then Rufio stood by his desk and ate in silence.

"What do you think, old friend?" Rufio said at last.

Neko set down Rufio's sword and dagger belts and water flask. "I believe Victoria will need to be active this day."

Rufio washed down the porridge with some cool water. "I agree."

"It's unfortunate that Diocles isn't here to record it."

"No, it's just as well that he's not. His literary flourishes need more scope. The Hill of Scorpions was sweeping and grand"—he smiled—"or at least Diocles made it seem that way. This place is sharp and harsh and corrosive. War is different out here. In the grit and the salt. A pitiless land spawns pitiless people."

"But aren't the Suebi pitiless, too?"

"There's a savagery to these eastern barbarians that I've never seen in anyone else. Killing a German is like striking down a lion. Fighting these Asiatics is like battering a thousand mad weasels. There's no glory here."

"But glory never exists among outside things but only within the hearts of the glorious." Neko smiled his knowing smile. "Is that not so?"

Rufio smiled back. "Armor."

Rufio remained quiet as Neko helped him put on his subarmalis and mail lorica. He omitted his greaves to avoid irritating his horse's sides.

Rufio held the heavy chain armor up at the waist as Neko fastened the swordbelt, and then Rufio let the small flap drop over the belt so the weight of the mail would now be carried partly by his hips. While Neko fastened the dagger belt around him, Rufio absently slid his right hand around Flavia's torque on his left wrist.

Neko waited for a moment and then handed him his cloak and left the room.

Rufio walked over to his little table. He pulled the cloak up from behind him and draped it over his head. Then he dropped to one knee before the red porphyry statue of Victoria.

Never did he ask anything for himself, regardless of what others might have thought. Only of his men did he speak. Today he knelt longer than he usually did, and he prayed that Victoria's wings would embrace his men as tenderly as they had always enveloped him.

When he was done, he stood and set his cloak aside. He noticed that Neko had returned and was standing by the door with his helmet.

"I'll see you before the sun sets," Rufio said, taking the helmet.

Neko nodded, and Rufio stepped outside.

Nimbus was waiting for him. Rufio held the reins and rubbed him on the forehead. He pushed the red fly fringe out of the way and pressed his lips to the side of Nimbus's face just below his left eye and gently held them there affectionately. Nimbus lowered his head and sighed softly. Rufio caressed him again and then tied his helmet to the saddle and mounted.

The aroma of cooking food wafted along the street outside of the barracks block. The moon was still up and many of his men were already in full armor and leading their horses back from the pens. No soldier in any army likes getting up early, but Rufio had trained his troops well. Long ago, when his hair was black, he had heard an old centurion in Egypt tell an optio, "Always make your men rise in the dark. Soon they won't know how not to."

That lesson had stuck. Rufio saw, after only about a month of steady routine, that the clock inside a man became more accurate than any absurd water clock anyone had yet devised. His men would get up early without being ordered simply because their bodies commanded that they do.

He rode along and spoke quietly with them or shared a joke. They smiled or teased him back. Rufio was continually amused at how people unfamiliar with fighting men always had the most bizarre notions about them. The patricians in Rome regarded them as barely sentient and pathetically crude, especially because so many of the soldiers hailed from rural areas. It ministered to the sense of their soulless self-importance for senators to speak of them, when they referred to them at all, as if one needed to cleanse one's mouth afterward. One surely risked defiling his tongue with a recitation of their vulgarities. Yet, as Rufio knew, soldiers were among the most courteous and polite of men. Living a daily life of hierarchical discipline and prudent speech, these quiet warriors, justly feared along the rivers of Hell, were more confidently soft-spoken and serene than nine out of ten people babbling in the streets of Rome.

Other Romans took a view opposite from that of the desiccated elite. Instead they believed that soldiers, especially before battle, were roiling with martial passion and a sensual craving for the profane delights of the battlefield. Such fantasists would have been stunned to learn that fighting men rarely spoke of fighting and almost never did so beforehand. They preferred quiet moments checking their gear or praying to their gods or simply relishing the small pleasure of tossing a few scraps to a hungry dog in the street.

When Rufio had finished chatting with the soldiers of his century, he rode along the barracks toward where Decius had dismounted to help straighten the lorica of one of his newer men. Although a bit embarrassing, small gestures like that also meant a great deal to an uncertain soldier.

When the trooper left, Rufio said, "Would you help me with mine?"

Decius mounted his horse and laughed, but not with his usual energy.

Rufio bent down and asked for a few figs from a soldier standing by his horse nearby and then handed one to Decius.

"Is everything all right?" Rufio asked.

"In this cauldron?"

Rufio had learned long ago that when Decius chose not to answer a question he just tossed out another question to deflect it.

"The centurion," Rufio said. "The king of those who bring comfort. But who consoles the consolers? Allow Silver Hair to help polish your corroded bronze."

This time Decius's laugh was genuine. He made a gesture, and the two old friends rode along the barracks block together.

"How well do you sleep before battle?" Decius asked.

"Soundly."

"I do, too. Except for last night. I kept thinking about Gaul."

"Nothing strange in that."

"But it was the oddest thing. . . ." Decius shook his head. "A few months ago in Gaul, I scooped up a little sparrow drowning in a barrel. I dried him and warmed him and fed him. Then I let him go. But he wouldn't go. Not far anyway. . . ."

Rufio smiled. "Like a centurion. If he gets thrown out of the fort, where on earth can he fly to?"

Decius turned and looked at Rufio with a serious expression. "I hadn't thought of that."

"I was just joking."

"Ever since then, I've fed him. Every day. He comes to the window ledge mornings and late afternoons and jumps on my wrist and takes seeds from the back of my hand. I asked Corbulus from the Third Cohort to feed him for me while we're gone."

Rufio remained quiet.

"I have a woman in Aquabona," Decius said. "A wonderful Sequani woman. . . ."

"Yes, I know."

"But last night all I could think of was that delicate little bird waiting there. Trusting. Waiting for me to come home and feed him. And how much I want to get back there to do that."

Rufio smiled in the darkness. "Such a small thing. . . ."

Decius looked at him. "I guess that's always true, isn't it?"

"The smallest things are always the greatest things."

"I don't know why I never realized that before. Not until I rode into to this desolation."

"You had to come a long way to find it, though, didn't you?"

"Yes," he said with a smile. "But it was worth the trip."

The other four centurions could be seen riding toward the Principia up the street. The tribune and Bellator were seated on their horses just in front of it.

"I'll be there," Rufio said as he saw Matthias coming.

Decius went on ahead.

"Let's go together," Rufio said as the Judaean rode up. "All is well?"

"I hope it is," he said as they rode toward the Principia. "I don't want to be a fool. And a disaster to my men."

"Disaster? What do you mean?"

"On the battlefield a few hours from now."

"Don't worry about that. Your men are looking very fine. And they have trust in you. So does the tribune."

"You're not just being polite?"

"Have I ever been?"

Matthias laughed. "You were very harsh when you first arrived here. Where did that go?"

"Harsh? Toward the sons of David? You sound like Bellator."

"You've changed. Toward us I mean. Softened."

"Changed?" he said with a laugh. "Ask anyone—Rufio's flaws are carved in marble."

"Perhaps. But Elah has been known to write deeply even on tablets of stone."

That remark startled him, and touched him as well. "My friend, we'll do what we can together to keep the barbarians at bay."

Rufio and Matthias joined the other centurions in front of the Principia. Bellator left Crus's side and brought his horse into line with the centurions.

"Comrades," Crus said. "Anything to report?"

"The cohort is ready," Rufio answered quietly.

"I want to take the field in one hour."

"Tribune, the cohort can depart in half that," Rufio said.

"Excellent." Crus looked at Matthias. "On the march, I want our Judaean soldiers in the center."

"It'll be done, tribune," Matthias said.

"The First and Second centuries take the van, Fifth and Sixth the flanks, Third and Fourth the rear." Crus let his gaze glide over his officers. "I want to thank all of you for everything you've done for Rome. And for your tribune. The journey, the training, and above all your patience in a land that tries all men's patience." He paused and then said, "I'd planned to say to you today that we don't have to win, just keep those hard-riding savages off the throats of the Judaeans—that if we simply fight to a draw, we triumph." He grinned. "But whom am I talking to? Let's send their blistered asses all the way back to the Euphrates!"

The centurions roared with laughter.

"All right," Crus said. "Let's ride!"

55

MEN ARE LEAST SAFE FROM WHAT SUCCESS INDUCES THEM NOT TO FEAR.

LIVIUS

Faint light was spreading on the eastern horizon as the Roman and Judaean formation descended into the dry riverbed. Enormous chalky cliffs of perfectly flat horizontal layers towered on both sides of the troops as they moved on. The horses had been watered so well that few of them were tempted to try to veer off to the full wooden troughs that they passed.

From the van, Crus turned and inspected the soldiers behind him. No one knew how to hold formation like Romans. The Judaeans in the center looked a bit ragged, but still much better than they had just a month earlier.

Riding beside Crus, Bellator said, "Now that it's bright enough, it's time to spread out."

The old decurion signaled and the two centuries in front fanned into a wide and thin screen. The centuries on the flanks and at the rear did likewise.

Crus looked to Bellator for an explanation.

"In the dark, we have to ride a tight formation so some of the troops don't drift away and get lost, but when the sun comes up that's not necessary."

"But why spread out so much?"

"When saving space isn't important, a broad screen is best. Your troops can scan more terrain as they move and so the formation has less chance of being surprised." He turned to Arrianus, who was riding next to him. "Go on ahead, all the way to the widest part of the riverbed. Let us know if you see any movement or scouts."

Without a word, he cantered away down the big wash.

Crus continued to survey the surrounding cliffs. He wanted to remember every detail for the grandchildren who would sit with him someday around a fireside in the Alban Hills, the future home that Rufio had imagined for him on an uneasy day before the battle at Scorpion Hill. As the sun rose higher, the golden color of the walls and bluffs lightened, and he found himself squinting at the fierce brightness that seemed to challenge the fragile eyes of men. Occasionally the flat layers would give way to eerie swirls in the cliff faces, as if some bored god or idle titan had taken a finger and dreamily sketched on a superhuman scale. The entire expanse dazzled him with an utterly ferocious beauty that would have been incomprehensible to him just a few months before.

After about another quarter hour, Crus called a rest halt. The Romans dismounted and checked tack and tightened saddle girths. Then all of them sat in the shade of their horses and drank. The Judaeans had no choice but to sit in the sun.

Crus stayed mounted and rode about among his troops. They were taut, as they should have been, but confident, and they teased him to relieve their tension. About ten minutes later, he ordered them to remount, and they did so with a fluidity and grace that made him proud to be one of them, let alone their commander.

Dust from far down the riverbed showed that Arrianus was returning. Crus trotted back to his position at the head of the column.

Arrianus galloped up. "They're waiting for us," he said, breathing heavily.

"Relax," Bellator said. He offered Arrianus his own water flask.

"Thank you. I still have mine." He looked at Crus. "They're on the flat just above the grade leading down into this riverbed. They're dismounted and they have their horses lying down beside them."

"How could you see them from here?" Crus asked.

"I couldn't. I wanted to get a look at the whole area, so I rode to the raised spot from where the tribune and the decurion are going to watch the battle. From there they were obvious, like flies on a corpse."

"Well done. Tell the other centurions what you've seen." Crus turned and signaled to the troops behind him, and they moved off as smoothly as a wave rolling down a stream.

The eastern sun was slicing their eyes by the time that Crus and Bellator and Arrianus reached the little dry wash draining off to the left. The formation moved on while the three of them turned away and climbed to the flat plain from which they would see the battlefield below.

When they reached the top, Crus gazed across the gorge to the flatland beyond. Shimmering warm waves rippled skyward from the surface. The Parthians and their mounts lying on the ground were easily visible, but the upsurges of heat deformed them into seemingly grotesque creatures, poised now to pillage without purpose a meaningless and lifeless netherworld.

The three men dismounted. Below them and to the north they could see their troops entering the gorge. The two centuries in the van pulled off to the flanks and allowed the broad front of the three Judaean ranks to be completely exposed. The First Century and Fifth Century formed two columns of four riders in a rank on the right, while the Second Century and Sixth Century assembled into parallel files on the Judaean left. The Third Century dropped back into reserve on the right flank, and the Fourth Century did likewise on the left.

"Tribune." Arrianus pointed across the gorge.

The Parthians were getting their horses on their feet. Even that small amount of activity started stirring up dust.

"Do you think the centurions can see that?" Crus asked Bellator.

"They see it. Arrianus, your eyes are better than mine. Can you make out any horns?"

Arrianus studied the gathering mass. "No."

Bellator nodded. "The Parthians like to blow horns to unnerve their enemies, but I don't think they'll do it today. They want surprise. They'll charge down that grade without warning."

Suddenly Crus felt so afraid for his men that he started quivering. He took two steps backward behind Arrianus's line of vision.

Bellator laid a soothing hand on Crus's shoulder.

"It's all right, tribune," Arrianus said without turning around. "All of us shake."

The Parthians began mounting.

"Soon," Bellator said.

Crus looked at the Judaeans below. Their bows hung from their shoulders and were invisible because of the Roman infantry shields they held in front of them. Crus wondered how they could stand so still. Were they that brave? Or that terrified?

He looked back at the high plain. The Parthians were all mounted now. At this distance and with the dust, no red-capped rider could be seen.

Bellator took a sip from his flask to wet his lips. "Hold onto your animals."

Crus and Arrianus gripped their horses' reins, and Bellator raised the bronze boar-headed horn to the heavens.

Rufio's tension conveyed itself to his horse, and Nimbus was nervous and stiff between his rider's legs. Rufio pulled one rein gently back and then the other to flex his neck and soften him, and then they peeled off from the front of the formation to the flank.

The First Century took the far right, with the Fifth Century to Rufio's left and the Third to the rear. Metellus was riding to the right of the entire double column. All the horses were twitchy and alert, ears constantly moving and nostrils snorting out salt and sand stirred up from the surface of the gorge.

"You're not nearly as impressive without your wolf skin," Rufio said to his signifer as they rode on.

"Calpurnia claims I'd be handsome covered even in rags and ashes."

"How is your Gallic princess? And the little one?"

"Very well. Of course, Calpurnia would have liked to come with the cohort, but not all are so blessed with the favor of the centurion."

"Flavia is my archery teacher."

"I'd forgotten. And all in the First Century are certain that no one is as skilled as Flavia at the delicate mysteries of unstringing the centurion's bowstring."

Rufio bit down hard to stop from laughing and gave Metellus the imitation of a glare. "You're on the edge, signifer."

"I know," he answered with mock weariness, "but isn't that the fate of all who toil in the cause of Caesar?"

Not as adept with blade or brawl as some, the sandy-haired signifer, ironically so un-Roman in appearance, was nonetheless one of Rufio's greatest treasures. He was among the most quick-thinking soldiers Rufio had ever known, and yet he concealed it with an offhand air that many misunderstood. Having him here on the flank of the column was to Rufio a source of comfort that Metellus would never have imagined. His unself-conscious valor by Rufio's side in the mud of Gaul had shown the spine of Rome to all who had been privileged to see. And, to Metellus, jumping down a well to save a child was no more an act of bravery than brushing out the mane of his horse. After all, the signifer would have argued, would any true Roman not have done the same?

"What is it?" Metellus asked as Rufio looked at him.

"I was just thinking about the little girl in the well."

Metellus smiled, and it was not a mocking smile this time. "That's interesting, because I was, too."

Rufio studied the three long Judaean ranks to his left. They stood as still as pillars with their shields before them. Matthias commanded from the far right of the first rank. Rufio had advised him otherwise, but he had insisted. Beyond them, Rufio could make out Decius at the front rank of the Second Century on the Judaeans' left flank.

"Rufio," Metellus said and pointed forward.

Parthian bowmen, now mounted, could be seen readying themselves at the top of the grade above the riverbed. Through the heat waves and the dust, Rufio saw a rider raise his right hand.

A hideous blast on Bellator's carnyx shattered the air when the Parthian lowered his arm and the alien army swept down to its destiny.

Muffled by the soft surface, the hoofbeats of the Turanian horses seemed eerily distant, echoes heard only at the moment of waking on the edge of a dream. White dust enveloped all except the horsemen in front, but on they all came with the terrifying confidence of the courageous or the mad.

As the first riders cleared the grade and raced into the chasm, Rufio could hear Matthias shout a command. The Judaeans dropped their shields and gripped they bows. Each man nocked an arrow but held his weapon relaxed before him.

No more than five hundred feet distant were the Parthian horsemen when the front rank of Judaeans unleashed their first torrent. Wails of pain from the horses mixed with the cries of men as the wounded and the dead tumbled into the powder of the abyss. The second Judaean rank now launched its own shower of missiles in a great arc toward the hated foe. More screams and crippling and death filled the gorge, but now the Parthian bowmen could at last see through the dust. On a trumpet command, they halted in a single orderly mass, and their first storm of arrows tore into the Judaeans. Young men fell with arrows slicing through their faces or splintering their legs. The third rank ignored or failed to hear Matthias's command to shoot, and the Judaeans scrambled for the big Roman shields to protect themselves.

Rufio turned toward the high plain behind him and signaled to Bellator, and the old warrior blew two long blasts from the carnyx.

"Now!" Rufio shouted, unsheathing his sword, and the First and Fifth Centuries began their canter toward the invaders, as did the Second and Sixth on the opposite side of the field.

A trumpet sounded again from deep within the Parthian throng, and the entire horde of horseman suddenly whirled and galloped off.

Startled at this early use of the false retreat, Rufio raised his hand for a halt, and Metellus shouted the command down the columns. Across the field, the other centuries stopped as well.

About three hundred feet away, the inchoate swarm of Parthian riders began reassembling. What had seemed moments earlier like nothing more organized than chaotic streams of oil swirling across a plate now began to take sensible shape.

"What on earth is that?" Metellus said.

The Parthian horsemen started forming files of their own, four massive columns five ranks across. A flash of red could be seen flitting among the gathering riders.

Two volleys of Judaean arrows swished overhead and tore into the Parthians, but they never broke ranks and they seemed to absorb it almost as their due.

"They're better drilled than we thought," Rufio said to himself as much as to Metellus.

"Look how they're positioning," Metellus said, peering through the dust.

"Your eyes are sharper than mine. What is it?"

"Five swordsmen in the first rank, five archers in the second, then five more swordsmen, five more archers—all the way down each column. What *is* this?"

At that instant Rufio knew that he had made a disastrous mistake. Allowing Yahlavi to carry back tales of heavy Roman cavalry would have intimidated any rational leader of lightly armed bowmen, but now he realized that Durena was not even halfway sane but, rather, half-mad in his brilliance. Men who were not trained in the sword were about to use swords to screen their comrades against seasoned Roman swordsmen. And for what purpose, to what end? For petty booty? To earn the tentative benevolence of a petulant tyrant? None of this was remotely comprehensible to an arrogant race ever eager to boast that it had been suckled by a wolf. Rufio's intuitive self-assurance had been its own undoing. There was no sense to this, and that was the brilliance of it. Who could have foreseen it? These men with little skill would crudely hack to death Romans and Jews and in the course of it would die in the hundreds in the appalling suicidal fatalism of the East.

Another shriek of a Parthian trumpet rocked the walls of the abyss, and the four columns of Asiatic horsemen charged across the white riverbed. Rufio raised a hand, Bellator's carnyx blew twice, and the Romans dashed straight at them.

The Arabian horses were brilliant, and Bellator's training of the men held true. The Romans neatly avoided the scattered acacias, and the files kept their formation on this hideous field meant for nothing but the despairing wails of the doomed.

When the Parthian column facing the First Century saw that the Romans seemed about to crash into them, the Parthians stopped suddenly, and the entire column bunched up.

Rufio fronted the attack, and the first Roman horsemen tore into the Parthian first rank. A black-bearded Parthian flailed his sword at Rufio with mindless bravery, but the Roman pivoted out of the way. The Parthian swords were as short as the Roman blades, and each man struggled to reach his foe. At last in desperation the Parthian charged directly at Rufio's horse. The two great mounts crashed together at their chests. In his fury, Nimbus whipped his head around and pinned his ears and bit savagely at the Turanian horse's face. The animal squealed horribly as Nimbus's teeth tore into his upper lip. The Turanian pulled back, but Nimbus bit all the more deeply. With no choice left, the anguished horse finally bucked in his despair. The rider flew out of the saddle straight into Rufio. The Parthian landed across Nimbus's neck right in front of Rufio's saddle, with his eyes only inches from the Roman's. Rufio smashed the ebony pommel of his sword into the Parthian's face. Teeth and bones splintered and Rufio slammed him again in the forehead. The Parthian's fingers clawed at Rufio's mail, but he slipped to the ground while still managing to hold onto his sword.

The Parthian stabbed upward at Nimbus's belly, but Rufio kicked the Parthian's wrist and diverted the thrust. The unhorsed warrior struggled to one knee, and Rufio sliced down at an angle and caught the edge his jaw. His chin flew off like the chopped end of a loaf of hard bread. The Parthian dropped his sword and reached up to feel for the part of his face that was no longer there, and Rufio's blade came down into the side of his neck and finished the agony.

The four Romans to Rufio's left were slicing into the Parthians in front them, but during the fighting the Parthian archers directly behind had the chance to unleash their arrows at the Judaeans.

In just a few moments, three of the five Parthians before Rufio's men were dead on the ground and their horses scattered. Yet even before Rufio had time to order his first four men to roll back, the two surviving Parthians in the front had already begun to peel off and the first archers along with them. Five fresh Parthian horsemen armed with swords charged the Roman front rank.

The black stallion before Rufio was braver than the last, and his rider's eyes flashed with the confidence of his wild race. With ears pinned, his horse bolted straight at Nimbus. Rufio reined to his left and slashed down into the animal's skull and the shiny black head split like a rotted log. The horse's front legs buckled and Rufio cut upward at the face of the Parthian tumbling forward in a downward arc, and man and rider were dead in an instant.

"Metellus!" Rufio shouted.

The signifer galloped over from the right, his sword already bloodied.

"Ride across the field and tell the other centurions to stay with the first rank. Not to roll back with their men. We need them at the front."

Metellus nodded and was off.

"And watch your rear, soldier!" Rufio yelled, but the signifer was already gone.

56

WE ARE IN THE POWER OF NOTHING WHEN ONCE WE HAVE DEATH IN OUR OWN POWER.

SENECA

Crus stared in confusion at the chaos. Bellator was down on one knee and studying the battlefield like a master latrunculi player planning his moves.

"Everything looks wrong," Crus said. "What's happening down there?"

"Nothing that we expected. I'd never have thought Durena would chance that. Risk so many of his men by having them attack with swords. That man is audacity in the flesh."

"But look how many men he's already lost."

"Dozens in just a few minutes, but he's managed to shield his archers from the toughest cohort in Gaul and allow his bowmen to rip into the Judaeans."

"How can we help from here?"

Bellator seemed not hear. "The Judaeans are too close. They don't need that short range. They're shooting arrows at men without armor. They need to pull back to protect themselves better. To make the Parthian arrow shots weaker. And they can still take down those archers. Arrianus! Mount up! And make sure you carry your shield."

Arrianus was instantly in the saddle.

"Ride down to Rufio and tell him that the Jews should withdraw at least another two hundred feet. They're bleeding there for no reason. He'll have you to take the order to Matthias. After that, ride across the field and tell Decius on the left flank what's about to happen. Go!"

Arrianus dashed off.

Still down on one knee, Bellator leaned forward with his forearms folded against his other thigh and continued analyzing the battleground. "Is it a surprise that Crassus died in the sands? Or that Antonius crawled home in shame?"

Crus said nothing.

"It probably seems like confusion to you, but it isn't," Bellator said. "Forget that you're looking at men and horses and examine the pattern. Two columns on the right coming down and swirling to their left and the two on the other side of the field riding down and sweeping to the right. Durena knows how vulnerable his archers are, so instead of the usual Parthian tactic of staying out of range — which he knows he can't do because of the Judaean archers — he's keeping them moving all the time. Then he came up with this idea of screening his own bowmen with swordsmen."

"But those men haven't been trained to fight with swords on horseback — have they?"

"No, but that's no good fortune for us."

"I don't understand."

"Ask a Greek wrestler if he'd rather face another wrestler or a brute from the streets. He'll choose the wrestler every time. The wrestler is predictable. You can counter him. A criminal who jumps out of an alley does things that are so ridiculous they succeed because no one expects them. It's the same here. Seasoned soldiers fighting these half-trained swordsmen is like philosophers trying to debate lunatics."

"But haven't our centurions fought men like this before?"

Again Bellator appeared not to hear. "Look at that." He shook his head. "I haven't seen anything like it in years. In northern Spain there are fighting horsemen who have a maneuver that's overwhelming. The attackers ride in a circle and hit a massed enemy with javelins and then spin immediately away. We call it the Cantabrian gallop. It's not identical with this but this is close and just as brutal. By the blood of Mars, these Parthians were born for war!"

Crus stepped away and took hold of his horse's reins and mane and sprang into the saddle.

"I've had enough leading from the rear," he said and raced off.

He galloped along the riverbed and dashed into the wide chasm where Hell had found its home. Held in tightly by the walls of the gorge, the wails of wounded horses were horrifying. At that instant, and for no reason that he could grasp, he had the most absurd vision, that of self-satisfied senators dining in their summer homes in the Alban hills. How could he ever explain this to them? How could he even try?

The First and Second Centuries had already pulled back to rest at the end of the columns on the right and left, with the Fifth and Sixth taking their places in the front line. Crus saw Arrianus finish speaking to Rufio at the back of the column and then sprint off across the field toward the Judaeans.

"I'll deal with them!" Crus shouted to Arrianus, who signaled that he had heard and galloped off to speak with Decius on the left flank.

When Crus reached the Judaean ranks, for the first time he felt pity for these quarrelsome Jews. They had endured a terrible beating. The fallen were everywhere, scattered like a flock of birds blasted dead by a storm. Soldiers stumbled over the corpses in their attempts to maintain their three ranks.

"Get those bodies out of there!" Crus shouted. He jumped from his horse and helped some of the men drag the dead out of the way. "Maintain your formation! Give yourself space!"

He looked around for Matthias. "Spread out!" Crus yelled.

"Tribune."

Crus turned to see Matthias coming toward him. His drawn face was the color of pale mold on a slab of old cheese. A glancing arrow had opened up his left cheek. It was still seeping.

"Pull your men back at least two hundred feet," Crus said. "You're too close here. Leave the dead. Can you do that?"

"I can."

Crus smiled at him. "Your men will be fine. Just get back. And pick up as many Parthian arrows as you can when you go."

Crus leaped back into the saddle and galloped over to the right flank.

"Describe the situation," he said to Rufio at the end of the column.

"They're sacrificing their men to wear us down," Rufio answered, watching the mounted swordsmen hacking at the Romans in front of them. "The Parthians are exhausting us with their own blood. This makes the Germans look sane."

Crus stared at the circling archers. "Some of them seem to be out of arrows."

"Some are, but they're holding formation."

"Are they waiting for the camels?"

Three blows from the carnyx boomed a signal down from Bellator.

"There's the answer," Rufio said.

On the high plain east of the riverbed dust from the camels betrayed their approach.

"Arrows and water," Rufio said in exasperation. "But we're not finished yet." He looked for Valerius at the end of the column. "You're in command!" he shouted to his optio. "Order the men to dismount and check their girths." He made a kissing sound to Nimbus and they raced off toward the Roman left flank.

57

ENERGETIC MEN AVAIL A PEOPLE FAR MORE THAN THE WITTY AND THE SLY.

PLAUTUS

"I got the message from Arrianus," Decius said, wiping the sweat that was dripping from his face onto his horse's neck.

"New message," Rufio said as Nimbus stopped at the edge of the Second Century. "Did you see the camels?"

"I can see the dust."

"Before their columns withdraw for water and arrows we're going to attack again. I have no idea if this will work, but we have to try to break their will. I want—."

"Will is what they have plenty of," Decius said with a harsh smile.

"Let's try to knock some of it away. Get your century to the middle of the field right in front of the Judaeans. My century will be next to you. We—."

"Do you want to flank them?"

"Not in this place. We could try it, but I don't want to risk it. It's too tight. Before they break off for supplies, the First and Second Centuries are going to shoot straight up the middle between both pairs of their columns. They'll never expect it, and there's enough space for us. We'll ride in twos instead of fours. We'll fly up there like fire through straw. We'll hit them from the inside out. They'll try to swing toward us, but they can do it only one man at a time. They won't be able to pivot entire groups of five. There's no space for that. They can't defy geometry. Tell your men to ignore the archers and take down the swordsmen."

Before Decius could answer, Rufio galloped back across the field. He could hear Decius's century following. He passed Crus, who was on foot and encouraging the Judaeans and helping them maintain their formation. Matthias was leaning against a shield and not looking well.

"All ready?" Rufio asked when he reached his men.

"Ready," Valerius said.

"Metellus, next to me." Rufio ordered. "A column of twos."

The entire century swung out of the line and cantered behind him to the center of the field. Decius and the Second Century were already there.

"They're starting to pull back." Decius gestured toward the Parthian riders lowering their swords and bows.

"Then let's move," Rufio said and looked over his shoulder toward his men. "Straight up the space in the middle like a blade through pig fat." He turned again to the front and unsheathed his sword and raised it. "Now!" he shouted.

Both centuries erupted to life and streaked eastward once more into the heart of the battlefield.

The other centuries were still hammering all four columns from the front, and so the First and the Second flew by before the Parthians realized it. When Rufio and Metellus reached the end of the Parthian column, the First Century swung to the right in a double file and attacked instantly. Stunned, the horsemen recoiled from this second onslaught. Rufio and Metellus sliced into the swordsmen between two ranks of archers. The Parthians flailed their blades wildly as they struggled to turn the entire rank in the tight space, but the Romans cut them down. Horses fell on top of one another, squealing in terror and pain. Yet Rufio heard nothing as he chopped and stabbed more deeply into the row of warriors. Soon he lost sight and even awareness of the men to his right and left. At that instant, only one man at a time could he see, an embodiment of the fevered dreams of an Asiatic despot. And there he tumbled beneath Rufio's blade to the sand of Judaea.

As though echoing from the edge of the earth, a trumpet wailed, shocking Rufio out of his smothering silence. Suddenly he was engulfed by the clanging and shrieking of a world gone mad. He looked to right and left and witnessed something he could never have dared imagine. In what seemed like a single motion, every man in the Parthian column swung to the rear without even brushing the horseman beside him. Each rank stayed perfectly in place, but every rider swiveled like an arrowhead spun on its point. Three more trumpet blasts rang out and then the riders bolted to the east before the Romans could even inhale. Rufio pivoted Nimbus and saw that the columns Decius had been battling had done likewise.

The two Roman centuries were left standing alone on the battleground.

Rufio paused to catch his breath and sheath his sword.

Decius rode up beside him. "Has any man ever heard of anything like that?"

Rufio shook his head. "It's one of the most incredible things I've seen in my life."

"They can't outfight us, but they can outride us. And they still have enough men to wear us down to nothing."

Rufio remained silent.

"Old friend . . . ?"

Rufio looked at Decius.

"Share your thoughts."

Rufio turned and gazed at the Parthians riding off to their camel train for more water and arrows. "They have skills we can barely even dream of. But they're missing something. And that one thing is more important than everything else." He looked back at Decius. "Did you see the terror in their eyes when we hit them from the flank?"

Decius hesitated, and then said, "I did."

"They don't have what every good centurion has had since the wars with Carthage." He smiled, and yet not with arrogance but with his own distinctive tranquility. "They lack the flexibility to improvise."

After making sure that none of his men had been wounded, he led his century back across the battlefield, with Decius and his men close behind. The other four centurions had already ordered their troops out of the line to the rear. All knew that they were in the lull before the final gale.

Rufio stopped in front of the Judaeans and dismounted. Color had returned to Matthias's face, and he seemed to have recovered some of his strength. He and Crus were tending the wounded Judaeans. All the centurions now gathered around, and Bellator and Arrianus came riding in from the high plain to the west.

"It'll take hours for the Parthians to water their horses," Rufio said to his officers. "I want to rotate one century at a time back to the troughs to water our animals and to bring some wagons up to cart away the wounded." He looked at Decius. "We'll start with the Second Century and finish with mine." Rufio turned to Crus for confirmation.

"Do it," the tribune said to the centurions, and they went off to organize the watering of their mounts. "Let's rest." He pulled off his helmet, and he and Rufio and Bellator and Arrianus sat on the ground in the shadows of their horses. "Matthias, please join us. Decius, stay for a bit."

The big centurion dropped to the ground next to his horse, and Matthias sat beside Crus.

Rufio took a drink from his flask and remained quiet for a while. "We've learned a few things," he said finally. "We struck them with converging columns and killed many of them, but they endured it. Then we split their columns and tried to cut them from the inside out and they evaded it." He looked at Decius. "Thoughts?"

"Our men fought like titans, but it isn't enough. We know now that fine swordsmen who are new riders are no match for mediocre swordsmen who are brilliant riders."

Rufio turned to Matthias. "How many men have you lost?"

"At least eighty wounded and about thirty-five killed."

Rufio was surprised. "That's a brutal tally." He paused, and then said, "With almost half the Judaeans out of the battle, we have to guard the rest. This isn't a struggle for Rome but a fight for the existence of Judaea. For the survival of the eastern gate. If the Judaeans are slaughtered, we've lost, no matter how many Romans live to return to Gaul."

"Are you thinking we should pull the troops out?" Crus asked.

"No, tribune," Rufio said. "Matthias, you know how to form the turtle. When the final action starts, that's what I want to see. Pure tactical defense. There's no dishonor in that. You've bled enough. If you use the turtle at this range with our shields, you're invulnerable to their arrows. I've tested them. Let the Parthians waste their arrows on you. We need you to do that."

"Then we will," he said with recovering strength.

"As for us . . ." Rufio laughed and it lightened the mood. "I have no idea." He turned to Bellator. "What do you think, you old stud?"

Bellator seemed grimmer than he usually did, even on bad days. "I have some unhappy information for you. The camel train that's replenishing them right now — it's only about fifty camels. Arrianus counted them."

"I'm certain," Arrianus said.

Rufio turned away toward the battlefield.

After a long silence, Crus said, "I'm missing the meaning of this. Why is it bad that they have fewer camels than Yahlavi told us?"

"Tribune, they don't have fewer," Decius said.

Crus turned to Rufio. "Centurion . . . ?"

"We're in serious danger now," Rufio answered, still staring at the wasteland in front of him. "Their tactics are as clear at this moment as if I could see inside Durena's mind." He turned back to his tribune. "By the time they're done resupplying their troops in a few hours, the other fifty camels are already going to be riding here with more water and arrows. Durena is cycling them back and forth. If it's true that they've tapped into one of the cisterns of the Nabataeans—and we cannot risk believing that it *isn't* true—they can do this forever. At least with regard to water. They'll run out of arrows eventually, but not until they've worn us down."

"Since they outnumber us by so much," Bellator said, "my guess is that Durena will field only half his troops at one time, too. He'll rotate them. He knows we don't have the numbers to do that. All of our men have to fight all the time to hold them off. The Parthians will grind us down to exhaustion and collapse."

"And then what?" Matthias asked.

Rufio turned with a look of sadness toward his Judaean comrade. "We'd have to withdraw."

Matthias stared at him for a long time. "And then the Parthians have won."

"If we retire from the field," Rufio said, "the entire East will know that the security promised by Rome is hollow. This kingdom will shake—and the old lion may fall from his throne. And the Parthians will have won."

"Rufio," Crus said.

Rufio turned toward him.

"We cannot win, can we?" Crus asked.

Rufio tried to find some moisture in his mouth to wet his lips as he turned and looked once more out onto the battleground. "We cannot win."

Minutes passed in silence.

"Silver Hair."

Rufio turned back to Bellator. "Yes?"

"We don't have to win."

Everyone looked at Bellator.

"Explain what you mean," Crus said.

"We just have to break their will." He smiled at Rufio. "How many times have you told me that? Have you forgotten?"

"Apparently I have."

"I want details," Crus said.

"It's so obvious that no one is even thinking of it," Bellator said. "We have to kill or cripple as many of them as possible *before* the next camel train arrives. Make them use up their arrows *now*. And we continue pummeling their swordsmen without letup and fight them to a draw. That'll be enough. Rufio is giving Durena too much credit. They're not Romans—they're not accustomed to fighting with swords. We drain them dry so that even if they rotate their men in and out we wear them down. Exhaust them. With no energy and no arrows left they'll *have* to retire. Is that impossible for us to do? No, it's not impossible."

"But it's not likely either," Decius said.

Bellator scowled. "How likely is it that a bloated monstrosity like you would die on a sweating horse in a Judaean wilderness? Who would ever have thought that possible? Likely? What has likely to do with life?"

Decius laughed. "Golden-tongued as always."

"What do you think?" Crus said to Rufio.

Rufio smiled at Bellator. "I think the old stable rat is a wise man. Or a madman." He took a long deep breath and let it out slowly. "There's only one way even to attempt what he's suggesting—hold nothing in reserve. And I've never done that in my life. We'd have to strike them with everything at once. Then . . . then it's conceivable. But it's a desperate act. Our men will have to fight as if they're convinced they can never be killed— or as if they're certain that nothing can save them. Then it's possible—just possible."

Crus stood up. "Let's water and rest our troops and our horses and prepare for the final throw of the dice."

He turned away and walked alone out onto the battlefield.

After Bellator and Arrianus went off to water their mounts and Decius rode back to rejoin his century, Rufio touched Matthias on the arm.

"A few words," Rufio said, and the two of them led their horses by the reins and walked off together.

"There's one thing I want you to realize," Rufio said. "The Second Cohort has been honored to share this battleground with you and your brave troops."

Matthias gazed at him in disbelief and then quickly looked away.

"If my friend Diocles back in Rome decides to write an account of this, it won't simply be about a pack of grumbling Romans with blistered lips and grit between their teeth defending the eastern gate"—he gestured all around him—"here, in the rectum of the world. It'll be about the pride of Judaea making a stand."

Matthias turned back, tears rolling down his face.

"As far away as the Tiber, people will know of Judaean valor," Rufio said. His voice was soft, caring. "On that I swear a sacred oath—soldier to soldier." His eyes smiled at Matthias. "Friend to friend."

He grabbed Nimbus by the mane and swung into the saddle.

"One more thing," Rufio said, smiling down on the Judaean. "Ask Elah if he'll consider giving us one last push so we can bring this day to an end."

Matthias grinned through his tears. "It'll be done."

58

BETWEEN THE DOG AND THE WOLF.

ROMAN SAYING

Rufio and Crus sat on their horses and gazed east at the gathering Parthian troops.

"Durena should never have taken so long to water his animals," Rufio said. "Now the sun is in *his* eyes."

"What do these Asiatics know about organization?" Crus said.

Rufio smiled. "The tribune rides with us?"

"Do you think I'm going to go home and tell Lucia that my men bled while I watched from far away?"

"Knot your reins. You don't want to lose them in the field. And stay to my right. Near my sword hand. If you die, I'm the one who'll have to go to Rome and explain to that poor maiden that I let the tribune expire beneath Parthian blades—when really it'll probably be because he slipped off his horse and broke his neck."

Crus smiled and looked back toward the enemy. "It seems like a different formation this time."

"Bellator was right. I think that I might have overestimated Durena. I hate when Bellator is right. . . ."

"I can't make out what they're doing."

"He's abandoning his version of the Cantabrian gallop. That's the first mistake he's made today. Our charge up the middle that didn't bring down a single Parthian might decide this battle. And it was just a quick improvisation that I thought up at that moment to salvage a failing situation. But it scared him. Scared him into folly. Look. . . ."

Instead of forming the multiple columns from the previous assault, the Parthian mounted swordsmen assembled now into a single mass in front of the archers.

"He's giving us exactly the fat target I expected the first time," Rufio said. "He should have kept the two moving Spanish circles and just fielded a straight column of fives between them to seal the hole. That would have been hard for us to split. But he's worried now. Worried because of a desperate Roman's half-thought-out attempt to deal with the unthinkable."

Crus looked at Rufio. "You should have been a cavalryman. You're intuitive on horseback. There's still time."

"No, I love my men too—." He stopped suddenly and said no more.

Crus smiled. "That's all right. I know you do."

Rufio pivoted Nimbus on the hindquarter, and Crus turned his horse as well.

Mounted before them in columns of four files of twenty ranks each stood all six centuries of the Second Cohort. Watered and rested, they presented the fierce confidence, tinged with just the proper amount of positive tension, that was the stamp of all triumphant armies.

"This is the final strike," Rufio said to his troops. "Six columns—six blades into the belly of the enemy." He folded his hands across the front of his saddle. "Behind you is a village where the people feel little but fear and longing and despair. We're Romans, so we can never share those sentiments, but we can understand them. We won't desert these people. As one of my fine officers said, if we can abandon a child, we might as well roll up the Empire right now." With a low voice, he said, "Tribune," and backed Nimbus four steps to leave Crus in the lead before him.

"One thing only," Crus said. "As I told you earlier, that performance on the deck of the ship was sluggish. In a few weeks' time I have a dinner engagement in Caesarea—so be quick about it!"

The men laughed, and Crus backed his horse until it was even with Nimbus.

Rufio raised a hand to Matthias, whose three ranks stood holding their big shields about a hundred feet behind the Romans. Matthias signaled back.

Rufio checked to see that all the optios were in position at the rear of each column, and then he and Crus took their places at the head of the First Century on the right of the line.

"Stay with me," Rufio said to Metellus.

"Always," Metellus answered in a serious tone that was rare for him.

"Tribune," Rufio said, "we're ready."

"Let's finish it!" Crus sliced his hand through the air, and the cohort moved off.

The six centuries began crossing the bleak arena at an easy trot. Rufio caught a burst of movement among the Parthians. Evidently Durena had expected, for some inexplicable reason, that the Romans would wait until he was ready, and now his troops were scrambling for position. The mounted archers raced to their places at least two hundred feet to the rear of the other troops for maximum protection, but this would greatly weaken the force of the arrows shot at the Judaeans. At that range, their arrows would never penetrate even chain mail, let alone laminated Roman shields. Rufio was certain Durena knew this, but the Parthian commander must have felt, after the initial contacts and the quick retreat of his bowmen, that they were far too vulnerable to the Romans to be risked at a closer range.

"Bellator was wrong," Rufio said to Crus. "Look."

Durena had decided not to hold any of his swordsmen in reserve. All of them rapidly formed up in ranks before the archers.

"That's a mistake," Rufio said. "We can risk not having reserves because we have the fort behind us. Durena has nothing. And besides that, he's putting too many horsemen into too small a space. They won't be able to maneuver the way they did before."

"How many does it look like to you?" Crus asked.

"About four hundred. Maybe a few less. I figured we killed at least a hundred."

"And five hundred archers behind them," Crus said. "And they have swords, too."

"It's never easy for Romans. Never."

When the cohort came at a trot to within about a hundred and fifty feet of the Parthians, Rufio raised his hand.

"Now!" he shouted.

The carnyx blew from the high plain behind them, and the first rank of each century erupted and dashed across the riverbed and into the face of the enemy.

Surprised by the sudden furious surge, the Parthians charged, but the momentum was all with the Romans.

The young Parthian before Rufio seemed stunned that the Roman had leaped upon him so quickly. The Parthian's weak thrust did nothing but cause Rufio a fleeting flash of pity before Rufio cut him down.

He turned to his right. Crus was battling a brawny rider who looked strong enough to chop a tree with his sword. Crus eluded a sweep of his blade and then slashed upward in a backhand "X" from left to right, and his sword sliced through the Parthian's cheek and cropped the end of his nose. Blood spurted from the center of the

Parthian's face onto his horse, and the warrior exploded with a bestial sound and thrust his sword at the tribune.

Already off balance and slipping from his saddle to the right, Crus tried to pull away, but his horse panicked at his rider dangling from the side. Crus struggled to right himself on the terrified animal, and now the Parthian veered around to the flailing tribune's defenseless left. The Parthian's sword came shearing down at Crus's left thigh when Rufio's blade split the warrior's skull from the crown to the chin. The corpse slid from the horse and was trampled underfoot, and his mount galloped off to the west.

Rufio dropped his reins across Nimbus's neck and swept around to the right of the tribune's horse and pulled him up into the saddle.

"Are you cut?" Rufio shouted.

"No! Go to the men!"

Rufio grabbed his reins and swung around the flank of Crus's horse and raced back into his position on line.

Maimed horses and butchered Asians cluttered the ground before the Romans.

"Roll!" Rufio shouted, and the first rank peeled to right or left as if they had been born to do it.

Rufio looked across the battlefield, and the forward ranks of the other centuries were rolling as well. He turned back to the west. Arrows sailed overhead toward the Judaeans, formed up now with their shields over their heads and all around them. Some of the missiles never reached their targets, while the rest clattered uselessly against the heavy Roman shields.

Rufio knew that Durena would be desperate to shorten the distance.

The second rank of Romans galloped into line.

"Hit them!" Rufio shouted as if he were conducting a training drill, and the soldiers sliced into the Parthians with a controlled intensity as overwhelming as it was terrifying.

Behind the Parthians, Rufio could see a flash of red as Durena dashed about to shore up his attack. His troops pushed onward to shorten the distance to the Judaeans, but now the Parthian commander was getting a lesson that the Macedonians had learned long ago at the point of Roman blades. The only troops in the line who mattered were those in contact with the enemy. The rest were just an encumbrance. Whether they were on foot or horse counted for nothing. Like a horde of befuddled hoplites, the Parthian horsemen had become victims of their own sluggish mass. The troops in the first rank absorbed all the punishment, while those packed in the rear had no access to the front and could do nothing but inadvertently shove their comrades forward to exhaustion and death.

"Metellus!" Rufio shouted, but the signifer was already beside him. "Ride to the other centurions. Tell them to look for Durena to open up his lines. He's going to try to get his fresh troops up here. Tell the centurions to use their own judgment—not to wait for orders from me."

Metellus galloped off across the field.

"Roll!" one of Rufio's troopers shouted, and the first rank peeled off as smoothly as dancers and cantered back to the end of the column, while the next four horsemen galloped into line against the Parthians.

"Look at that," Crus said.

Most of the archers had stopped shooting at the Judaeans.

"They're running out of arrows," Rufio said. "And they know it's useless at that range anyway. Get ready."

"Ready for what?"

Rufio waited and it came quickly.

The useless Parthian horsemen at the rear suddenly spread out and opened up irregular slots between the files. Immediately the battered fighters at the front swung around.

"Now!" Rufio roared.

The moment the worn out Parthian swordsmen retired to allow their comrades to replace them, the Romans shot forth like the Assyrians of old. Straight down the makeshift alleys they flew, the six centuries surging through the startled Parthian ranks like javelins piercing putrid flesh.

Rufio and Crus dived with the First Century far into the Parthian body. Recovering from their surprise, some of the Parthian veterans charged the Romans with a courage that could have ennobled the damned.

A gray-bearded warrior, creased and scarred, raced toward them.

Rufio pivoted to the left to bring his right hand into play, but Nimbus stumbled in the sand, and Rufio slammed forward into his neck. Pushing himself back to regain his seat, he snapped his head around and glimpsed just a few feet away a battle-worn face marred with the fury of hereditary hate. Rufio clearly saw the point of the Parthian's sword, and sun glinted off the blade. Nimbus pinned his ears and lashed out to bite as the sword came down toward the center of the horse's skull. Suddenly Rufio's vision was blocked as Crus's mount sprang in front of them. Rufio heard the Parthian's weapon bang against the tribune's helmet, but Crus stayed in the saddle. A seemingly endless groan of anguish and despair rose above the clamor, and the Parthian fell at Nimbus's feet with Crus's sword still buried in his chest.

Rufio stretched down and swept the blade out of the carcass and tossed it to Crus.

"Over there!" Crus shouted and pointed.

Rufio spun around toward the open lane of horsemen just as the archers in the rear unleashed a volley against the Romans. Missiles shot by them, and some struck their mail or glanced off their helmets. The range was far too great for the arrows to do injury to armored men, except to their faces or to their limbs. Or to their horses.

And then something in Rufio shattered. For the first time in more than twenty years in the legions, he lost control. The thought of an arrow from an Asiatic barbarian driving through Nimbus's face launched him without thought into the Parthians all around him. With the pitiless rage of a Sargon gone mad, he stabbed and slashed every creature within reach. Faces gaped at him in their final terror, but he cared nothing and heard nothing as he killed, except the hammering of the pulse within his head. Men and horses died and fell and took a year to hit the earth, and all in an endless and engulfing silence.

A carnyx blast expelled him from his private realm of slaughter.

"How many times?" he managed to say to Crus as he struggled to recover his reason.

"Three blasts," Crus shouted.

Rufio looked to Bellator on the high plain behind them. "Are you sure?"

"I'm certain."

Rufio turned back toward the tribune. Crus was spattered with the blood of horses and men, some no doubt from Rufio's sword.

"Look!" Crus yelled.

Rufio pivoted and saw a train of at least fifty camels racing into the riverbed about a quarter-mile off.

"More arrows," Rufio said in near despair.

The Parthian bowmen cheered as they saw their comrades rushing forward with supplies. The archers pulled back to meet them, and the swordsmen also broke contact to recover and regroup.

"They'll have enough arrows now to tear up all our horses," Rufio said. "If we try to hold our position, they all die. And we die."

"Should I order a withdrawal?" Crus asked in disbelief. "Can we still screen the Judaeans?"

Rufio looked back at Matthias and his troops. They were resting with their shields down, out of range but also out of choices if the Romans pulled back and deserted them to save their horses.

Rufio stared down at Nimbus and suddenly felt an eerie calmness. He stroked the left side of Nimbus's neck. The horse's left ear cocked backward and Rufio leaned over and gazed sadly into that trusting eye.

"If you die on this field, my friend," he whispered, still leaning over Nimbus's withers, "we'll ride together to Paradise." He spoke as serenely as a man enveloped in a spell. "I'll never abandon you now."

The simultaneous squeals of dozens of horses could have splintered a man's sanity. It sounded as if an entire herd had been hurled shrieking in terror into the blackest rivers of Acheron.

"In the name of all the gods at once . . . !" Rufio yelled.

Across the battleground, horses riddled with arrows bolted or crumpled, and riders tumbled to the crusted sands.

"Nabataeans!" Crus shouted.

With that uniquely rolling glide, the camels raced in a giant wedge deep into the bowels of the abyss. Two bowmen in each saddle launched their lethal darts into the panicked horsemen, and walls of earth or ranks of men blocked the Parthians on all sides.

As if of a single mind, all the centurions barked to their troops, and the six centuries sprang once more upon the invaders. There was no place left for them to go.

Dressed in black and wrapped in a dark red head-cloth, the leader of the camel warriors shot arrow after arrow as quickly and mercilessly as bolts from Zeus. Every missile found its mark.

Before arrows and blades, the surrounded Parthians died in their hundreds and finally collapsed in the face of slavery or death.

The centurions tended the wounded while the optios assembled the Parthian prisoners. They had fought valiantly, but after being shredded from two directions their spirit was spent. There was no resistance.

Rufio's century had suffered no fatalities, but there were eighteen injured men to transport back to the fort. Twelve of them were still able to sit a saddle, but the other six had to be lifted onto the wagons, which were now being brought forward from their positions by the troughs in the riverbed.

When Rufio had finished with his wounded, he rode across the battlefield. Stepping around dead men and dying horses, Nimbus walked over to the two Nabataeans sitting on a camel at the far end of the killing ground.

Haritat pulled the side of his red head-cloth down from his face. One of his sons was sitting behind him.

The Roman and the Nabataean just stared at each other for a few moments.

Finally Rufio spread his arms in a question that needed no words.

"The fools stole our water." Haritat's eyes creased in what might have been the trace of a smile.

"Is that the only reason?"

"There was but one other." He turned to the east and pointed. On a ridge above the riverbed, the late day sun struck a woman sitting astride a beautiful gray Arabian mare and gazing down at them. "The huntress thought that perhaps—just this once—Victoria might like a bit of help from the hand of Haritat." Then he smiled a smile that flashed like a shooting star across the desert night.

Rufio grinned at the dark chieftain.

"Rufio!"

He looked to his right and saw Valerius riding up.

"Durena . . ."

"Where?" Rufio asked.

Valerius gestured and then pivoted his horse and rode east across the battlefield.

Rufio clicked to Nimbus and trotted behind Valerius around dead horses and shattered men. Rufio heard hoofbeats behind him, and he turned and saw Bellator riding to join them.

The three of them came up to several Romans gathered by a fallen Parthian. Crus was already there. Rufio and Bellator dismounted, and the soldiers standing around stepped away.

Decius was down on one knee and holding Durena up at the waist and allowing him to lean back against his bent leg. The Parthian had a Nabataean arrow piercing him just below the right shoulder. His pale tunic was already scabbing over with blood.

Rufio walked up to him. The tattered red cap still covered Durena's head. Rufio bent down and pulled it off.

"My men," Durena said with startling strength. "Spare my men. No crucifixions."

"We don't crucify soldiers," Crus said.

Rufio turned to Valerius. "Tell Matthias to collect the Parthian survivors. Have him take the ten strongest to kill all the horses that are maimed beyond hope. The First Century will guard the rest of these curs until we're finished on this field. If they resist, tell Matthias that the Judaeans can kill them all or enslave them if they wish. But if the Parthians submit and refuse to act like fools, let each one take a Turanian horse, a water flask, and whatever rations he can find and ride out of here before the sun sets. We want them out of Judaea now. They can die beyond the Euphrates." He turned to Durena. "Fair?"

"Yes," he said hoarsely but seemed to be searching for some ruse.

"I didn't expect gratitude," Rufio said, reading his thoughts. He looked at Decius and pointed with his chin at the arrow. "Is it all the way through?"

Decius nodded and spread his thumb and forefinger apart about six inches.

"We almost crushed you, didn't we?" Durena said.

Rufio remained silent.

"I've never been frightened by Romans before. . . . But when Yahlavi told me about all the cavalry, then I knew I had to be afraid for my men."

"You were wise to fear," Bellator said. "You should have withdrawn."

"I decided to change tactics instead."

Bellator nodded. "It was well done. Your men ride like Spaniards. And that's a compliment."

"Spaniards ride like *us*," he answered, grimacing in pain. "And *that's* a compliment. If it weren't for those Nabataeans . . ."

"You shouldn't have stolen their water," Rufio said.

"That's what brought Haritat down on top of us?" Durena asked Rufio with a sudden burst of life.

"You should know—know better than anyone—that out here it's *always* about water."

"*That's* what aroused that lord of death?"

Rufio smiled, but more to himself than to Durena. "Not just that."

"Let me die here among my loyal troops," Durena said and looked down at the crusting wound. "Even Durena isn't tough enough to survive this."

"Even Durena?" Rufio said. "You're not tough at all. Fortuna spared you."

"A Roman goddess? Why?"

"She has her ways."

Durena seemed resigned to his own extinction. "Her ways are not my ways."

"You have no say in the matter."

Durena twisted his head around to Decius. "Stand me up so I can die on my feet like a man."

"Leave him where he is," Rufio said. "Die like a man? Someone who was going to kill Judaean children at their mothers' breasts?"

"I would never have done that." His eyelids drooped and his head sagged forward.

While Durena's eyes were still closed, Rufio nodded to Decius.

"We'll bring you back to health and then take you to Rome," Rufio said.

Durena opened his eyes and looked up at him.

"If the tribune is granted a triumph, you'll march in chains before his chariot in the streets below the Palatinum. Then he can have you flung into the Tullianum and strangled there slowly and at his leisure. Like Vercingetorix."

Durena stared at Crus. "So much for Roman honor. You won't let me die like a soldier should die. You won't—."

Rufio glanced at Decius, and the centurion gripped the arrow behind the head and whipped it all the way through and out the back with one powerful sweep.

Durena sucked in air and held his mouth open for a long breath that he seemed unable to let go. Then he slumped back against Decius.

Rufio smiled. "I had to get your attention."

"No strangling in Rome?" Durena said, still struggling for air.

"For a little scuffle like this?" Rufio said, laughing. "Not worth the inconvenience." He looked at Decius. "After all of our injured are cared for, have some of your men put him in a wagon and take him back to the fort. I'm sure Neko has an exotic tincture to cure the wounds and the illusions of Asiatic madmen." He turned and walked away.

Durena smiled through his pain.

Rufio went back to Nimbus, and when his horse looked at him Rufio tried to ignore the lump clogging his throat and the moisture annoying his eyes. He draped his right arm over the animal's neck and caressed his forehead with his other hand and just stared quietly at the horse's soft gaze. Finally, pressing his cheek to the left side of Nimbus's face beneath that understanding eye, he murmured to him and inhaled the sweet primeval scent. He rubbed his knuckles gently against the soft area behind Nimbus's mouth and rested his face against him for a long time until his tears disappeared, and then he whispered, "Let's go home, my friend. To a land where the grass grows soft and green."

Taking the reins, he gripped Nimbus's mane and leaped into the saddle and rode off to entrust the fallen to eternity.

59

ANYONE, EVEN A COWARD, MAY TAKE UP ARMS, BUT ONLY THE VICTORS CAN SAY WHEN THEY ARE TO BE LAID DOWN.

SALLUST

*J*ust twelve of our men were killed in the battle, but the Judaeans lost about thirty-eight soldiers, according to Arrianus. Twenty-six of our horses needed to be destroyed and a much larger number of crippled Turanians had to be slaughtered.

Judaeans do not burn their dead as Romans do but bury them and do it quickly. The tribune has left this, as well as every other detail relating to the Judaean troops, in Matthias's capable hands. Bellator told me that the tribune is gradually withdrawing from daily interaction with the Judaeans in preparation for turning over to Matthias full command.

Rufio and Metellus are completing all the documents that record everything that has happened. The tribune will present these to Sabinus when we return to Gaul. Rufio said that Rome has made its statement here, and we will leave as soon as all of our wounded men have healed enough to travel. Knowing these fine soldiers, I am sure that will be soon.

We have no doctor, but Neko's Egyptian elixirs seem as effective as Greek potions, and the injured men are doing well. Rufio spends as much time with them as he can, and his presence is the true magic. I believe that his soldiers struggle to recover as quickly as possible simply to avoid disappointing him. I smile when I think of that because Rufio would never feel that way, but I know he allows his men to believe it for their own good.

Durena is recovering slowly. Yahlavi never leaves his side and tends to all his needs. These men now have no country. They realize that their king would shame them or kill them. I overheard Yahlavi say that they have resigned themselves to being enslaved by the Judaeans. They will be slaves, but not where they believe. They do not know it yet, but Rufio told me that Crus is

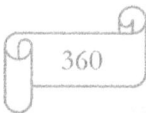

going to take the loyal Yahlavi to Gaul as his servant, and Rufio has decided that Durena has a new life before him as a horse trainer with the Twenty-fifth Legion. Romans are absolutely ruthless with their enemies, but, once those enemies fall, matters are different. Provided that the men of the Tiber decide not to chop off one of the hands of each of their captives, they can reveal a comradeship that would baffle every Sequani I know.

Rufio smiled when he saw Morlana sitting on the ground in an empty horse pen and playing with the black and white puppy in her lap. He leaned with both arms against a top rail and took quiet pleasure in the little girl's laughter while the puppy licked her face as if it were the most important task on earth.

Rufio turned at the footsteps behind him and saw Matthias walking up.

"Did that dog just wander in here?" Rufio said.

"I gave it to her," Matthias answered as he came over to the fence and leaned on the rail.

"I thought Judaeans didn't keep dogs as pets," Rufio said good-naturedly.

"We don't. She's not a Judaean."

Matthias sounded distant.

"Then . . . ?"

"I gave the dog to her to watch over her. The Dog of the Canaanites is very protective. She calls him Pirate because of the black eye patch."

"Does she need protection?"

Matthias continued staring forward. "More than she knows."

Rufio gazed at the side of his face. "What's wrong?"

The Judaean remained quiet.

"Matthias . . . ."

"I'm just concerned about the little one. About what will happen to her."

"What will that be?"

"She has no family," he answered, as if that alone were reply enough.

"Then what will happen?" Rufio said in a tone that showed his growing annoyance.

Matthias hesitated a long time and finally turned toward Rufio, "She'll be a beggar." He seemed embarrassed and looked away again. "Or a prostitute. Probably both."

"You say that like it's a law from Olympus."

"She has no family. So it might as well be on our tablets from Sinai."

Rufio gazed back at Morlana. The puppy had fallen asleep in her lap. She was stroking it gently, and Paki had come up and was licking its head in a motherly way.

"Harsh lands breed harsh people," Rufio said. "A brutal reality that I've learned in my many years in the legions."

"Please don't say that."

"You wouldn't look so sad if you didn't know it was true." He pushed himself off the rail. "I'm sick of the desert."

"It's easy for rich Romans to condemn a poor people who —."

"Matthias," Rufio said, laying a hand on his left shoulder, "I'm not condemning. I'm too tired to condemn." He turned away. "It's time for this old soldier to go home."

Neko was busy packing Rufio's gear when Flavia walked into the office.

"Valerius just came through looking for the Camel Queen of Gaul," Neko said with a gentle smile. "There's someone to see you down by the remains of the gyrus."

"Do you know who, Neko?"

"I do not."

"Thank you."

She hurried off into the darkness. By the time she reached the quarter of the gyrus that was still standing, a trace of moonlight washed across the figure on the other side of the fragment of wall. As with a man on horseback, only his head and shoulders were visible behind what was left of the boards, but there was still enough light for her to see more than Rufio had been able to make out that night in the blackness.

He was bearded like a Greek, and his torso was naked except for a bow on one shoulder and a dark cloak thrown carelessly across his bare chest. Despite his height, Flavia could see no horse beneath him behind the scrap of wall that remained.

"You are leaving soon," he said with an accent from some distant land.

"Yes," she answered softly.

"You will be safe. Poseidon indulges my whims."

"Poseidon?"

"The Romans call him Neptune." Her visitor unleashed a smile that could have melted marble. "These Romans always get everything right but the name."

Flavia moistened her lips. "Thank you for what you've done—for watching over those I love. And over me."

"It has been a unique delight."

"Can I repay in some way?"

"Ah, but you just did."

She dreaded having him go. "You're so kind. Might I call on you again someday? If I'm in need? Will you hear my voice?"

"Always will I listen for the musical rhythms of Gaul. You know where I can be found."

She hesitated, suddenly feeling an almost pleasurable fear. "On Mount Pelion?"

"Yes." Then he pointed to the heavens. "Or up there."

Now he seemed to be waiting for her to speak.

"Farewell," she said.

"For now," he answered with that devastating smile, and in an explosion of hoofbeats he was gone.

Rufio always felt that evening in the desert was the gods' apology. As he and Nimbus made their way down a narrow defile to the battlefield, the erosive air of the day was barely a memory. The Salt Sea helped, since it had no other outlet than to vaporize to the sky, and so it softened the air more than was common in such caustic wastes.

The white walls of the gorge were now washed with gold, and the faintest hints on the ground of grayish blue shadows had been transmuted into lavender and the deepest purple.

Rufio rode Nimbus into the chasm. All the blood on the battlefield had turned black, as had the bodies of the dead. If these dark Parthian corpses had once been soldiers, they did not seem so now. To Rufio, indifferent to the Parthian dead, far more monstrous were the carcasses of the horses, struck down for the petty follies of heartless men. All their lives these animals had desired but two things, ample nourishment and the security promised to them by their masters. And here they had fallen, in a lifeless abyss empty of sustenance and ridden to their deaths by men who could not save even themselves.

Nimbus stepped around the cadavers with the poise of a race of horses bred by warriors and so inured to the reek of death. Yet there was little stench here, unlike most battlefields Rufio had known. The nauseatingly sweet odor that always seemed so preposterous in these horrid landscapes was scarcely noticeable. Death in the desert had its own rituals. The drying air often mummified before it putrefied, discouraging even the flies from their usual fetid feasts. Most of these cadavers would not bloat and explode but would desiccate and endure with the tenacity of the natron-packed corpses of half-forgotten pharaohs.

Rufio rode along the edge of the field to take in the entire expanse. It seemed smaller than it had just a few days ago. Already his memory was attempting to deceive him, as it did every man who had ever fought. In a few years, his mind would imbue the killing ground with a vastness it never had. To a soldier challenging mortality, there were no minor battlegrounds.

So Rufio stopped and studied it now. He stroked Nimbus's neck and spoke softly to him and fixed this place in his mind forever. Yet even those who thought they knew Rufio well would have been surprised to learn that his ultimate reason was not so he could absorb its lessons or write a chronicle or recall it in a mellow recounting around his fireside in years to come. He was attempting to preserve it accurately not so he could remember it, but so that now, once and for all, he could be done with it.

60

HAPPY THREE TIMES AND MORE ARE THOSE WHOM AN UNBROKEN BOND HOLDS, AND WHOSE LOVE, NOT TORN APART BY COMPLAINTS, WILL NOT DISSOLVE BEFORE THE FINAL DAY.

HORACE

*T*he word of Salario is fine and true. His ship was already docked at Caesarea when the cohort arrived. One thing he did not expect, though, was the sight of more than eighty horses to be transported with the troops. However, after the battle with the pirates, his loyalty to Rufio, and perhaps even to Rome, is such that he raised no objection. Beakless, too, was there to greet us. This surprised me because I had gotten the feeling that there might have been some bad feeling between him and Rufio. Yet they greeted one another cheerfully as old comrades.

The tribune had allowed all of the centurions and optios and signifers to bring their horses, and then he had let Rufio decide how to deal with the other soldiers who did not want to bid farewell to their animals. Rufio held a lottery with every tent group and one man from each was permitted to bring his mount back to Gaul. Even the seven out of eight who lost the lottery seemed deeply affected by Rufio's gift to the fortunate few. I am always fascinated by how the toughest soldiers can be moved by seemingly the smallest gesture. I think that not even a year's worth of silver would have touched them half as deeply. For me, living these harsh and demanding months with these men has been wondrous.

Crus was standing before Herod on the marble dais and giving a sharp and lucid summary of the clash with the Parthians. Rufio stood behind the tribune and to his left.

Herod seemed more relaxed than he had before—more the confident lion in his lair. Rufio assumed this was due to the fact that it was much easier for him to be tranquil when Romans were marching out rather than marching in.

"We would speak with the centurion now," Herod said when Crus had completed his account. "Our people thank you for your valor."

The tribune stepped back and Rufio moved forward.

"The King of Judaea honors the fighting men of Rome," Herod said with the sincerity of an old warrior.

"My men are grateful, my lord."

"We presume our people treated you with kindness. They are thankful that you came."

"And, my lord, we suspect they will be even more thankful when we sail."

A wise smile narrowed Herod's eyes. "And the fort on the southern border?"

"In Matthias's loyal and prudent hands."

"We neglected to question the tribune about captives."

"There were just a few."

"And were they executed?"

"They were not, my lord."

"Mercy?"

"No, my lord. They were returned to the babbling Parthian king as battered mementoes of Herod's wrath. The dead teach no lessons, but the bloody always do."

Herod nodded. "Wisely spoken."

"May Rome make a request?"

"Rome may."

"A promotion for Matthias."

"It has already been done."

"Rome thanks the king."

Rufio watched as Herod looked down the hall of his sycophants at the two men standing far off.

"And those?" Herod said.

"The younger is the personal servant of the tribune. The older is one of my horse trainers."

"They look like Persians." Herod's eyes narrowed. "Are they Persians?"

"So I am led to believe, my lord."

Herod's gaze seemed to search Rufio's soul. "This court has rarely seen such contented looking slaves."

"The king is wise enough to know that some slaves are happier even than some freeborn citizens. Happier even than some great men."

"Ah, yes," Herod said, looking suddenly weary and sad. "Will the centurion ever return to Judaea?"

"If such is the will of Caesar. I'm sworn to his will."

"Ah, the oath. The sacramentum."

Rufio smiled. "Yes, my lord."

"We would like you to return. Perhaps not with armor and blades but for rest and quiet talk. Can not Sebastos grant a small request to an old king?"

"He can, my lord."

"Excellent. We leave it to you to make the petition for us."

"At our next dinner together on the Palatinum, my lord, I'll put him to the question."

Herod smiled shrewdly. "And if you return, would it not be possible, perhaps just once, for the King of Judaea to hunt lions with a man who kills not for pleasure but for Rome?"

Stunned, Rufio just stared at Herod for a moment and then exploded in laughter.

The old tyrant roared with a laugh that drowned out Rufio and shook the throne room with as pure and unfettered a joy as that royal hall had not heard in years beyond number.

Tens of thousands of racing fanatics in the Circus Maximus created a sound that seemed eerily ominous when heard from the hidden spaces beyond the stands, like the mysterious far-off roar rising from the depths of an ocean shell.

Other than doves of dubious virtue, women were rare in these secret enclaves of men and chariots. Yet women with Rufio would be another matter. He was well-known to the charioteers, and his martial fame also unlatched many doors, including the unspoken proscription against females in these masculine haunts.

The four dozen horses were twitchy and nervous now, for they knew what was coming. Men greased axles and checked tack and took a moment to pray to whatever gods they honored.

"Do you think maybe he's not here today?" Flavia asked, looking around.

"Rufio!" boomed a voice from deep within the staging area.

Rufio smiled. "He's such a quiet man."

They made their way among sweating animals and toiling men to the blonde-bearded driver in a red tunic who had been making a few final adjustments to his horseless chariot.

"You look scorched, centurion," the charioteer said. "I suspect a desert adventure."

"This," Rufio said with an expansive gesture, "is Crestus, the pride of Germania."

Like all charioteers, Crestus was short, especially for a German, but he was massive in the shoulders. He made a slight bow to Flavia.

"And this woman I know," Crestus said. "This must be Flavia of the Sequani."

Flavia turned to Rufio in surprise.

"You can read?" Rufio said in mock amazement. "Diocles has a Suebi admirer! The forest gods will shake."

Crestus looked suddenly humble. "One of the senator's servants read it to me."

"I'm honored to meet you," Flavia said.

"Diocles was far too restrained in his description," Crestus answered. "He deserves a stern rebuke."

Flavia smiled.

"But one thing he did not explain," Crestus went on. "Who on earth is this?"

He reached down and seized Morlana by the waist.

She shrieked and laughed simultaneously as he raised her high above his head. While she was still giggling, he set her down on the front edge of the chariot.

"A Suebi daughter?" he said, looking at Rufio.

Morlana turned toward Rufio. "Yes," she said softly in her native language, but her eyes whispered far more.

Rufio wanted to answer Crestus, but for once he did not know what to say, and his throat was too tight to speak.

Crestus grinned at Morlana. "Can this be true?"

As if in answer, she smiled and jumped down from the chariot and slid her thin arms around Rufio's waist.

Crestus put his hands on his hips and stared down at them. "A Roman centurion and a Sequani archer and a Suebi princess. What can this possibly mean?"

"Don't you know?" Rufio said, reaching for Flavia's hand and squeezing Morlana tightly against his side as she gazed up at him with love and awe. "It means," he said, laughing, "that it's not time to roll up the Empire just yet."

www.ingramcontent.com/pod-product-compliance
Lightning Source LLC
LaVergne TN
LVHW041206250326
834689LV00016BA/149/J